14- 4

THE VIKING PORTABLE LIBRARY
POETS OF THE ENGLISH LANGUAGE

Elizabethan and Jacobean Poets

The Viking Portable Library

Each Portable Library volume is made up of representative works of a favorite modern or classic author, or is a comprehensive anthology on a special subject. The format is designed for compactness and for pleasurable reading. The books average about 700 pages in length. Each is intended to fill a need not hitherto met by any single book. Each is edited by an authority distinguished in his field, who adds a thoroughgoing introductory essay and other helpful material. Most "Portables" are available both in durable cloth and in stiff paper covers.

The Viking Portable Library

POETS OF THE
ENGLISH LANGUAGE

Edited by

W. H. AUDEN

and

NORMAN HOLMES PEARSON

POETS OF THE ENGLISH LANGUAGE

Elizabethan
AND
Jacobean
POETS

Marlowe to Marvell

NEW YORK · THE VIKING PRESS

Grateful acknowledgment is made to the following
for permission to reprint selections. P. J. and A. E.
Dobell, Tunbridge Wells: the poems by William
Strode and by Thomas Traherne; The Catholic
University of America, Washington, D. C., excerpts
from *Recusant Poets*, edited by Louise Imogen
Guiney: "A Prayer to the Holy Trinity" by
Richard Stanyhurst, "At Fotheringay" by Robert
Southwell, "To Saint Mary Magdalen" by Henry
Constable, "Upon the Crucifix" and "On the Reed
of Our Lord's Passion" by William Alabaster, and
the anonymous "Hierusalem, my happie home" and
"A Lament for Our Lady's Shrine at Walsingham."

Contents

v

CONTENTS

CONTENTS

CONTENTS

Introduction

The desire of the Protestants for a Bible and a liturgy in the vernacular, and the desire of the new aristocracy for secular culture combined to make the sixteenth and seventeenth centuries one of the great periods of translations. Translation is fruitful in two ways. First, it introduces new kinds of sensibility and rhetoric —for example, the Petrarchan love convention; and fresh literary forms—for example, the pastoral. It does not particularly matter if the translators have understood their originals correctly; often, indeed, misunderstanding is, from the point of view of the native writer, more profitable. Second, and perhaps even more important, the problem of finding an equivalent meaning in a language with a very different structure from the original develops the syntax and vocabulary of the former. It would be difficult to overestimate the debt which the technique of English verse owes to the exercise of making rhymed versions of the Psalms and translating Vergil and Ovid. Along with this interest in translation went an intense interest in words and verbal experiment. Theories about poetry, about prosody, about diction, affectations of every kind, flourished. The schoolmasters of literature frown on affectation as silly and probably unhealthy. They are wrong. Only stupid people are without affectations and only dishonest ones think of themselves as rational. In literature, as in life, there can be no growth without them, for affectation, passionately adopted and loyally obeyed, is one of the chief forms of self-discipline by which the human sensibility can raise itself by its own bootstraps.

The schoolmasters dismiss, for instance, the Euphuists and imagine that, because Shakespeare laughs at them in *Love's Labour's Lost* and *Hamlet*, they have him on their side. In fact, throughout his career, the diction, the figures of speech, the cadences of his poetry are profoundly indebted to the Euphuist movement, and he knew it.

Shakespeare's poetry exhibits, in its most fully developed forms, the characteristics of most of his contemporaries: the range of vocabulary from the most Latinate to the most vulgar, from

> I never did like mollestation view
> On the enchafed Flood.

to

> The Kitchen Malkin Pinnes
> Her richest Lockram 'bout her reechie necke.

the daring use of one part of speech as another,

> The smiles of Knaves
> Tent in my cheekes

> With every gale and vary of their masters

the concretion of abstractions,

> Murd'ring Impossibility, to make
> What cannot be, slight worke.

and the rapid shifting of metaphor to the edge of nonsense,

> The hearts
> That spaniel'd me at heels, to whom I gave
> Their wishes, do dis-Candie, melt their sweets
> On blossoming Cæsar; and this Pine is barkt
> That over-top'd them all.

Such a range of possibilities is dangerous, however, for all but the greatest artists. As Mr. T. S. Eliot has remarked, if you try to imitate Dante and fail you will only be dull, but if you try to imitate Shakespeare and fail, you will make a fool of yourself. The lesser Elizabethan poets frequently do, and the reader must put up with a great many lines of fustian for the sake of a few lines of splendor.

THE LYRIC

In medieval English poetry, the poems are usually either short lyrics in the strict sense (poems intended to be sung), or long poems (allegorical, narrative, or didactic), intended to be recited or read over more than one evening. In the sixteenth century the sung lyric develops to keep pace with the development of music, both in solos and madrigals. The simple ballad measures develop into complicated variable stanzas with studied rhythmical tricks which depend on the music for their effect; for example:

> All you that love, or lov'd before,
>   The Fairie Queene Proserpina
> Bids you increase that loving humour more:
>   They that yet have not fed
> On delight amorous,
>   She vowes that they shall lead
>   Apes in Avernus.
>
>   Campion, *A Booke of Ayres*

or,

> Slow, slow, fresh fount, keepe time with my salt teares;
>   Yet slower, yet, O faintly gentle springs:
> List to the heavy part the musique beares,
>   Woe weepes out her division, when shee sings.
>   Droupe hearbs, and flowres;
>   Fall griefe in showres;

>   Our beauties are not ours:
>   O, I could still
> (Like melting snow upon some craggie hill,)
>   drop, drop, drop, drop,
> Since natures pride is, now, a wither'd daffodill.
>   Jonson, *Cynthia's Revels*

In addition, a new kind of poem develops, the poem of concentrated reflection, lyric in length, but not for singing. Its archetype, both in manner and structure, is the Italian sonnet, which is then broken up into stanzas and extended. The development of the sonnet and the reflective lyric from Wyatt through Fulke Greville to Donne is an interesting example of the relation of poets to a convention. There can be no art without a convention which emphasizes certain aspects of experience as important and dismisses others to the background. A new convention is a revolution in sensibility. It appeals to and is adopted by a generation because it makes sense of experiences which previously had been ignored. Every convention in its turn, when it has done its work, becomes reactionary and needs to be replaced. Its effects, however, do not disappear; its successor embodies them.

The Petrarchan love convention with which Tudor poetry begins, for instance, is not the same as the earlier Provençal convention. The Lady does not so much inspire noble actions in a warrior as be the cause of the emotions about which a poet writes. For such a convention, the most suitable kind of lady has a good character but says No, and the most suitable poet is one with a gentle and rather passive temperament but with the introvert's capacity for deep and sustained emotion. When, either by temperament or on occasion, the poet's feelings are frivolous or transient, the convention of seriousness leads to the most boring kind of rhetoric. Nor is it well suited to situations in which the behavior of the beloved is such that there is as much hatred as love in the relation or in which the feelings of the lover are consciously and violently sensual.

Shakespeare in his sonnets and Donne in his early love lyrics wrestle with the convention and break through it, but at the same time neither of them can write as if the *Amor* religion of fidelity and deification of the beloved had never existed. It is precisely the conflict between their natural situation—that is, one that can always occur to lovers—and a historical ideal of love unknown to antiquity that is the new experience which their poetry expresses.

BLANK VERSE

It was perhaps more luck than deliberate choice which led to the adoption of unrhymed decasyllabics as the standard meter for drama. It might quite easily have been rhymed fourteeners. Further, the first essays in blank-verse drama did not look very promising. A playgoer familiar with the technical virtuosity of some of the rhymed miracle and morality plays, in which the kind of meter employed by a character was in itself revealing, might well have thought *Gorboduc,* with its monotonous iambic stomp, a lapse into barbarism.

Even when Marlowe has developed his mighty line, one wearies of a meter so continuously fortissimo, and is tempted to feel that the hero is a prisoner of the verse, compelled to be continuously grand and in a perpetual passion because that is all the meter is capable of. Certainly no one reading Surrey's translation of the *Æneid:*

> The Grekes toward the palace rushed fast,
> And, cover'd with engines, the gates beset,
> And rered up ladders against the walles;
> Under the windowes scaling by their steppes,

Fencéd with sheldes in their left hands, whereon
They did receive the darts, while their right hands
Griped for hold th'embatel of the wall.
The Troyans on the other part rend down
The turrets hye and eke the palace roofe;
With such weapons they shope them to defend,
Seing al lost, now at the point of death.
The gilt sparres and the beams then threw they down,
Of old fathers the proud and royal workes

could have foreseen that within a generation this meter
would become capable of such music and complexity as

                    Then beganne
A top i' th' Chaser, a Retyre: Anon
A Rowt, confusion thicke; forthwith they flye
Chickens, the way which they stopt Eagles: Slaves,
The strides the Victors made: and now our Cowards,
Like Fragments in hard Voyages became
The life o' th' need: having found the backe doore open
Of the unguarded hearts: heavens, how they wound,
Some slaine before, some dying; some their Friends
O'er-borne i' th' former wave: ten chac'd by one,
Are now each one the slaughter-man of twenty:
Those that would dye or ere resist, are growne
The mortall bugs o' th' Field.
                    Shakespeare, *Cymbeline*
or,
                    This deare houre,
A doughtie Don is taken, with my Dol;
And thou maist make his ransome, what thou wilt,
My Dousabel: He shall be brought here fetter'd
With thy faire lookes, before he sees thee; and throwne
In a downe-bed, as darke as any dungeon;
Where thou shalt keepe him waking with thy drum;
Thy drum, my Dol, thy drum; till he be tame
As the poore blackbirds were i' the great frost,
Or bees are with a bason; and so hive him

I' the swan-skin coverlid and cambrick sheets,
Till he worke honey and waxe, my little Gods-guift.
Jonson, *The Alchemist*

Given that there were going to be Shakespeare and Jonson to use it, blank verse was a fortunate choice, for no other meter could have allowed so much freedom of inversion, elision, varying of the caesura, etc., without collapsing into doggerel or prose.

Freedom, however, is a snare for the second-rate. If, outside the plays of Shakespeare and Jonson, only one work of the period, *The Changeling*, approaches being a satisfactory stage play, if the average Elizabethan play is a hodgepodge containing a few magnificent scenes or poetic passages, the freedom permitted in its verse and its construction is in some measure responsible.

GENERAL

The sixteenth and seventeenth centuries cover a period of revolutionary change in our civilization. Revolutions are rare. Just as most illnesses are temporary derangements, recovery from which means a restoration of normal functioning as it was before the attack—and it is only on rare occasions that sickness is a symptom of a profound change in the organism after which health itself will have a new meaning—so, while a revolution is always accompanied by war, few wars are revolutionary.

Further, it is only after a revolution is over that it is recognizable as such; its contemporaries are always mistaken about what they are doing. The Revolutionary Party imagines that it is the revolution to end revolutions, that it is destined to make the world anew; the Counter-revolutionary Party imagines that what is happening is no revolution but a revolt which must and can be crushed without any radical change taking place.

Thus the Reformers believed that the work of the previous Papal Revolution was to be swept from the earth, while the Papacy believed it was dealing with another heresy like the Albigensian revolt, which could be made to disappear. Neither anticipated or desired a Christendom in permanent schism, with all the consequences to life and thinking which this would involve for both.

As cultural examples of these consequences, take two: Catholic baroque art and Lutheran music. The Reformers denounced religious images; the Counter Reformation reaffirmed them more exuberantly than ever, but its conception of the nature of the image and its attitude towards the materials of which the image is made were very different from what they had been before the debate started. Previously the human figure had usually been thought of as we think of a friend—as a rational person to be encountered face to face; in baroque painting it becomes a natural object in space, to be regarded from any angle or perspective, and of which the eye is no more significant than the foot; it is the body in movement—or the will of man, rather than his reason—on which the interest is concentrated. Similarly, in baroque architecture the architect is no longer the midwife who brings forth from matter its latent soul but the potter whose will imposes on a neutral substance whatever shape he fancies. The defiant assertion in baroque of the visual simply as visual, its deliberate theatricality, its use of the *trompe l'oeil,* are signs that for Catholicism too the old confidence in a simple relation between Faith and Works has been lost. Nature can be exploited for religious purposes, but she herself is secular.

The Reformers, on the other hand, while depriving

their congregations of visual images and pilgrimages, could not destroy the idea of Corpus Christi which the Papal Revolution had established; to hold their converts they had to replace the Catholic expressions of unity which they had destroyed with a new one, namely music, which goes further than they realized, for it transcends all doctrinal differences.

The political consequence of this revolution was the emergence of centralized national states and the exaltation of the power of the secular Prince. Luther deliberately glorified the Christian Magistrate, without whose support he could not have survived, and in defending itself the Papacy was compelled to do the same. The right of the subject to revolt against a prince who violates natural law, a doctrine held by St. Thomas, was denied by both parties.

This political revolution went further in England than in any other country, and only in England did the political change precede the religious. The real symbolic revolutionary act of Henry VIII was not his severance from Rome but his execution of Sir Thomas More in 1535, for the Lord Chancellor was by tradition the King's conscience, the voice of natural law. This was going too far for the West, which has never been able to accept Byzantinism, and the excess was corrected in 1649 with the execution of Charles I, in whose person Sir Thomas More is avenged, and the voice of natural law returns as the Public Spirit of the House of Commons.

If the concept of the Machiavellian villain has more fascination for English dramatists than for French or Spanish, it is possible that this was because they had such first-hand experience under the Tudors of Machiavellian politics. For political acumen combined with

unscrupulousness, the Continent can show no figure before Richelieu to match Henry VIII or Burghley. Similarly, the emergence of a purely secular English drama
with little overt reference to religious beliefs was perhaps encouraged by an unwillingness to look too closely
at the reasons for the nation's having become Protestant.
The new nobility, who patronized the players, was dis-
charging one of the duties of the Church whose money
it had stolen; a religious drama would have reminded
men of events which were better forgotten.

The mythical hero of the Papal Revolution was the
Knight-Errant, the epic hero who, tamed by Christianity
and the love of a noble woman, fights and triumphs in
the service of the law of justice and the faith of Mother
Church. He is both good and successful. The representative heroes of the sixteenth century are three:

1. *The Machiavellian Prince* who believes neither in
God nor in woman but only in himself. He has the secular virtues of will and cunning and is, unless or until he
falls, successful. But good he is not. At his best he is
Prince Hal, at his worst, Iago.

2. *Don Quixote,* the Knight of Faith, who has no epic
virtues and knows it, but who believes he is called to
perform the tasks of the Knight-Errant. He is like the
Machiavellian Prince in that he is capable of acting. He
is his opposite in that he does not love himself and his
actions are totally ineffective. He is good and a worldly
failure.

3. *Hamlet,* the man without faith either in himself or
in God, who defines his existence in terms of others: "I
am the man whose mother married his uncle who murdered his father." He would like to become what the
Greek hero is, a creature of situation. Unable to achieve
this, he cannot act, only "act" in the theatrical sense,

that is, play at possibilities. He is neither good like Don Quixote nor evil like the Prince, because, unlike either of them, he is incapable of action; he can only reflect.

All three myths mark the emergence into consciousness of an attitude which Charles Williams has aptly called the "Quality of Disbelief." At its best this means an awareness and acceptance of the paradoxes involved in all human feelings, beliefs, and actions. The irony of Cervantes and Montaigne, the way in which Pascal examines his relation to God, and Donne his relation to women, have much in common. At its worst this attitude leads either to cheap complacency or to the nihilistic despair which produces the demonic Iago, who spends his destructive life proving that life has no meaning, or the paralyzed Hamlet, who will not wager but remains trapped in the snare of self-reflection.

DRAMA

Civilization appears to alternate between periods in which the dominating ideal is masculine and those in which it is feminine. The sixteenth century is marked by a revolt against *La donna gentile* and the Motherhood of the Church, in favor of the spectacular violent male and the Fatherhood of God. (In response to the rejection of the Madonna by the Reformation, Catholicism encouraged the cult of St. Joseph.) The female does not come into her own again until the Romantic Movement. Perhaps drama, as distinct from ritual, only flourishes in such periods, and even then only so long as the emphasis is on the masculine will, for when, as in the eighteenth century, the ideal is the masculine reason, drama wanes.

Internal and External Drama. It is difficult, perhaps impossible, for any of us to form a complete picture of life, because, for that, we have to reconcile and combine two completely different impressions—that of life as each of us experiences it in his own person, and that of life as we observe it in others.

When I observe myself, the *I* which observes is unique, but not individual; it has only a power to recognize, compare, judge, and choose: the self which it observes is neither unique nor individual, but rather a succession of states of feeling or desire. Necessity in my world means two things, the givenness of whatever state of myself is at any moment present, and the obligatory freedom of my ego. Similarly, action in my world has a special sense; I act toward my states of being, not toward the stimuli which provoked them; *my* action, in fact, is the giving or withholding of permission to myself to act. It is impossible for me to act in ignorance, for any world is by definition that which I know; it is not even, strictly speaking, possible for me to be self-deceived, for if I know I am deceiving myself, I am at once no longer doing so; I can never believe that I do not know what is good for me. Again, I cannot say that I am fortunate or unfortunate, for these words apply only to my self.

If I try, then, to present my own experience of life in dramatic form, the play will be of the allegorical morality type, like *Everyman*. The hero will be the rational willing *I* that chooses, and the other characters, states of the self, pleasant and unpleasant, good and bad, for or against which the hero's choices are made. The aim of the hero is to attain true felicity; the play is a comedy if he succeeds and a tragedy if he fails. The plot can only be a succession of incidents in time, and the passing of time from birth to death the only necessity; all else is free choice.

If now I turn round and, deliberately putting aside anything I know about myself, scrutinize other human beings as objectively as I can, I see a very different world. I do not see states of being but individuals in states, say of anger, each of them different, and caused by different stimuli, that is, I see people acting in a situation, and the situation and the action are all I see; I never see another choose between alternative actions, only the action he does take. I cannot therefore tell whether he has free will or not, I only know that he is fortunate or unfortunate in his circumstances. I often see him acting in ignorance of facts about his situation which I know; I cannot, however, so long as I remain completely detached and objective, ever say for certain that in a given situation he is deceiving himself. To recognize self-deception I have to combine both the objective and subjective pictures—I learn to recognize self-deception in myself by observing others, and self-deception in others by observing myself.

If I try to present the objective version in dramatic form, the play will be of the type of Sophoclean tragedy, in which the hero is a man in an exceptional situation. The drama will consist, not in the choices he freely makes, but in the actions which the situation obliges him to take. His motive will not be ultimate felicity, but some concrete satisfaction of desire, and the tragedy will lie in the knowledge, granted to the audience but withheld from him, that in fact his actions are going to have the opposite effect.

The pure drama of consciousness, and the pure drama of situation, are alike in that their characters have no existence outside what they do and the situation they happen to be in. The audience knows all about them that there is to know. One cannot imagine, therefore, writing a book about the characters in Greek tragedy, or the characters in the morality plays; they themselves have said all there is to say. The fact that it has been and will always remain possible to write books about Shakespeare's characters, in which completely contradictory conclusions are reached, indicates that the Elizabethan play is different from either, being, in fact, an attempt to synthesize both into a new, more complicated type.

Actually, of course, the Elizabethan dramatists knew and owed very little to classical drama. The closet tragedies of Seneca may have had some influence upon their style of rhetoric, the comedies of Plautus and Terence provided a few comic situations and devices, but Elizabethan drama would probably be pretty much the same if they had never been known at all. Even the comedies of Ben Jonson, the most learned of all the playwrights, owe much more to the morality play than to Latin comedy. Take away Everyman, substitute one of the seven deadly sins as the hero, set the other six in league to profit from his obsession, and one has the basic pattern of the Jonsonian comedy of humors.

The link between the medieval play and the Elizabethan is the chronicle play. If few of the pre-Shakespearian chronicle plays except Marlowe's *Edward II* are now readable, nothing could have been more fortunate for Shakespeare's development as a dramatist than his being compelled for his livelihood—judging by the early poems his natural taste was for something much less coarse—to face the problems which the chronicle play poses.

The writer of a chronicle play cannot, like the Greek tragedians who have a significant myth as subject, select his situations; he has to take whatever history offers, the humdrum as well as the startling, those in which a character is the victim of a situation, and those in which he creates one. He can therefore have no narrow theory of aesthetic propriety which separates the tragic from the comic, no theory of heroic *areté* which can pick one historical character and reject another. Finally, the study of the human individual involved in political action, and of the moral ambiguities in which history abounds, cures any tendency toward a simple moralizing of characters into good or bad, or any equating of success and failure with virtue and vice.

The Elizabethan drama inherited from the mystery and morality plays three important and very un-Greek conceptions:

The significance of time. Whereas time in Greek drama is simply the time it takes for the situation of the hero to be revealed, in Elizabethan drama it is what the hero creates with what he does and suffers, the medium in which he realizes his potential nature.

The significance of choice. In a Greek tragedy everything that could have been otherwise has already happened before the play begins, and it is impossible at any point in the play to call out to the hero, "Don't choose this, choose that." He is already in the trap. In an Elizabethan tragedy, in *Othello,* for example, there is no point before he actually murders Desdemona when it would be impossible for him to control his jealousy, discover the truth, and convert the tragedy into a comedy. Vice versa, there is no point in a comedy like *The Two Gentlemen of Verona* where the wrong turning could not be taken and the conclusion be tragic.

The significance of suffering. To the Greeks suffering is retributive, a punishment for sin or vice. In tragedy the hero who suffers is the fortunate and gifted man whom everyone would like to be, and whose suffering therefore they sympathetically share. In comedy the hero, or rather the butt, is the ridiculous man who nobody wants to be, and whose suffering is, therefore, not felt by the audience. But in Shakespeare—Jonson's comedies are in this sense classical and non-Christian—suffering and misfortune are not in themselves a punishment. It is true that they would not exist if man had never fallen into sin, but precisely because he has, suffering is a necessary accompaniment to his salvation, to be accepted as an occasion for grace or as a process of purgation. Those who try to refuse suffering not only fail to avoid it but are plunged deeper into sin and suffering. Thus the difference between Shakespeare's tragedies and comedies is not that characters suffer in the one and not in the other, but that in comedy the suffering leads to self-knowledge, repentance, forgiveness, love, and in tragedy it leads in the opposite direction into self-blindness, defiance, hatred.

Even in so light-hearted a comedy as *Love's Labour's Lost* the decisive events involve real suffering. The princess is brought by the death of her father to the realization that she loves Biron, and at the same time to the insight that what he lacks, without which he cannot know the meaning of love, is a knowledge of suffering, hence the task of visiting hospitals for a year which she makes a precondition of their marriage.

If Shakespearean comedy is full of a sympathetic joy which classical comedy excludes, Shakespearean tragedy, on the other hand, is more terrifying than classical tragedy. In the latter the curtain falls on disaster, but also on justice done and knowledge of the truth gained; whereas in the former the disaster, for the hero, is in vain. He has suffered, but without gaining any comprehension of himself or his action, and he dies in despair, damned.

Whereas in Greek drama the hero and the chorus argue the truth out between them, in Elizabethan drama the hero receives no such help. He stands there alone, he makes his soliloquy to a silent chorus, the audience, who are expected by the playwright to supply the appropriate lines themselves. An Elizabethan play, therefore, is always at the mercy of the audience; if they are lazy or unperceptive, its significance and meaning are diminished and blurred.

THE METAPHYSICAL POETS

"Metaphysical" is a somewhat misleading term, for it suggests that the poets to whom it is applied had a unique interest in the science of Being, in contrast, say, to "Nature" poets. This is not the case: the subject matter of Donne and his followers is not essentially different from that of most poets. What characterizes them is, first, certain habits of metaphor: instead of drawing their images from mythology, imaginative literature of the past, or direct observation of nature, they take their analogies from technical and scientific fields of knowledge, from, for example, cartography:

> My face in thine eye, thine in mine appeares,
> And true plaine hearts doe in the faces rest,
> Where can we finde two better hemisphæres
> Without sharp North, without declining West?
>
> Donne

or mathematics:

> As Lines, so Loves oblique may well
> Themselves in every Angle greet:
> But ours so truly Paralel,
> Though infinite can never meet.
>
> Marvell

Secondly they are particularly intrigued by paradoxes, both of logic and emotion:

> For I
> Except you enthrall mee, never shall be free,
> Nor ever chaste, except you ravish mee.
>
> Donne

> My God, my God, though I be clean forgot,
> Let me not love Thee if I love Thee not.
>
> Herbert

Both the technical term and the paradox had appeared in poetry before Donne and were to continue after Traherne, but elsewhere they are peripheral, not central to the style.

It seems possible—it is not provable—that the disruption of traditional values, cosmological and political, which was occurring at the beginning of the seventeenth century encouraged this cast of mind and that metaphysical poetry is the reflection of a peculiar tension between faith and skepticism.

This would in part account for the rediscovery of these poets in our century after two centuries of neglect, a revival of popularity which has gone so far, indeed, that it is now not without its dangers. It has become necessary to remind readers that, great poets as Donne, Herbert, and Marvell are, their kind of poetry is not the only kind. The danger of thinking so has been increased by the development of certain methods of critical analysis which work particularly well with metaphysical poetry but perhaps not so well with other kinds. It is always wise to remember that, if a certain critical theory fails to do much with a certain kind of poetry, the fault may lie in the theory, not in the poetry. As one of the metaphysicals himself has said,

> Is all good structure in a winding stair?

Too exclusive a taste is always an indiscriminate taste. If a person asserts that he worships Donne but abhors Pope, or vice versa, one suspects that he does not really appreciate his favorite.

General Principles

The exuberant richness of Christopher Marlowe's *Hero and Leander* serves as an introduction to this volume, somewhat as the sobered classicism of Marvell's "Horatian Ode" marks a point of departure. Midway, though not precisely halfway, comes the triumph of Shakespeare's *Anthony and Cleopatra.* With some polite and preliminary trepidation between themselves, the editors approached the choice of a single poetical drama to serve as outstanding and as an example of a genre in which the Elizabethan achievement has never been equaled in the English language. The same title came immediately to each mind. Additional space would have admitted Jonson's *The Alchemist* as a demonstration of a somewhat different success, yet his masque, *The Vision of Delight,* does help to widen the understanding of how brilliantly the Elizabethans realized the possibilities of the dramatic craft.

Fortunately it has been possible to include generous selections of longer poems from the period, and this should prove a welcome change from the usual emphasis on songs and briefer lyrics. Of this latter type, others than those selected for this volume might have been chosen from the almost anonymous wealth which its poets provided. But on this score anthologists must be permitted at least as much leeway as their critics, and freshness of choice may give refreshment to the reader.

TEXTS

As in the first volume of the series, the editors have retained the contemporary appearance of the texts of the poems, on the basis that modernization of spelling, punctuation, and capitalization detracts from the intended meaning and tonal qualities of the poem. Such variations from a true "diplomatic" text as exist have been made sparingly and only to avoid absolute misunderstanding. Thus the text of *Anthony and Cleopatra,* taken from the Second Folio, has been only minimally altered. In the enthusiasm of modern editors for modernizing punctuation and spelling, for example, they have in many instances, to all intents and purposes, substituted new lines.

The reader will be given useful, though not infallible, assistance in his reading—which should always be done with the ear as well as the eye—if he will remember that a capitalized word is usually stressed, and that spelling helps to give syllabic values, and that Elizabethan punctuation is not so much based on strict grammatical logic as on oratorical phrasing. For example, the progression of values of the comma, semi-colon, colon, and period (or "full stop" as the British call it) roughly follows a sequence of proportionally increasing rests or breath pauses. If the Elizabethans did not follow this absolutely, and though scholarship cannot accept the rule in finality, nevertheless it seems to work in practice.

SUPPLEMENTARY DATA

We have not tried to supply biographical data on the poets, although the dates of their births and deaths will be found with the poems, and those of their principal works in the charts which are a supplement to each volume. The amount of biographical data which could have been supplied within the volumes would in actuality have been meaningless. For such study there are published biographies which it would have been folly to attempt to summarize in a few lines. We have preferred to print more poems.

If there is anything in the nature of biography in the various volumes, it is the autobiography of the poetical imagination and fancy as it has been expressed in poems. Comments on this autobiography occur in the introductions to each volume, which are meant not to be definitive but to suggest as freshly as possible the problems with which poetry has coped. Instead of biographical data for each poet, therefore, we have drawn up tables in which, on one side, is given the direct course of poetry and, on the other, are to be found certain of the cultural and societal events which had formative effect. These will be of some help, we trust, toward seeing the course of poetry in historical perspective.

A Calendar of British and American Poetry

GENERAL BACKGROUND	DATE	DIRECT HISTORY
Robynson, first English translation of More's *Utopia*	1551	Wyatt, *Certayne Psalmes drawn into English Meter*
Wilson, *The Art of Rhetoric*	1553	
Temporary reconciliation of England to Rome under Mary	1554	
Index Expurgatorius drawn up by the Council of Trent	1557	*The Book of Songs and Sonnets* ("Tottel's Miscellany"): including lyrics by Wyatt, Surrey, Vaux, etc.
		Surrey, *Certain Books* [2nd and 4th] *of Virgil's Aeneid:* first English blank verse
John Knox returns to Scotland	1559	Baldwin, ed., *A Mirror for Magistrates*
Matthew Parker made Archbishop of Canterbury		Jasper Heywood, *Troas:* first English translation of Seneca
Hoby, *The Courtyer*, translation of Castiglione	1561	
	1562	Broke, *History of Romeus and Juliet*
End of the Council of Trent	1563	Googe, *Eclogs, Epitaphs and Sonnets*
Foxe, *Actes and Monuments* ("Book of Martyrs")		Sackville, *The Complaint of Henrie Duke of Buckinghame*
Fabricius, *De re poetica*	1565	Norton and Sackville, *Gorboduc:* first blank-verse tragedy, printed
	1566	Udall, *Ralph Roister Doister;* written 1553
Painter, *The Palace of Pleasure:* collection of *novelle*	1566–67	Golding, *The XV Books of P. Ovidius Naso's Work entitled Metamorphoses*
Bishops' Bible	1568	
	1569	Ingelend, *The Disobedient Child:* "prodigal son" play
Ascham, *The Scholemaster*	1570	
Euclid's *Elements of Geometry* first translated into English		
Latimer, *Frutefull Sermons*	1571	Edwards, *Damon and Pithias:* earliest extant court drama

GENERAL BACKGROUND	DATE	DIRECT HISTORY
Massacre of St. Bartholomew	1572	
	1573	Gascoigne, *A Hundredth Sundric Flowres:* experiments in versification
		Jocasta: translation of Italian translation of Euripides, first Greek tragedy in English
		The Masque for Lord Montacute: first printed masque
Gascoigne, *The Noble Art of Venerie or Hunting*	1575	Breton, *Small Handful of Fragrant Flowers*
		Gascoigne, *Certain Notes of Instruction concerning the Making of Verse or Rime in English*
The first Blackfriars built: first private theater	1576	Gascoigne, *The Steel Glass:* first original poem in blank verse
Pettie, *A Petite Pallace of Pettie his Pleasure*		
The Theatre built: first public theater		
Holinshed, *Chronicles*	1577	
Peacham, *The Garden of Eloquence*		
Lyly, *Euphues, the Anatomy of Wit*	1578	
Frampton, translation of travels of Marco Polo	1579	Spenser, *The Shepheardes Calender*
Lodge, *Defence of Stage Plays*		
North, translation of Plutarch's *Lives*		
Lyly, *Euphues and his England*	1580	
Montaigne, *Essais*		
Tasso, *Gerusalemme liberata* published	1581	
Mulcaster, *Right Writing of our English Tongue*	1582	Stanyhurst, *The First Four Books of Virgil His Aeneid*
Lyly, *Campaspe; Sapho and Phao*	1584	Peele, *The Arraignment of Paris*
Camden, *Britannia*	1586	Webbe, *A Discourse of English Poetrie:* prosody
Historia vom D. Johann Fausten	1587	Turberville, *Tragical Tales:* chiefly from Boccaccio
	1588	Byrd, *Psalms, Sonnets, and Songs*
Greene, *Menaphon*	1589	Puttenham, *The Arte of English Poesie*
Hakluyt, *Voyages*	1589– 1600	
Galileo, *Sermones de motu gravium*	1590	Marlowe, *Tamburlaine the Great*

GENERAL BACKGROUND	DATE	DIRECT HISTORY
Lodge, *Rosalynde*	1590	Spenser, *The Faerie Queene,* books I–III
Sidney, *Arcadia*		
Janssen's invention of the microscope	c.1590	
Harington, translation of Ariosto's *Orlando Furioso*	1591	Sidney, *Astrophel and Stella*
		The Troublesome Reign of King John: first historical drama
Establishment of Presbyterianism in Scotland	1592	Constable, *Diana*
		Daniel, *Delia*
Greene, *Groatsworth of Witte Bought with a Million of Repentance; A Disputation between a hee Conny-Catcher and a shee Conny-Catcher*		Kyd, *The Spanish Tragedy*
		The Lamentable and True Tragedy of M. Arden of Feversham in Kent: first domestic drama
	1593	Drayton, *Idea*
		Sir Thomas More
		The Phoenix Nest: including lyrics by Dyer, Raleigh, Lodge, Peele, Breton, etc.
		Shakespeare, *Venus and Adonis*
Fairfax, *Godfrey of Bulloigne,* translation of Tasso's *Gerusalemme liberata*	1594	Barnfield, *The Affectionate Shepherd*
		Chapman, *The Shadow of Night*
		Daniel, *Cleopatra*
		Greene, *Friar Bacon and Friar Bungay*
		Greene and Lodge, *A Looking Glass for London and England*
		Lodge, *The Wounds of Civil War*
		Marlowe, *Edward the Second*
		Morley, *Madrigals to Four Voices*
		Shakespeare, *The Rape of Lucrece; Titus Andronicus*
Richard Hooker, *Of the Lawes of Ecclesiasticall Politie*	1594–97	
	1595	Barnes, *A Divine Century of Spiritual Sonnets*
		Sidney, *The Defence of Poesie;* written about 1583
		Southwell, *Moeoniae*
		Spenser, *Amoretti; Ephithalamion*
Carew, *The Excellence of the English Tongue*	1595–96	
Ralegh, *The Discoverie of Guiana*	1596	Davies, *Orchestra*
		Griffin, *Fidessa*

GENERAL BACKGROUND	DATE	DIRECT HISTORY
	1596	Spenser, *The Faerie Queene*, books IV–VI
Bacon, *Essayes* Gabriel Harvey, *The Trimming of Thomas Nashe*	1597	Dowland, *The First Book of Songs* Drayton, *England's Heroical Epistles* Shakespeare, *Romeo and Juliet; Richard III*
Florio, *A Worlde of Wordes:* Italian-English dictionary Meres, *Palladis Tamia; Wits Treasury*	1598	Breton, *A Solemn Passion of the Soul's Love* Marlowe, *Hero and Leander* *A Most Pleasant Comedy of Mucedorus;* 12 editions before 1640 Shakespeare, *Love's Labour's Lost*
Blundeville, *The Art of Logike* Opening of Globe Playhouse	1599	Daniel, *Musophilus* Davies, *Nosce Teipsum* Peele, *David and Bethsabe*
First charter granted an English East India Company Peri's *Euridice:* first extant opera	1600	Allot, ed., *England's Parnassus:* miscellany of verse Bodenham, ed., *England's Helicon:* miscellany of verse Dekker, *The Shoemaker's Holiday* Nashe, *Summer's Last Will*
	1600–49	William Strode; greater part of poetry not published until 1907
	1601	Jonson, *Cynthia's Revels; Every Man in his Humour*
Bodleian Library opened	1602	Campion, *Art of English Poesie* Jonson, *Poetaster*
Florio, translation of Montaigne	1603	Daniel, *Defense of Rhyme* Jonson, *Sejanus* Shakespeare, *Hamlet*
	1604	Breton, *Passionate Shepherd* Marlowe, *Doctor Faustus:* written c.1590 Marston, *The Malcontent*
King James Version of the Bible	1604–11	
Bacon, *Advancement of Learning* Cervantes, *Don Quixote,* first part, published	1605	Drayton, *Certain Small Poems*
	1606	Drayton, *Poems Lyric and Pastoral* *The Return from Parnassus:* Cambridge drama

GENERAL BACKGROUND	DATE	DIRECT HISTORY
Founding of Jamestown Colony Monteverdi's *Orfeo* performed at Mantua	1607	Chapman, *Bussy D'Ambois* Heywood, *A Woman Killed with Kindness* Jonson, *Volpone* Shakespeare, *Anthony and Cleopatra* acted; first published in First Folio, 1623 Tourneur (?), *The Revenger's Tragedy*
Hall, *Characters of Vertues and Vices* Lippershey invents the telescope	1608	Shakespeare, *King Lear*
Avisa Relation oder Zeitung, first newspaper Dekker, *The Gul's Hornebooke*	1609	Shakespeare, *Sonnets*
	1610	Campion, *Two Books of Airs* Daniel, *Tethys Festival* Giles Fletcher, *Christ's Victory and Triumph* John Fletcher, *The Faithful Shepherdess* Richard Rich, *News from Virginia*
	c.1610	Shakespeare, *The Tempest* acted
	1611	Donne, *Anatomy of the World*
Brinsley, *Ludus literarius: or the Grammar Schoole* Heywood, *An Apology for Actors* Purchas, *Purchas his Pilgrimage* Shelton, translation of *Don Quixote*	1612	Jonson, *The Alchemist* Textor, *Epitheta:* helps in composing verse Webster, *The White Divel*
	1612–20	
Galileo, *Istoria e dimostrazioni delle macchie solari:* discovery that the sun turns on its axis Globe Playhouse burned	1613	
Overbury, *Characters*	1614	
Ralegh, *The History of the World*	1616	Chapman completes translation of *Whole Works* of Homer Drummond of Hawthornden, *Poems* Jonson, *Works,* first folio
	1617	Jonson, *Vision of Delight* presented; published in 1640 folio
Outbreak of the Thirty Years' War	1618	Chapman, translation of Hesiod's *Georgics*

GENERAL BACKGROUND	DATE	DIRECT HISTORY
First importation of Negro slaves into Virginia	1619	Beaumont and Fletcher, *The Maid's Tragedy*
		Pavier quartos: first attempt to collect Shakespeare
Arrival of Pilgrims at Plymouth	1620	Beaumont and Fletcher, *Philaster*
Bacon, *Novum Organum*		
Burton, *The Anatomy of Melancholy*	1621	
Mun, *A Discourse of Trade from England unto the East Indies*		
	1622	Shakespeare, *Othello*
Drummond of Hawthornden, *Cypress Grove*	1623	Browne, "On the Countess Dowager of Pembroke," in Camden's *Remains*
		Drummond of Hawthornden, *Flowers of Sion*
		Shakespeare, First Folio
		Webster, *The Dutchesse of Malfi*
Herbert of Cherbury, *De Veritate*	1624	Chapman, translation of *Battle of Frogs and Mice*
		Donne, *Devotions upon Emergent Occasions*
Grotius, *De jure belli ac pacis*	1625	
New Amsterdam founded		
Donne, *Five Sermons*	1626	
Roper, *The Life of Syr T. More*		
	1627	Drayton, *Shepherd's Sirena; The Moon Calf*
Kepler, *Tabulae Rudolphinae:* astronomical tables of Tycho Brahe	1627–30	
Bernini begins tomb of Urban VIII (rise of Baroque)	1628	
Harvey, *Exercitatio anatomica de motu cardis et sanguinis in animalibus*		
Mun, *England's Treasure by Forraign Trade* written	1630	Drayton, *Muses Elizium* (*Noah's Floud*, etc.)
Galileo, *Dialogo dei due massimi sistemi del mondo*	1632	
	1633	Cowley, *Poetical Blossoms*
		Donne, *Poems*
		Phineas Fletcher, *The Purple Island*
		Ford, *The Broken Heart; 'Tis Pity She's a Whore*
		George Herbert, *The Temple*
		Massinger, *A New Way to Pay Old Debts*

GENERAL BACKGROUND	DATE	DIRECT HISTORY
	1634	Carew, *Coelum Britannicum* John Fletcher (and Shakespeare?), *The Two Noble Kinsmen*
Founding of the French Academy	1635	Quarles, *Emblems*
Founding of Harvard College	1636	
	1637?–74	Thomas Traherne; poems not published until 1903
Descartes, *Discours de la méthode* Hobbes, *A Briefe of the Art of Rhetorique*	1637	Milton, *Comus, a Masque Presented at Ludlow Castle*
New Sweden founded	1638	Milton, "Lycidas," in *Obsequies to . . . Edward King*
Bay Psalm Book: first book printed in English colonies in America Jonson, *Timber: or, Discoveries* Walton, *The Life and Death of Dr. Donne*	1640	Beaumont, *Poems* Carew, *Poems*
Browne, *Religio Medici* Milton, *The Reason of Church-Government Urg'd against Prelaty* Outbreak of Civil War	1642	Denham, *Cooper's Hill*
Milton, *The Doctrine and Discipline of Divorce*	1643	
Milton, *Areopagitica* Roger Williams, *The Bloudy Tenent of Persecution for Cause of Conscience, Discussed*	1644	
	1644–1729	Edward Taylor; poems chiefly published 1939
	1645	Milton, *Poems* Waller, *Poems*
	1646	Crashaw, *Steps to the Temple* Shirley, *Poems* Suckling, *Fragmenta Aurea* Vaughan, *Poems*
	1647	Beaumont and Fletcher, *Comedies and Tragedies* Cowley, *The Mistress*
End of Thirty Years' War Fox founds Society of Friends	1648	Herrick, *Hesperides*
Donne, *Fifty Sermons* England as commonwealth; execution of Charles I	1649	Lovelace, *Lucasta*
	1650	Anne Bradstreet, *The Tenth*

GENERAL BACKGROUND	DATE	DIRECT HISTORY
	1650	*Muse lately sprung up in America*
		Marvell, "An Horatian Ode upon Cromwel's Return from Ireland"
	1650–55	Vaughan, *Silex Scintillans*
Hobbes, *Leviathan*	1651	Cleveland, *Poems*
Taylor, *The Rule and Exercises of Holy Dying*		D'Avenant, *Gondibert,* with critical preface, and Hobbes' *Answer to D'Avenant*
		Vaughan, *Olor Iscanus*
Urquhart, translation of Rabelais, books I–II	1653	Fanshawe, translation of *The Lusiad* of Camoëns
Walton, *The Compleat Angler*		Lawes, *Aires and Dialogues,* containing Townshend's "Dialogue"
		Middleton and Rowley, *The Changeling*
		Strode, *Floating Island*
Johnson, *A History of New-England*	1654	
	1656	Cowley, *Poems,* with critical preface
		Drummond of Hawthornden, *Poems*
	1657	Henry King, *Poems*
		Poole, *The English Parnassus: Or, A Help to English Poesie*
Browne, *Hydriotaphia, Urne-Buriall*	1658	
Baxter, *A Holy Commonwealth*	1659	Lovelace, *Posthume Poems*
Molière, *Les Précieuses ridicules*		Shirley, *The Contention of Ajax and Ulysses, for the Arms of Achilles*
Boyle, *New Experiments Physico-Mechanical*	1660	
Founding of the Royal Society		
Restoration of the English monarchy		
Beginning of personal government of Louis XIV: *"L'état, c'est moi";* Court of Versailles established	1661	
Fuller, *The History of the Worthies of England*	1662	Wigglesworth, *The Day of Doom*
	1662–78	Butler, *Hudibras*
Boyle, *Experiments and Considerations touching Colours*	1664	
New Netherlands captured by English, and rechristened New York		

GENERAL BACKGROUND	DATE	DIRECT HISTORY
Boyle, *Occasional Reflections*	1665	Herbert of Cherbury, *Occasional Verses*
The Great Plague		
Bunyan, *Grace Abounding to the Chief of Sinners*	1666	Philip Pain, *Daily Meditations:* apparently first original verse printed in English colonies in America
The Great Fire of London		
Molière, *Le Misanthrope*		
Racine, *Andromaque*	1667	Milton, *Paradise Lost*
Sprat, *The History of the Royal-Society of London*		
Dryden, *Of Dramatick Poesie*	1668	
La Fontaine, *Fables,* books I–VI		
Dryden made first poet laureate	1670	Dryden, *The Tempest,* redacted from Shakespeare's play
First celebration of Feast of Sacred Heart, originated by Jean Eudes		Wigglesworth, *Meat Out of the Eater*
Pascal, *Pensées*		
	1671	Milton, *Paradise Regained; Samson Agonistes*
	1672	Dryden, *The Conquest of Granada*
	1673	Dryden, *Marriage A-la-Mode*
Boileau, *L'Art poétique*	1674	
Traherne, *Christian Ethicks*	1675	Rochester, *A Satyr Against Mankind*
Wren starts rebuilding St. Paul's Cathedral		
Wycherley, *The Country-Wife*		
	1676	Dryden, *Aurung-Zebe*
Racine, *Phèdre*	1677	
Wycherley, *The Plain-Dealer*		
Bunyan, *The Pilgrim's Progress,* Part I	1678	Dryden, *All for Love*
	1680	Roscommon, *translation of Horace's Art of Poetry*
	1681	Marvell, *Miscellaneous Poems*
	1681–82	Dryden, *Absalom and Achitophel*
	1682	Dryden, *MacFlecknoe; Religio Laici*
		John Sheffield, Duke of Buckingham, *An Essay upon Poetry*
Ashmolean Museum founded	1683	
Boyle, *Memoirs for the Natural History of Humane Blood*	1684	Roscommon, *An Essay on Translated Verse*
Leibniz's theory of the infinitesimal calculus made public		
	1685	Rochester, *Valentinian*
Newton, *Philosophiae naturalis principia mathematica*	1687	

GENERAL BACKGROUND	DATE	DIRECT HISTORY
Aphra Behn, *Oroonoko; or, the Royal Slave:* a novel	1688	
La Bruyère, *Les Caractères*		
The Glorious Revolution		
Purcell, *Dido and Aeneas:* an opera	1689	Cotton, *Poems on Several Occasions*
Locke, *Essay concerning Human Understanding; Two Treatises*	1690	
Temple, "An Essay upon the Ancient and Modern Learning": a defense of classicism		
Bank of England chartered	1691	
Langbaine, *An Account of the English Dramatick Poets:* first scholarly study of Shakespeare		
	1694	Dryden, *Love Triumphant*
	1697	Dryden, *Alexander's Feast*
Collier, *A Short View of the Immorality and Profaneness of the English Stage*	1698	

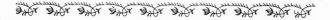

THE VIKING PORTABLE LIBRARY

Poets of the English Language

VOLUME II: MARLOWE TO MARVELL

Christopher Marlowe

(1564–1593)

FROM *Hero and Leander*

THE FIRST SESTYAD

Heros description and her Loves,
The Phane of Venus; *where he moves*
His worthie Love-suite, and attaines;
Whose blisse the wrath of Fates restraines,
For Cupids *grace to* Mercurie,
Which tale the Author doth implie.

On *Hellespont* guiltie of True-loves blood,
In view and opposit two citties stood,
Seaborderers, disjoin'd by *Neptunes* might:
The one *Abydos,* the other *Sestos* hight.
At *Sestos, Hero* dwelt; *Hero* the faire,
Whom young *Apollo* courted for her haire,
And offred as a dower his burning throne,
Where she should sit for men to gaze upon.
The outside of her garments were of lawne,
The lining purple silke, with guilt starres drawne,
Her wide sleeves greene, and bordered with a grove,
Where *Venus* in her naked glory strove,
To please the carelesse and disdainfull eies
Of proud *Adonis* that before her lies.
Her kirtle blew, whereon was many a staine,
Made with the blood of wretched Lovers slaine.
Upon her head she ware a myrtle wreath,
From whence her vaile reacht to the ground beneath.

1

Her vaile was artificiall flowers and leaves,
Whose workmanship both man and beast deceaves.
Many would praise the sweet smell as she past,
When t'was the odour which her breath foorth cast,
And there for honie bees have sought in vaine,
And beat from thence, have lighted there againe.
About her necke hung chaines of peble stone,
Which lightned by her necke, like Diamonds shone.
She ware no gloves, for neither sunne nor wind
Would burne or parch her hands, but to her mind,
Or warme or coole them, for they tooke delite
To play upon those hands, they were so white.
Buskins of shels all silvered used she,
And brancht with blushing corall to the knee;
Where sparrowes pearcht, of hollow pearle and gold,
Such as the world would woonder to behold:
Those with sweet water oft her handmaid fils,
Which as shee went would cherupe through the bils.
Some say, for her the fairest *Cupid* pyn'd,
And looking in her face, was strooken blind.
But this is true, so like was one the other,
As he imagyn'd *Hero* was his mother.
And oftentimes into her bosome flew,
About her naked necke his bare armes threw,
And laid his childish head upon her brest,
And with still panting rockt, there tooke his rest.
So lovely faire was *Hero, Venus* Nun,
As nature wept, thinking she was undone;
Because she tooke more from her than she left,
And of such wondrous beautie her bereft:
Therefore in signe her treasure suffred wracke,
Since *Heroes time,* hath halfe the world beene blacke.
Amorous *Leander,* beautifull and yoong,
(Whose tragedie divine *Musæus* soong)
Dwelt at *Abidus:* since him dwelt there none,

For whom succeeding times make greater mone.
His dangling tresses that were never shorne,
Had they beene cut, and unto *Colchos* borne,
Would have allur'd the vent'rous youth of *Greece*
To hazard more than for the golden Fleece.
Faire *Cinthia* wisht his armes might be her spheare,
Greefe makes her pale, because she mooves not there.
His bodie was as straight as *Circes* wand,
Jove might have not sipt out *Nectar* from his hand.
Even as delicious meat is to the tast,
So was his necke in touching, and surpast
The white of *Pelops* shoulder. I could tell ye,
How smooth his brest was, and how white his bellie,
And whose immortall fingars did imprint
That heavenly path, with many a curious dint,
That runs along his backe, but my rude pen
Can hardly blazon foorth the loves of men,
Much lesse of powerfull gods: let it suffise,
That my slacke muse sings of *Leanders* eies,
Those orient cheekes and lippes, exceeding his
That leapt into the water for a kis
Of his owne shadow, and despising many,
Died ere he could enjoy the love of any.
Had wilde *Hippolitus Leander* seene,
Enamoured of his beautie had he beene,
His presence made the rudest paisant melt,
That in the vast uplandish countrie dwelt,
The barbarous *Thratian* soldier moov'd with nought,
Was moov'd with him, and for his favour sought.
Some swore he was a maid in mans attire,
For in his lookes were all that men desire,
A pleasant smiling cheeke, a speaking eye,
A brow for love to banquet royallie,
And such as knew he was a man would say,
Leander, thou art made for amorous play:

Why art thou not in love, and lov'd of all?
Though thou be faire, yet be not thine owne thrall.
　The men of wealthie *Sestos*, everie yeare,
(For his sake whom their goddesse held so deare,
Rose-cheekt *Adonis*) kept a solemne feast.
Thither resorted many a wandring guest,
To meet their loves; such as had none at all,
Came lovers home from this great festivall.
For everie street like to a Firmament
Glistered with breathing stars, who where they went,
Frighted the melancholie earth, which deem'd
Eternall heaven to burne, for so it seem'd,
As if another *Phaeton* had got
The guidance of the sunnes rich chariot.
But far above the loveliest *Hero* shin'd,
And stole away th'inchaunted gazers mind,
For like Sea-nimphs inveigling harmony,
So was her beautie to the standers by.
Nor that night-wandring pale and watrie starre
(When yawning dragons draw her thirling carre
From *Latmus* mount up to the glomie skie,
Where crown'd with blazing light and majestie,
She proudly sits) more over-rules the flood,
Than she the hearts of those that neere her stood.
Even as, when gawdie Nymphs pursue the chace,
Wretched *Ixions* shaggie footed race,
Incenst with savage heat, gallop amaine
From steepe Pine-bearing mountains to the plaine:
So ran the people foorth to gaze upon her,
And all that view'd her, were enamour'd on her.
And as in furie of a dreadfull fight,
Their fellowes being slaine or put to flight,
Poore soldiers stand with fear of death dead strooken,
So at her presence all surpris'd and tooken,
Await the sentence of her scornefull eies:

He whom she favours lives, the other dies.
There might you see one sigh, another rage,
And some (their violent passions to asswage)
Compile sharpe satyrs, but alas too late,
For faithfull love will never turne to hate.
And many seeing great princes were denied,
Pyn'd as they went, and thinking on her died.
On this feast day, O cursed day and hower,
Went *Hero* thorow *Sestos*, from her tower
To *Venus* temple, where unhappilye,
As after chaunc'd, they did each other spye.
So faire a church as this, had *Venus* none,
The wals were of discoloured *Jasper* stone,
Wherein was *Proteus* carved, and o'rehead,
A livelie vine of greene sea agget spread;
Where by one hand, light headed *Bacchus* hoong,
And with the other, wine from grapes out wroong.
Of Christall shining faire the pavement was,
The towne of *Sestos* cal'd it *Venus* glasse.
There might you see the gods in sundrie shapes,
Committing headdie ryots, incest, rapes:
For know, that underneath this radiant floure
Was *Danaes* statue in a brazen tower,
Jove slylie stealing from his sisters bed,
To dallie with *Idalian Ganimed*,
And for his love *Europa* bellowing loud,
And tumbling with the Rainbow in a cloud:
Blood-quaffing *Mars* heaving the yron net,
Which limping *Vulcan* and his *Cyclops* set:
Love kindling fire, to burne such townes as *Troy*,
Sylvanus weeping for the lovely boy
That now is turn'd into a *Cypres* tree,
Under whose shade the Wood-gods love to bee.
And in the midst a silver altar stood;
There *Hero* sacrificing turtles blood,

Vaild to the ground, vailing her eie-lids close,
And modestly they opened as she rose:
Thence flew Loves arrow with the golden head,
And thus *Leander* was enamoured.
Stone still he stood, and evermore he gazed,
Till with the fire that from his count'nance blazed,
Relenting *Heroes* gentle heart was strooke,
Such force and vertue hath an amorous looke.

    It lies not in our power to love, or hate,
For will in us is over-rul'd by fate.
When two are stript long ere the course begin,
We wish that one should loose, the other win;
And one especiallie doe we affect
Of two gold Ingots like in each respect.
The reason no man knowes, let it suffise,
What we behold is censur'd by our eies.
Where both deliberat, the love is slight,
Who ever lov'd, that lov'd not at first sight?

    He kneel'd, but unto her devoutly praid;
Chast *Hero* to her selfe thus softly said:
Were I the saint hee worships, I would heare him,
And as shee spake those words, came somewhat nere
    him.
He started up, she blusht as one asham'd;
Wherewith *Leander* much more was inflam'd.
He toucht her hand, in touching it she trembled,
Love deepely grounded, hardly is dissembled.
These lovers parled by the touch of hands,
True love is mute, and oft amazed stands.
Thus while dum signs their yeelding harts entangled,
The aire with sparkes of living fire was spangled,
And night deepe drencht in mystie *Acheron*
Heav'd up her head, and halfe the world upon
Breath'd darkenesse forth (darke night is *Cupids* day).
And now begins *Leander* to display

Loves holy fire, with words, with sighs and teares,
Which like sweet musicke entred *Heroes* eares,
And yet at everie word shee turn'd aside,
And alwaies cut him off as he replide.
At last, like to a bold sharpe Sophister,
With chearefull hope thus he accosted her.

    Faire creature, let me speake without offence,
I would my rude words had the influence,
To lead thy thoughts as thy faire lookes doe mine,
Then shouldst thou bee his prisoner who is thine.
Be not unkind and faire, mishapen stuffe
Are of behaviour boisterous and ruffe.
O shun me not, but heare me ere you goe,
God knowes I cannot force love, as you doe.
My words shall be as spotlesse as my youth,
Full of simplicitie and naked truth.
This sacrifice (whose sweet perfume descending,
From *Venus* altar to your footsteps bending)
Doth testifie that you exceed her farre,
To whom you offer, and whose Nunne you are.
Why should you worship her? her you surpasse,
As much as sparkling Diamonds flaring glasse.
A Diamond set in lead his worth retaines,
A heavenly Nimph, belov'd of humane swaines,
Receives no blemish, but oft-times more grace,
Which makes me hope, although I am but base,
Base in respect of thee, divine and pure,
Dutifull service may thy love procure,
And I in dutie will excell all other,
As thou in beautie doest exceed Loves mother.
Nor heaven, nor thou, were made to gaze upon,
As heaven preserves all things, so save thou one.
A stately builded ship, well rig'd and tall,
The Ocean maketh more majesticall:
Why vowest thou then to live in *Sestos* here,

Who on Loves seas more glorious wouldst appeare?
Like untun'd golden strings all women are,
Which long time lie untoucht, will harshly jarre,
Vessels of Brasse oft handled, brightly shine,
What difference betwixt the richest mine
And basest mold, but use? for both, not us'de,
Are of like worth. Then treasure is abus'de,
When misers keepe it; being put to lone,
In time it will returne us two for one.
Rich robes themselves and others do adorne,
Neither themselves nor others, if not worne.
Who builds a pallace and rams up the gate,
Shall see it ruinous and desolate.
Ah simple *Hero,* learne thy selfe to cherish,
Lone women like to emptie houses perish.
Lesse sinnes the poore rich man that starves himselfe,
In heaping up a masse of drossie pelfe,
·Than such as you: his golden earth remains,
Which after his disceasse, some other gains.
But this faire jem, sweet in the losse alone,
When you fleet hence, can be bequeath'd to none.
Or if it could, downe from th'enameld skie
All heaven would come to claime this legacie,
And with intestine broiles the world destroy,
And quite confound natures sweet harmony.
Well therefore by the gods decreed it is,
We humane creatures should enjoy that blisse
One is no number, mayds are nothing then,
Without the sweet societie of men.
Wilt thou live single still? one shalt thou bee,
Though never-singling *Hymen* couple thee.
Wild savages, that drinke of running springs,
Thinke water farre excels all earthly things:
But they that dayly tast neat wine, despise it.
Virginitie, albeit some highly prise it,

Compar'd with marriage, had you tried them both,
Differs as much as wine and water doth.
Base boullion for the stampes sake we allow,
Even so for mens impression do we you,
By which alone, our reverend fathers say,
Women receave perfection everie way.
This idoll which you terme *Virginitie,*
Is neither essence subject to the eie,
No, nor to any one exterior sence,
Nor hath it any place of residence,
Nor is't of earth or mold celestiall,
Or capable of any forme at all.
Of that which hath no being doe not boast,
Things that are not at all are never lost.
Men foolishly doe call it vertuous,
What vertue is it that is borne with us?
Much lesse can honour bee ascrib'd thereto,
Honour is purchac'd by the deedes wee do.
Beleeve me *Hero,* honour is not wone,
Untill some honourable deed be done.
Seeke you for chastitie, immortall fame,
And know that some have wrong'd *Dianas* name?
Whose name is it, if she be false or not,
So she be faire, but some vile toongs will blot?
But you are faire (aye me) so wondrous faire,
So yoong, so gentle, and so debonaire,
As *Greece* will thinke, if thus you live alone,
Some one or other keepes you as his owne.
Then *Hero* hate me not, nor from me flie,
To follow swiftly blasting infamie.
Perhaps, thy sacred Priesthood makes thee loath,
Tell me, to whom mad'st thou that heedlesse oath?
    To *Venus,* answered shee, and as shee spake,
Foorth from those two tralucent cesternes brake
A streame of liquid pearle, which downe her face

Made milk-white paths, wheron the gods might trace
To *Joves* high court. Hee thus replide: The rites
In which Loves beauteous Empresse most delites,
Are banquets, Dorick musicke, midnight-revell,
Plaies, maskes, and all that stern age counteth evill.
Thee as a holy Idiot doth she scorne,
For thou in vowing chastitie hast sworne
To rob her name and honour, and thereby
Commit'st a sinne far worse than perjurie,
Even sacrilege against her Deitie,
Through regular and formall puritie.
To expiat which sinne, kisse and shake hands,
Such sacrifice as this *Venus* demands.

 Thereat she smild, and did denie him so,
As put thereby, yet might he hope for mo.
Which makes him quickly re-enforce his speech,
And her in humble manner thus beseech.

 Though neither gods nor men may thee deserve,
Yet for her sake whom you have vow'd to serve,
Abandon fruitlesse cold Virginitie,
The gentle queene of Loves sole enemie.
Then shall you most resemble *Venus* Nun,
When *Venus* sweet rites are perform'd and done.
Flint-brested *Pallas* joies in single life,
But *Pallas* and your mistresse are at strife.
Love *Hero* then, and be not tirannous,
But heale the heart, that thou hast wounded thus,
Nor staine thy youthfull years with avarice,
Faire fooles delight to be accounted nice.
The richest corne dies, if it be not reapt,
Beautie alone is lost, too warily kept.
These arguments he us'de, and many more,
Wherewith she yeelded, that was woon before.
Heroes lookes yeelded, but her words made warre,
Women are woon when they begin to jarre.

Thus having swallow'd *Cupids* golden hooke,
The more she striv'd, the deeper was she strooke.
Yet evilly faining anger, strove she still,
And would be thought to graunt against her will.
So having paus'd a while, at last shee said:
Who taught thee Rhethoricke to deceive a maid?
Aye me, such words as these should I abhor,
And yet I like them for the Orator.

   With that *Leander* stoopt, to have imbrac'd her,
But from his spreading armes away she cast her,
And thus bespake him: Gentle youth forbeare
To touch the sacred garments which I weare.
Upon a rocke, and underneath a hill,
Far from the towne (where all is whist and still,
Save that the sea playing on yellow sand,
Sends foorth a ratling murmure to the land,
Whose sound allures the golden *Morpheus*
In silence of the night to visite us.)
My turret stands, and there God knowes I play
With *Venus* swannes and sparrowes all the day.
A dwarfish beldame beares me companie,
That hops about the chamber where I lie,
And spends the night (that might be better spent)
In vaine discourse, and apish merriment.
Come thither. As she spake this, her toong tript,
For unawares (*Come thither*) from her slipt,
And sodainly her former colour chang'd,
And here and there her eies through anger rang'd.
And like a planet, mooving severall waies,
At one selfe instant, she poore soule assaies,
Loving, not to love at all, and everie part
Strove to resist the motions of her hart.
And hands so pure, so innocent, nay such,
As might have made heaven stoope to have a touch,
Did she uphold to *Venus,* and againe

Vow'd spotlesse chastitie, but all in vaine.
Cupid beats downe her praiers with his wings,
Her vowes above the emptie aire he flings:
All deepe enrag'd, his sinowie bow he bent,
And shot a shaft that burning from him went,
Wherewith she strooken look'd so dolefully,
As made Love sigh, to see his tirannie.
And as she wept, her teares to pearle he turn'd,
And wound them on his arme, and for her mourn'd.
Then towards the pallace of the destinies,
Laden with languishment and griefe he flies,
And to those sterne nymphs humblie made request,
Both might enjoy ech other, and be blest.
But with a ghastly dreadfull countenaunce,
Threatning a thousand deaths at everie glaunce,
They answered Love, nor would vouchsafe so much
As one poore word, their hate to him was such.
Harken a while, and I will tell you why:
Heavens winged herrald, *Jove-borne Mercury,*
The selfe-same day that he asleepe had layd
Inchaunted Argus, spied a countrie mayd,
Whose carelesse haire, in stead of pearle t'adorne it,
Glist'red with deaw, as one that seem'd to skorne it:
Her breath as fragrant as the morning rose,
Her mind pure, and her toong untaught to glose.
Yet prowd she was, (for loftie pride that dwels
In tow'red courts, is oft in sheapheards cels.)
And too too well the faire vermilion knew,
And silver tincture of her cheekes, that drew
The love of everie swaine: On her, this god
Enamoured was, and with his snakie rod,
Did charme her nimble feet, and made her stay,
The while upon a hillocke downe he lay,
And sweetly on his pipe began to play,
And with smooth speech her fancie to assay,

Till in his twining armes he lockt her fast,
And then he woo'd with kisses, and at last,
As sheap-heards do, her on the ground hee layd,
And tumbling in the grasse, he often strayd
Beyond the bounds of shame, in being bold
To eie those parts, which no eie should behold.
And like an insolent commaunding lover,
Boasting his parentage, would needs discover
The way to new *Elisium:* but she,
Whose only dower was her chastitie,
Having striv'ne in vaine, was now about to crie,
And crave the helpe of sheap-heards that were nie.
Herewith he stayd his furie, and began
To give her leave to rise: away she ran,
After went *Mercurie,* who us'd such cunning,
As she to heare his tale, left off her running.
Maids are not woon by brutish force and might,
But speeches full of pleasure and delight.
And knowing *Hermes* courted her, was glad
That she such lovelinesse and beautie had
As could provoke his liking, yet was mute,
And neither would denie, nor graunt his sute.
Still vowd he love, she wanting no excuse
To feed him with delaies, as women use,
Or thirsting after immortalitie,—
All women are ambitious naturallie,—
Impos'd upon her lover such a taske,
As he ought not performe, nor yet she aske.
A draught of flowing *Nectar* she requested,
Wherewith the king of Gods and men is feasted.
He readie to accomplish what she wil'd,
Stole some from *Hebe* (*Hebe Joves* cup fil'd),
And gave it to his simple rustike love,
Which being knowne (as what is hid from *Jove?*)
He inly storm'd, and waxt more furious

Than for the fire filcht by *Prometheus,*
And thrusts him down from heaven. he wandring here,
In mournfull tearmes, with sad and heavie cheare
Complaind to *Cupid. Cupid* for his sake,
To be reveng'd on Jove did undertake,
And those on whom heaven, earth, and hell relies,
I mean the Adamantine Destinies,
He wounds with love, and forst them equallie
To dote upon deceitfull *Mercurie.*
They offred him the deadly fatall knife,
That sheares the slender threads of humane life,
At his faire feathered feet the engins layd,
Which th'earth from ougly *Chaos* den up-wayd:
These he regarded not, but did intreat,
That Jove, usurper of his fathers seat,
Might presently be banisht into hell,
And aged *Saturne* in *Olympus* dwell.
They granted what he crav'd, and once againe
Saturne and *Ops* began their golden raigne.
Murder, rape, warre, lust and trecherie,
Were with *Jove* clos'd in *Stigian* Emprie.
But long this blessed time continued not:
As soone as he his wished purpose got,
He recklesse of his promise did despise
The love of th'everlasting Destinies.
They seeing it, both Love and him abhor'd,
And *Jupiter* unto his place restor'd.
And but that Learning, in despight of Fate,
Will mount aloft, and enter heaven gate,
And to the seat of *Jove* it selfe advaunce,
Hermes had slept in hell with ignoraunce,
Yet as a punishment they added this,
That he and *Povertie* should alwaies kis.
And to this day is everie scholler poore,
Grosse gold from them runs headlong to the boore.

Likewise the angrie sisters thus deluded,
To venge themselves on *Hermes,* have concluded
That *Midas* brood shall sit in Honors chaire,
To which the *Muses* sonnes are only heire:
And fruitfull wits that in aspiring are,
Shall discontent run into regions farre;
And few great lords in vertuous deeds shall joy,
But be surpris'd with every garish toy;
And still inrich the loftie servile clowne,
Who with incroching guile keepes learning downe
Then muse not *Cupids* sute no better sped,
Seeing in their loves the Fates were iniured.

FROM *Tamburlaine the Great*

TAMBURLAINE. Nature that fram'd us of foure Ele-
    ments,
Warring within our breasts for regiment,
Doth teach us all to have aspyring minds:
Our soules, whose faculties can comprehend
The wondrous Architecture of the world:
And measure every wandring plannets course,
Still climing after knowledge infinite,
And alwaies mooving as the restles Spheares,
Wils us to weare our selves and never rest,
Untill we reach the ripest fruit of all,
That perfect blisse and sole felicitie,
The sweet fruition of an earthly crowne.

(Act II, scene vi, lines 869–80)

TAMBURLAINE. Ah faire *Zenocrate,* divine *Zenocrate,*
Faire is too foule an Epithite for thee,

That in thy passion for thy countries love,
And feare to see thy kingly Fathers harme,
With haire discheweld wip'st thy watery cheeks:
And like to *Flora* in her mornings pride,
Shaking her silver treshes in the aire,
Rain'st on the earth resolved pearle in showers,
And sprinklest Saphyrs on thy shining face,
Wher Beauty, mother to the Muses sits,
And comments vollumes with her Yvory pen:
Taking instructions from thy flowing eies,
Eies when that *Ebena* steps to heaven,
In silence of thy solemn Evenings walk,
Making the mantle of the richest night,
The Moone, the Planets, and the Meteors light.
There Angels in their christal armours fight
A doubtfull battell with my tempted thoughtes,
For Egypts freedom and the Souldans life:
His life that so consumes *Zenocrate,*
Whose sorrowes lay more siege unto my soule,
Than all my Army to *Damascus* walles.
And neither Perseans Soveraign, nor the Turk
Troubled my sences with conceit of foile,
So much by much, as dooth *Zenocrate.*
What is beauty saith my sufferings then?
If all the pens that ever poets held,
Had fed the feeling of their maisters thoughts,
And every sweetnes that inspir'd their harts,
Their minds, and muses on admyred theames:
If all the heavenly Quintessence they still
From their immortall flowers of Poesy,
Wherein as in a myrrour we perceive
The highest reaches of a humaine wit.
If these had made one Poems period
And all combin'd in Beauties worthinesse,
Yet should ther hover in their restlesse heads,

One thought, one grace, one woonder at the least,
Which into words no vertue can digest:
But how unseemly is it for my Sex
My discipline of armes and Chivalrie,
My nature and the terrour of my name,
To harbour thoughts effeminate and faint?
Save onely that in Beauties just applause,
With whose instinct the soule of man is toucht,
And every warriour that is rapt with love,
Of fame, of valour, and of victory
Must needs have beauty beat on his conceites,
I thus conceiving and subduing both
That which hath stoopt the tempest of the Gods,
Even from the fiery spangled vaile of heaven,
To feele the lovely warmth of shepheards flames,
And martch in cottages of strowed weeds,
Shal give the world to note for all my byrth,
That Vertue solely is the sum of glorie,
And fashions men with true nobility.
Who's within there?   (Act V, scene ii, lines 1916–72)

FROM *The Tragicall Historie of Doctor Faustus*

[*The End of Doctor Faustus*]

The clocke strikes eleven.
FAUSTUS. Ah Faustus,
Now hast thou but one bare hower to live,
And then thou must be damnd perpetually:
Stand stil you ever mooving spheres of heaven,
That time may cease, and midnight never come:
Faire Natures eie, rise, rise againe, and make
Perpetuall day, or let this houre be but

A yeere, a moneth, a weeke, a naturall day,
That Faustus may repent, and save his soule,
O lente, lente curite noctis equi:
The starres moove stil, time runs, the clocke wil strike,
The divel wil come, and Faustus must be damnd.
O Ile leape up to my God: who pulles me downe?
See see where Christs blood streames in the firmament.
One drop would save my soule, halfe a drop, ah my
    Christ.
Ah rend not my heart for naming of my Christ,
Yet wil I call on him: oh spare me *Lucifer!*
Where is it now? tis gone: And see where God
Stretcheth out his arme, and bends his irefull browes:
Mountaines and hilles, come, come, and fall on me,
And hide me from the heavy wrath of God.
No, no.
Then wil I headlong runne into the earth:
Earth gape. O no, it wil not harbour me:
You starres that raignd at my nativitie,
Whose influence hath alotted death and hel,
Now draw up Faustus like a foggy mist,
Into the intrailes of yon labring cloude,
That when you vomite foorth into the ayre,
My limbes may issue from your smoaky mouthes,
So that my soule may but ascend to heaven:
Ah, halfe the houre is past: *The watch strikes.*
Twil all be past anone:
Oh God,
If thou wilt not have mercy on my soule,
Yet for Christs sake, whose bloud hath ransomd me,
Impose some end to my incessant paine.
Let Faustus live in hel a thousand yeeres,
A hundred thousand, and at last be sav'd.
O no end is limited to damned soules,
Why wert thou not a creature wanting soule?

Or, why is this immortall that thou hast?
Ah *Pythagoras metemsucosis,* were that true,
This soule should flie from me, and I be changde
Unto some brutish beast: al beasts are happy,
For when they die,
Their soules are soone dissolved in elements,
But mine must live still to be plagde in hel:
Curst be the parents that ingendred me:
No Faustus, curse thy selfe, curse *Lucifer,*
That hath deprivde thee of the joyes of heaven:
The clocke striketh twelve.
O it strikes, it strikes: now body turne to ayre,
Or *Lucifer* wil beare thee quicke to hel:
Thunder and lightning.
O soule, be changde into little water drops,
And fal into the *Ocean,* nere be found:
My God, my God, looke not so fierce on me:
Enter divels.
Adders, and Serpents, let me breathe a while:
Ugly hell gape not, come not *Lucifer,*
Ile burne my bookes, ah *Mephastophilis.*

                              Exeunt with him.

Enter Chorus.

CHORUS. Cut is the branch that might have growne ful
    straight,
And burned is *Apolloes* Laurel bough,
That sometime grew within this learned man:
Faustus is gone, regard his hellish fall,
Whose fiendful fortune may exhort the wise,
Onely to wonder at unlawful things,
Whose deepenesse doth intise such forward wits,
To practise more than heavenly power permits.

       Terminat hora diem, Terminat Author opus.

                         (Lines 1419–end)

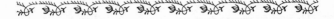

Sir Walter Ralegh

(1552?–1618)

The Passionate Mans Pilgrimage

SUPPOSED TO BE WRITTEN BY ONE AT THE POINT OF DEATH

Give me my Scallop shell of quiet,
My staffe of Faith to walke upon,
My Scrip of Joy, Immortall diet,
My bottle of salvation:
My Gowne of Glory, hopes true gage,
And thus Ile take my pilgrimage.

Blood must be my bodies balmer,
No other balme will there be given
Whilst my soule like a white Palmer
Travels to the land of heaven,
Over the silver mountaines,
Where spring the Nectar fountaines:
And there Ile kisse
The Bowle of blisse,
And drinke my eternall fill
On every milken hill.
My soule will be a drie before,
But after it, will nere thirst more.

And by the happie blisfull way
More peacefull Pilgrims I shall see,
That have shooke off their gownes of clay,

20

And goe appareld fresh like mee.
Ile bring them first
To slake their thirst,
And then to taste those Nectar suckets
At the cleare wells
Where sweetnes dwells,
Drawne up by Saints in Christall buckets.

And when our bottle and all we,
Are fild with immortalitie:
Then the holy paths weele travell
Strewde with Rubies thicke as gravell,
Seelings of Diamonds, Saphire floores,
High walles of Corall and Pearl Bowres.

From thence to heavens Bribeles hall
Where no corrupted voyces brall,
No Conscience molten into gold,
Nor forg'd accusers bought and sold,
No cause deferd, nor vaine spent Jorney,
For there Christ is the Kings Atturney:
Who pleades for all without degrees,
And he hath Angells, but no fees.

When the grand twelve million Jury,
Of our sinnes with sinfull fury,
Gainst our soules blacke verdicts give,
Christ pleades his death, and then we live,
Be thou my speaker taintles pleader,
Unblotted Lawyer, true proceeder,
Thou movest salvation even for almes:
Not with a bribed Lawyers palmes.

And this is my eternall plea,
To him that made Heaven, Earth and Sea,
Seeing my flesh must die so soone,
And want a head to dine next noone,

Just at the stroke when my vaines start and spred
Set on my soul an everlasting head.
Then am I readie like a palmer fit,
To tread those blest paths which before I writ.

The Lie

Goe soule the bodies guest
   upon a thankelesse arrant,
Fear not to touch the best
   the truth shall be thy warrant:
Goe since I needs must die,
   and give the world the lie.

Say to the Court it glowes,
   and shines like rotten wood,
Say to the Church it showes
   whats good, and doth no good.
If Church and Court reply,
   then give them both the lie.

Tell Potentates they live
   acting by others action,
Not loved unlesse they give,
   not strong but by affection.
If Potentates reply,
   give Potentates the lie.

Tell men of high condition,
   that mannage the estate,
Their purpose is ambition,
   their practise onely hate:
And if they once reply,
   then give them all the lie.

Tell them that brave it most,
    they beg for more by spending,
Who in their greatest cost
    like nothing but commending.
And if they make replie,
    then give them all the lie.

Tell zeale it wants devotion
    tell love it is but lust,
Tell time it meets but motion,
    tell flesh it is but dust.
And wish them not replie
    for thou must give the lie.

Tell age it daily wasteth,
    tell honour how it alters.
Tell beauty how she blasteth
    tell favour how it falters
And as they shall reply,
    give every one the lie.

Tell wit how much it wrangles
    in tickle points of nycenesse,
Tell wisedome she entangles
    her selfe in over wisenesse.
And when they doe reply
    straight give them both the lie.

Tell Phisicke of her boldnes,
    tell skill it is prevention:
Tell charity of coldnes,
    tell law it is contention,
And as they doe reply
    so give them still the lie.

Tell fortune of her blindnesse,
    tell nature of decay,

Tell friendship of unkindnesse,
   tell justice of delay.
And if they will reply,
   then give them all the lie.

Tell Arts they have no soundnesse,
   but vary by esteeming,
Tell schooles they want profoundnes
   and stand so much on seeming.
If Arts and schooles reply,
   give arts and schooles the lie.

Tell faith its fled the Citie,
   tell how the country erreth,
Tell manhood shakes off pittie,
   tell vertue least preferred.
And if they doe reply,
   spare not to give the lie.

So when thou hast as I,
   commanded thee, done blabbing,
Because to give the lie,
   deserves no lesse than stabbing,
Stab at thee he that will,
   no stab thy soule can kill.

Three thinges there bee that prosper up apace

(*Sometimes attributed to Ralegh*)

Three thinges there bee that prosper up apace
And flourish, whilest they growe a sunder farr,
But on a day, they meet all in one place,
And when they meet, they one an other marr;
And they bee theise, the wood, the weede, the wagg.

The wood is that, which makes the Gallow tree,
The weed is that, which stringes the Hangmans bagg,
The wagg my pritty knave betokeneth thee.
Marke well deare boy whilest theise assemble not,
Green springs the tree, hempe growes, the wagg is
   wilde,
But when they meet, it makes the timber rott,
It fretts the halter, and it choakes the childe.
   Then bless thee, and beware, and lett us praye,
   Wee part not with thee at this meeting day.

As you came from the holy land

(Sometimes attributed to Ralegh)

As you came from the holy land
   Of Walsinghame,
Mett you not with my tru love
   By the way as you came?

How shall I know your trew love,
   That have mett many one
As I went to the holy lande,
   That have come, that have gone?

She is neyther whyte nor browne,
   Butt as the heavens fayre:
There is none hathe a forme so divine
   In the earth or the ayre:

Such an one did I meet, good Sir,
   Suche an Angelyke face,
Who lyke a queene, lyke a nymph, did appere,
   By her gate, by her grace:

She hath lefte me here all alone,
  All allone as unknowne,
Who somtymes did me lead with her selfe
  And me lovde as her owne:

Whats the cause that she leaves you alone
  And a new waye doth take:
Who loved you once as her owne,
  And her joye did you make?

I have lovde her all my youth,
  Butt now ould as you see,
Love lykes not the fallyng frute
  From the wythered tree:

Know that love is a careless chylld
  And forgets promyse paste:
He is blynd, he is deaff, when he lyste
  And in faythe never faste:

His desyre is a dureless contente
  And a trustless joye;
He is wonn with a world of despayre
  And is lost with a toye:

Of women kynde suche indeed is the love
  Or the word Love abused,
Under which many chyldysh desyres
  And conceytes are excusde:

Butt Love is a durable fyre,
  In the mynde ever burnynge:
Never sycke, never ould, never dead,
  From itt selfe never turnynge.

Richard Stanyhurst

(1547–1618)

A Prayer to the Holy Trinity

Trinitee blessed, deitee coëqual,
Unitee sacred, God one eeke in essence,
Yeeld toe thy servaunt, pitifullye calling
        Merciful hyring.
Vertuus living dyd I long relinquish,
Thy wyl and precepts miserablye scorning,
Graunt toe mee, sinful pacient, repenting,
        Helthful amendment.
Blessed I judge hym, that in hert is healed:
Cursed I know hym, that in helth is harmed:
Thy physick therefore, toe me, wretch unhappye,
        Send, mye Redeemer.
Glorye too God, the father, and his onlye
Son, the protectoure of us earthlye sinners,
Thee sacred spirit, laborers refreshing,
        Stil be renowned. Amen.

Robert Southwell

(1561?–1595)

The Burning Babe

As I in hoarie Winters night
　　Stood shivering in the snow,
Surpriz'd I was with sudden heat,
　　Which made my heart to glow;
And lifting up a fearefull eye
　　To view what fire was neere,
A prettie Babe all burning bright
　　Did in the aire appeare;
Who, scorched with excessive heat,
　　Such flouds of teares did shed,
As though his flouds should quench his flames,
　　Which with his teares were bred:
Alas, (quoth he) but newly borne,
　　In fierie heats I frie,
Yet none approach to warme their hearts,
　　Or feele my fire but I;
My faultlesse brest the furnace is,
　　The fuell wounding thornes:
Love is the fire, and sighs the smoke,
　　The ashes shames and scornes;
The fuell justice layeth on,
　　And mercy blowes the coales,
The metall in this Furnace wrought,
　　Are mens defiled soules:
For which, as now on fire I am,

To worke them to their good,
So will I melt into a bath,
To wash them in my blood.
With this he vanisht out of sight,
And swiftly shrunke away,
And straight I called unto minde,
That it was Christmasse day.

At Fotheringay

The pounded spise both tast and sent doth please;
In fadinge smoke the force doth incense showe;
The perisht kernell springeth with increase;
The lopped tree doth best and soonest growe.

Gods spice I was, and poundinge was my due;
In fadinge breath my incense favoured best;
Death was my meane my kernell to renewe;
By loppinge shott I upp to heavenly rest.

Some thinges more perfit are in their decaye,
Like sparke that going out geeves clerest light:
Such was my happe, whose dolefull dying daye
Begane my joye and termed fortunes spight.

Alive a Queene, now dead I am a Saint;
Once *Mary* cald, my name now Martyr is;
From earthly raigne debarred by restrainte,
In liew wherof I raigne in heavenly blis.

My life, my griefe, my death, hath wrought my joye;
My freendes, my foyle, my foes, my weale procurd,
My speedie death hath scorned longe annoye,
And losse of life an endles life assurd.

My scaffolde was the bedd where ease I fownde;
The blocke a pillowe of eternall rest.
My headman cast mee in in blesfull sownde;
His axe cutt of my cares from combred brest.

Rue not my death, rejoyce at my repose;
It was no death to mee but to my woe,
The budd was opened to let owt the rose,
The cheynes unloosed to let the captive goe.

A Prince by birth, a prisoner by mishappe,
From crowne to crosse from throne to thrall I fell.
My right my ruth, my tytles wrought my trapp;
My weale my woe, my worldly heaven my hell.

By death from prisoner to a prince enhaunced;
From crosse to crowne from thrall to throne againe,
My ruth my righte, my trappe my styll advaunced
From woe to weale, from hell to heavenly raigne.

Times Goe by Turnes

The lopped tree
    In time may grow againe,
Most naked plants
    Renew both fruit and flowre:
The sorriest wight
    May finde release of paine,
The dryest soile
    Suck in some moistning showre.
Times goe by turnes,
    And chances chaunge by course,
From foule to faire,
    From better hap to worse.

The Sea of Fortune
   Doth not ever flow,
She drawes her favours
   To the lowest ebbe;
Her tides have equall times
   To come and goe,
Her Loome doth weave
   The fine and coursest webbe;
No joy so great,
   But runneth to an end:
No hap so hard,
   But may in fine amend.

Not alwayes Fall of leafe,
   Nor ever Spring,
No endlesse night,
   Nor yet eternall day:
The saddest Birds
   A season finde to sing,
The roughest storme
   A calme may soone allay.
Thus with succeeding turnes
   God tempereth all;
That man may hope to rise,
   Yet feare to fall.

A chance may winne
   That by mischaunce was lost,
That net that holds no great,
   Takes little fish;
In some things all,
   In all things none are crost:
Few all they need,
   But none have all they wish.
Unmedled joyes
   Here to no man befall:

Who least, hath some,
   Who most, hath never all.

Ensamples of Our Saviour

Our Saviour
   (Paterne of true holinesse)
Continuall praid
   Us by ensample teaching,
When he was baptized
   In the wildernesse,
In working miracles
   And in his preaching,
Upon the mount
   In garden grones of death,
At his last Supper
   At his parting breath.

O fortresse of the faithfull,
   Sure defence,
In which doth Christians
   Cognizance consist:
Their victories, their triumph
   Comes from thence,
So forcible, hellgates
   Cannot resist:
A thing whereby
   Both Angels, clouds, and starres,
At mans request
   Fight Gods revengefull warres.

Nothing more gratefull
   In the Highest eyes,

Nothing more firme
   In danger to protect us,
Nothing more forcible
   To pierce the skies,
And not depart
   Till mercy doe respect us:
And as the soule
   Life to the body gives,
So prayer revives
   The soule, by prayer it lives.

Henry Constable

(1562–1613)

To Saint Mary Magdalen

Blessed Offendour: who thyselfe haist try'd,
  How farr a synner differs from a Saynt
  Joyne thy wett eyes, with teares of my complaint,
  While I sighe for that grave, for which thow cry'd.
No longer let my synfull sowle, abyde
  In feaver of thy fyrst desyres faynte:
  But lett that love which last thy hart did taynt
  With panges of thy repentance, pierce my syde.
So shall my sowle, no foolysh vyrgyn bee
  With empty lampe: but lyke a Magdalen, beere
  For oyntment boxe, a breast with oyle of grace:
And so the zeale, which then shall burne in mee,
  May make my hart, lyke to a lampe appere
  And in my spouses pallace gyve me place.

Damelus' Song to His Diaphenia

Diaphenia like the Daffadown-dillie,
White as the Sunne, faire as the Lillie,
    Heigh hoe, how I doo love thee?
I doo love thee as my Lambs
Are beloved of their Dams,
    How blest were I if thou would'st proove me?

Diaphenia like the spreading Roses,
That in my sweetes all sweetes incloses,
     Faire sweete how I doo love thee?
I doo love thee as each flower,
Loves the Sunnes life-giving power.
     For dead, thy breath to life might moove me.

Diaphenia like to all things blessed,
When all thy praises are expressed,
     Deare Joy, how I doo love thee?
As the birds doo love the Spring:
Or the Bees their carefull King,
     Then in requite, sweet Virgin love me.

William Alabaster

(1567–1640)

Upon the Crucifix

Now I have found thee I will evermore
Embrace this standard where thou sitts above,
Feede greedie eies, and from hence never rove;
Sucke hungrie soule of this eternall store;
Issue my hart from thie two leaved dore,
And lett my lippes from kissinge not remove.
O that I weare transformed into love,
And as a plant might springe uppon this flower,
Like wandring Ivy or sweete honnie suckle:
How would I with my twine about it buckle,
And kisse his feete with my ambitious boughes,
And clyme along uppon his sacred brest,
And make a garland for his wounded browes:
Lord soe I am, if heare my thoughts may rest.

On the Reed of Our Lord's Passion

Long tyme hathe Christ (long tyme I must confesse)
Held mee a hollowe Reede within his hande,
That merited in Hell to make a brande
Had not his grace supplied mine emptines.
Oft time with languor and newfanglenes
Had I bene borne awaye like sifted sande,

36

When sinn and Sathan gott the upper hande,
But that his stedfast mercie did mee blesse.
Still let mee growe upon that livinge lande,
  Within that wounde which iron did impresse,
  And made a springe of bloud flowe from thie hand:
Then will I gather sapp, and rise, and stand
  That all that see this wonder maye expresse
  Upon this grounde how well growes barrennes.

Sir John Davies

(1569–1626)

FROM *Orchestra or A Poeme of Dauncing*

Dauncing (bright Lady) then began to bee,
When the first seeds whereof the World did spring,
The fire, ayre, earth, and water—did agree,
By Love's perswasion,—Nature's mighty King,—
To leave their first disordred combating;
   And in a daunce such measure to observe,
   As all the world their motion should perserve.

Since when, they still are carried in a round,
And changing, come one in another's place;
Yet doe they neither mingle nor confound,
But every one doth keepe the bounded space
Wherein the Daunce doth bid it turne or trace;
   This wondrous myracle did Love devise,
   For Dauncing is Love's proper exercise.

Like this, he fram'd the gods' eternall Bower,
And of a shapelesse and confusèd masse,
By his through-piercing and digesting power,
The turning vault of heaven formèd was;
Whose starry wheeles he hath so made to passe,
   As that their moovings do a musicke frame,
   And they themselves still daunce unto the same.

(Stanzas 17–19)·

38

Behold the *World*, how it is *whirled round*,
And for it is so *whirl'd*, is named so;
In whose large volume many rules are found
Of this new Art, which it doth fairely show;
For your quicke eyes in wandring too and fro
   From East to West, on no one thing can glaunce
   But if you marke it well, it seemes to daunce.

First you see fixt in this huge mirrour blew,
Of trembling lights, a number numberlesse:
Fixt they are nam'd, but with a name untrue,
For they all moove and in a Daunce expresse
That *great long yeare*, that doth containe no lesse
   Then threescore hundreds of those yeares in all,
   Which the sunne makes with his course naturall.

What if to you these sparks disordered seeme
As if by chaunce they had beene scattered there?
The gods a solemne measure doe it deeme,
And see a just proportion every where,
And know the points whence first their movings were;
   To which first points when all returne againe,
   The axel-tree of Heav'n shall breake in twaine.

Under that spangled skye, five wandring flames
Besides the King of Day, and Queene of Night,
Are wheel'd around, all in their sundry frames,
And all in sundry measures doe delight,
Yet altogether keepe no measure right;
   For by it selfe each doth it selfe advance,
   And by it selfe each doth a galliard daunce.

Venus, the mother of that bastard Love,
Which doth usurpe the World's great Marshal's name,
Just with the sunne her dainty feete doth move,
And unto him doth all the jestures frame;

Now after, now afore, the flattering Dame,
   With divers cunning passages doth erre,
   Still him respecting that respects not her.

For that brave Sunne the Father of the Day,
Doth love this Earth, the Mother of the Night;
And like a revellour in rich aray,
Doth daunce his galliard in his lemman's sight,
Both back, and forth, and sidewaies, passing light;
   His princely grace doth so the gods amaze,
   That all stand still and at his beauty gaze.

But see the Earth, when he approcheth neere,
How she for joy doth spring and sweetly smile;
But see againe her sad and heavy cheere
When changing places he retires a while;
But those blake cloudes he shortly will exile,
   And make them all before his presence flye,
   As mists consum'd before his cheerefull eye.

Who doth not see the measures of the Moone,
Which thirteene times she daunceth every yeare?
And ends her pavine thirteene times as soone
As doth her brother, of whose golden haire
She borroweth part, and proudly doth it weare;
   Then doth she coyly turne her face aside,
   Then halfe her cheeke is scarse sometimes discride.

Next her, the pure, subtile, and clensing Fire
Is swiftly carried in a circle even;
Though Vulcan be pronounst by many a lyer,
The only halting god that dwels in heaven:
But that foule name may be more fitly given
   To your false Fire, that farre from heaven is fall:
   And doth consume, waste, spoile, disorder all.

And now behold your tender nurse the *Ayre*
And common neighbour that ay runns around;
How many pictures and impressions faire
Within her empty regions are there found;
Which to your sences Dauncing doe propound.
  For what are *Breath, Speech, Ecchos, Musicke,*
    Winds,
  But Dauncings of the Ayre in sundry kinds?

For when you breath, the *ayre* in order moves,
Now in, now out, in time and measure trew;
And when you speake, so well she dauncing loves,
That doubling oft, and oft redoubling new,
With thousand formes she doth her selfe endew
  For all the words that from our lips repaire
  Are nought but tricks and turnings of the ayre.

Hence is her pratling daughter *Eccho* borne,
That daunces to all voyces she can heare;
There is no sound so harsh that shee doth scorne,
Nor any time wherein shee wil forbeare
The ayrie pavement with her feet to weare;
  And yet her hearing sence is nothing quick,
  For after time she endeth every trick.

And thou sweet *Musicke,* Dauncing's onely life,
The eare's sole happinesse, the ayre's best speach;
Loadstone of fellowship, charming-rod of strife,
The soft mind's Paradice, the sicke mind's leach;
With thine own tong, thou trees and stons canst teach,
  That when the Aire doth dance her finest measure,
  Then art thou borne, the gods and mens sweet pleas-
  ure.

Lastly, where keepe the *Winds* their revelry,
Their violent turnings, and wild whirling hayes,

But in the Ayre's tralucent gallery?
Where shee herselfe is turnd a hundreth wayes,
While with those Maskers wantonly she playes;
    Yet in this misrule, they such rule embrace,
    As two at once encomber not the place.

If then fire, ayre, wandring and fixed lights
In every province of the imperiall skie,
Yeeld perfect formes of dauncing to your sights,
In vaine I teach the eare, that which the eye
With certaine view already doth descrie.
    But for your eyes perceive not all they see,
    In this I will your Senses master bee.

For loe the *Sea* that fleets about the Land,
And like a girdle clips her solide waist,
Musicke and measure both doth understand;
For his great chrystall eye is alwayes cast
Up to the Moone, and on her fixèd fast;
    And as she daunceth in her pallid spheere,
    So daunceth he about his Center heere.

Sometimes his proud greene waves in order set,
One after other flow unto the shore;
Which, when they have with many kisses wet,
They ebbe away in order as before;
And to make knowne his courtly love the more,
    He oft doth lay aside his three-forkt mace,
    And with his armes the timorous Earth embrace.

Onely the Earth doth stand for ever still:
Her rocks remove not, nor her mountaines meet:
(Although some wits enricht with Learning's skill
Say heav'n stands firme, and that the Earth doth fleet,
And swiftly turneth underneath their feet)
    Yet though the Earth is ever stedfast seene,
    On her broad breast hath Dauncing ever beene.

For those blew vaines that through her body spred,
Those saphire streames which from great hils do spring.
(The Earth's great duggs; for every wight is fed
With sweet fresh moisture from them issuing):
Observe a daunce in their wilde wandering;
    And still their daunce begets a murmur sweet,
    And still the murmur with the daunce doth meet.

Of all their wayes I love *Maeander's* path,
Which to the tunes of dying swans doth daunce;
Such winding sleights, such turns and tricks he hath,
Such creeks, such wrenches, and such daliaunce;
That whether it be hap or heedlesse chaunce,
    In this indented course and wriggling play
    He seemes to daunce a perfect cunning *hay*.

But wherefore doe these streames for ever runne?
To keepe themselves for ever sweet and cleere:
For let their everlasting course be donne,
They straight corrupt and foule with mud appeare.
O yee sweet Nymphs that beautie's losse do feare,
    Contemne the drugs that Physicke doth devise,
    And learne of Love this dainty exercise.

See how those flowres that have sweet beauty too,
(The onely jewels that the Earth doth weare,
When the young Sunne in bravery her doth woo):
As oft as they the whistling wind doe heare,
Doe wave their tender bodies here and there;
    And though their daunce no perfect measure is,
    Yet oftentimes their musicke makes them kis.

What makes the vine about the elme to daunce,
With turnings, windings, and embracements round?
What makes the loadstone to the North advance
His subtile point, as if from thence he found
His chiefe attractive vertue to redound?

    Kind Nature first doth cause all things to love,
    Love makes them daunce and in just order move.

Harke how the birds doe sing, and marke then how
Jumpe with the modulation of their layes
They lightly leape, and skip from bow to bow:
Yet doe the cranes deserve a greater prayse
Which keepe such measure in their ayrie wayes,
    As when they all in order rankèd are,
     They make a perfect forme triangular.

In the chiefe angle flyes the watchfull guid,
And all the followers their heads doe lay
On their foregoers backs, on eyther side;
But for the captaine hath no rest to stay,
His head forewearied with the windy way,
    He back retires, and then the next behind,
    As his lieuetenaunt leads them through the wind.

But why relate I every singular?
Since all the World's great fortunes and affaires
Forward and backward rapt and whirled are,
According to the musicke of the spheares:
And Chaunge herselfe her nimble feete upbeares
    On a round slippery wheele that rowleth ay,
    And turnes all States with her impervous sway.

Learne then to daunce, you that are Princes borne,
And lawfull lords of earthly creatures all;
Imitate them, and thereof take no scorne,
For this new art to them is naturall—
And imitate the starres cœlestiall:
    For when pale Death your vital twist shall sever,
    Your better parts must daunce, with them for ever.

Thus Love perswades, and all the crowd of men
That stands around, doth make a murmuring;

As when the wind loosd from his hollow den,
Among the trees a gentle base doth sing,
Or as a brooke through peebles wandering;
    But in their looks they u'tered this plain speach,
    That they would learn to daunce, if Love would
      teach.

Then first of all he doth demonstrate plaine
The motions seaven that ar in Nature found,
Upward and *downeward, forth* and *backe againe,*
To this side and *to that,* and *turning round;*
Whereof a thousand brawles he doth compound,
    Which he doth teach unto the multitude,
    And ever with a turne they must conclude.

As when a Nimph arysing from the land,
Leadeth a daunce with her long watery traine
Down to the Sea; she wries to every hand,
And every way doth crosse the fertile plaine;
But when at last shee falls into the maine,
    Then all her traverses concluded are,
    And with the Sea her course is circulare.

Thus when at first Love had them marshallèd,
As earst he did the shapeless masse of things,
He taught them *rounds* and *winding heyes* to tread,
And about trees to cast themselves in rings:
As the two Beares, whom the First Mover flings
    With a short turn about heaven's axeltree,
    In a round daunce for ever wheeling bee.

But after these, as men more civell grew,
He did more grave and solemn measures frame,
With such faire order and proportion true,
And correspondence every way the same,
That no fault-finding eye did ever blame;

For every eye was movèd at the sight
With sober wondring, and with sweet delight.

(Stanzas 34–65)

FROM *Nosce Teipsum*

IN WHAT MANNER THE SOULE
IS UNITED TO THE BODY

But how shall we this *union* well expresse?
   Nought ties the *soule;* her subtiltie is such
   She moves the bodie, which she doth possesse,
   Yet no part toucheth, but by *Vertue's* touch.

Then dwels shee not therein as in a tent,
   Nor as a pilot in his ship doth sit;
   Nor as the spider in his web is pent;
   Nor as the waxe retaines the print in it;

Nor as a vessell water doth containe;
   Nor as one liquor in another shed;
   Nor as the heat doth in the fire remaine;
   Nor as a voice throughout the ayre is spread:

But as the faire and cheerfull *Morning light,*
   Doth here and there her silver beames impart,
   And in an instant doth herselfe unite
   To the transparent ayre, in all, and part:

Still resting whole, when blowes the ayre divide;
   Abiding pure, when th'ayre is most corrupted;
   Throughout the ayre, her beams dispersing wide,
   And when the ayre is tost, not interrupted:

So doth the piercing *Soule* the body fill,
   Being all in all, and all in part diffus'd;
   Indivisible, incorruptible still,
   Not forc't, encountred, troubled or confus'd.

And as the *sunne* above, the light doth bring,
   Though we behold it in the ayre below;
   So from th' Eternall Light the *Soule* doth spring,
   Though in the body she her powers doe show.

                       (*Lines* 897–1024)

Anonymous Lyrics

Hierusalem, my happie home

Hierusalem, my happie home,
    When shall I come to thee;
When shall my sorrowes have an end,
    Thy joyes when shall I see?

O happie harbour of the saintes,
    O sweete and pleasant soyle:
In thee noe sorrow may be founde,
    Noe greefe, noe care, noe toyle.

In thee noe sickenesse may be seene,
    Noe hurt, noe ache, noe sore;
There is no Death, nor uglie Devill,
    There is life for evermore.

Noe Dampishe mist is seene in thee,
    Nor could nor Darksome night;
There everie soule shines as the sunne,
    There god himselfe gives light.

There lust and lukar cannot dwell,
    There envie beares noe sway;
There is noe hunger, heate nor coulde,
    But pleasure everie way.

Hierusalem, Hierusalem,
    God grant I once may see
Thy endlesse joyes, and of the same
    Partaker aye to bee.

Thy wales are made of precious stones,
  Thy bulwarkes Diamondes square;
Thy gates are of right Orient pearle,
  Exceedinge riche and rare.

Thy terettes, and thy Pinacles
  With Carbuncles Doe shine;
Thy verie streetes are paved with gould,
  Surpassinge cleare, and fine.

Thy houses are of Ivorie,
  Thy windoes Cristale cleare;
Thy tyles are mad of beaten gold:
  O god that I were there!

Within thy gates nothinge doeth come
  That is not passinge cleane;
Noe spiders web, noe Durt, noe Dust,
  Noe filthe may there be seene.

Ay my sweete home, Hierusaleme,
  Would god I were in thee!
Would god my woes were at an end,
  Thy joyes that I might see!

Thy saintes are crownd with glorie great;
  They see god face to face;
They triumph still; they still rejoyce:
  Most happie is their case.

Wee that are heere in banishment
  Continuallie doe mourne;
We sighe and sobbe, we weepe and weale,
  Perpetually we groane.

Our sweete is mixt with bitter gaule;
  Our pleasure and such play,
Our joyes scarce last the lookeing on:
  Our sorrowes still remaine.

But there they live in such delight,
    Such pleasure and such play,
As that to them a thousand yeares
    Doth seeme as yesterday.

Thy Viniardes and thy Orchardes are
    Most beutifull and faire,
Full furnished with trees and fruites
    Most wonderful and rare.

Thy gardens and thy gallant walkes
    Continually are greene;
There groes such sweete and pleasant flowers
    As noe where eles are seene.

There is nector and Ambrosia made;
    There is muske and Civette sweete;
There manie a faire and daintie Drugge
    Are troden under feete.

There Cinomon, there sugar groes;
    There narde and balme abound:
What tounge can tell or hart conceive
    Thy joyes that there are found.

Thy happy Saints (Hierusalem)
    Doe bathe in endlesse blisse;
None but those blessed soules can tell
    How great thy glory is.

Quyt through the streetes with silver sound
    The flood of life doe flowe,
Upon whose bankes on everie syde
    The wood of life doth growe.

There trees for evermore beare fruite
    And evermore doe springe:
There evermore the Angels sit
    And evermore doe singe.

There David standes with harpe in hand
  As maister of the Queere:
Tenne thousand times that man were blest
  That might this musique heare.

Our Ladie singes magnificat
  With tune surpassinge sweete,
And all the virginns beare their partes,
  Sitinge above her feete.

Te Deum doth Sant Ambrose singe,
  Saint Augustine dothe the like,
Ould Simeon and Zacharie
  Have not their songes to seeke.

There Magdalene hath left her mone,
  And cheerefullie doth singe
With blessed saintes, whose harmonie
  In everie streete doth ringe.

Hierusalem, my happie home,
  Would god I were in thee!
Would god my woes were at an end,
  Thy joyes that I might see!

A Lament for Our Lady's Shrine
at Walsingham

In the wrackes of Walsingam
  Whom should I chuse,
But the Queene of Walsingham
  To be guide to my muse.
Then thou Prince of Walsingham,
  Graunt me to frame,

Bitter plaintes to rewe thy wronge,
  Bitter wo for thy name.
Bitter was it soe to see
  The seely sheepe
Murdred by the raveninge wolves
  While the sheephardes did sleep;
Bitter was it oh to vewe
  The sacred vyne,
Whiles the gardiners plaied all close,
  Rooted up by the swine;
Bitter, bitter, oh to behould,
  The grasse to growe
Where the walles of Walsingam
  So statly did shewe:
Such were the workes of Walsingam,
  While shee did stand;
Such are the wrackes as now do shewe
  Of that holy land.
Levell, Levell with the ground,
  The towres doe lye,
Which with their golden glitteringe tops
  Pearsed once to the skye;
Wher weare gates no gates ar nowe,
  The waies unknowen
Wher the presse of peares did passe
  While her fame far was blowen.
Oules do scrike wher the sweetest himnes
  Lately weer songe;
Toades, and serpentes hold ther dennes,
  Wher the Palmers did thronge.
Weepe, Weepe, o Walsingam,
  Whose dayes are nightes,
Blessinges turned to blasphemies,
  Holy deedes to dispites!
Sinne is wher our Ladie sate,

Heaven turned is to Hell;
Sathan sittes wher our Lord did swaye:
Walsingam, oh farewell!

Tom o' Bedlam's Song

From the hagg and hungrie goblin
That into raggs would rend ye,
And the spirit that stands by the naked man
In the Book of Moones defend yee!
That of your five sounde sences
You never be forsaken,
Nor wander from your selves with Tom
Abroad to begg your bacon.

While I doe sing "any foode, any feeding,
Feedinge, drinke or clothing,"
Come dame or maid, be not afraid,
Poor Tom will injure nothing.

Of thirty bare years have I
Twice twenty bin enragèd,
And of forty bin three tymes fifteene
In durance soundlie cagèd.
On the lordlie loftes of Bedlam,
With stubble softe and dainty,
Brave braceletts strong, sweet whips ding-dong,
With wholsome hunger plenty.

And nowe I sing, etc.

With a thought I tooke for Maudlin,
And a cruse of cockle pottage,
With a thing thus tall, skie blesse you all,
I befell into this dotage.
I slept not since the Conquest,

Till then I never wakèd,
Till the rogysh boy of love where I lay
Mee found and strip't mee naked.

And nowe I sing, etc.

When I short have shorne my sowre face
And swigg'd my horny barrel,
In an oaken inne I pound my skin
As a suite of guilt apparell.
The moon's my constant Mistrisse,
And the lowlie owle my morrowe,
The flaming Drake and the Nightcrowe make
Mee musicke to my sorrowe.

While I doe sing, etc.

The palsie plagues my pulses
When I prigg your pigs or pullen,
Your culvers take, or matchles make
Your Chanticleare, or sullen.
When I want provant, with Humfrie
I sup, and when benighted,
I repose in Powles with waking soules
Yet nevere am affrighted.

But I doe sing, etc.

I knowe more then Apollo,
For oft, when hee ly's sleeping,
I see the starres att bloudie warres
In the wounded welkin weeping;
The moone embrace her shepheard,
And the quene of Love her warryor,
While the first doth borne the star of morne,
And the next the heavenly Farrier.

While I doe sing, etc.

The Gipsie Snap and Pedro
Are none of Tom's comradoes.
The punk I skorne and the cut purse sworn
And the roaring boyes bravadoe.
The meeke, the white, the gentle,
Me handle touch and spare not
But those that crosse Tom Rynosseros
Doe what the panther dare not.

Although I sing, etc.

With an host of furious fancies,
Whereof I am commander,
With a burning speare, and a horse of aire,
To the wildernesse I wander.
By a knight of ghostes and shadowes
I summon'd am to tourney
Ten leagues beyond the wide world's end.
Me thinke it is noe journey.

Yet will I sing, etc.

Lady Greensleeves

Alas, my love, ye do me wrong,
    To cast me off discurteously:
And I have loved you so long,
    Delighting in your companie.

Greensleeves was all my joy,
    Greensleeves was my delight:
Greensleeves was my hart of gold,
    And who but Ladie Greensleeves.

I have been readie at your hand,
   To grant what ever you would crave.
I have both waged life and land,
   Your love and good will for to have.

     Greensleeves was all my joy, etc.

I bought thee kerchers to thy head,
   That were wrought fine and gallantly:
I kept thee both at boord and bed,
   Which cost my purse wel favouredly,

I bought thee peticotes of the best,
   The cloth so fine as fine might be:
I gave thee jewels for thy chest,
   And all this cost I spent on thee.

Thy smock of silk, both faire and white,
   With gold embrodered gorgeously:
Thy peticote of Sendall right:
   And thus I bought thee gladly.

Thy girdle of gold so red,
   With pearles bedecked sumptuously:
The like no other lasses had,
   And yet thou wouldst not love me,

Thy purse and eke thy gay guilt knives,
   Thy pincase gallant to the eie:
No better wore the Burgesse wives,
   And yet thou wouldst not love me.

Thy crimson stockings all of silk,
   With golde all wrought above the knee,
Thy pumps as white as was the milk,
   And yet thou wouldst not love me.

Thy gown was of the grossie green,
   Thy sleeves of Satten hanging by:

Which made thee be our harvest Queen,
    And yet thou wouldst not love me.

Thy garters fringed with the golde,
    And silver aglets hanging by,
Which made thee blithe for to beholde,
    And yet thou wouldst not love me.

My gayest gelding I thee gave,
    To ride where ever liked thee,
No Ladie ever was so brave,
    And yet thou wouldst not love me.

My men were clothed all in green,
    And they did ever wait on thee:
Al this was gallant to be seen,
    And yet thou wouldst not love me.

They set thee up, they took thee downe,
    They served thee with humilitie,
Thy foote might not once touch the ground,
    And yet thou wouldst not love me.

For everie morning when thou rose,
    I sent thee dainties orderly:
To cheare thy stomack from all woes,
    And yet thou wouldst not love me.

Thou couldst desire no earthly thing.
    But stil thou hadst it readily:
Thy musicke still to play and sing,
    And yet thou wouldst not love me.

And who did pay for all this geare,
    That thou didst spend when pleased thee?
Even I that am rejected here,
    And thou disdainst to love me.

Wel, I wil pray to God on hie,
  That thou my constancie maist see:
And that yet once before I die,
  Thou wilt vouchsafe to love me.

Greensleeves now farewel adue,
  God I pray to prosper thee:
For I am stil thy lover true,
  Come once againe and love me.

Airs and Madrigals

Come away, come sweet Love

Come away, come sweet Love,
The golden morning breakes:
All the earth, all the ayre,
Of love and pleasure speakes.
Teach thine armes then to embrace,
And sweet Rosie lips to kisse:
And mixe our soules in mutuall blisse.
Eyes were made for beauties grace,
Viewing, ruing Loves long paine:
Procur'd by beauties rude disdaine.

Come away, come sweet Love,
The golden morning wasts:
While the Sunne from his Sphere
His fierie arrowes casts,
Making all the shadowes flie,
Playing, staying in the Groave:
To entertaine the stealth of love.
Thither sweet Love let us hie
Flying, dying in desire:
Wing'd with sweet hopes and heavenly fire.

Come away, come sweet Love,
Doo not in vaine adiorne
Beauties grace that should rise
Like to the naked morne.
Lillies on the Rivers side,

And faire *Cyprian* flowers new blowne,
Desire no beauties but their owne.
Ornament is Nurse of pride,
Pleasure, measure, Loves delight:
Hast then sweet Love our wished flight.

Deare, if you change

Deare, if you change, Ile never chuse againe,
Sweete, if you shrinke, Ile never think of love;
Fayre, if you faile, Ile judge all beauty vaine,
Wise, if to weake, my wits Ile never prove.
    Deare, sweete, fayre, wise; change, shrinke nor be not
      weake,
    And on my faith, my faith shall never breake.

Earth with her flowers shall sooner heav'n adorne,
Heaven her bright stars through earths dim globe shall
      move,
Fire heate shall loose and frosts of flames be borne,
Ayre made to shine as blacke as hell shall prove:
    Earth, heaven, fire, ayre, the world transform'd shall
      view,
    E're I prove false to faith, or strange to you.

Fain would I change that note

Fain would I change that note
    To which fond Love hath charm'd me,
Long, long to sing by rote,
    Fancying that that harm'd me.
Yet when this thought doth come,

"Love is the perfect sum
   Of all delight,"
I have no other choice
Either for pen or voice,
   To sing or write.

O Love! they wrong thee much
   That say thy sweet is bitter;
When thy ripe fruit is such
   As nothing can be sweeter.
Fair house of joy and bliss
Where truest pleasure is,
   I do adore thee:
I know thee what thou art,
I serve thee with my heart
   And fall before thee.

Every bush new springing

Every bush new springing,
Every bird now singing,
Merrily sat poor Nicho,
Chanting troli lo loli lo,
Till her he had espied
On whom his hope relied,
Down a down, with a frown,
O she pulled him down.

A ha ha ha! this world doth passe

A ha ha ha! this world doth passe,
Most merily, most merily Ile bee sworne,
For many an honest Indian Asse

Goes for a unicorne.
> Farra diddle diddle dyno,
> This is idle idle fyno.

Tygh hygh, tygh hygh! O sweet delight,
He tickles this age that can
Call Tulliæ's Ape a Marmasyte,
And Ledæ's Goose a swan.
> Farra diddle diddle dyno,
> This is idle idle fyno.

So so so so! fine English dayes,
For false play is no reproch,
For that he doth the Cochman prayse,
May safely use the Coch.
> Farra diddle diddle dyno,
> This is idle idle fyno.

The silver Swanne, who living had no Note

The silver Swanne, who living had no Note,
When death approacht unlockt her silent throat,
Leaning her breast against the reedie shore,
Thus sung her first and last, and sung no more:
Farewell all joyes, O death come close mine eyes,
More Geese than Swannes now live, more fooles than
   wise.

Since Bonny-boots was dead

Since Bonny-boots was dead, that so divinely
Could toot and foot it, (O he did it finely!)
> We ne'er went more a-Maying
> Nor had that sweet fa-laing.

Weepe O mine eyes

Weepe O mine eyes,
Weepe O mine eyes, and cease not;
(Alas) these your spring-tides,
Me-thinkes increase not.
O when begin you,
To swell so high that I may drowne me in you?
O when begin you,
To swell so high, that I may drowne me in you?
That I may drowne me in you?

Weepe you no more, sad fountaines

Weepe you no more, sad fountaines,
    What need you flowe so fast:
Looke how the snowie mountaines,
    Heav'ns sunne doth gently waste.
But my sunnes heav'nly eyes
    View not your weeping,
    That nowe lie sleeping:
Softly, now softly lies sleeping.

Sleepe is a reconciling,
    A rest that peace begets:
Doth not the sunne rise smiling,
    When faire at ev'n he sets?
Rest you, then rest sad eyes,
    Melt not in weeping,
    While she lies sleeping:
Softly, now softly lies sleeping.

George Peele

(1556–1596)

Fair Maiden

FROM *The Old Wives Tale*

COREBUS. Come wench, are we almost at the well.

ZELANTO. Ay, *Corebus* we are almost at the Well now, ile go fetch some water: sit downe while I dip my pitcher in.

VOYCE.   Gently dip: but not too deepe;
           For feare you make the goulden beard to
                weepe.

A head comes up with eares of Corne, and she combes them in her lap.

           Faire maiden white and red,
           Combe me smoothe, and stroke my head:
           And thou shalt have some cockell bread.
           Gently dippe, but not too deepe,
           For feare thou make the goulden beard to
                weep.
           Faire maide, white and redde,
           Combe me smooth, and stroke my head;
           And every haire, a sheave shall be,
           And every sheave a goulden tree.

Song

FROM *The Old Wives Tale*

When as the Rie reach to the chin,
And chopcherrie chopcherrie ripe within,
Strawberries swimming in the creame,
And schoole boyes playing in the streame:
Then O, then O, then O my true love said,
Till that time come againe,
Shee could not live a maid.

Hot sunne, coole fire, temperd with sweet aire

FROM *David and Bethsabe*

Hot sunne, coole fire, temperd with sweet aire,
Black shade, fair nurse, shadow my white haire,
Shine sun, burne fire, breath aire, and ease mee,
Black shade, fair nurse, shroud me and please me,
Shadow (my sweet nurse) keep me from burning,
Make not my glad cause, cause of mourning.
   Let not my beauties fire,
   Enflame unstaied desire,
   Nor pierce any bright eye,
   That wandreth lightly.

A Sonet

FROM *Polyhymnia*

His Golden lockes, Time hath to Silver turn'd,
O Time too swift, ô Swiftnesse never ceasing:
His Youth gainst Time and Age hath ever spurn'd
But spurn'd in vain, Youth waineth by increasing.
    Beauty, Strength, Youth, are flowers, but fading seen,
    Dutie, Faith, Love are roots, and ever greene.

His Helmet now, shall make a hive for Bees,
And Lovers Sonets, turn'd to holy Psalmes:
A man at Armes must now serve on his knees,
And feede on praiers, which are Age his almes.
    But though from Court to Cottage he depart,
    His Saint is sure of his unspotted heart.

And when he saddest sits in homely Cell,
Heele teach his Swaines this Carroll for a Song,
Blest be the heartes that wish my Soveraigne well,
Curst be the soules that thinke her any wrong.
    Goddesse, allow this aged man his right,
    To be your Beads-man now, that was your Knight.

Thomas Lodge

(1558?–1625)

Rosalynde's Madrigall

FROM *Rosalynde*

Love in my bosome like a Bee
    Doth sucke his sweete:
Now with his wings he playes with me,
    Now with his feete.
  Within mine eyes he makes his nest,
  His bed amidst my tender brest,
  My kisses are his dayly feast,
  And yet he robs me of my rest,
    Ah wanton, will ye?

And if I sleepe, then pearcheth he
    With pretty flight,
And makes his pillow of my knee
    The livelong night.
  Strike I my lute, he tunes the string,
  He musicke playes if so I sing,
  He lends me every lovely thing;
  Yet cruell he my heart doth sting.
    Whist wanton, still ye.

Else I with Roses every day
    Will whip you hence:
And binde you when you long to play,
    For your offence.
  Ile shut mine eyes to keep you in,

Ile make you fast it for your sinne,
Ile count your power not worth a pinne,
And what hereby shall I winne,
    If he gainsay me?

What if I beate the wanton boy
    With many a rod?
He wil repay me with annoy,
    Because a God.
  Then sit thou safely on my knee,
  And let thy bower my bosome be;
  Lurke in mine eies I like of thee.
  O *Cupid* so thou pittie me,
    Spare not but play thee.

Montanus' Sonnet

FROM *Rosalynde*

Phoebe sate,
Sweet she sate,
   Sweet sate Phoebe when I saw her,
White her brow,
Coy her eye;
   Brow and eye, how much you please me!
Words I spent,
Sighs I sent,
   Sighs and words could never draw her,
Oh my Love,
Thou art lost,
   Since no sight could ever ease thee.

Phoebe sat
By a Fount,

Sitting by a Fount I spide her,
Sweet her touch,
Rare her voyce:
    Touch and voice, what may distaine you?
As she sung,
I did sigh,
    And by sighs whilst that I tride her,
Oh mine eyes
You did loose,
    Her first sight whose want did pain you.

Phoebes flockes,
White as wooll,
    Yet were Phoebes locks more whiter.
Phoebes eyes,
Dovelike mild,
    Dovelike eyes, both mild and cruell,
Montan sweares,
In your lampes
    He will die for to delight her,
Phoebe yeeld,
Or I die:
    Shall true hearts be fancies fuell?

Robert Greene

(1558?–1592)

In Praise of His Loving and Best-Beloved Fawnia

FROM *Pandosto*

Ah! were she Pitiful as she is Fair,
  Or but as mild as she is seeming so,
Then were my Hopes greater than my Despair;
  Then all the World were Heaven, nothing Woe.
Ah! were her Heart relenting as her Hand,
  That seems to melt even with the mildest touch,
Then knew I where to seat me in a Land
  Under the wide Heavens, but yet not such:
So as she shews, so seems the budding Rose,
  Yet sweeter far than is an earthly Flower;
Sovereign of Beauty! like the Spray she grows,
  Compass'd she is with Thorns and canker'd Flower:
Yet were she willing to be pluck'd and worn,
She would be gather'd, tho she grew on Thorn.

Ah! when she sings, all Musick else be still,
  For none must be compared to her Note;
Ne'er breath'd such Glee from *Philomela's* Bill,
  Nor from the Morning-finger's swelling Throat:
Ah! when she riseth from her blissful Bed,
  She comforts all the World, as doth the Sun;
And at her sight, the Night's foul Vapour's fled:

When she is set, the gladsom Day is done:
O glorious Sun! imagine me the West,
Shine in my Arms, and set thou in my Breast.

Hexametra Alexis in Laudem Rosamundi

FROM *Greene's Mourning Garment*

Oft have I heard my liefe *Coridon* report on a love-day,
When bonny maides doe meete with the Swaines in the
vally by *Tempe*,
How bright eyd his *Phillis* was, how lovely they glanced,
When fro th' Aarches Eben black, flew lookes as a light-
ning,
That set a fire with piercing flames even hearts adaman-
tine:
Face Rose hued, Cherry red, with a silver taint like a
Lilly.
Venus pride might abate, might abash with a blush to
behold her.
Phoebus wyers compar'd to her haires unworthy the
praysing.
Junoes state, and *Pallas* wit disgrac'd with the Graces,
That grac'd her, whom poore *Coridon* did choose for a
love-mate:
Ah, but had *Coridon* now seene the starre that *Alexis*
Likes and loves so deare, that he melts to sighs when he
sees her.
Did *Coridon* but see those eyes, those amorous eyelids,
From whence fly holy flames of death or life in a mo-
ment.
Ah, did he see that face, those haires that *Venus, Apollo*
Basht to behold, and both disgrac'd, did grieve, that a
creature

Should exceed in hue, compare both a god and a god-
   desse:
Ah, had he seene my sweet Paramour the saint of *Alexis,*
Then had he sayd, *Phillis,* sit downe surpassed in all
   points,
For there is one more faire then thou, beloved of *Alexis.*

Doron's Description of Samela

FROM *Menaphon*

Like to *Diana* in her Summer weede
Girt with a crimson roabe of brightest die,
          goes faire *Samela.*
Whiter than be the flockes that straggling feede,
When washt by *Arethusa,* faint they lie:
          is faire *Samela.*
As faire *Aurora* in her morning gray
Deckt with the ruddie glister of her love,
          is faire *Samela.*
Like lovely *Thetis* on a calmèd day,
When as her brightnesse *Neptunes* fancie move,
          shines faire *Samela.*
Her tresses gold, her eyes like glassie streames,
Her teeth are pearle, the breast of yvorie
          of faire *Samela.*
Her cheekes like rose and lilly yeeld foorth gleames,
Her browes bright arches framde of ebonie:
          thus faire *Samela.*
Passeth faire *Venus* in her bravest hiew,
And *Juno* in the shew of maiestie,
          for she is *Samela.*
Pallas in wit, all three if you will view,
For beautie, wit, and matchlesse dignitie
          yeeld to *Samela.*

Sephestia's Song to Her Childe

FROM *Menaphon*

Weepe not my wanton! smile upon my knee!
When thou art olde, ther's grief inough for thee!
    Mothers wagge, pretie boy.
    Fathers sorrow, fathers joy.
    When thy father first did see
    Such a boy by him and mee,
    He was glad, I was woe.
    Fortune changde made him so,
    When he left his pretie boy,
    Last his sorowe, first his joy.

Weepe not my wanton! smile upon my knee!
When thou art olde, ther's griefe inough for thee!
    Streaming teares that never stint,
    Like pearle drops from a flint,
    Fell by course from his eyes,
    That one anothers place supplies:
    Thus he grievd in everie part,
    Teares of bloud fell from his hart,
    When he left his pretie boy,
    Fathers sorrow, fathers joy.

Weepe not my wanton! smile upon my knee!
When thou art olde, ther's griefe inough for thee!
    The wanton smilde, father wept;
    Mother cride, babie lept:
    More he crowde, more we cride;
    Nature could not sorowe hide.
    He must goe, he must kisse

Childe and mother, babie blisse:
For he left his pretie boy,
Fathers sorowe, fathers joy.

Weepe not my wanton! smile upon my knee!
When thou art olde, ther's grief inough for thee!

Doron's Jigge

FROM *Arcadia*

Through the shrubs as I can cracke,
　　For my Lambes pretty ones,
　　Mongst many little ones,
Nymphes I meane, whose haire was blacke,
　　　　As the Crow,
　　　　Like the snow,
Her face and browes shine I weene,
　　I saw a little one,
　　A bonny pretty one,
As bright, buxome, and as sheene,
　　　　As was she
　　　　On her knee,
That lulled the God, whose arrowes warmes,
　　Such merry little ones,
　　Such faire fac'de pretty ones,
As dally in loves chiefest harmes:
　　　　Such was mine,
　　　　Whose gray eyne
Made me love. I gan to woo
　　This sweet little one,
　　This bonny pretty one,
I wooed hard a day or two,
　　　　Till she bad,
　　　　Be not sad,

Woo no more, I am thine owne,
   Thy deerest little one,
   Thy truest pretty one:
Thus was faith and firme love showne,
     As behoves
     Shepheards loves.

Song

FROM *Greene's Farewell to Folly*

Sweet are the thoughts that savour of content,
   The quiet mind is richer then a crowne:
Sweet are the nights in carelesse slumber spent,
   The poore estate scornes fortunes angrie frowne:
Such sweet content, such mindes, such sleep, such blis
   Beggars injoy, when Princes oft do mis.

The homely house that harbors quiet rest,
   The cottage that affoords no pride, nor care:
The meane that grees with Countrie musick best,
   The sweet consort of mirth and musicks fare:
Obscured life sets downe a type of blis,
   A minde content both crowne and kingdome is.

Thomas Nashe

(1567–1601)

Song

FROM *Summer's Last Will and Testament*

Adieu, farewell earths blisse,
This world uncertaine is,
Fond are lifes lustfull joyes,
Death proves them all but toyes,
None from his darts can flye;
I am sick, I must dye:
    Lord, have mercy on us.

Rich men, trust not in wealth,
God cannot buy you health;
Phisick himselfe must fade.
All things to end are made,
The plague full swift goes bye;
I am sick, I must dye:
    Lord, have mercy on us.

Beauty is but a flowre,
Which wrinckles will devoure,
Brightnesse falls from the ayre,
Queenes have died yong and faire,
Dust hath closde *Helens* eye.
I am sick, I must dye:
    Lord, have mercy on us.

Strength stoopes unto the grave,
Wormes feed on *Hector* brave,

Swords may not fight with fate,
Earth still holds ope her gate.
Come, come, the bells do crye.
I am sick, I must dye:
     Lord, have mercy on us.

Wit with his wantonesse
Tasteth deaths bitternesse:
Hels executioner
Hath no eares for to heare
What vaine art can reply.
I am sick, I must dye:
     Lord, have mercy on us.

Haste therefore eche degree,
To welcome destiny:
Heaven is our heritage,
Earth but a players stage,
Mount wee unto the sky.
I am sick, I must dye:
     Lord, have mercy on us.

Summer's Farewell

FROM *Summer's Last Will and Testament*

This is the last stroke my toungs clock must strike,
My last will, which I will that you performe.
My crowne I have disposde already of.
Item, I give my withered flowers and herbes,
Unto dead corses, for to decke them with.
My shady walkes to great mens servitors,
Who in their masters shadowes walke secure.
My pleasant open ayre, and fragrant smels,

To Croyden and the grounds abutting round.
My heate and warmth to toyling labourers,
My long dayes to bondmen, and prisoners,
My shortest nights to young marrièd soules,
My drought and thirst to drunkards quenchlesse
    throates;
My fruites to *Autumne,* my adopted heire,
My murmuring springs, musicians of sweete sleepe,
To murmuring male-contents, whose well tun'd cares,
Channel'd in a sweete falling quaterzaine,
Do lull their eares asleepe, listning themselves.
And finally,—O words, now clense your course!—
Unto *Eliza* that most sacred Dame,
Whom none but Saints and Angels ought to name;
All my faire dayes remaining, I bequeath
To waite upon her till she be returnd.
Autumne, I charge thee, when that I am dead,
Be prest and serviceable at her beck,
Present her with thy goodliest ripened fruites;
Unclothe no Arbors where she ever sate,
Touch not a tree, thou thinkst she may passe by.
And *Winter,* with thy wrythen frostie face,
Smoothe up thy visage, when thou lookst on her,
Thou never lookst on such bright majestie:
A charmed circle draw about her court,
Wherein warme dayes may daunce, and no cold come;
On seas let winds make warre, not vexe her rest,
Quiet inclose her bed, thought flye her brest.
Ah, gracious Queene, though *Summer* pine away,
Yet let thy flourishing stand at a stay!
First droupe this universals aged frame,
E're any malady thy strength should tame:
Heaven raise up pillers to uphold thy hand,
Peace may have still his temple in thy land.
Loe, I have said! this is the totall summe.

Autumne and *Winter,* on your faithfulnesse
For the performance I do firmely builde.
Farewell, my friends, *Summer* bids you farewell,
Archers, and bowlers, all my followers,
Adieu, and dwell with desolation;
Silence must be your masters mansion:
Slow marching thus, discend I to the feends.
Weepe heavens, mourne earth, here *Summer* ends.

*Heere the Satyres and Wood-nimphes carry him out,
singing as he came in.*

(Lines 1969–2029)

Edmund Bolton

(1575?–1633?)

A Palinode

As withereth the Primrose by the river,
As fadeth Sommers-sunne from gliding fountaines;
As vanisheth the light blowne bubble ever,
As melteth snow upon the mossie Mountaines.
So melts, so vanisheth, so fades, so withers,
The Rose, the shine, the bubble and the snow,
Of praise, pompe, glorie, joy (which short life gathers,)
Faire praise, vaine pompe, sweet glory, brittle joy.
The withered Primrose by the mourning river,
The faded Sommers-sunne from weeping fountaines:
The light-blowne bubble, vanished for ever,
The molten snow upon the naked mountaines,
    Are Emblems that the treasures we up-lay,
    Soone wither, vanish, fade, and melt away.

For as the snowe, whose lawne did over-spread
Th' ambitious hills, which Giant-like did threat
To pierce the heaven with theyr aspiring head,
Naked and bare doth leave their craggie seate.
When as the bubble, which did emptie flie
The daliance of the undiscerned winde:
On whose calme rowling waves it did relie,
Hath shipwrack made, where it did daliance finde:
And when the Sun-shine which dissolv'd the snow,
Cullourd the bubble with a pleasant varie,

And made the rathe and timely Primrose grow,
Swarth clowdes with-drawne (which longer time doth
    tarie)
  Oh what is praise, pompe, glory, joy, but so
  As shine by fountaines, bubbles, flowers or snow?

Bartholomew Griffin

(?–1602)

Faire is my love

FROM *Fidessa*

Faire is my love that feedes among the Lillies,
   The Lillies growing in that pleasant garden,
Where Cupids mount that welbeloved hill is,
   And where that little god himselfe is warden.
See where my Love fits in the beds of spices,
   Beset all round with Camphere, Myrrhe and Roses,
And interlac'd with curious devices,
   Which her from all the world apart incloses.
There doth she tune her Lute for her delight,
   And with sweet musick makes the ground to move.
Whil'st I (poore I) doe sit alone in heavie plight,
   Wayling alone my unrespected love,
Not daring rush into so rare a place,
That gives to her and she to it a grace.

(xxxvii)

Samuel Daniel

(1562–1619)

Song

FROM *Tethys Festival*

Are they shadowes that we see?
And can shadowes pleasure give?
Pleasures onely shadowes bee
Cast by bodies we conceive,
And are made the thinges we deeme,
In those figures which they seeme.
But these pleasures vanish fast,
Which by shadowes are exprest:
Pleasures are not, if they last,
In their passing, is their best.
Glory is most bright and gay
In a flash, and so away.
Feed apace then greedy eyes
On the wonder you behold.
Take it sodaine as it flies
Though you take it not to hold:
When your eyes have done their part,
Thought must length it in the hart.

Sonnets

Faire is my Love, and cruell as she's faire;
Her brow shades frownes, although her eyes are sunny,
Her smiles are lightning, though her pride dispaire;
And her disdaines are Gall, her favours Hunny.
A modest Maide, deckt with a blush of honor,
Whose feete doe treade greene pathes of youth and love,
The wonder of all eyes that looke uppon her:
Sacred on earth, design'd a Saint above.
Chastitie and Beautie, which were deadly foes,
Live reconciled friends within her brow:
And had she pity to conjoine with those,
Then who had heard the plaints I utter now.
    For had she not beene faire, and thus unkinde,
    My Muse had slept, and none had knowne my
      minde.

                                    (*vi*)

Care-charmer Sleepe, sonne of the sable night,
Brother to death, in silent darknes borne:
Relieve my languish, and restore the light,
With darke forgetting of my cares returne.
And let the day be time enough to morne
The shipwracke of my ill-adventred youth:
Let waking eyes suffice to waile their scorne,
Without the torment of the nights untruth.
Cease dreames, th'Images of day desires,
To modell foorth the passions of the morrow:
Never let rising Sunne approve you liers,
To adde more griefe to aggravate my sorrow.
    Still let me sleepe, imbracing clowdes in vaine;
    And never wake to feele the dayes disdayne.

                                    (*xliv*)

O Fearfull, frowning Nemesis

FROM *The Tragedy of Cleopatra*

CHORUS. O Fearfull, frowning *Nemesis,*
   Daughter of Justice, most severe,
   That art the worlds great arbitresse,
   And Queene of causes raigning here:
Whose swift-sure hand is ever neere
   Eternall justice, righting wrong:
   Who never yet deferrest long
   The prowds decay, the weakes redresse:
But through thy power every where,
   Dooest raze the great, and raise the lesse
   The lesse made great doest ruine too,
   To shew the earth what heaven can doe.

Thou from darke-clos'd eternitie,
   From thy blacke clowdy hidden seat,
   The worlds disorders doest discry:
   Which when they swell so proudly great,
Reversing th'order nature set,
   Thou giv'st thy all counfounding doome,
   Which none can know before it come.
   Th'inevitable destenie,
Which neither wit nor strength can let,
   Fast chain'd unto necessity,
   In mortall things doth order so,
   Th'alternate course of weale or woe.

Oh how the powre of heaven does play
   With travailèd mortality:
   And doth their weakenesse still betray,

In their best prosperitie:
When beeing lifted up so hie,
　　They looke beyond themselves so farre,
　　That to themselves they take no care;
　　Whilst swift confusion downe doth lay,
Their late prowd mounting vanity:
　　Bringing their glory to decay,
　　And with the ruine of their fall,
　　Extinguish people, state and all.

But is it Justice that all we
　　The innocent poore multitude,
　　For great mens faults should punisht be,
　　And to destruction thus pursude?
O why should th'heavens us include,
　　Within the compasse of their fall,
　　Who of themselves procurèd all?
　　Or doe the gods (in close) decree,
Occasion take how to extrude
　　Man from the earth with crueltie?
　　Ah no, the gods are ever just,
　　Our faults excuse their rigor must.

This is the period Fate set downe,
　　To Egypts fat prosperitie:
　　Which now unto her greatest growne,
　　Must perish thus, by course must die.
And some must be the causers why
　　Their revolution must be wrought:
　　As borne to bring their state to nought.
　　To change the people and the crowne,
And purge the worlds iniquitie:
　　Which vice so farre hath overgrowne,
　　As we, so they that treate us thus,
　　Must one day perish like to us.

　　　　　　　　　　　(Act III, scene ii)

A *Pastorall*

O Happy golden Age,
   Not for that Rivers ranne
   With streames of milke, and hunny dropt from trees,
   Not that the earth did gage
   Unto the husband-man
   Her voluntary fruites, free without fees:
   Not for no cold did freeze,
   Nor any cloud beguile,
   Th'eternall flowring Spring
   Wherein liv'd every thing,
   And whereon th'heavens perpetually did smile,
   Not for no ship had brought
   From forraine shores, or warres or wares ill sought.
But onely for that name,
   That Idle name of wind:
   That Idoll of deceit, that empty sound
   Call'd *Honor,* which became
   Thy tyrant of the minde:
   And so torments our Nature without ground,
   Was not yet vainly found:
   Nor yet sad griefes imparts
   Amidst the sweet delights
   Of joyfull amorous wights.
   Nor were his hard lawes knowne to free-borne hearts.
   But golden lawes like these
   Which nature wrote. *That's lawfull which doth please.*
Then amongst flowres and springs
   Making delightful sport,
   Sate Lovers without conflict, without flame,
   And Nymphs and shepheards sings

Mixing in wanton sort
Whisp'rings with Songs, then kisses with the same
Which from affection came:
The naked virgin then
Her Roses fresh reveales,
Which now her vaile conceales.
The tender Apples in her bosome seene,
And oft in Rivers cleere
The Lovers with their Loves consorting were.
Honor, thou first didst close
   The spring of all delight:
   Denying water to the amorous thirst
   Thou taught'st faire eyes to lose
   The glory of their light.
   Restrain'd from men, and on themselves reverst.
   Thou in a lawne didst first
   Those golden haires incase,
   Late spred unto the wind;
   Thou mad'st loose grace unkind,
   Gav'st bridle to their words, art to their pace.
   O Honour it is thou
   That mak'st that stealth, which love doth free allow.
It is thy worke that brings
   Our griefes, and torments thus:
   But thou fierce Lord of Nature and of Love,
   The quallifier of Kings,
   What doest thou here with us
   That are below thy power, shut from above?
   Goe and from us remove,
   Trouble the mighties sleepe,
   Let us neglected, base,
   Live still without thy grace,
   And th'use of th'ancient happy ages keepe.
   Let's love, this life of ours
   Can make no truce with time that all devours.

Let's love: the sun doth set, and rise againe,
But when as our short light
Comes once to set, it makes eternall night.

Love is a sicknesse

FROM *Hymens Triumph*

Love is a sicknesse full of woes,
   All remedies refusing:
A plant that with most cutting growes,
   Most barren with best using.
        Why so?
More we enjoy it, more it dyes,
If not enjoy'd, it sighing cries
        Hey ho.

Love is a torment of the minde,
   A tempest everlasting;
And Jove hath made it of a kinde,
   Not well, nor full nor fasting.
        Why so?
More we enjoy it, more it dies,
If not enjoy'd, it sighing cries,
        Hey ho.

Ulysses and the Siren

SYREN. Come worthy Greeke, *Ulisses* come
Possesse these shores with me:
The windes and Seas are troublesome,

And heere we may be free.
　　Here may we sit, and view their toile
That travaile in the deepe,
And joy the day in mirth the while,
And spend the night in sleepe.

ULISSES. Faire Nimph, if fame, or honor were
To be attaynd with ease,
Then would I come, and rest with thee,
And leave such toyles as these.
　　But here it dwels, and here must I
With danger seeke it forth,
To spend the time luxuriously
Becomes not men of worth.

SYREN. *Ulisses,* O be not deceiv'd
With that unreall name:
This honour is a thing conceiv'd,
And rests on others fame.
　　Begotten onely to molest
Our peace, and to beguile
(The best thing of our life) our rest,
And give us up to toile.

ULISSES. Delicious Nimph, suppose there were
Nor honour, nor report,
Yet manlines would scorne to weare
The time in idle sport.
　　For toyle doth give a better touch,
To make us feele our joy;
And ease findes tediousnesse as much
As labour yeelds annoy.

SYREN. Then pleasure likewise seemes the shore,
Whereto tends all your toyle,
Which you forgo to make it more,
And perish oft the while.

Who may disporte them diversly,
Finde never tedious day,
And ease may have varietie,
As well as action may.

ULISSES. But natures of the noblest frame
These toyles, and dangers please,
And they take comfort in the same,
As much as you in ease.
  And with the thought of actions past
Are recreated still;
When pleasure leaves a touch at last,
To shew that it was ill.

SYREN. That doth opinion onely cause,
That's out of custome bred,
Which makes us many other lawes
Then ever Nature did.
  No widdowes waile for our delights,
Our sportes are without bloud,
The world we see by warlike wights
Receives more hurt then good.

ULISSES. But yet the state of things require
These motions of unrest,
And these great Spirits of high desire,
Seeme borne to turne them best.
  To purge the mischiefes that increase,
And all good order mar:
For oft we see a wicked peace
To be well chang'd for war.

SYREN. Well, well *Ulisses* then I see,
I shall not have thee heere,
And therefore I will come to thee,
And take my fortunes there.

SAMUEL DANIEL

I must be wonne that cannot win,
Yet lost were I not wonne:
For beauty hath created bin,
T'undoo, or be undonne.

Thomas Campion

(1567–1620)

Followe thy faire sunne, unhappy shadowe

Followe thy faire sunne, unhappy shadowe,
Though thou be blacke as night,
And she made all of light,
Yet follow thy faire sun, unhappie shadowe.

Follow her whose light thy light depriveth,
Though here thou liv'st disgrac't,
And she in heaven is plac't,
Yet follow her whose light the world reviveth.

Follow those pure beames whose beautie burneth,
That so have scorched thee,
As thou still blacke must bee,
Til her kind beames thy black to brightnes turneth.

Follow her while yet her glorie shineth:
There comes a luckles night,
That will dim all her light;
And this the black unhappie shade devineth.

Follow still since so thy fates ordained;
The Sunne must have his shade,
Till both at once doe fade,
The Sun still proud, the shadow still disdained.

Harke, al you ladies that do sleep

Harke, al you ladies that do sleep;
   The fayry queen Proserpina
Bids·you awake and pitie them that weep.
   You may doe in the darke
What the day doth forbid;
   Feare not the dogs that barke,
     Night will have all hid.

But if you let your lovers mone,
   The Fairie Queene Proserpina
Will send abroad her Fairies ev'ry one,
   That shall pinch blacke and blew
Your white hands and faire armes
   That did not kindly rue
     Your Paramours harmes.

In Myrtle Arbours on the downes
   The Fairie Queene Proserpina,
This night by moone-shine leading merrie rounds
   Holds a watch with sweet love,
Downe the dale, up the hill;
   No plaints or groanes may move
     Their holy vigill.

All you that will hold watch with love,
   The Fairie Queene Proserpina
Will make you fairer then Diones dove;
   Roses red, Lillies white,
And the cleare damaske hue,
   Shall on your cheekes alight:
     Love will adorne you.

All you that love, or lov'd before,
  The Fairie Queene Proserpina
Bids you encrease that loving humour more:
  They that yet have not fed
On delight amorous,
  She vowes that they shall lead
    Apes in Avernus.

When thou must home to shades of under ground

When thou must home to shades of under ground,
And there ariv'd, a newe admired guest,
The beauteous spirits do ingirt thee round,
White Iope, blith Hellen, and the rest,
To heare the stories of thy finisht love
From that smoothe toong whose musicke hell can move;

Then wilt thou speake of banqueting delights,
Of masks and revels which sweete youth did make,
Of Turnies and great challenges of knights,
And all these triumphes for thy beauties sake:
When thou hast told these honours done to thee,
Then tell, O tell, how thou didst murther me.

Rose-cheekt Laura, come

Rose-cheekt *Laura,* come
Sing thou smoothly with thy beawties
Silent musick, either other
    Sweetely gracing.

Lovely formes do flowe
From concent devinely framed;
Heav'n is musick, and thy beawties
Birth is heavenly.

These dull notes we sing
Discords neede for helps to grace them;
Only beawty purely loving
Knowes no discord,

But still mooves delight,
Like cleare springs renu'd by flowing,
Ever perfet, ever in them-
selves eternall.

Never weather-beaten Saile more willing bent to shore

Never weather-beaten Saile more willing bent to shore,
Never tyred Pilgrims limbs affected slumber more,
Than my wearied spright now longs to flye out of my
troubled brest.
O come quickly, sweetest Lord, and take my soule to
rest.

Ever-blooming are the joys of Heav'ns high paradice,
Cold age deafes not there our eares, nor vapour dims
our eyes:
Glory there the Sun outshines, whose beames the
blessed onely see;
O come quickly, glorious Lord, and raise my spright
to thee.

Kinde are her answeres

Kinde are her answeres,
  But her performance keeps no day;
Breaks time, as dancers
  From their own Musicke when they stray:
  All her free favors and smooth words,
Wing my hopes in vaine.
O did ever voice so sweet but only fain?
  Can true love yeeld such delay,
  Converting joy to pain?

Lost is our freedome,
  When we submit to women so:
Why doe wee neede them,
  When in their best they worke our woe?
  There is no wisedome
Can alter ends, by Fate prefixt.
O why is the good of man with evill mixt?
  Never were days yet cal'd two,
  But one night went betwixt.

Thrice tosse these Oaken ashes in the ayre

Thrice tosse these Oaken ashes in the ayre,
Thrice sit thou mute in this inchanted chayre;
And thrice three times tye up this true loves knot,
And murmur soft, shee will, or shee wil not.

Goe burn these poy'snous weedes in yon blew fire,
These Screech-owles fethers and this prickling bryer;
This Cypresse gathered at a dead mans grave;
That all thy feares and cares, an end may have.

Then come, you Fayries, dance with me a round;
Melt her hard hart with your melodious sound:
In vaine are all the charms I can devise:
She hath an Arte to breake them with her eyes.

There is a Garden in her face

There is a Garden in her face,
Where Roses and white Lillies grow;
    A heav'nly paradice is that place,
Wherein all pleasant fruits doe flow.
    There Cherries grow, which none may buy
    Till Cherry ripe themselves doe cry.

Those Cherries fayrely doe enclose
Of Orient Pearle a double row;
    Which when her lovely laughter showes,
They look like Rose-buds fill'd with snow.
    Yet them nor Peere nor Prince can buy,
    Till Cherry ripe themselves doe cry.

Her Eyes like Angles watch them still;
Her Browes like bended bowes doe stand,
    Threatning with piercing frownes to kill
All that attempt with eye or hand
    Those sacred Cherries to come nigh,
    Till Cherry ripe themselves doe cry.

What faire pompe have I spide of glittering Ladies

What faire pompe have I spide of glittering Ladies;
With locks sparckled abroad, and rosie Coronet
On their yvorie browes, trackt to the daintie thies
With roabs like *Amazons,* blew as Violet,
With gold Aiglets adornd, some in a changeable
Pale; with spangs wavering taught to be moveable.

Then those Knights that a farre off with dolorous view-
ing
Cast their eyes hetherward; loe, in an agonie,
All unbrac'd, crie aloud, their heavie state ruing:
Moyst cheekes with blubbering, painted as *Ebonie*
Blacke; their feltred haire torne with wrathful hand:
And whiles astonied, starke in a maze they stand.

But hearke! what merry sound! what sodaine harmonie!
Looke looke neere the grove where the Ladies doe tread
With their Knights the measures waide by the melodie.
Wantons! whose travesing make men enamoured;
Now they faine an honor, now by the slender wast
He must lift hir aloft, and seale a kisse in hast.

Streight downe under a shadow for wearines they lie
With pleasant daliance, hand knit with arme in arme,
Now close, now set aloof, they gaze with an equall eie,
Changing kisses alike; streight with a false alarme,
Mocking kisses alike, powt with a lovely lip.
Thus drownd with jollities, their merry daies doe slip.

But stay! now I discerne they goe on a Pilgrimage
Towards Loves holy land, faire *Paphos* or *Cyprus.*

Such devotion is meete for a blithesome age;
With sweet youth, it agrees well to be amorous.
Let olde angrie fathers lurke in an Hermitage:
Come, weele associate this jolly Pilgrimage!

So quicke, so hot, so mad is thy fond sute

So quicke, so hot, so mad is thy fond sute,
So rude, so tedious growne, in urging mee,
That faine I would with losse make thy tongue mute,
And yeeld some little grace to quiet thee:
    An houre with thee I care not to converse,
    For I would not be counted too perverse,

But roofes too hot would prove for men all fire;
And hils too high for my unused pace;
The grove is charg'd with thornes and the bold bryer;
Gray Snakes the meadowes shrowde in every place:
    A yellow Frog, alas, will fright me so,
    As I should start and tremble as I goe.

Since then I can on earth no fit roome finde,
In heaven I am resolv'd with you to meete,
Till then, for Hopes sweet sake, rest your tir'd minde,
And not so much as see mee in the streete:
    A heavenly meeting one day wee shall have,
    But never, as you dreame, in bed, or grave.

Shall I come, sweet Love, to thee

Shall I come, sweet Love, to thee,
    When the ev'ning beames are set?
Shall I not excluded be?

Will you finde no fained lett?
Let me not, for pitty, more,
Tell the long houres at your dore.

Who can tell what theefe or foe,
   In the covert of the night,
For his prey will worke my woe,
   Or through wicked foule despight:
So may I dye unredrest,
Ere my long love be possest.

But to let such dangers passe,
   Which a lovers thoughts disdaine,
'Tis enough in such a place
   To attend loves joyes in vaine.
Doe not mocke me in thy bed,
While these cold nights freeze me dead.

Michael Drayton

(1563–1631)

FROM *Idea*

Nothing but No and I, and I and No,
How fals it out so strangely you reply?
I tell yee (Faire) ile not be answered so,
With this affirming No, denying I.
I say, I Love, you sleightly answere I:
I say, You Love, you peule me out a No:
I say, I Die, you Eccho me with I:
Save mee I Crie, you sigh me out a No;
Must Woe and I, have naught but No and I?
No I, am I, if I no more can have;
Answere no more, with Silence make reply,
And let me take my selfe what I doe crave,
   Let No and I, with I and you be so:
   Then answere No and I, and I and No.

(v)

You not alone, when You are still alone,
O God from You, that I could private be,
Since You one were, I never since was one,
Since You in Me, my selfe since out of Me,
Transported from my Selfe, into Your being,
Though either distant, present yet to either,
Senselesse with too much Joy, each other seeing
And onely absent, when Wee are together.

Give Me my Selfe, and take your Selfe againe,
Devise some meanes, but how I may forsake You,
So much is Mine, that doth with You remaine,
That taking what is Mine, with Me I take You;
   You doe bewitch Me, O that I could flie,
    From my Selfe You, or from your owne Selfe I.

                             (*xi*)

Deare, why should you command me to my Rest,
When now the Night doth summon all to sleepe?
Me thinkes this Time becommeth Lovers best;
Night was ordayn'd, together Friends to keepe:
How happy are all other living Things,
Which though the Day dis-joyne by sev'rall flight,
The quiet Ev'ning yet together brings,
And each returnes unto his Love at Night?
O, Thou that art so courteous else to all!
Why should'st thou, Night, abuse me onely thus,
That ev'ry Creature to his kind do'st call,
And yet 'tis thou do'st onely sever us?
   Well could I wish, it would be ever Day,
    If when Night comes, you bid me goe away.

                           (*xxxvii*)

Calling to minde since first my Love begun,
Th' incertaine Times oft varying in their Course,
How Things still unexpectedly have runne,
As't please the Fates, by their resistlesse force:
Lastly, mine Eyes amazedly have seene
Essex great fall, *Tyrone* his Peace to gaine,
The quiet end of that Long-living Queene,
This Kings faire Entrance, and our Peace with *Spaine*,

We and the *Dutch* at length our Selves to sever;
Thus the World doth, and evermore shall Reele:
Yet to my Goddesse am I constant ever;
How e're blind Fortune turne her giddie Wheele:
    Though Heaven and Earth, prove both to me untrue,
    Yet am I still inviolate to You.

                                    (*li*)

Since ther's no helpe, Come let us kisse and part,
Nay, I have done: You get no more of Me,
And I am glad, yea glad withall my heart,
That thus so cleanly, I my Selfe can free,
Shake hands for ever, Cancell all our Vowes,
And when We meet at any time againe,
Be it not seene in either of our Browes,
That We one jot of former Love reteyne;
Now at the last gaspe, of Loves latest Breath,
When his Pulse fayling, Passion speechlesse lies,
When Faith is kneeling by his bed of Death,
And Innocence is closing up his Eyes,
    Now if thou would'st, when all have given him over,
    From Death to Life, thou might'st him yet recover.

                                    (*lxi*)

FROM *The Third Eclogue*

ROWLAND. Stay, *Thames,* to heare my Song, thou great
        and famous Flood,
Beta alone the *Phoenix* is of all thy watry Brood,
    The Queene of Virgins onely Shee,
    The King of Floods allotting Thee

Of all the rest, be joyfull then to see this happy Day,
Thy *Beta* now alone shall be the Subject of my Lay.

With daintie and delightsome straynes of dapper Veri-
       layes:
Come lovely Shepheards, sit by me, to tell our *Beta's*
       prayse,
    And let us sing so high a Verse,
    Her soveraigne Vertues to rehearse:
That little Birds shall silent sit to heare us Shepheards
       sing,
Whilst Rivers backward bend their course, and flow up
      to their spring.

Range all thy Swans, faire *Thames,* together on a ranke,
And place them each in their degree upon thy winding
      Banke,
    And let them set together all,
    Time keeping with the Waters fall:
And crave the tunefull *Nightingale* to helpe them with
      her Lay,
The *Woosell* and the *Throstle-Cocke,* chief musike of
      our May.

See what a troupe of Nymphs, come leading Hand in
      Hand,
In such a number that well-neere they take up all the
      Strand:
    And harke how merrily they sing,
    That makes the Neigh'bring Meddowes ring,
And *Beta* comes before alone, clad in a purple Pall,
And as the Queene of all the rest doth weare a Coronall.

Trim up her golden Tresses with *Apollo's* sacred Tree,
Whose Tutage and especiall care I wish her still to bee,
    That for his Darling hath prepar'd,
    A glorious Crowne as her reward,

Not such a golden Crowne as haughtie *Caesar* weares,
But such a glittering starry one as *Ariadne* beares.

Mayds, get the choycest Flowres, a Garland and en-
twine,
Nor Pinks, nor Pansies, let there want, be sure of Eglan-
tine,
    See that there be store of Lillyes,
    (Call'd of Shepheards Daffadillyes)
With Roses Damaske, White, and Red, the dearest
Flower-de-lice,
The Cowslip of *Jerusalem,* and Clove of *Paradise.*

O thou great Eye of Heaven, the Dayes most dearest
Light,
With thy bright Sister *Cynthia,* the Glorie of the Night,
    And those that make yee seven,
    To us the neer'st of Heaven,
And thou, O gorgeous *Iris,* with all thy Colours dy'd,
When shee streames forth her Rayes, then dasht is all
your pride.

In thee, whilst shee beholds (O Flood) her heavenly
Face,
The Sea-Gods in their watry Armes would gladly her
imbrace,
    The intising *Syrens* in their layes,
    And *Tritons* doe resound her prayse,
Hasting with all the speed they can unto the spacious
Sea,
And through all *Neptunes* Court proclaim our *Beta's*
holyday.

O evermore refresh the Roote of the fat Olive Tree,
In whose sweet shaddow ever may thy Banks preserved
bee.
    With Bayes that Poets doe adorne,

And Mirtles of chaste Lovers worne,
That faire may be the Fruit, the Boughes preserv'd by
        peace,
And let the mournefull Cypres die, and here for ever
        cease.

Weele strew the Shore with Pearle, where *Beta* walks
    , alone,
And we will pave her Summer Bower with the rich
        Indian stone,
        Perfume the Ayre and make it sweet,
        For such a Goddesse as is meet,
For if her Eyes for purity contend with *Titans* Light,
No marvaile then although their Beames doe dazle hu-
        mane sight.

Sound lowde your Trumpets then from *Londons* loftiest
        Towers,
To beate the stormie Tempests back, and calme the
        raging Showers,
        Set the Cornet with the Flute,
        The Orpharion to the Lute,
Tuning the Taber and the Pipe to the sweet Violons,
And mocke the Thunder in the Ayre with the lowd
        Clarions.

Beta, long may thine Altars smoke with yeerely Sacri-
        fice,
And long thy sacred Temples may their high Dayes
        solemnize,
        Thy Shepheards watch by Day and Night,
        Thy Mayds attend thy holy Light,
And thy large Empire stretch her Armes from East in to
        the West,
And *Albion* on the *Appenines* advance her conquering
        Crest.

                                        (Lines 49–120)

To the New Yeere

Rich Statue, double-faced,
With Marble Temples graced,
  To rayse thy God-head hyer,
In flames where Altars shining,
Before thy Priests divining,
  Doe od'rous Fumes expire.

Great *Janus,* I thy pleasure,
With all the *Thespian* Treasure,
  Doe seriously pursue;
To th' passed yeere returning,
As though the old adjourning,
  Yet bringing in the new.

Thy ancient Vigils yeerely,
I have observed cleerely,
  Thy Feasts yet smoaking bee;
Since all thy store abroad is,
Give something to my Goddesse,
  As hath been us'd by thee.

Give her th' *Eoan* brightnesse,
Wing'd with that subtill lightnesse,
  That doth trans-pierce the Ayre;
The Roses of the Morning
The rising Heav'n adorning,
  To mesh with flames of Hayre.

Those ceaselesse Sounds, above all,
Made by those Orbes that move all,
  And ever swelling there,

Wrap'd up in Numbers flowing,
Them actually bestowing,
   For Jewels at her Eare.

O Rapture great and holy,
Doe thou transport me wholly,
   So well her forme to vary,
That I aloft may beare her,
Whereas I will insphere her
   In Regions high and starry.

And in my choise Composures,
The soft and easie Closures,
   So amorously shall meet;
That ev'ry lively Ceasure
Shall tread a perfect Measure,
   Set on so equall feet.

That Spray to fame so fertle,
The Lover-crowning Mirtle,
   In Wreaths of mixed Bowes,
Within whose shades are dwelling
Those Beauties most excelling,
   Inthron'd upon her Browes.

Those Paralels so even,
Drawne on the face of Heaven,
   That curious Art supposes,
Direct those Gems, whose cleerenesse
Farre off amaze by neerenesse,
   Each Globe such fire incloses.

Her Bosome full of Blisses,
By nature made for Kisses,
   So pure and wond'rous cleere,
Whereas a thousand Graces
Behold their lovely Faces,
   As they are bathing there.

O, thou selfe-little blindnesse,
The kindnesse of unkindnesse,
    Yet one of those divine;
Thy Brands to me were lever,
Thy Fascia, and thy Quiver,
And thou this Quill of mine.

This Heart so freshly bleeding,
Upon it owne selfe feeding,
    Whose wounds still dropping be;
O Love, thy selfe confounding,
Her coldnesse so abounding,
    And yet such heat in me.

Yet if I be inspired,
Ile leave thee so admired,
    To all that shall succeed,
That were they more then many,
'Mongst all, there is not any,
    That Time so oft shall reed.

Nor Adamant ingraved,
That hath been choisely'st saved,
    Idea's Name out-weares;
So large a Dower as this is,
The greatest often misses,
    The Diadem that beares.

To His Valentine

Muse, bid the Morne awake,
    Sad Winter now declines,
Each Bird doth chuse a Make,
    This day's Saint *Valentines*;
For that good Bishops sake
Get up, and let us see,

What Beautie it shall bee,
   That Fortune us assignes.

But lo, in happy How'r,
   The place wherein she lyes,
In yonder climbing Tow'r,
   Gilt by the glitt'ring Rise;
O *Jove!* that in a Show'r,
As once that Thund'rer did,
When he in drops lay hid,
   That I could her surprize.

Her Canopie Ile draw,
   With spangled Plumes bedight,
No Mortall ever saw
   So ravishing a sight;
That it the Gods might awe,
And pow'rfully trans-pierce
The Globie Universe,
   Out-shooting ev'ry Light.

My Lips Ile softly lay
   Upon her heav'nly Cheeke,
Dy'd like the dawning Day,
   As polish'd Ivorie sleeke:
And in her Eare Ile say;
O, thou bright Morning-Starre,
'Tis I that come so farre,
   My Valentine to seeke.

Each little Bird, this Tyde,
   Doth chuse her loved Pheere,
Which constantly abide
   In Wedlock all the yeere,
As Nature is their Guide:
So may we two be true,

This yeere, nor change for new,
   As Turtles coupled were.

The Sparrow, Swan, the Dove,
   Though *Venus* Birds they be,
Yet are they not for Love
   So absolute as we:
For Reason us doth move;
They but by billing woo:
Then try what we can doo,
   To whom each sense is free.

Which we have more than they,
   By livelyer Organs sway'd,
Our Appetite each way
   More by our Sense obay'd:
Our Passions to display,
This Season us doth fit;
Then let us follow it,
   As Nature us doth lead.

One Kiss in two let's breake,
   Confounded with the touch,
But halfe words let us speake,
   Our Lip's imploy'd so much;
Untill we both grow weake,
With sweetnesse of thy breath;
O smother me to death:
   Long let our Joyes be such.

Let's laugh at them that chuse
   Their Valentines by lot,
To weare their Names that use,
   Whom idly they have got:
Such poore choise we refuse,
Saint *Valentine* befriend;
We thus this Morne may spend,
   Else Muse, awake her not.

To the Virginian Voyage

You brave Heroique Minds,
Worthy your Countries Name,
    That Honour still pursue,
    Goe, and subdue,
Whilst loyt'ring Hinds
Lurke here at home, with shame.

Britans, you stay too long,
Quickly aboord bestow you,
    And with a merry Gale
    Swell your stretch'd Sayle,
With Vowes as strong,
As the Winds that blow you.

Your Course securely steere,
West and by South forth keepe,
    Rocks, Lee-shores, nor Sholes,
    When *Eolus* scowles,
You need not feare,
So absolute the Deepe.

And cheerefully at Sea,
Successe you still intice,
    To get the Pearle and Gold,
    And ours to hold,
Virginia,
Earth's onely Paradise.

Where Nature hath in store
Fowle, Venison, and Fish,
    And the fruitfull'st Soyle,

Without your Toyle,
Three Harvests more,
All greater then your wish.

And the ambitious Vine
Crownes with his purple Masse,
   The Cedar reaching hie
   To kisse the Sky,
The Cypresse, Pine
And use-full Sassafras.

To whose, the golden Age
Still Natures lawes doth give,
   No other Cares that tend,
   But Them to defend
From Winters age,
That long there doth not live.

When as the Lushious smell
Of that delicious Land,
   Above the Seas that flowes,
   The cleere Wind throwes,
Your Hearts to swell
Approching the deare Strand.

In kenning of the Shore
(Thanks to God first given,)
   O you the happy'st men,
   Be Frolike then,
Let Cannons roare,
Frighting the wide Heaven.

And in Regions farre
Such *Heroes* bring yee foorth,
   As those from whom We came,
   And plant Our name,
Under that Starre
Not knowne unto our North.

And as there Plenty growes
Of Lawrell every where,
  Apollo's Sacred tree,
  You it may see,
A Poets Browes
To crowne, that may sing there.

Thy Voyage attend,
Industrious *Hackluit*,
  Whose Reading shall inflame
  Men to seeke Fame,
And much commend
To after-Times thy Wit.

A *Skeltoniad*

The Muse should be sprightly,
Yet not handling lightly
Things grave; as much loath,
Things that be slight, to cloath
Curiously: To retayne
The Comelinesse in meane,
Is true Knowledge and Wit.
Nor me forc'd Rage doth fit,
That I thereto should lacke
Tabacco, or need Sacke,
Which to the colder Braine
Is the true *Hyppocrene;*
Nor did I ever care
For great Fooles, nor them spare.
Vertue, though neglected,
Is not so dejected,
As vilely to descend

To low Basenesse their end;
Neyther each ryming Slave
Deserves the Name to have
Of Poet: so the Rabble
Of Fooles, for the Table,
That have their Jests by Heart,
As an Actor his Part,
Might assume them Chayres
Amongst the Muses Heyres.
Parnassus is not clome
By every such Mome;
Up whose steepe side who swerves,
It behoves t' have strong Nerves;
My Resolution such,
How well, and not how much
To write, thus doe I fare,
Like some, few good that care
(The evill sort among)
How well to live, and not how long.

The Cryer

Good Folke, for Gold or Hyre,
But helpe me to a Cryer;
For my poore Heart is runne astray
After two Eyes, that pass'd this way.
     O yes, O yes, O yes,
       If there be any Man,
       In Towne or Countrey, can
       Bring me my Heart againe,
       Ile please him for his paine;
And by these Marks I will you show,
That onely I this Heart doe owe.

It is a wounded Heart,
Wherein yet sticks the Dart,
Ev'ry piece sore hurt throughout it,
Faith, and Troth, writ round about it:
It was a tame Heart, and a deare,
   And never us'd to roame;
But having got this Haunt, I feare
   'Twill hardly stay at home.
For Gods sake, walking by the way,
   If you my Heart doe see,
Either impound it for a Stray,
   Or send it backe to me.

FROM *The Shepheards Sirena*

[*The Jovial Shepheard's Song*]

Neare to the Silver *Trent,*
   Sirena dwelleth:
Shee to whom Nature lent
   All that excelleth:
By which the *Muses* late,
   And the neate *Graces,*
Have for their greater state
   Taken their places:
Twisting an *Anadem,*
   Wherewith to Crowne her,
As it belong'd to them
   Most to renowne her.

CHORUS: *On thy Bancke,*
   In a Rancke,
   Let thy Swanes sing her,
And with their Musick,
   Along let them bring her.

Tagus and *Pactolus*
  Are to thee Debter,
Nor for their gould to us
  Are they the better:
Henceforth of all the rest,
  Be thou the River,
Which as the daintiest,
  Puts them downe ever,
For as my precious one,
  O'r thee doth travell,
She to Pearle Parragon
  Turneth thy gravell.

  On thy Bancke, etc.

Our mournefull *Philomell*,
  That rarest Turner,
Henceforth in *Aperill*
  Shall wake the sooner,
And to her shall complaine
  From the thicke Cover,
Redoubling every straine
  Over and over:
For when my Love too long
  Her Chamber keepeth;
As though it suffered wrong,
  The Morning weepeth.

Oft have I seene the Sunne,
  To doe her honour,
Fix himselfe at his noone,
  To looke upon her,
And hath guilt every Grove,
  Every Hill neare her,
With his flames from above,
  Striving to cheere her,

And when shee from his sight
   Hath her selfe turned,
He as it had beene night,
   In Cloudes hath mourned:

The Verdant Meades are seene,
   When she doth view them,
In fresh and gallant Greene,
   Straight to renewe them,
And every little Grasse
   Broad it selfe spreadeth,
Proud that this bonny Lasse
   Upon it treadeth:
Nor flower is so sweete
   In this large Cincture
But it upon her feete
   Leaveth some Tincture.

The Fishes in the Flood,
   When she doth Angle,
For the Hooke strive a good
   Them to intangle;
And leaping on the Land
   From the cleare water,
Their Scales upon the sand
   Lavishly scatter;
Therewith to pave the mould
   Whereon she passes,
So her selfe to behold,
   As in her glasses.

When shee lookes out by night,
   The Starres stand gazing,
Like Commets to our sight
   Fearefully blazing,
As wondring at her eyes,

With their much brightnesse,
Which so amaze the skies,
    Dimming their lightnesse,
The raging Tempests are Calme,
    When shee speaketh,
Such most delightsome balme,
    From her lips breaketh.

In all our *Brittany,*
    Ther's not a fayrer,
Nor can you fitt any:
    Should you compare her.
Angels her eye-lids keepe
    All harts surprizing,
Which looke whilst she doth sleepe
    Like the Sunnes rising:
She alone of her kinde
    Knoweth true measure,
And her unmatched mind
    Is Heavens treasure:

Fayre *Dove* and *Darwine* cleere
    Boast yee your beauties,
To *Trent* your Mistres here
    Yet pay your duties,
My Love was higher borne
    Tow'rds the full Fountaines,
Yet she doth *Moorland* scorne,
    And the *Peake* Mountaines;
Nor would she none should dreame,
    Where she abideth,
Humble as is the streame,
    Which by her slydeth,

Yet my poore Rusticke *Muse,*
    Nothing can move her,

Nor the meanes I can use,
   Though her true Lover:
Many a long Winters night
   Have I wak'd for her,
Yet this my piteous plight,
   Nothing can stirre her.
All thy Sands silver *Trent*
   Downe to the *Humber,*
The sighes that I have spent
   Never can number.

(Lines 165–331)

FROM *The Moone-Calfe*

It was not long e're he perceiv'd the skies
Setled to raine, and a black cloud arise,
Whose foggy grosnesse so oppos'd the light,
As it would turne the noone-sted into night.
When the winde came about with all his power,
Into the tayle of this approching shower,
And it to lighten presently began;
Quicker then thought, from East to West that ran:
The Thunder following did so fiercely rave,
And through the thick clouds with such fury drave,
As Hell had been set open for the nonce,
And all the Divels heard to rore at once:
And soone the Tempest so outragious grew,
That it whole hedgerowes by the roots up threw,
So wondrously prodigious was the weather,
As heven and earth had meant to goe together:
And downe the shower impetuously doth fall,
Like that which men the *Hurricano* call:
As the grand Deluge had beene come againe,
And all the World should perish by the raine.

And long it lasted; all which time this man
Hid in the Cave doth in his judgement scan,
What of this inundation would ensue,
For he knew well the Prophecie was true:
And when the shower was somwhat over-past,
And that the skies began to cleare at last:
To the Caves mouth he softly put his eare,
To listen if he any thing could heare:
What harme this storme had done, and what became
Of those that had been sowsed in the same.
No sooner he that nimble Organ lent
To the Caves mouth; but that incontinent
There was a noyse as if the Garden Beares,
And all the Dogs together by the eares,
And those of *Bedlam* had enlarged bin,
And to behold the Bayting had come in:
Which when he heard, he knew too well alasse,
That what had beene fore-told, was come to passe;
Within himselfe good man, he reasoned thus:
Tis for our sinnes, this plague is falne on us.
Of all the rest, though in my wits I be,
(I thanke my Maker) yet it greeveth me,
To see my Country in this piteous case;
Woe's me that ever that so wanted grace:
But when as man once casts off vertue quite,
And doth in sinne and beastlinesse delight,
We see how soone God turnes him to a Sot:
To showe my selfe yet a true Patriot,
Ile in amongst them, and if so, that they
Be not accurst of God, yet, yet I may,
By wholesome counsell (if they can but heare)
Make them as perfect as at first they were,
And thus resolv'd goes this good poore man downe;
When at the entrance of the Neighbouring Towne,
He meetes a woman, with her Buttocks bare,

Got up a stride upon a wall-eyde Mare,
To runne a Horse-race, and was like to ride
Over the good man: but he stept aside;
And after her, another that bestroad
A Horse of Service, with a Lance she rode
Arm'd, and behinde her on a Pillian satt
Her frantique Husband, in a broad-brim'd Hatt,
A Maske and Safeguard; and had in his hand
His mad Wifes Distaffe for a ryding Wand:
Scarse from these mad folke, had he gone so farre,
As a strong man, will eas'ly pitch a Barre:
But that he found a Youth in Tissue brave,
(A daintier man one would not wish to have)
Was courting of a loathsome mezzeld Sowe,
And in his judgement, swore he must alowe
Hers, the prime Beauty, that he ever sawe,
Thus was she sued to (by that prating Dawe)
Who, on a dunghill in the loathsome gore,
Had farrowed ten Pigs scarce an houre before.
At which this man in melancholly deepe,
Burst into laughter, like before to weepe.
Another foole, to fit him for the weather,
Had arm'd his heeles with Cork, his head with feather;
And in more strange and sundry colours clad,
Then in the Raine-bowe ever can be had:
Stalk'd through the Streets, preparing him to flie,
Up to the Moone upon an Embassie.
Another seeing his drunken Wife disgorge
Her pamperd stomack, got her to a Forge,
And in her throat the Feverous heat to quench
With the Smiths horne, was giving her a Drench:
One his next Neighbour haltred had my force,
So frantique, that he tooke him for a Horse,
And to a Pond was leading him to drinke;
It went beyond the wit of man to thinke,

The sundry frenzies that he there might see,
One man would to another married be:
And for a Curate taking the Towne Bull,
Would have him knit the knot: another Gull
Had found an Ape was chained to a Stall,
Which he to worship on his knees doth fall;
To doe the like and doth his Neighbours get,
Who in a Chaire this ill-fac'd Munky set,
And on their shoulders lifting him on hie,
They in Procession beare him with a crie;
And him a Lord will have at least, if not,
A greater man: another sort had got
About a Pedlar, who had lately heard,
How with the mad men of this Ile it far'd:
And having nothing in his Pack but toyes,
Which none except meere mad men, and fond boyes
Would ever touch; thought verily that he
Amongst these Bedlams, would a gayner be,
Or else loose all; scarce had he pitch'd his Pack,
E're he could scarcely say, what doe yee lack:
But that they throng'd about him with their mony,
As thick as Flyes about a Pot of hony;
Some of these Lunaticks, these frantique Asses,
Gave him Spurryalls for his farthing Glasses:
There should you see another of these Cattell,
Give him a pound of silver for a Rattle;
And there another that would needsly scorse,
A costly Jewell for a Hobby-Horse:
For Bells, and Babies, such as children small,
Are ever us'd to solace them withall:
Those they did buy at such a costly rate,
That it was able to subvert a State.

(Lines 651–772)

FROM *Noah's Floud*

Eternall and all-working God, which wast
Before the world, whose frame by thee was cast,
And beatifi'd with beamefull lampes above,
By thy great wisedome set how they should move
To guide the seasons, equally to all,
Which come and goe as they doe rise and fall.
My mighty Maker, O doe thou infuse
Such life and spirit into my labouring Muse,
That I may sing (what but from Noah thou hid'st)
The greatest thing that ever yet thou didst
Since the Creation; that the world may see
The Muse is heavenly, and deriv'd from thee.
O let thy glorious Angell which since kept
That gorgeous *Eden,* where once *Adam* slept;
When tempting *Eve* was taken from his side,
Let him great God not onely be my guide,
But with his fiery Faucheon still be nie,
To keepe affliction farre from me, that I
With a free soule thy wondrous workes may show,
Then like that Deluge shall my numbers flow,
Telling the state wherein the earth then stood,
The Gyant race, the universall flood.
The fruitfull earth being lusty then and strong,
Like to a Woman, fit for love, and young,
Brought forth her creatures mighty, not a thing
Issu'd from her, but a continuall spring
Had to increase it, and to make it flourish,
For in her selfe she had that power to nourish
Her Procreation, that her children then
Were at the instant of their birth, halfe men.

Men then begot so soone, and got so long,
That scarcely one a thousand men among
But he ten thousand in his time might see,
That from his loynes deriv'd their Pedegree.
The full-womb'd Women, very hardly went
Out their nine months, abundant nature lent
Their fruit such thriving, as that once waxt quicke,
The large-limb'd mother, neither faint nor sicke,
Hasted her houre by her abundant health,
Nature so plaid the unthrift with her wealth,
So prodigally lavishing her store
Upon the teeming earth, then wasting more
Then it had need of: not the smallest weed
Knowne in that first age, but the naturall seed
Made it a Plant, to these now since the Floud,
So that each Garden look'd then like a Wood:
Beside, in Med'cen, simples had that power,
That none need then the Planetary houre
To helpe their working, they so juycefull were.
The Winter and the Spring time of the yeare
Seem'd all one season: that most stately tree
Of *Libanus,* which many times we see
Mention'd for talenesse in the holy Writ,
Whose tops the clouds oft in their wandring hit,
Were shrubs to those then on the earth that grew;
Nor the most sturdy storme that ever blew
Their big-growne bodies, to the earth ere shooke,
Their mighty Rootes, so certaine fastening tooke;
Cover'd with grasse, more softe than any silke,
The Trees dropt honey, and the Springs gusht milke:
The Flower-fleec't Meadow, and the gorgeous grove,
Which should smell sweetest in their bravery, strove;
No little shrub, but it some Gum let fall,
To make the cleere Ayre aromaticall:
Whilst to the little Birds melodious straines,

The trembling Rivers tript along the Plaines.
Shades serv'd for houses, neither Heate nor Cold
Troubl'd the yong, nor yet annoy'd the old:
The batning earth all plenty did afford,
And without tilling (of her owne accord)
That living idly without taking paine
(Like to the first) made every man a *Caine*.

(*Lines* 1–72)

George Chapman

(1559?–1634)

FROM *Bussy D'Ambois*

TAMYRA. Now all the peacefull regents of the night,
Silently-gliding exhalations,
Languishing windes, and murmuring fals of waters,
Sadnesse of heart, and ominous securenesse,
Enchantments, dead sleepes, all the friends of rest,
That ever wrought upon the life of man,
Extend your utmost strengths; and this charm'd houre
Fix like the Center; make the violent wheeles
Of Time and Fortune stand; and Great Existens
(The Makers treasurie) now not seeme to bee,
To all but my approaching friends and mee:
They come, alas they come, feare, feare and hope
Of one thing, at one instant fight in mee:
I love what most I loath, and cannot live
Unlesse I compasse that which holds my death:
For life's meere death loving one that loathes me,
And he I love will loth me, when he sees
I flie my sex, my vertue, my Renowne,
To runne so madly on a man unknowne.
See, see a Vault is opening that was never
Knowne to my Lord and husband, nor to any
But him that brings the man I love, and me;
How shall I looke on him? how shall I live
And not consume in blushes, I will in;
And cast my selfe off, as I ne're had beene.

(*Act II, scene ii*)

128

BUSSY. Ile sooth his plots: and strow my hate with smiles
Till all at once the close mines of my heart
Rise at full date, and rush into his bloud:
Ile bind his arme in silke, and rub his flesh,
To make the vaine swell, that his soule may gush
Into some kennell, where it longs to lie,
And policy shall be flanckt with policy
Yet shall the feeling center where wee meet
Grone with the wait of my approaching feet:
Ile make th' inspired threshals of his Court
Sweat with the weather of my horrid steps
Before I enter: yet will I appeare
Like calme security, before a ruine;
A Politician, must like lightening melt
The very marrow, and not taint the skin:
His wayes must not be seene: the superficies
Of the greene center must not taste his feet:
When hell is plow'd up with his wounding tracts:
And all his harvest reap't by hellish facts.

(Act IV, scene ii)

MONSIEUR. Now shall we see, that nature hath no end
In her great works, responsive to their worths,
That she that makes so many eies, and soules,
To see and fore-see, is starke blinde herselfe:
And as illiterate men say Latine prayers
By rote of heart, and daily iteration;
Not knowing what they say: So nature layes
A deale of stuffe together, and by use,
Or by the meere necessitie of matter,
Ends such a worke, fills it, or leaves it empty,
Of strength, or vertue, error or cleare truth;
Not knowing what she does; but usually
Gives that which she calls merit to a man,

And beliefe must arrive him on huge riches,
Honour, and happinesse, that effects his ruine;
Even as in ships of warre, whose lasts of powder
Are laid (men think) to make them last, and guard,
When a disorder'd sparke that powder taking,
Blowes up with sodaine violence and horror
Ships that (kept empty) had sail'd long with terror.

(Act V, scene ii)

The Shadow of Night

HYMNUS IN NOCTEM

Great Goddesse to whose throne in Cynthian fires,
This earthlie Alter endlesse fumes exspires,
Therefore, in fumes of sighes and fires of griefe,
To fearefull chances thou sendst bold reliefe,
Happie, thrise happie, Type, and nurse of death,
Who breathlesse, feeds on nothing but our breath,
In whom must vertue and her issue live,
Or dye for ever; now let humor give
Seas to mine eyes, that I may quicklie weepe
The shipwracke of the world: or let soft sleepe
(Binding my sences) lose my working soule,
That in her highest pitch, she may controule
The court of skill, compact of misterie,
Wanting but franchisement and memorie
To reach all secrets: then in blissfull trance,
Raise her (deare Night) to that perseverance,
That in my torture, she all earths may sing,
And force to tremble in her trumpeting
Heavens christall temples: in her powrs implant

Skill of my griefs, and she can nothing want.
  Then like fierce bolts, well rammd with heate and cold
In Joves Artillerie; my words unfold,
To breake the labyrinth of everie eare,
And make ech frighted soule come forth and heare,
Let them breake harts, as well as yeelding ayre,
That all mens bosoms (pierst with no affaires,
But gaine of riches) may be lanced wide,
And with the threates of vertue terrified.
  Sorrowes deare soveraigne, and the queene of rest,
That when unlightsome, vast, and indigest
The formelesse matter of this world did lye,
Fildst every place with thy Divinitie,
Why did thy absolute and endlesse sway,
Licence heavens torch, the scepter of the Day,
Distinguisht intercession to thy throne,
That long before, all matchlesse rulde alone?
Why letst thou order, orderlesse disperse,
The fighting parents of this universe?
When earth, the ayre, and sea, in fire remaind,
When fire, the sea, and earth, the ayre containd,
When ayre, the earth, and fire, the sea enclosde
When sea, fire, ayre, in earth were indisposde,
Nothing, as now, remainde so out of kinde,
All things in grosse, were finer than refinde,
Substance was sound within, and had no being,
Now forme gives being; all our essence seeming,
Chaos had soule without a bodie then,
Now bodies live without the soules of men,
Lumps being digested; monsters, in our pride.
  And as a wealthie fount, that hils did hide,
Let forth by labor of industrious hands,
Powres out her treasure through the fruitefull strands,
Seemely divided to a hundred streames,
Whose bewties shed such profitable beames,

And make such Orphean Musicke in their courses,
That Citties follow their enchanting forces,
Who running farre, at length ech powres her hart
Into the bosome of the gulfie desart,
As much confounded there, and indigest,
As in the chaos of the hills comprest:
So all things now (extract out of the prime)
Are turnd to chaos, and confound the time.

A stepdame Night of minde about us clings,
Who broodes beneath her hell obscuring wings,
Worlds of confusion, where the soule defamde,
The bodie had bene better never framde,
Beneath thy soft, and peace-full covert then,
(Most sacred mother both of Gods and men)
Treasures unknowne, and more unprisde did dwell;
But in the blind borne shadow of this hell,
This horrid stepdame, blindnesse of the minde,
Nought worth the sight, no sight, but worse then blind,
A Gorgon that with brasse, and snakie brows,
(Most harlot-like) her naked secrets shows:
For in th' expansure, and distinct attire,
Of light, and darcknesse, of the sea, and fire,
Of ayre, and earth, and all, all these create,
First set and rulde, in most harmonious state,
Disjunction showes, in all things now amisse,
By that first order, what confusion is:
Religious curb, that manadgd men in bounds,
Of publique wellfare; lothing private grounds,
(Now cast away, by selfe-lov's paramores)
All are transformd to Calydonian bores,
That kill our bleeding vines, displow our fields,
Rend groves in peeces; all things nature yeelds
Supplanting: tumbling up in hills of dearth,
The fruitefull disposition of the earth,
Ruine creates men: all to slaughter bent,

Like envie, fed with others famishment.
    And what makes men without the parts of men,
Or in their manhoods, lesse then childeren,
But manlesse natures? all this world was namde
A world of him, for whom it first was framde,
(Who (like a tender Chevrill,) shruncke with fire
Of base ambition, and of selfe-desire,
His armes into his shoulders crept for feare
Bountie should use them; and fierce rape forbeare,
His legges into his greedie belly runne,
The charge of hospitalitie to shunne)
In him the world is to a lump reverst,
That shruncke from forme, that was by forme disperst,
And in nought more then thanklesse avarice,
Not rendring vertue her deserved price.
Kinde Amalthaea was transferd by Jove,
Into his sparckling pavement, for her love,
Though but a Goate, and giving him her milke,
Basenesse is flintie; gentrie softe as silke,
In heavens she lives, and rules a living signe
In humane bodies: yet not so divine,
That she can worke her kindnesse in our harts.
    The sencelesse Argive ship, for her deserts,
Bearing to Colchos, and for bringing backe,
The hardie Argonauts, secure of wracke,
The fautor and the God of gratitude,
Would not from number of the starres exclude.
A thousand such examples could I cite,
To damne stone-pesants, that like Typhons fight
Against their Maker, and contend to be
Of kings, the abject slaves of drudgerie:
Proud of that thraldome: love the kindest lest,
And hate, not to be hated of the best.
    If then we frame mans figure by his mind,
And that at first, his fashion was assignd,

Erection in such God-like excellence
For his soules sake, and her intelligence:
She so degenerate, and growne deprest,
Content to share affections with a beast,
The shape wherewith he should be now indude,
Must beare no signe of mans similitude.
Therefore Promethean Poets with the coles
Of their most geniale, more-then-humane soules
In living verse, created men like these,
With shapes of Centaurs, Harpies, Lapithes,
That they in prime of erudition,
When almost savage vulgar men were growne,
Seeing them selves in those Pierean founts,
Might mend their mindes, asham'd of such accounts.
So when ye heare, the sweetest Muses sonne,
With heavenly rapture of his Musicke, wonne
Rockes, forrests, floods, and winds to leave their course
In his attendance: it bewrayes the force
His wisedome had, to draw men growne so rude
To civill love of Art, and Fortitude.
And not for teaching others insolence,
Had he his date-exceeding excellence
With soveraigne Poets, but for use applyed,
And in his proper actes exemplified;
And that in calming the infernall kinde,
To wit, the perturbations of his minde,
And bringing his Eurydice from hell,
(Which Justice signifies) is proved well.
But if in rights observance any man
Looke backe, with boldnesse lesse then Orphean,
Soone falls he to the hell from whence he rose:
The fiction then would temprature dispose,
In all the tender motives of the minde,
To make man worthie his hel-danting kinde.
The golden chaine of Homers high device

Ambition is, or cursed avarice,
Which all Gods haling being tyed to Jove,
Him from his setled height could never move:
Intending this, that though that powrefull chaine
Of most Herculean vigor to constraine
Men from true vertue, or their pristine states
Attempt a man that manlesse changes hates,
And is enobled with a deathlesse love
Of things eternall, dignified above:
Nothing shall stirre him from adorning still
This shape with vertue, and his powre with will.

   But as rude painters that contend to show
Beasts, foules or fish, all artlesse to bestow
On every side his native counterfet,
Above his head, his name had neede to set:
So men that will be men, in more then face,
(As in their foreheads) should in actions place
More perfect characters, to prove they be
No mockers of their first nobilitie:
Else may they easly passe for beasts or foules:
Soules praise our shapes, and not our shapes our soules.

   And as when Chloris paints th'ennamild meads,
A flocke of shepherds to the bagpipe treads
Rude rurall dances with their countrey loves:
Some a farre off observing their removes,
Turnes, and returnes, quicke footing, sodaine stands,
Reelings aside, od actions with their hands;
Now backe, now forwards, now lockt arme in arme,
Now hearing musicke, thinke it is a charme,
That like loose froes at Bacchanalean feasts,
Makes them seeme franticke in their barraine jestes;
And being clusterd in a shapelesse croude,
With much lesse admiration are allowd.
So our first excellence, so much abusd,
And we (without the harmonie was usd,

When Saturnes golden scepter stroke the strings
Of Civill governement) make all our doings
Savour of rudenesse, and obscuritie,
And in our formes shew more deformitie,
Then if we still were wrapt, and smoothered
In that confusion, out of which we fled.

  And as when hosts of starres attend thy flight,
(Day of deepe students, most contentfull night)
The morning (mounted on the Muses stead)
Ushers the sonne from Vulcans golden bed,
And then from forth their sundrie roofes of rest,
All sorts of men, to sorted taskes addrest,
Spreade this inferiour element: and yeeld
Labour his due: the souldier to the field,
States-men to counsell, Judges to their pleas,
Merchants to commerce, mariners to seas:
All beasts, and birds, the groves and forrests range,
To fill all corners of this round Exchange,
Till thou (deare Night, ô goddesse of most worth)
Letst thy sweet seas of golden humor forth
And Eagle-like dost with thy starrie wings,
Beate in the foules, and beasts to Somnus lodgings,
And haughtie Day to the infernall deepe,
Proclaiming scilence, studie, ease, and sleepe.
All things before thy forces put in rout,
Retiring where the morning fir'd them out.

  So to the chaos of our first descent,
(All dayes of honor, and of vertue spent)
We basely make retrait, and are no lesse
Then huge impolisht heapes of filthinesse.
Mens faces glitter, and their hearts are blacke,
But thou (great Mistresse of heavens gloomie racke)
Art blacke in face, and glitterst in thy heart.
There is thy glorie, riches, force, and Art;
Opposed earth, beates blacke and blewe thy face,

And often doth thy heart it selfe deface,
For spite that to thy vertue-famed traine,
All the choise worthies that did ever raigne
In eldest age, were still preferd by Jove,
Esteeming that due honor to his love.
There shine they: not to sea-men guides alone,
But sacred presidents to everie one.
There fixt for ever, where the Day is driven,
Almost foure hundred times a yeare from heaven.
In hell then let her sit, and never rise,
Till Morns leave blushing at her cruelties.
   Meane while, accept, as followers of thy traine,
(Our better parts aspiring to thy raigne)
Vertues obscur'd, and banished the day,
With all the glories of this spongie sway,
Prisond in flesh, and that poore flesh in bands
Of stone, and steele, chiefe flowrs of vertues Garlands.
   O then most tender fortresse of our woes,
That bleeding lye in vertues overthroes,
Hating the whoredome of this painted light:
Raise thy chast daughters, ministers of right,
The dreadfull and the just Eumenides,
And let them wreake the wrongs of our disease,
Drowning the world in bloud, and staine the skies
With their split soules, made drunke with tyrannies.
   Fall Hercules from heaven in tempestes hurld,
And cleanse this beastly stable of the world:
Or bend thy brasen bow against the Sunne,
As in Tartessus, when thou hadst begunne
Thy taske of oxen: heat in more extreames
Then thou wouldst suffer, with his envious beames:
Now make him leave the world to Night and dreames.
Never were vertues labours so envy'd
As in this light: shoote, shoote, and stoope his pride:
Suffer no more his lustfull rayes to get

The Earth with issue: let him still be set
In Somnus thickets: bound about the browes
With pitchie vapours, and with Ebone bowes.
   Rich-tapird sanctuarie of the blest,
Pallace of Ruth, made all of teares, and rest,
To thy blacke shades and desolation,
I consecrate my life; and living mone,
Where furies shall for ever fighting be,
And adders hisse the world for hating me,
Foxes shall barke, and Night-ravens belch in grones,
And owles shall hollow my confusions:
There will I furnish up my funerall bed,
Strewd with the bones and relickes of the dead.
Atlas shall let th'Olimpick burthen fall,
To cover my untombed face withall.
And when as well, the matter of our kind,
As the materiall substance of the mind,
Shall cease their revolutions, in abode
Of such impure and ugly period,
As the old essence, and insensive prime:
Then shall the ruines of the fourefold time,
Turnd to that lumpe (as rapting Torrents rise)
For ever murmure forth my miseries.
   Ye living spirits then, if any live,
Whom like extreames, do like affections give,
Shun, shun this cruell light, and end your thrall,
In these soft shades of sable funerall:
From whence with ghosts, whom vengeance holds from
     rest,
Dog-fiends and monsters hanting the distrest,
As men whose parents tyrannie hath slaine,
Whose sisters rape, and bondage do sustaine.
But you that ne'er had birth, nor ever prov'd,
How deare a blessing tis to be belov'd,

Whose friends idolatrous desire of gold,
To scorne, and ruine have your freedome sold:
Whose vertues feele all this, and shew your eyes,
Men made of Tartar, and of villanies:
Aspire th'extraction, and the quintessence
Of all the joyes in earths circumference:
With ghosts, fiends, monsters: as men robd and rackt,
Murtherd in life: from shades with shadowes blackt·
Thunder your wrongs, your miseries and hells,
And with the dismall accents of your knells,
Revive the dead, and make the living dye
In ruth, and terror of your torturie:
Still all the powre of Art into your grones,
Scorning your triviall and remissive mones,
Compact of fiction, and hyperboles,
(Like wanton mourners, cloyd with too much ease)
Should leave the glasses of the hearers eyes
Unbroken, counting all but vanities.
But paint, or else create in serious truth,
A bodie figur'd to your vertues ruth,
That to the sence may shew what damned sinne,
For your extreames this Chaos tumbles in.
But wo is wretched me, without a name:
Vertue feeds scorne, and noblest honor, shame:
Pride bathes in teares of poore submission,
And makes his soule, the purple he puts on.
   Kneele then with me, fall worm-like on the ground,
And from th'infectious dunghill of this Round,
From mens brasse wits, and golden foolerie,
Weepe, weepe your soules, into felicitie:
Come to this house of mourning, serve the night,
To whom pale day (with whoredome soked quite)
Is but a drudge, selling her beauties use
To rapes, adultries, and to all abuse.

Her labors feast imperiall Night with sports,
Where Loves are Christmast, with all pleasures sorts:
And whom her fugitive, and far-shot rayes
Disjoyne, and drive into ten thousand wayes,
Nights glorious mantle wraps in safe abodes,
And frees their neckes from servile labors lodes:
Her trustie shadowes, succour men dismayd,
Whom Dayes deceiptfull malice hath betrayd:
From the silke vapors of her Iveryport,
Sweet Protean dreames she sends of every sort:
Some taking formes of Princes, to perswade
Of men deject, we are their equals made,
Some clad in habit of deceased friends,
For whom we mournd, and now have wisht amends,
And some (deare favour) Lady-like attyrd,
With pride of Beauties full Meridian fir'd:
Who pitie our contempts, revive our harts:
For wisest Ladies love the inward parts.

If these be dreames, even so are all things else,
That walke this round by heavenly sentinels:
But from Nights port of horne she greets our eyes
With graver dreames inspir'd with prophesies,
Which oft presage to us succeeding chances,
We prooving that awake, they shew in trances.
If these seeme likewise vaine, or nothing are
Vaine things, or nothing come to vertues share:
For nothing more then dreames, with us shee findes:
Then since all pleasures vanish like the windes,
And that most serious actions not respecting
The second light, are worth but the neglecting,
Since day, or light, in anie qualitie,
For earthly uses do but serve the eye.
And since the eyes most quicke and dangerous use,
Enflames the heart, and learnes the soule abuse,
Since mournings are preferd to banquettings,

And they reach heaven, bred under sorrowes wings.
Since Night brings terror to our frailties still,
And shameless Day, doth marble us in ill.
 All you possest with indepressed spirits,
Indu'd with nimble, and aspiring wits,
Come consecrate with me, to sacred Night
Your whole endevours, and detest the light.
Sweete Peaces richest crowne is made of starres,
Most certaine guides of honord Marinars,
No pen can any thing eternall wright,
That is not steept in humor of the Night.
 Hence beasts, and birds to caves and bushes then,
And welcome Night, ye noblest heires of men,
Hence Phebus to thy glassie strumpets bed,
And never more let Themis daughters spred,
Thy golden harnesse on thy rosie horse,
But in close thickets run thy oblique course.
 See now ascends, the glorious Bride of Brides,
Nuptials, and triumphs, glittring by her sides,
Juno and Hymen do her traine adorne,
Ten thousand torches round about them borne:
Dumbe Silence mounted on the Cyprian starre,
With becks, rebukes the winds before his carre,
Where she advanst; beates downe with cloudie mace,
The feeble light to blacke Saturnius pallace:
Behind her, with a brase of silver Hynds,
In Ivorie chariot, swifter than the winds,
Is great Hyperions horned daughter drawne
Enchantresse-like, deckt in disparent lawne,
Circkled with charmes, and incantations,
That ride huge spirits, and outragious passions:
Musicke, and moode, she loves, but love she hates,
(As curious Ladies do, their publique cates)
This traine, with meteors, comets, lightenings,
The dreadfull presence of our Empresse sings:

Which grant for ever (ô eternall Night)
Till vertue flourish in the light of light.

Explicit Hymnus.

FROM *Euthymiæ Raptus or The Teares
of Peace*

And, now gives Time, her states description.
Before her flew Affliction, girt in storms,
Gasht all with gushing wounds; and all the formes
Of bane, and miserie, frowning in her face;
Whom Tyrannie, and Injustice, had in Chace;
Grimme Persecution, Povertie, and Shame;
Detraction, Envie, foule Mishap and lame;
Scruple of Conscience; Feare, Deceipt, Despaire;
Slaunder, and Clamor, that rent all the Ayre;
Hate, Warre, and Massacre; uncrowned Toyle;
And Sickenes (t'all the rest, the Base, and Foile)
Crept after; and his deadly weight, trode downe
Wealth, Beautie, and the glorie of a Crowne.
These ushered her farre off; as figures given,
To showe, these Crosses borne, make peace with
    heaven:
But now (made free from them) next her, before;
Peacefull, and young, Herculean silence bore
His craggie Club; which up, aloft, hee hild;
With which, and his forefingers charme hee stild
All sounds in ayre; and left so free, mine eares,
That I might heare, the musique of the Spheres,
And all the Angels, singing, out of heaven;
Whose tunes were solemne (as to Passion given)
For now, that Justice was the Happinesse there

For all the wrongs to Right, inflicted here.
Such was the Passion that Peace now put on;
And on, all went; when soudainely was gone
All light of heaven before us; from a wood
Whose sight, fore-seene (now lost) amaz'd wee stood,
The Sunne still gracing us; when now (the Ayre
Inflam'd with Meteors) we discoverd, fayre,
The skipping Gote; the Horses flaming Mane;
Bearded, and trained Comets; Starres in wane;
The burning sword; the Firebrand, flying Snake;
The Lance; the Torch; the Licking fire; the Drake:
And all else Metors, that did ill abode;
The thunder chid; the lightning leapt abrode;
And yet, when Peace came in, all heaven was cleare;
And then, did all the horrid wood appeare;
Where mortall dangers, more then leaves did growe;
In which wee could not, one free steppe bestowe;
For treading on some murtherd Passenger,
Who thither, was by witchcraft, forc't to erre,
Whose face, the bird hid, that loves Humans best;
That hath the bugle eyes, and Rosie Breast;
And is the yellow Autumns Nightingall.

(*Conclusio, lines* 1090–1135)

A Hymne to Our Saviour on the Crosse

Haile great Redeemer, man, and God, all haile,
Whose fervent agonie, tore the temples vaile,
Let sacrifices out, darke Prophesies
And miracles: and let in, for all these,
A simple pietie, a naked heart,
And humble spirit, that no lesse impart,

And prove thy Godhead to us, being as rare,
And in all sacred powre, as circulare.
Water and blood mixt, were not swet from thee
With deadlier hardnesse: more divinitie
Of supportation, then through flesh and blood,
Good doctrine is diffusde, and life as good.
O open to me then, (like thy spread armes
That East and West reach) all those misticke charmes
That hold us in thy life and discipline:
Thy merits in thy love so thrice divine;
It made thee, being our God, assume our man;
And like our Champion Olympian,
Come to the field gainst Sathan, and our sinne:
Wrastle with torments, and the garland winne
From death and hell; which cannot crown our browes
But blood must follow: thornes mixe with thy bowes
Of conquering Lawrell, fast naild to thy Crosse,
Are all the glories we can here engrosse.
Prove then to those, that in vaine glories place
Their happiness here: they hold not by thy grace,
To those whose powres, proudly oppose thy lawes,
Oppressing Vertue, giving Vice applause:
They never manage just authoritie,
But thee in thy deare members crucifie.
  Thou couldst have come in glorie past them all,
With powre to force thy pleasure, and empale
Thy Church with brasse, and Adamant, that no swine,
Nor theeves, nor hypocrites, nor fiends divine
Could have broke in, or rooted, or put on
Vestments of Pietie, when their hearts had none:
Or rapt to ruine with pretext, to save:
Would pompe, and radiance, rather not out brave
Thy naked truth, then cloath, or countnance it
With grace, and such sincerenesse as is fit:
But since true pietie weares her pearles within,

And outward paintings onely pranke up sinne:
Since bodies strengthned, soules go to the wall;
Since God we cannot serve and Beliall;
Therefore thou putst on, earths most abject plight,
Hid'st thee in humblesse, underwentst despight,
Mockerie, detraction, shame, blowes, vilest death.
These, thou, thy souldiers taughtst to fight beneath:
Mad'st a commanding President of these,
Perfect, perpetuall: bearing all the keyes
To holinesse, and heaven. To these, such lawes
Thou in thy blood writst: that were no more cause
T'enflame our loves, and fervent faiths in thee,
Then in them, truths divine simplicitie,
Twere full enough; for therein we may well
See thy white finger furrowing blackest hell,
In turning up the errors that our sence
And sensuall powres, incurre by negligence
Of our eternall truth-exploring soule.
All Churches powres, thy writ word doth controule;
And mixt it with the fabulous Alchoran,
A man might boult it out, as floure from branne;
Easily discerning it, a heavenly birth,
Brake it but now out, and but crept on earth.
Yet (as if God lackt mans election,
And shadowes were creators of the Sunne)
Men must authorise it: antiquities
Must be explor'd, to spirit, and give it thies,
And controversies, thicke as flies at Spring,
Must be maintain'd about th'ingenuous meaning;
When no stile can expresse it selfe so cleare,
Nor holds so even, and firme a character.
Those mysteries that are not to be reacht,
Still to be striv'd with, make them more impeacht:
And as the Mill fares with an ill pickt grist,
When any stone, the stones is got betwist,

Rumbling together, fill the graine with grit;
Offends the eare, sets teeth an edge with it:
Blunts the pict quarrie so, twill grinde no more,
Spoyles bread, and scants the Millars custom'd store.
So in the Church, when controversie fals,
It marres her musicke, shakes her batterd wals,
Grates tender consciences, and weakens faith;
The bread of life taints, and makes worke for Death;
Darkens truths light, with her perplext Abysmes,
And dustlike grinds men into sects and schismes.
And what's the cause? the words deficiencie?
In volume, matter, perspecuitie?
Ambition, lust, and damned avarice,
Pervert, and each the sacred word applies
To his prophane ends; all to profite given,
And pursnets lay to catch the joyes of heaven.
   Since truth, and reall worth, men seldome sease,
Impostors most, and sleightest learnings please.
And, where the true Church, like the nest should be
Of chast, and provident Alcione:
(To which is onely one straight orifice,
Which is so strictly fitted to her sise,
That no bird bigger then her selfe, or lesse,
Can pierce and keepe it, or discerne th'accesse:
Nor which the sea it selfe, on which tis made,
Can ever overflow, or once invade);
Now wayes so many to her Altars are,
So easie, so prophane, and populare:
That torrents charg'd with weeds, and sin-drownd
       beasts,
Breake in, lode, cracke them: sensuall joyes and feasts
Corrupt their pure fumes: and the slendrest flash
Of lust, or profite, makes a standing plash
Of sinne about them, which men will not passe.
Looke (Lord) upon them, build them wals cf brasse,

To keepe prophane feete off: do not thou
In wounds and anguish ever overflow,
And suffer such in ease, and sensualitie,
Dare to reject thy rules of humble life:
The minds true peace, and turne their zeales to strife,
For objects earthly, and corporeall.
A tricke of humblesse now they practise all,
Confesse their no deserts, habilities none:
Professe all frailties, and amend not one:
As if a priviledge they meant to claime
In sinning by acknowledging the maime
Sinne gave in Adam: Nor the surplussage
Of thy redemption, seeme to put in gage
For his transgression: that thy vertuous paines
(Deare Lord) have eat out all their former staines;
That thy most mightie innocence had powre
To cleanse their guilts: that the unvalued dowre
Thou mad'st the Church thy spouse, in pietie,
And (to endure paines impious) constancie,
Will and alacritie (if they invoke)
To beare the sweete lode, and the easie yoke
Of thy injunctions, in diffusing these
(In thy perfection) through her faculties:
In every fiver, suffering to her use,
And perfecting the forme thou didst infuse
In mans creation: made him cleare as then
Of all the frailties, since defiling men.
And as a runner at th'Olympian games,
With all the luggage he can lay on, frames
His whole powres to the race, bags, pockets, greaves
Stuft full of sand he weares, which when he leaves,
And doth his other weightie weeds uncover,
With which halfe smotherd, he is wrapt all over:
Then seemes he light, and fresh as morning aire;
Guirds him with silkes, swaddles with roulers faire

His lightsome body: and away he scoures
So swift, and light, he scarce treads down the flowrs:
So to our game proposde, of endlesse joy
(Before thy deare death) when we did employ,
Our tainted powres; we felt them clogd and chain'd
With sinne and bondage, which did rust, and raign'd
In our most mortall bodies: but when thou
Strip'dst us of these bands, and from foote to brow
Guirt, rold, and trimd us up in thy deserts:
Free were our feete, and hands; and spritely hearts
Leapt in our bosoms; and (ascribing still
All to thy merits: both our powre and will
To every thought of goodnesse, wrought by thee;
That divine scarlet, in which thou didst die
Our cleansd consistence; lasting still in powre
T'enable acts in us, as the next howre
To thy most saving, glorious sufferance)
We may make all our manly powers advance
Up to thy Image; and these formes of earth,
Beauties and mockeries, matcht in beastly birth:
We may despise, with still aspiring spirits
To thy high graces, in thy still fresh merits:
Not touching at this base and spongie mould,
For any springs of lust, or mines of gold.
    For else (milde Saviour, pardon me to speake)
How did thy foote, the Serpents forhead breake?
How hath the Nectar of thy vertuous blood,
The sinke of Adams forfeit overflow'd?
How doth it set us free, if we still stand
(For all thy sufferings) bound both foote and hand
Vassals to Sathan? Didst thou onely die,
Thine owne divine deserts to glorifie,
And shew thou couldst do this? O were not those
Given to our use in powre? If we shall lose
By damn'd relapse, grace to enact that powre:

And basely give up our redemptions towre,
Before we trie our strengths, built all on thine,
And with a humblesse, false, and Asinine,
Flattering our senses, lay upon our soules
The burthens of their conquests, and like Moules
Grovell in earth still, being advanc't to heaven:
(Cowes that we are) in heards how are we driven
To Sathans shambles? Wherein stand we for
Thy heavenly image, Hels great Conqueror?
Didst thou not offer, to restore our fall
Thy sacrifice, full, once, and one for all?
If we be still downe, how then can we rise
Againe with thee, and seeke crownes in the skies?
But we excuse this; saying, We are but men,
And must erre, must fall: what thou didst sustaine
To free our beastly frailties, never can
With all thy grace, by any powre in man
Make good thy Rise to us: O blasphemie
In hypocriticall humilitie!
As we are men, we death and hell controule,
Since thou createdst man a living soule:
As everie houre we sinne, we do like beasts:
Heedlesse, and wilfull, murthering in our breasts
Thy saved image, out of which, one cals
Our humane soules, mortall celestialls:
When casting off a good lifes godlike grace,
We fall from God; and then make good our place
When we returne to him: and so are said
To live: when life like his true forme we leade,
And die (as much as can immortall creature):
Not that we utterly can ceasse to be,
But that we fall from life's best qualitie.
    But we are tost out of our humane Throne
By pied and Portean opinion;
We vouch thee onely, for pretext and fashion,

And are not inward with thy death and passion.
We slavishly renounce thy royaltie
With which thou crownst us in thy victorie:
Spend all our manhood in the fiends defence,
And drowne thy right, in beastly negligence.

God never is deceiv'd so, to respect,
His shade in Angels beauties, to neglect
His owne most cleare and rapting lovelinesse:
Nor Angels dote so on the species
And grace given to our soule (which is their shade)
That therefore they will let their owne formes fade.
And yet our soule (which most deserves our woe,
And that from which our whole mishap doth flow)
So softn'd is, and rapt (as with a storme)
With flatteries of our base corporeall forme,
(Which is her shadow) that she quite forsakes
Her proper noblesse, and for nothing takes
The beauties that for her love, thou putst on;
In torments rarefied farre past the Sunne.

Hence came the cruell fate that Orpheus
Sings of Narcissus: who being amorous
Of his shade in the water (which denotes
Beautie in bodies, that like water flotes)
Despisd himselfe, his soule, and so let fade
His substance for a never-purchast shade.
Since soules of their use, ignorant are still,
With this vile bodies use, men never fill.

And, as the Suns light, in streames ne're so faire
Is but a shadow, to his light in aire,
His splendor that in aire we so admire,
Is but a shadow to his beames in fire:
In fire his brightnesse, but a shadow is
To radiance fir'd, in that pure brest of his:
So as the subject on which thy grace shines,

Is thicke, or cleare; to earthe or heaven inclines;
So that truths light showes; so thy passion takes;
With which, who inward is, and thy breast makes
Bulwarke to his breast, against all the darts
The foe stil shoots more, more his late blow smarts,
And sea-like raves most, where tis most withstood.
He tasts the strength and vertue of thy blood:
He knows that when flesh is most sooth'd, and grac't,
Admir'd and magnified, ador'd, and plac't
In height of all the blouds Idolatry,
And fed with all the spirits of Luxury,
One thought of joy, in any soule that knowes
Her owne true strength, and thereon doth repose;
Bringing her bodies organs to attend
Chiefly her powres, to her eternall end;
Makes all things outward; and the sweetest sin,
That ravisheth the beastly flesh within;
All but a fiend, prankt in an Angels plume:
A shade, a fraud, before the wind a fume.
   Hayle then divine Redeemer, still all haile,
All glorie, gratitude, and all availe,
Be given thy all-deserving agonie;
Whose vineger thou Nectar mak'st in me,
Whose goodnesse freely all my ill turnes good:
Since thou being crusht, and straind throgh flesh and
      blood:
Each nerve and artire needs must tast of thee.
What odour burn'd in ayres that noisome be,
Leaves not his sent there? O then how much more
Must thou, whose sweetnesse swet eternall odour,
Stick where it breath'd, and for whom thy sweet
      breath,
Thou freely gav'st up, to revive his death?
Let those that shrink then as their conscience lodes,

That fight in Sathans right, and faint in Gods,
Still count them slaves to Sathan. I am none:
Thy fight hath freed me, thine thou mak'st mine owne.

O then (my sweetest and my onely life)
Confirme this comfort, purchast with thy griefe,
And my despisde soule of the world, love thou:
No thought to any other joy I vow.
Order these last steps of my abject state,
Straite on the marke a man should levell at:
And grant that while I strive to forme in me,
Thy sacred image, no adversitie
May make me draw one limme, or line amisse:
Let no vile fashion wrest my faculties
From what becomes that Image. Quiet so
My bodies powres, that neither weale nor wo,
May stirre one thought up, gainst thy freest will.
Grant, that in me, my mindes waves may be still:
The world for no extreme may use her voice;
Nor Fortune treading reeds, make any noise.

Amen.

Complaine not whatsoever Need invades,
But heaviest fortunes beare as lightest shades.
Ανέχου καὶ Απέχου.

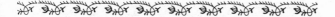

John Marston

(1575?–1634)

FROM *The Malcontent*

MALEVOLE. I cannot sleepe, my eyes ill neighbouring
   lids
Will holde no fellowship: O thou pale sober night,
Thou that in sluggish fumes all sence doost steepe:
Thou that gives all the world full leave to play,
Unbendst the feebled veines of sweatie labour;
The gally-slave that, all the toilesome day,
Tugges at his oare against the stubburne wave,
Straining his rugged veines; snores fast:
The stooping sith-man that doth barbe the field,
Thou makest winke sure: in night all creatures sleepe,
Onely the Malecontent that gainst his fate,
Repines and quarrells, alas hee's goodman tell-clocke;
His sallow jaw-bones sinke with wasting mone,
Whilst others beds are downe, his pillowes stone.

(*Act III, scene i*)

William Shakespeare

(1564–1616)

Sonnets

Musick to heare, why hear'st thou musick sadly,
Sweets with sweets warre not, joy delights in joy:
Why lov'st thou that which thou receavst not gladly,
Or else receav'st with pleasure thine annoy?
If the true concord of well tuned sounds,
By unions married do offend thine eare,
They do but sweetly chide thee, who confounds
In singlenesse the parts that thou should'st beare:
Marke how one string sweet husband to an other,
Strikes each in each by mutuall ordering;
Resembling sire, and child, and happy mother,
Who all in one, one pleasing note do sing:
   Whose speechlesse song being many, seeming one,
   Sings this to thee thou single wilt prove none.

(viii)

Shall I compare thee to a Sommers day?
Thou art more lovely and more temperate:
Rough windes do shake the darling buds of Maie,
And Sommers lease hath all too short a date:
Sometime too hot the eye of heaven shines,
And often is his gold complexion dimm'd,
And every faire from faire some-time declines,
By chance, or natures changing course untrim'd:

154

But thy eternall Sommer shall not fade,
Nor loose possession of that faire thou ow'st,
Nor shall death brag thou wandr'st in his shade,
When in eternall lines to time thou grow'st,
  So long as men can breath or eyes can see,
  So long lives this, and this gives life to thee.

(xviii)

Devouring time blunt thou the Lyons pawes,
And make the earth devoure her owne sweet brood,
Plucke the keene teeth from the fierce Tygers yawes,
And burne the long liv'd Phaenix in her blood,
Make glad and sorry seasons as thou fleet'st,
And do what ere thou wilt swift-footed time
To the wide world and all her fading sweets:
But I forbid thee one most hainous crime,
O carve not with thy howers my loves faire brow,
Nor draw noe lines there with thine antique pen,
Him in thy course untainted doe allow,
For beauties patterne to succeding men.
  Yet doe thy worst ould Time dispight thy wrong,
  My love shall in my verse ever live young.

(xix)

When in disgrace with Fortune and mens eyes,
I all alone beweepe my out-cast state,
And trouble deafe heaven with my bootlesse cries,
And looke upon my selfe and curse my fate.
Wishing me like to one more rich in hope,
Featur'd like him, like him with friends possest,
Desiring this mans art, and that mans skope,
With what I most injoy contented least,
Yet in these thoughts my selfe almost despising,

Haplye· I thinke on thee, and then my state,
(Like to the Larke at breake of daye arising)
From sullen earth sings himns at Heavens gate,
   For thy sweet love remembred such welth brings,
   That then I skorne to change my state with Kings.

(xxix)

When to the Sessions of sweet silent thought,
I sommon up remembrance of things past,
I sigh the lacke of many a ́thing I sought,
And with old woes new waile my deare times waste:
Then can I drowne an eye (un-us'd to flow)
For precious friends hid in deaths dateles night,
And weepe a fresh loves long since canceld woe,
And mone th'expence of many a vannisht sight.
Then can I greeve at greevances fore-gon,
And heavily from woe to woe tell ore
The sad account of fore-bemoaned mone,
Which I new pay as if not payd before.
   But if the while I thinke on thee (deare friend)
   All losses are restord, and sorrowes end.

(xxx)

Thy bosome is indeared with all hearts,
Which I by lacking have supposed dead,
And there raignes Love and all Loves loving parts,
And all those friends which I thought buried.
How many a holy and obsequious teare
Hath deare religious love stolne from mine eye,
As interest of the dead, which now appeare,
But things remov'd that hidden in there lie.
Thou art the grave where buried love doth live,
Hung with the tropheis of my lovers gon,

Who all their parts of me to thee did give,
That due of many, now is thine alone.
  Their images I lov'd, I view in thee,
  And thou (all they) hast all the all of me.

(xxxi)

Not marble, nor the guilded monument,
Of Princes shall out-live this powrefull rime,
But you shall shine more bright in these contents
Then unswept stone, besmeer'd with sluttish time.
When wastefull warre shall *Statues* over-turne,
And broiles roote out the worke of masonry,
Nor *Mars* his sword, nor warres quick fire shall burne:
The living record of your memory.
Gainst death, and all oblivious emnity
Shall you pace forth, your praise shall stil finde roome,
Even in the eyes of all posterity
That weare this world out to the ending doome.
  So til the judgement that your selfe arise,
  You live in this, and dwell in lovers eies.

(lv)

Being your slave what should I doe but tend,
Upon the houres, and times of your desire?
I have no precious time at al to spend;
Nor services to doe til you require.
Nor dare I chide the world without end houre,
Whilst I (my soveraine) watch the clock for you,
Nor thinke the bitternesse of absence sowre,
When you have bid your servant once adieue.
Nor dare I question with my jealious thought,
Where you may be, or your affaires suppose,
But like a sad slave stay and thinke of nought

Save where you are, how happy you make those.
  So true a foole is love, that in your Will,
    (Though you doe any thing) he thinkes no ill.

(lvii)

Is it thy wil, thy Image should keepe open
My heavy eielids to the weary night?
Dost thou desire my slumbers should be broken,
While shadowes like to thee do mocke my sight?
Is it thy spirit that thou send'st from thee
So farre from home into my deeds to prye,
To find out shames and idle houres in me,
The skope and tenure of thy Jelousie?
O no, thy love though much, is not so great,
It is my love that keepes mine eie awake,
Mine owne true love that doth my rest defeat,
To plaie the watch-man ever for thy sake.
  For thee watch I, whilst thou dost wake elsewhere,
  From me farre off, with others all too neere.

(lxi)

    Sinne of selfe-love possesseth al mine eie,
    And all my soule, and al my every part;
    And for this sinne there is no remedie,
    It is so grounded inward in my heart.
    Me thinkes no face so gratious is as mine,
    No shape so true, no truth of such account,
    And for my selfe mine owne worth do define,
    As I all other in all worths surmount.
    But when my glasse shewes me my selfe indeed
    Beated and chopt with tand antiquitie,
    Mine owne selfe love quite contrary I read
    Selfe, so selfe loving were iniquity,

'Tis thee (my selfe) that for my selfe I praise,
Painting my age with beauty of thy daies.

(lxii)

Tyr'd with all these for restfull death I cry,
As to behold desert a begger borne,
And needie Nothing trimd in jollitie,
And purest faith unhappily forsworne,
And gilded honor shamefully misplast,
And maiden vertue rudely strumpeted,
And right perfection wrongfully disgrac'd,
And strength by limping sway disabled,
And arte made tung-tide by authoritie,
And Folly (Doctor-like) controuling skill,
And simple-Truth miscalde Simplicitie,
And captive-good attending Captaine ill.
 Tyr'd with all these, from these would I be gone,
 Save that to dye, I leave my love alone.

(lxvi)

That time of yeare thou maist in me behold,
When yellow leaves, or none, or few doe hange
Upon those boughes which shake against the could,
Bare ruin'd quiers, where late the sweet birds sang.
In me thou seest the twi-light of such day,
As after Sun-set fadeth in the West,
Which by and by blacke night doth take away,
Deaths second selfe that seals up all in rest.
In me thou seest the glowing of such fire,
That on the ashes of his youth doth lye,
As the death bed, whereon it must expire,
Consum'd with that which it was nurrisht by.

This thou percev'st, which makes thy love more
    strong,
To love that well, which thou must leave ere long.

(*lxxiii*)

So are you to my thoughts as food to life,
Or as sweet season'd shewers are to the ground;
And for the peace of you I hold such strife,
As twixt a miser and his wealth is found.
Now proud as an injoyer, and anon
Doubting the filching age will steale his treasure,
Now counting best to be with you alone,
Then betterd that the world may see my pleasure,
Some-time all ful with feasting on your sight,
And by and by cleane starved for a looke,
Possessing or pursuing no delight
Save what is had, or must from you be tooke.
    Thus do I pine and surfet day by day,
    Or gluttoning on all, or all away.

(*lxxv*)

Farewell thou art too deare for my possessing,
And like enough thou knowst thy estimate,
The Charter of thy worth gives thee releasing:
My bonds in thee are all determinate.
For how do I hold thee but by thy granting,
And for that ritches where is my deserving?
The cause of this faire guift in me is wanting,
And so my pattent back againe is swerving.
Thy selfe thou gav'st, thy owne worth then not knowing,
Or mee to whom thou gav'st it, else mistaking,
So thy great guift upon misprision growing,
Comes home againe, on better judgement making.

Thus have I had thee as a dreame doth flatter,
In sleepe a King, but waking no such matter.

(lxxxvii)

Then hate me when thou wilt, if ever, now,
Now while the world is bent my deeds to crosse,
Joyne with the spight of fortune, make me bow,
And doe not drop in for an after losse:
Ah doe not, when my heart hath scapte this sorrow,
Come in the rereward of a conquerd woe,
Give not a windy night a rainie morrow,
To linger out a purposd over-throw.
If thou wilt leave me, do not leave me last,
When other pettie griefes have done their spight,
But in the onset come, so shall I taste
At first the very worst of fortunes might.
    And other straines of woe, which now seeme woe,
    Compar'd with losse of thee, will not seeme so.

(xc)

They that have powre to hurt, and will doe none,
That doe not do the thing, they most do showe,
Who moving others, are themselves as stone,
Unmooved, could, and to temptation slow:
They rightly do inherrit heavens graces,
And husband natures ritches from expence,
They are the Lords and owners of their faces,
Others, but stewards of their excellence:
The sommers flowre is to the sommer sweet,
Though to it selfe, it onely live and die,
But if that flowre with base infection meete,
The basest weed out-braves his dignity:

For sweetest things turne sowrest by their deedes,
Lillies that fester, smell far worse then weeds.

(xciv)

Let me not to the marriage of true mindes
Admit impediments, love is not love
Which alters when it alteration findes,
Or bends with the remover to remove.
O no, it is an ever fixed marke
That lookes on tempests and is never shaken;
It is the star to every wandring barke,
Whose worths unknowne, although his higth be taken.
Lov's not Times foole, though rosie lips and cheeks
Within his bending sickles compasse come,
Love alters not with his breefe houres and weekes,
But beares it out even to the edge of doome:
    If this be error and upon me proved,
    I never writ, nor no man ever loved.

(cxvi)

Tis better to be vile then vile esteemed,
When not to be, receives reproach of being,
And the just pleasure lost, which is so deemed,
Not by our feeling, but by others seeing.
For why should others false adulterat eyes
Give salutation to my sportive blood?
Or on my frailties why are frailer spies;
Which in their wils count bad what I think good?
Noe, I am that I am, and they that levell
At my abuses, reckon up their owne,
I may be straight though they them-selves be bevel
By their rancke thoughtes, my deedes must not be
    shown

Unlesse this generall evill they maintaine,
All men are bad and in their badnesse raigne.

(cxxi)

Th'expence of Spirit in a waste of shame
Is lust in action, and till action, lust
Is perjurd, murdrous, blouddy, full of blame,
Savage, extreame, rude, cruell, not to trust,
Injoyd no sooner but dispised straight,
Past reason hunted, and no sooner had
Past reason hated as a swollowed bayt,
On purpose layd to make the taker mad.
Made in pursut and in possession so,
Had, having, and in quest, to have extreame,
A blisse in proofe and provd a very wo,
Before a joy proposd behind a dreame,
    All this the world well knowes yet none knowes well,
    To shun the heaven that leads men to this hell.

(cxxix)

When my love sweares that she is made of truth,
I do beleeve her though I know she lyes,
That she might thinke me some untuterd youth,
Unlearned in the worlds false subtilties.
Thus vainely thinking that she thinkes me young,
Although she knowes my dayes are past the best,
Simply I credit her false speaking tongue,
On both sides thus is simple truth supprest:
But wherefore sayes she not she is unjust?
And wherefore say not I that I am old?
O loves best habit is in seeming trust,
And age in love, loves not t'have yeares told.

Therefore I lye with her, and she with me,
And in our faults by lyes we flattered be.

(cxxxviii)

In faith I doe not love thee with mine eyes,
For they in thee a thousand errors note,
But 'tis my heart that loves what they dispise,
Who in dispight of view is pleasd to dote.
Nor are mine eares with thy toungs tune delighted,
Nor tender feeling to base touches prone,
Nor taste, nor smell, desire to be invited
To any sensuall feast with thee alone:
But my five wits, nor five sences can
Diswade one foolish heart from serving thee,
Who leaves unswai'd the likenesse of a man,
Thy proud hearts slave and vassall wretch to be:
    Onely my plague thus farre I count my gaine,
    That she that makes me sinne, awards me paine.

(cxli)

Two loves I have of comfort and dispaire,
Which like two spirits do sugiest me still,
The better angell is a man right faire:
The worser spirit a woman collour'd il.
To win me soone to hell my femall evill,
Tempteth my better angel from my sight,
And would corrupt my saint to be a divel:
Wooing his purity with her fowle pride.
And whether that my angel be turn'd finde,
Suspect I may, yet not directly tell,
But being both from me both to each friend,
I gesse one angel in an others hel.

Yet this shal I nere know but live in doubt,
Till my bad angel fire my good one out.

(cxliv)

My love is as a feaver longing still,
For that which longer nurseth the disease,
Feeding on that which doth preserve the ill,
Th'uncertaine sicklie appetite to please:
My reason the Phisition to my love,
Angry that his prescriptions are not kept
Hath left me, and I desperate now approove,
Desire is death, which Phisick did except.
Past cure I am, now Reason is past care,
And frantick madde with ever-more unrest,
My thoughts and my discourse as mad mens are,
At random from the truth vainely exprest.
      For I have sworne thee faire, and thought thee bright,
      Who art as black as hell, as darke as night.

(cxlvii)

Love is too young to know what conscience is,
Yet who knowes not conscience is borne of love,
Then gentle cheater urge not my amisse,
Least guilty of my faults thy sweet selfe prove.
For thou betraying me, I doe betray
My nobler part to my grose bodies treason,
My soule doth tell my body that he may,
Triumph in love, flesh staies no farther reason,
But rysing at thy name doth point out thee,
As his triumphant prize, proud of this pride,
He is contented thy poore drudge to be
To stand in thy affaires, fall by thy side.
      No want of conscience hold it that I call,
      Her love, for whose deare love I rise and fall.

(cli)

Poore soule the center of my sinfull earth,
My sinfull earth these rebbell powres that thee array,
Why dost thou pine within and suffer dearth
Painting thy outward walls so costlie gay?
Why so large cost having so short a lease,
Dost thou upon thy fading mansion spend?
Shall wormes inheritors of this excesse
Eate up thy charge? is this thy bodies end?
Then soule live thou upon thy servants losse,
And let that pine to aggravat thy store;
Buy tearmes divine in selling houres of drosse:
Within be fed, without be rich no more,
   So shalt thou feed on death, that feeds on men,
   And death once dead, ther's no more dying then.

(cxlvi)

FROM *The Rape of Lucrece*

O opportunity thy guilt is great,
Tis thou that execut'st the traytors treason:
Thou sets the wolfe where he the lambe may get,
Who ever plots the sinne thou poinst the season,
Tis thou that spurn'st at right, at law, at reason,
   And in thy shadie Cell where none may spie him,
   Sits sin to ceaze the soules that wander by him.

Thou makest the vestall violate her oath,
Thou blowest the fire when temperance is thawd,
Thou smotherst honestie, thou murthrest troth,
Thou fowle abbettor, thou notorious bawd,
Thou plantest scandall, and displacest lawd.
   Thou ravisher, thou traytor, thou false theefe,
   Thy honie turnes to gall, thy joy to greefe.

Thy secret pleasure turnes to open shame,
Thy private feasting to a publicke fast,
Thy smoothing titles to a ragged name,
Thy sugred tongue to bitter wormwood tast,
Thy violent vanities can never last.
   How comes it then, vile opportunity
   Being so bad, such numbers seeke for thee?

When wilt thou be the humble suppliants friend
And bring him where his suit may be obtained?
When wilt thou sort an howre great strifes to end?
Or free that soule which wretchednes hath chained?
Give phisicke to the sicke, ease to the pained?
   The poore, lame, blind, hault, creepe, cry out for thee,
   But they nere meet with oportunitie.

The patient dies while the Phisitian sleepes,
The Orphane pines while the oppressor feedes.
Justice is feasting while the widow weepes.
Advise is sporting while infection breeds.
Thou graunt'st no time for charitable deeds.
   Wrath, envy, treason, rape, and murthers rages,
   Thy heinous houres wait on them as their Pages.

When Trueth and Vertue have to do with thee,
A thousand crosses keepe them from thy aide:
They buie thy helpe, but sinne nere gives a fee,
He gratis comes, and thou art well apaide,
As well to heare, as graunt what he hath saide.
   My *Colatine* would else have come to me,
   When *Tarquin* did, but he was staied by thee.

Guilty thou art of murther, and of theft,
Guilty of perjurie, and subornation,
Guilty of treason, forgerie, and shift,
Guilty of incest that abhomination,
An accessarie by thine inclination.

To all sinnes past and all that are to come,
From the creation to the generall doome.

Misshapen time, copesmate of ugly night,
Swift subtle post, carrier of grieslie care,
Eater of youth, false slave to false delight:
Base watch of woes, sins packhorse, vertues snare.
Thou noursest all, and murthrest all that are.
    O heare me then, injurious shifting time,
    Be guiltie of my death since of my crime.

Why hath thy servant opportunity
Betraide the howres thou gav'st me to repose?
Canceld my fortunes, and inchained me
To endlesse date of never-ending woes?
Times office is to fine the hate of foes,
    To eate up errours by opinion bred,
    Not spend the dowrie of a lawfull bed.

Times glorie is to calme contending Kings,
To unmaske falshood, and bring truth to light,
To stampe the seale of time in aged things,
To wake the morne, and Centinell the night,
To wrong the wronger till he render right,
    To ruinate proud buildings with thy howres,
    And smeare with dust their glitring golden towrs.

To fill with worme-holes stately monuments,
To feede oblivion with decay of things,
To blot old bookes, and alter their contents,
To plucke the quils from auncient ravens wings,
To drie the old oakes sappe, and cherish springs:
    To spoile Antiquities of hammerd steele,
    And turne the giddy round of Fortunes wheele.

To shew the beldame daughters of her daughter,
To make the child a man, the man a childe,
To slay the tygre that doth live by slaughter,

To tame the Unicorne, and Lion wild,
To mocke the subtle in themselves beguild,
  To cheare the Plowman with increasefull crops,
  And wast huge stones with little water drops.

(*Lines 876–959*)

The Phoenix and the Turtle

Let the bird of lowdest lay,
On the sole *Arabian* tree,
Herauld sad and trumpet be:
To whose sound chaste wings obay.

But thou shriking harbinger,
Foule precurrer of the fiend,
Augour of the fevers end,
To this troupe come thou not neere.

From this Session inderdict
Every soule of tyrant wing,
Save the Eagle feath'red King,
Keepe the obsequie so strict.

Let the Priest in Surples white,
That defunctive Musicke can,
Be the death-devining Swan,
Lest the *Requiem* lacke his right.

And thou treble dated Crow,
That thy sable gender mak'st,
With the breath thou giv'st and tak'st,
Mongst our mourners shalt thou go.

Here the Antheme doth commence,
Love and Constancie is dead,

Phoenix and the *Turtle* fled,
In a mutuall flame from hence.

So they loved as love in twaine,
Had the essence but in one,
Two distincts, Division none,
Number there in love was slaine.

Hearts remote, yet not asunder;
Distance and no space was seene,
Twixt this *Turtle* and his Queene;
But in them it were a wonder.

So betweene them Love did shine,
That the *Turtle* saw his right,
Flaming in the *Phoenix* sight;
Either was the others mine.

Propertie was thus appalled,
That the selfe was not the same:
Single Natures double name,
Neither two nor one was called.

Reason in it selfe confounded,
Saw Division grow together,
To themselves yet either neither,
Simple were so well compounded.

That it cried, how true a twaine,
Seemeth this concordant one,
Love hath Reason, Reason none,
If what parts, can so remaine.

Whereupon it made this *Threne*,
To the *Phoenix* and the *Dove*,
Co-supremes and starres of Love,
As *Chorus* to their Tragique Scene.

THRENOS

Beautie, Truth, and Raritie,
Grace in all simplicitie,
Here enclosde, in cinders lie.

Death is now the *Phoenix* nest,
And the *Turtles* loyall brest,
To eternitie doth rest.

Leaving no posteritie,
Twas not their infirmitie,
It was married Chastitie.

Truth may seeme, but cannot be,
Beautie bragge, but tis not she,
Truth and Beautie buried be.

To this urne let those repaire,
That are either true or faire,
For these dead Birds, sigh a prayer.

Songs from the Plays

FROM *Love's Labour's Lost*

When Dasies pied, and Violets blew,
And Cuckow-buds of yellow hew:
And Ladie-smockes all silver white,
Doe paint the Medowes with delight,
The Cuckow then on everie tree,
Mockes married men, for thus sings he,
Cuckow.
Cuckow, Cuckow: O word of feare,
Unpleasing to a married eare.

When Shepheards pipe on Oaten strawes,
And merry Larkes are Ploughmens clockes:

When Turtles tread, and Rookes and Dawes,
And Maidens bleach their summer smockes:
The Cuckow then on every tree
Mockes married men; for thus sings he,
Cuckow.
Cuckow, Cuckow: O word of feare,
Unpleasing to a married eare.

FROM *Love's Labour's Lost*

When Isicles hang by the wall,
And Dicke the Shepheard blowes his naile;
And Tom beares Logges into the hall,
And Milke comes frozen home in paile:
When blood is nipt, and wayes be fowle,
Then nightly sings the staring Owle
Tu-whit to-who.
   A merrie note,
    While greasie Joan doth keele the pot.

When all aloud the winde doth blow,
And coffing drownes the Parsons saw:
And birds sit brooding in the snow,
And Marrians nose lookes red and raw:
When roasted Crabs hisse in the bowle,
Then nightly sings the staring Owle,
Tu-whit to-who:
   A merrie note,
    While greasie Joan doth keele the pot.

FROM *As You Like It*

Blow, blow, thou winter winde,
Thou art not so unkinde, as mans ingratitude;
Thy tooth is not so keene, because thou art not seene,
   Although thy breath be rude.

Heigh ho, sing heigh ho, unto the greene holly,
Most friendship, is fayning; most Loving, meere folly:
  The heigh ho, the holly,
  This Life is most jolly.

Freize, freize, thou bitter skie that dost not bight so
    nigh,
  As benefitts forget:
Though thou the waters warpe, thy sting is not so
    sharpe,
  As friend remembred not.
    Heigh ho, sing the holly,
    This Life is most jolly.

FROM *Twelfth Night*

Come away, come away death,
And in sad cypresse let me be laide,
Fie away, fie away breath,
I am slaine by a faire cruell maid.
  My shrowd of white, stucke all with yew, O prepare
    it.
  My part of death no one so true did share it.

Not a flower, not a flower sweete
On my blacke coffin, let there be strewne:
Not a friend, not a friend greet
My poore corpse, where my bones shall be throwne:
  A thousand thousand sighes to save, lay me O where
  Sad true lover never find my grave, to weepe there.

FROM *Twelfth Night*

When that I was and a little tiny Boy,
  With hey, ho, the winde and the raine:
A foolish thing was but a toy,
  For the raine it raineth every day.

But when I came to mans estate,
   With hey, ho, the winde and the raine:
Gainst Knaves and Theeves men shut their gate,
   For the raine it raineth every day.

But when I came alas to wive,
   With hey, ho, the winde and the raine:
By swaggering could I never thrive,
   For the raine it raineth every day.

But when I came unto my beds,
   With hey, ho, the winde and the raine:
With tosspots still had drunken heads,
   For the raine it raineth every day.

A great while ago the world begon,
   With hey, ho, the winde and the raine.
But that's all one, our Play is done,
   And wee'l strive to please you every day.

FROM *Cymbeline*

GUIDERIUS. Feare no more the heate o' th' Sun,
Nor the furious Winters rages,
Thou thy worldly task hast done,
Home art gon, and tane thy wages.
Golden Lads, and Girles all must,
As Chimney-Sweepers come to dust.

ARVIRAGUS. Feare no more the frowne o' th' Great,
Thou art past the Tirants stroake,
Care no more to cloath and eate,
To thee the Reede is as the Oake:
The Scepter, Learning, Physicke must,
All follow this and come to dust.

GUIDERIUS. Feare no more the Lightning flash.
ARVIRAGUS. Nor th' all-dreaded Thunderstone.
GUIDERIUS. Feare not Slander, Censure rash.
ARVIRAGUS. Thou hast finish'd Joy and mone.
BOTH. All Lovers young, all Lovers must,
Consigne to thee and come to dust.

GUIDERIUS. No Exorciser harme thee,
ARVIRAGUS. Nor no witch-craft charme thee.
GUIDERIUS. Ghost unlaid forbeare thee.
ARVIRAGUS. Nothing ill come neere thee.
BOTH. Quiet consummation have,
And renowned be thy grave.

FROM *The Merchant of Venice*

Tell me where is fancie bred,
Or in the heart, or in the head:
How begot, how nourished.   Replie, replie.
It is engendred in the eyes,
With gazing fed, and Fancie dies,
In the cradle where it lies:
Let us all ring Fancies knell.
Ile begin it.
Ding, dong, bell,
     ALL. Ding, dong, bell.

FROM *Much Ado About Nothing*

Sigh no more Ladies, sigh no more,
Men were deceivers ever,
One foote in Sea, and one on shore,
To one thing constant never,
Then sigh not so, but let them goe,

And be you blithe and bonnie,
Converting all your sounds of woe,
Into hey nony nony.

Sing no more ditties, sing no moe,
Of dumps so dull and heavy,
The fraud of men were ever so,
Since summer first was leavy,
Then sigh not so, but let them goe,
And be you blithe and bonny,
Converting all your sounds of woe,
Into hey nony nony.

FROM *The Winter's Tale*

When Daffadils begin to peere,
With heigh the Doxy over the dale,
Why then comes in the sweet o' the yeere.
For the red blood raigns in the winters pale.

The white sheete bleaching on the hedge,
With hey the sweet birds, O how they sing:
Doth set my pugging tooth an edge,
For a quart of Ale is a dish for a King.

The Larke, that tirra-Lyra chaunts,
With heigh, with heigh the Thrush and the Jay:
Are Summer songs for me and my Aunts,
While we lye tumbling in the hay.

FROM *Hamlet*

And will he not come again?
And will he not come again?
No, no, he is dead,

Go to thy death-bed,
He never will come again.
His beard as white as snow.
All flaxen was his pole:
He is gone, he is gone,
And we cast away mone,
Gramercy on his Soule.

FROM *The Tempest*

ARIEL. Come unto these yellow sands,
    And then take hands:
Curtsied when you have, and kist
    The wilde waves whist:
Foote it featly heere, and there, and sweete Sprights the
    burthen beare.
(*Burthen dispersedly.*)
Harke, harke, bowgh-wawgh: the watch-Dogges barke,
    Bowgh-wawgh.
ARIEL. Hark, hark, I heare the straine of strutting Chan-
    ticlere
    Cry cockadidle-dowe.

FROM *The Tempest*

Full fadom five thy Father lies,
Of his bones are Corrall made:
Those are pearles that were his eyes,
Nothing of him that doth fade,
But doth suffer a Sea-change
Into something rich, and strange:
Sea-Nimphs hourly ring his knell.
                    Burthen: ding dong.
Hearke now I heare them; ding-dong bell.

Anthony and Cleopatra

DRAMATIS PERSONÆ

Anthony
Octavius Cæsar } *triumvirs*
Lepidus

Sextus Pompeius

Domitius Enobarbus
Ventidius
Eros
Scarus   } *friends to Anthony*
Decretas
Demetrius
Philo

Mecenas
Agrippa
Dolabella
Proculeius   } *friends to Cæsar*
Thyreus
Gallus

Menas
Menecrates   } *friends to Pompey*
Varrius

Taurus, *lieutenant-general to Cæsar*
Camidius, *lieutenant-general to Anthony*
Silius, *an officer in Ventidius' army*
Euphronius, *an ambassador from Anthony to Cæsar*

Alexas
Mardian (*a eunuch*) } *attendants on Cleopatra*
Diomedes

Seleucus, *treasurer to Cleopatra*
A Soothsayer
A Clown

Cleopatra, queen of Egypt

Charmian ⎱
Iras ⎰ *attendants on Cleopatra*

Octavia, sister to Cæsar, and wife to Anthony

Officers, Soldiers, Messengers, and other attendants.

Scene—Several parts of the Roman Empire.

Enter Demetrius, and Philo.

PHILO. Nay, but this dotage of our Generall
Ore-flowes the measure: those his goodly eyes
That o're the files and Musters of the Warre,
Have glow'd like plated Mars:
Now bend, now turne
The Office and Devotion of their view
Upon a Tawny Front. His Captaines heart,
Which in the scuffles of great fights hath burst
The Buckles on his brest, reneages all temper,
And is become the Bellowes and the Fan
To coole a Gypsies Lust.
*Enter Anthony, Cleopatra, her Ladies; the Traine, with
Eunuchs fanning her.*
                              Looke where they come:
Take but good note, and you shall see in him
The triple Pillar of the world transform'd
Into a Strumpets Foole. Behold and see.

CLEOPATRA. If it be Love indeed, tell me how much.

ANTHONY. Theres beggery in the love that can be
    reckon'd.

CLEOPATRA. Ile set a bourne how farre to be belov'd.

ANTHONY. Then must thou needes find out new heaven,
    new Earth.

Enter a Messenger.

MESSENGER. Newes (my good Lord) from Rome.

ANTHONY.   Rate me, the summe.

CLEOPATRA. Nay heare them *Anthony*.

Fulvia perchance is angry: Or who knowes,
If the scarse-bearded *Cæsar* have not sent
His powerfull Mandate to you. Doe this, or this;
Take in that Kingdome, and infranchise that:
Perform't, or else we damne thee.

ANTHONY.   How, my Love?

CLEOPATRA. Perchance? Nay, and most like;
You must not stay heere longer, your dismission
Is come from *Cæsar,* therefore heare it *Anthony*.
Wheres *Fulvias* Processe? (*Cæsars* I would say) both?
Call in the Messengers: As I am Egypts Queene,
Thou blushest *Anthony,* and that blood of thine
Is *Cæsars* homager: else so thy cheeke payes shame,
When shrill-tongu'd *Fulvia* scolds. The Messengers.

ANTHONY. Let Rome in Tyber melt, and the wide Arch
Of the raing'd Empire fall: Heere is my space.
Kingdomes are clay: Our dungy earth alike
Feeds Beast as Man; the Noblenesse of life
Is to doe thus: when such a mutuall paire,
And such a twaine can doo't, in which I bind,
On paine of punishment, the world to weete
We stand up Peerelesse.

CLEOPATRA.   Excellent falshood:
Why did he marry *Fulvia,* and not love her?
Ile seeme the Foole I am not. *Anthony* will be himselfe.

ANTHONY. But stirr'd by *Cleopatra*.
Now for the love of love, and her soft houres,
Lets not confound the time with Conference harsh;
Theres not a minute of our lives should stretch
Without some pleasure now. What sport to night?

CLEOPATRA. Heare the Ambassadors.

ANTHONY.   Fye wrangling Queene:
Whom every thing becomes, to chide, to laugh,

To weepe: whose every passion fully strives
To make it selfe (in Thee) faire, and admir'd.
No Messenger but thine, and all alone, to night
We'll wander through the streets, and note
The qualities of people. Come my Queene,
Last night you did desire it. Speake not to us.

Exeunt with the Traine.

DEMETRIUS. Is *Cæsar* with *Anthonius* priz'd so slight?
PHILO. Sir sometimes when he is not *Anthony*,
He comes too short of that great Property
Which still should goe with *Anthony*.
DEMETRIUS. I am full sorry, that he approves the common
Lyar, who thus speakes of him at Rome; but I will hope
Of better deeds to morrow. Rest you happy.   *Exeunt.*

Enter Enobarbus, Lamprius, a Soothsayer, Rannius, Lucillius, Charmian, Iras, Mardian the Eunuch, and Alexas.

CHARMIAN. Lord *Alexas*, sweet *Alexas*, most any thing *Alexas*, almost most absolute *Alexas*, wheres the Soothsayer that you prais'd so to th' Queene? Oh that I knew this Husband, which you say, must change his hornes with Garlands.
ALEXAS. Soothsayer.
SOOTHSAYER. Your will?
CHARMIAN. Is this the man? Is't you sir that know things?
SOOTHSAYER. In Natures infinite booke of Secrecy, a little I can read.
ALEXAS. Shew him your hand.
ENOBARBUS. Bring in the Banket quickly: Wine enough, *Cleopatras* health to drinke.
CHARMIAN. Good sir, give me good Fortune.

SOOTHSAYER. I make not, but forsee.

CHARMIAN. Pray then, foresee me one.

SOOTHSAYER. You shall be yet farre fairer then you are.

CHARMIAN. He meanes in flesh.

IRAS. No, you shall paint when you are old.

CHARMIAN. Wrinkles forbid.

ALEXAS. Vex not his prescience, be attentive.

CHARMIAN. Hush.

SOOTHSAYER. You shall be more beloving, then beloved.

CHARMIAN. I had rather heate my Liver with drinking.

ALEXAS. Nay, heare him.

CHARMIAN. Good now some excellent Fortune. Let mee
be married to three Kings in a forenoone, and Widdow them all: Let me have a Child at fifty, to whom
Herod of Jewry may doe Homage. Finde me to marry
me with *Octavius Cæsar,* and companion me with
my Mistris.

SOOTHSAYER. You shall out-live the Lady whom you
serve.

CHARMIAN. Oh excellent, I love long life better then
Figs.

SOOTHSAYER. You have seene and proved a fairer former
fortune, then that which is to approach.

CHARMIAN. Then belike my Children shall have no
names:

Prethee how many Boyes and Wenches must I have.

SOOTHSAYER. If every of your wishes had a wombe, and
foretell every wish, a Million.

CHARMIAN. Out Foole, I forgive thee for a Witch.

ALEXAS. You thinke none but your sheets are privy to
your wishes.

CHARMIAN. Nay come, tell *Iras* hers.

ALEXAS. We'll know all our Fortunes.

ENOBARBUS. Mine, and most of our Fortunes to night,
shall be drunke to bed.

IRAS. Theres a Palme presages Chastity, if nothing else.

CHARMIAN. E'ne as the ore-flowing Nylus presageth Famine.

IRAS. Goe, you wild Bedfellow, you cannot Soothsay.

CHARMIAN. Nay, if an oyly Palme be not a fruitfull Prognostication, I cannot scratch mine eare. Prethee tell her but a worky day Fortune.

SOOTHSAYER. Your Fortunes are alike.

IRAS. But how, but how, give me particulars.

SOOTHSAYER. I have said.

IRAS. Am I not an inch of Fortune better than she?

CHARMIAN. Well, if you were but an inch of Fortune better than I: where would you choose it.

IRAS. Not in my husbands Nose.

CHAIRMIAN. Our worser thoughts heavens mend. *Alexas* —come, his Fortune, his Fortune. Oh let him marry a woman that cannot go, sweet *Isis,* I beseech thee, and let her dye too, and give him a worse, and let worse follow worse, till the worst of all follow him laughing to his grave, fifty-fold a Cuckold. Good *Isis* heare me this Prayer, though thou deny me a matter of more waight: good *Isis* I beseech thee.

IRAS. Amen, deere Goddesse, heare that prayer of the people. For, as it is a heart-breaking to see a handsome man loose-wiv'd, so it is a deadly sorrow, to behold a foule Knave uncuckolded: Therefore deare *Isis* keepe *decorum,* and Fortune him accordingly.

CHARMIAN. Amen.

ALEXAS. Loe now, if it lay in their hands to make me a Cuckold, they would make themselves Whores, but they'ld doo't.

Enter Cleopatra.

ENOBARBUS. Hush, here comes *Anthony.*

CHARMIAN.   Not he, the Queene.

CLEOPATRA. Saw you my Lord?

ENOBARBUS.   No Lady.

CLEOPATRA.   Was he not here?

CHARMIAN. No Madame.

CLEOPATRA. He was dispos'd to mirth, but on the sodaine

A Roman thought hath strooke him.

Enobarbus?

ENOBARBUS. Madam.

CLEOPATRA. Seeke him, and bring him hither: where's
Alexas?

ALEXAS. Here at your service. My Lord approaches.

Enter Anthony with a Messenger.

CLEOPATRA. We will not looke upon him;

Goe with us.   *Exeunt.*

MESSENGER. *Fulvia* thy Wife,

First came into the Field.

ANTHONY. Against my Brother *Lucius?*

MESSENGER. Ay, but soone that Warre had end,

And the times state

Made friends of them, joynting their force 'gainst
Cæsar.

Whose better issue in the warre from Italy,

Upon the first encounter drave them.

ANTHONY.   Well, what worst?

MESSENGER. The nature of bad newes infects the Teller.

ANTHONY. When it concernes the Foole or Coward: On.

Things that are past, are done, with me. Tis thus,

Who tels me true, though in his Tale lye death,

I heare him as he flatter'd.

MESSENGER. *Labienus* (this is stiffe-newes)

Hath with his Parthian Force

Extended Asia: from Euphrates his conquering

Banner shooke, from Syria to Lydia,

And to Ionia, whilst—

ANTHONY. *Anthony* thou wouldst say.

MESSENGER.   Oh my Lord.

ANTHONY. Speake to me home,
Mince not the generall tongue, name
Cleopatra as she is call'd in Rome:
Raile thou in *Fulvia's* phrase, and 'taunt my faults
With such full License, as both Truth and Malice
Have power to utter. Oh then we bring forth weeds,
When our quicke windes lye still, and our illes told us
Is as our earing: fare thee well awhile.

MESSENGER. At your Noble pleasure.   *Exit Messenger.*

Enter another Messenger.

ANTHONY. From *Scicion* how the newes? Speake there.

1 MESSENGER. The man from *Scicion*,
Is there such an one?

2 MESSENGER. He stayes upon your will.

ANTHONY. Let him appeare:
These strong Egyptian Fetters I must breake,
Or loose my selfe in dotage.

Enter another Messenger with a Letter.

What are you?

3 MESSENGER. *Fulvia* thy wife is dead.

ANTHONY.   Where dyed she.

MESSENGER. In *Scicion*, her length of sicknesse,
With what else more serious,
Importeth thee to know, this beares.

ANTHONY.   Forebeare me:
Theres a great Spirit gone, thus did I desire it:
What our contempts doe often hurle from us,
We wish it ours againe. The present pleasure,
By revolution lowring, does become
The opposite of it selfe: she's good being gon,
The hand could plucke her backe, that shov'd her on.
I must from this Queene breake off,
Ten thousand harmes, more than the illes I know
My idlenesse doth hatch.

Enter Enobarbus.

How now *Enobarbus.*

ENOBARBUS. Whats your pleasure, Sir?

ANTHONY. I must with haste from hence.

ENOBARBUS. Why then we kill all our Women. We see
how mortall an unkindnesse is to them; if they suffer
our departure, death's the word.

ANTHONY. I must be gone.

ENOBARBUS. Under a compelling an occasion, let women
dye. It were pitty to cast them away for nothing;
though betweene them and a great cause, they should
be esteemed nothing. *Cleopatra* catching but the least
noyse of this, dyes instantly: I have seene her, dye
twenty times upon farre poorer moment: I do think
there is mettle in death, which commits some loving
acte upon her, she hath such a celerity in dying,

ANTHONY. She is cunning past mans thought.

ENOBARBUS. Alacke sir no; her passions are made of
nothing but the finest part of pure love. We cannot
call her winds and waters, sighes and teares: They
are greater stormes and Tempests then Almanackes
can report. This cannot be cunning in her; if it be, she
makes a showre of Raine as well as love.

ANTHONY. Would I had never seene her.

ENOBARBUS. Oh sir, you had then left unseene a won-
derfull peece of worke, which not to have been blest
withall, would have discredited your Travaile.

ANTHONY. *Fulvia* is dead.

ENOBARBUS. Sir.

ANTHONY. *Fulvia* is dead.

ENOBARBUS. *Fulvia?*

ANTHONY. Dead.

ENOBARBUS. Why sir, give the gods a thankefull Sacrifice: when it pleaseth their Deities to take the wife of
a man from him, it shewes to man the Tailors of the

earth: comforting therein, that when old Robes are
worne out, there are members to make new. If there
were no more Women but *Fulvia,* then had you indeed a cut, and the case to be lamented: This griefe
is crown'd with Consolation, your old Smocke brings
fourth a new Petticoate, and indeed the teares live in
an Onion, that should water this sorrow.

ANTHONY. The businesse she hath broached in the State,
Cannot endure my absence.

ENOBARBUS. And the businesse you have broach'd heere
cannot be without you, especially that of *Cleopatras,*
which wholly depends on your abode.

ANTHONY. No more like Answers:
Let our Officers
Have notice what we purpose. I shall breake
The cause of our Expedience to the Queene,
And get her leave to part. For not alone
The death of *Fulvia,* with more urgent touches
Doe strongly speake to us: but the Letters too
Of many our contriving friends in Rome,
Petition us at home. *Sextus Pompeius*
Hath given the dare to *Cæsar,* and commands
The Empire of the Sea. Our slippery people,
Whose Love is never link'd to the deserver,
Till his deserts are past, begin to throw
Pompey the great, and all his Dignities
Upon his Sonne, who high in Name and Power,
Higher then both in blood and life, stands up
For the maine Souldier. Whose quality going on,
The sides o'th' world may danger. Much is breeding,
Which like the Coursers heire, hath yet but life,
And not a Serpents poyson. Say our pleasure,
To such whose place is under us, requires
Our quicke remove from hence.

ENOBARBUS. I shall doo't.   *Exeunt.*

Enter Cleopatra, Charmian, Alexas, and Iras.

CLEOPATRA. Where is he?

CHARMIAN. I did not see him since.

CLEOPATRA. See where he is,
Who's with him, what he does:
I did not send you. If you finde him sad,
Say I am dauncing: if in Myrth, report
That I am sodaine sicke. Quickly, and returne.

CHARMIAN. Madam, me thinkes if you did love him
   deerely
You doe not hold the method, to enforce
The like from him.

CLEOPATRA. What should I doe I doe not?

CHARMIAN. In each thing give him way, crosse him in
   nothing.

CLEOPATRA. Thou teachest like a foole: the way to lose
   him.

CHARMIAN. Tempt him not so too farre. I wish forbeare,
In time we hate that which we often feare.

Enter Anthony.

But heere comes *Anthony*.

CLEOPATRA.   I am sicke, and sullen.

ANTHONY. I am sorry to give breathing to my purpose.

CLEOPATRA. Helpe me away deere *Charmian*, I shall
   fall;
It cannot be thus long, the sides of Nature
Will not sustaine it.

ANTHONY.   Now my deerest Queene.

CLEOPATRA. Pray you stand farther from me.

ANTHONY.   Whats the matter?

CLEOPATRA. I know by that same eye theres some good
   newes.
What sayes the married woman: you may goe?
Would she had never given you leave to come;

Let her not say tis I that keepe you heere,
I have no power upon you: Hers you are.

ANTHONY.   The gods best know.

CLEOPATRA.   Oh never was there Queene
So mightily betrayed: yet at the first
I saw the Treasons planted.

ANTHONY.   *Cleopatra.*

CLEOPATRA. Why should I thinke you can be mine, and
    true
(Though you swearing shake the Throaned gods)
Who have been false to *Fulvia?*
Riotous madnesse,
To be entangled with those mouth-made vowes,
Which breake themselves in swearing.

ANTHONY.   Most sweet Queene.

CLEOPATRA. Nay pray you seeke no colour for your
    going,
But bid farewell, and goe:
When you sued staying,
Then was the time for words: No going then,
Eternity was in our Lippes and Eyes;
Blisse in our browes bent: none our parts so poore,
But was a race of heaven. They are so still,
Or thou the greatest Souldier of the world,
Art turn'd the greater Lyar.

ANTHONY.   How now Lady?

CLEOPATRA. I would I had thy inches, thou should'st
    know
There were a heart in Egypt.

ANTHONY.   Heare me Queene:
The strong necessity of Time, commands
Our Services a while: but my full heart
Remaines in use with you. Our Italy,
Shines o're with civill Swords; *Sextus Pompeius*
Makes his approches to the Port of Rome:

Equality of two Domesticke powers,
Breed scrupulous faction: The hated growne to strength
Are newly growne to Love: The condemn'd *Pompey*,
Rich in his Fathers honour, creepes apace
Into the hearts of such, as have not thrived
Upon the present state, whose numbers threaten,
And quietnesse growne sicke of rest, would purge
By any desperate change. My more particular,
And that which most with you should safe my going,
Is *Fulvias* death.

CLEOPATRA. Though age from folly could not give me
    freedom,
It does from childishnesse. Can *Fulvia* dye?

ANTHONY. Shee's dead my Queene,
Looke here, and at thy Soveraigne leysure reade
The Garboyles she awak'd: at the last, best,
See when, and where she dyed.

CLEOPATRA.   O most false love!
Where be the sacred Viols thou shoul'dst fill
With sorrowfull water? Now I see, I see,
In *Fulvias* death, how mine receiv'd shall be.

ANTHONY. Quarrell no more, but be prepar'd to know
The purposes I beare: which are, or cease,
As you shall give th' advice. By the fire
That quickens Nylus slime, I goe from hence
Thy Souldier, Servant, making Peace or Warre,
As thou affectst.

CLEOPATRA. Cut my Lace, *Charmian* come,
But let it be, I am quickly ill, and well,
So *Anthony* loves.

ANTHONY.   My precious Queene forbeare,
And give true evidence to his Love, which stands
An honourable Triall.

CLEOPATRA.   So *Fulvia* told me.
I prythee turne aside, and weepe for her,

Then bid adiew to me, and say the teares
Belong to Egypt. Good now, play one Scene
Of excellent dissembling, and let it looke
Like perfect honour.

ANTHONY.   You'l heat my blood no more?

CLEOPATRA. You can doe better yet: but this is meetly.

ANTHONY. Now by my Sword.

CLEOPATRA.   And Target. Still he mends.
But this is not the best. Looke prythee *Charmian*,
How this *Herculean* Roman does become
The carriage of his chafe.

ANTHONY. Ile leave you Lady.

CLEOPATRA.   Courteous Lord, one word:
Sir, you and I must part, but that's not it:
Sir, you and I have lov'd, but there's not it:
That you know well, something it is I would:
Oh, my oblivion is a very *Anthony*.
And I am all forgotten.

ANTHONY.   But that your Royalty
Holds Idlenesse your subject, I should take you
For idlenesse it selfe.

CLEOPATRA.   'Tis sweating labour,
To beare such Idlenesse so neare the heart
As *Cleopatra* this. But Sir, forgive me,
Since my becommings kill me, when they do not
Eye well to you. Your Honor calls you hence.
Therefore be deafe to my unpittied Folly,
And all the Gods go with you. Upon your Sword
Sit lawrel'd victory, and smooth successe
Be strew'd before your feete.

ANTHONY.   Let us go.
Come: Our separation so abides and flies,
That thou residing heere, goest yet with me,
And I hence fleeting, heere remaine with thee.
Away.   *Exeunt.*

Enter Octavius reading a Letter, Lepidus, and their Traine.

CÆSAR. You may see, *Lepidus,* and henceforth know,
It is not *Cæsars* Naturall vice, to hate
One great Competitor. From Alexandria
This is the newes: he fishes, drinkes, and wastes
The Lampes of night in revells: Is not more manlike
Then *Cleopatra:* nor the Queene of *Ptolomy*
More Womanly then he. Hardly gave audience
Or did vouchsafe to thinke he had Partners. You
Shall finde there a man, who is th' abstract of all faults
That all men follow.

LEPIDUS.   I must not thinke
There are evils enow to darken all his goodnesse;
His faults in him seeme as the Spots of heaven,
More fiery by nights Blacknesse; Hereditary
Rather then purchaste: what he cannot change,
Then what he chooses.

CÆSAR. You are too indulgent. Lets graunt it is not
Amisse to tumble on the bed of *Ptolemy,*
To give a Kingdome for a Mirth, to sit
And keepe the turne of Tipling with a Slave,
To reele the streets at noone, and stand the Buffet
With knaves that smell of sweate: Say this becomes him
(As his composure must be rare indeed,
Whom these things cannot blemish), yet must *Anthony*
No way excuse his foyles, when we doe beare
So great waight in his Lightnesse. If he filld
His vacancy with his Voluptuousnesse,
Full surfets, and the drinesse of his bones,
Call on him for't. But to confound such time,
That drummes him from his sport, and speakes as lowd
As his owne State, and ours, tis to be chid:
As we rate Boyes, who being mature in knowledge,

Pawne their experience to their present pleasure,
And to rebell to judgement.

Enter a Messenger.

LEPIDUS. Heeres more newes.

MESSENGER. Thy biddings have beene done, and every
    houre
Most Noble *Cæsar*, shalt thou have report
How tis abroad. *Pompey* is strong at Sea,
And it appeares, he is belov'd of those
That only have feard *Cæsar:* to the Ports
The discontents repaire, and mens reports
Give him much wrong'd.

CÆSAR.   I should have knowne no lesse.
It hath bin taught us from the primall state,
That he which is, was wisht, untill he were:
And the ebb'd man,
Ne're lov'd, till ne're worth love,
Comes fear'd, by being lack'd. This common body
Like to a Vagobond Flagge upon the Streame,
Goes to, and backe, lacking the varrying tyde,
To rot it selfe with motion.

MESSENGER. *Cæsar* I bring thee word,
Menacrates and *Menas* famous Pyrates
Makes the Sea serve them, which they eare and wound
With keeles of every kind. Many hot inrodes
They make in Italy, the borders Maritime
Lacke blood to thinke on't, and flush youth revolt:
No Vessell can peepe forth, but tis as soone
Taken as seene: for *Pompeyes* name strikes more
Then could his Warre resisted.

CÆSAR.   *Anthony,*
Leave thy lascivious Vassailes. When thou once
Wert beaten from *Medena*, where thou shewst
Hirsius, and *Pansa* Consuls, at thy heele
Did famine follow, whom thou foughtst against,

(Though daintily brought up) with patience more
Then Savages could suffer. Thou didst drinke
The stale of horses, and the gilded Puddle
Which Beasts would cough at. Thy pallat then did daine
The roughest Berry, on the rudest Hedge.
Yea, like the Stagge, when Snow the Pasture sheets,
The barkes of Trees thou browsedst. On the Alpes,
It is reported thou didst eate strange flesh,
Which some did dye to looke on: And all this
(It wounds thine honor that I speake it now)
Was borne so like a Souldiour, that thy cheeke
So much as lank'd not.

LEPIDUS.   Tis pitty of him.

CÆSAR. Let his shames. quickely
Drive him to Rome: tis time we twaine
Did shew our selves i'th' Field, and to that end
Assemble we immediate counsell; *Pompey*
Thrives in our Idlenesse.

LEPIDUS.   To morrow *Cæsar*,
I shall be furnisht to informe you rightly
Both what by Sea and Land I can be able
To front this present time.

CÆSAR. Till which encounter, it is my businesse too.
    Farewell.

LEPIDUS. Farewell my Lord, what you shall know meane
    time
Of stirres abroad, I shall beseech you Sir
To let me be partaker.

CÆSAR. Doubt not sir, I knew it for my bond.   *Exeunt.*

Enter Cleopatra, Charmian, Iras, and Mardian.

CLEOPATRA. *Charmian.*

CHARMIAN. Madam.

CLEOPATRA. Ha, ha, give me to drinke *Mandragoras.*

CHARMIAN. Why Madam?

CLEOPATRA. That I might sleepe out this great gap of
time:

My *Anthony* is away.

CHARMIAN.   You thinke of him too much.

CLEOPATRA. O tis Treason.

CHARMIAN.   Madam, I trust not so.

CLEOPATRA. Thou, Eunuch *Mardian?*

MARDIAN.   Whats your highnesse pleasure?

CLEOPATRA. Not now to heare thee sing. I take no pleasure

In ought an Eunuch has: Tis well for thee,

That being unseminaried, thy freer thoughts

May not flye forth of Egypt, Hast thou Affections?

MARDIAN. Yes gracious Madam.

CLEOPATRA. Indeed?

MARDIAN. Not indeed Madam, for I can doe nothing

But what indeed is honest to be done:

Yet have I fierce Affections, and thinke

What Venus did with Mars.

CLEOPATRA.   Oh *Charmian;*

Where thinkst thou he is now? Stands he, or sits he?

Or does he walke? Or is he on his Horse?

Oh happy horse to beare the weight of *Anthony!*

Doe bravely horse, for wot'st thou whom thou moov'st,

The demy *Atlas* of this Earth, the Arme

And Burgonet of man. Hes speaking now,

Or murmuring, wheres my Serpent of old Nyle,

(For so he calls me:) Now I feed my selfe

With most delicious poyson. Thinke on me

That am with Phebus amorous pinches blacke,

And wrinkled deepe in time. Broad-fronted *Cæsar,*

When thou wast heere above the ground, I was

A morsell for a Monarke; and great *Pompey*

Would stand and make his eyes grow in my brow,

There would he anchor his Aspect, and dye

With looking on his life.

Enter Alexas from Cæsar

ALEXAS.   Soveraigne of Egypt, haile.

CLEOPATRA. How much unlike art thou *Marke Anthony?*
Yet comming from him, that great Med'cine hath
With his Tinct gilded thee.
How goes it with my brave *Marke Anthony?*

ALEXAS. Last thing he did (deere Queene)
He kist the last of many doubled kisses,
This Orient Pearle. His speech stickes in my heart.

CLEOPATRA. Mine eare must plucke it thence.

ALEXAS. Good friend, quoth he:
Say the firme Roman to great Egypt sends
This treasure of an Oyster: at whose foote
To mend the petty present, I will peece
Her opulent Throne, with Kingdomes. All the East,
(Say thou) shall call her Mistris. So he nodded,
And soberly did mount an Arme-gaunt Steed,
Who neigh'd so hye, that what I would have spoke,
Was beastly dumbe by him.

CLEOPATRA.   What was he, sad, or merry?

ALEXAS. Like to the time o' th' yeare, betweene the ex-
    tremes
Of hot and cold, he was nor sad nor merry.

CLEOPATRA. Oh well divided disposition: Note him:
Note him, good *Charmian,* tis the man; but note him.
He was not sad, for he would shine on those
That make their lookes by his. He was not merry,
Which seem'd to tell them, his remembrance lay
In Egypt with his joy, but betweene both.
Oh heavenly mingle! Bee'st thou sad, or merry,
The violence of either thee becomes,
So do's it no man else. Metst thou my Posts?

ALEXAS. Ay, Madam, twenty severall Messengers.
Why doe you send so thicke?

CLEOPATRA. Who's borne that day, when I forget to send to *Anthony*, shall dye a Begger. Inke and paper, *Charmian*. Welcome my good *Alexas*. Did I *Charmian*, ever love *Cæsar* so?

CHARMIAN.   Oh that brave *Cæsar!*

CLEOPATRA. Be chok'd with such another Emphasis! Say the brave *Anthony*.

CHARMIAN.   The valiant *Cæsar.*

CLEOPATRA. By *Isis*, I will give thee bloody teeth, If thou with *Cæsar* Paragon againe My man of men.

CHARMIAN.   By your most gracious pardon, I sing but after you.

CLEOPATRA.   My Sallad dayes, When I was greene in judgement, cold in blood, To say, as I said then. But come, away, Get me Inke and Paper, He shall have every day severall greeting, or Ile unpeople Ægypt.   *Exeunt.*

Enter Pompey, Menecrates, and Menas in warlike manner.

POMPEY. If the great gods be just, they shall assist The deeds of justest men.

MENECRATES. Know worthy *Pompey*, that which they do delay, they not deny.

POMPEY. Whiles we are sutors to their Throne, decayes the thing we sue for.

MENECRATES. We, ignorant of our selves, Begge often our owne harmes, which the wise Powers Deny us for our good: so finde we profit By loosing of our Prayers.

POMPEY. I shall do well: The People love me, and the Sea is mine;

My powers are Cressent, and my Auguring hope
Sayes it will come to' th' full. *Marke Anthony*
In Ægypt sits at dinner, and will make
No warres without doores. *Cæsar* gets money where
He looses hearts: *Lepidus* flatters both,
Of both is flatter'd: but he neither loves,
Nor either cares for him.

MENECRATES. *Cæsar* and *Lepidus* are in the field,
A mighty strength they carry.

POMPEY. Where have you this? Tis false.

MENECRATES.   From *Silvius* Sir.

POMPEY. He dreames: I know they are in Rome together
Looking for *Antony:* but all the charmes of Love,
Salt *Cleopatra* soften thy wand lip,
Let witchcraft joyne with beauty, Lust with both!
Tye up the Libertine in a field of Feasts,
Keepe his Braine fuming. Epicurean Cookes,
Sharpen with cloylesse sawce his Appetite,
That sleepe and feeding may prorogue his Honour,
Even till a Lethied dulnesse—
Enter Varrius.

                              How now *Varrius?*

VARRIUS. This is most certaine, that I shall deliver:
Marke Anthony is every houre in Rome
Expected. Since he went from Ægypt, 'tis
A space for farther travaile,

POMPEY.   I could have given lesse matter
A better eare. *Menas,* I did not thinke
This amorous Surfetter would have donn'd his Helme
For such a petty Warre: His Souldiership
Is twice the other twaine: But let us reare
The higher our Opinion, that our stirring
Can from the lap of Ægypts Widdow, plucke
The neere Lust-wearied *Anthony.*

MENECRATES.   I cannot hope,

Cæsar and *Anthony* shall well greet together;
His Wife that's dead, did trespasses to *Cæsar*,
His Brother warr'd upon him, although I thinke
Not mov'd by *Anthony*.

POMPEY. I know not, *Menas*,
How lesser Enmities may give way to greater,
Were't not that we stand up against them all:
'Twer pregnant they should square betweene them-
selves,
For they have entertained cause enough
To draw their swords: but how the feare of us
May Ciment their divisions, and binde up
The petty difference, we yet not know:
Bee't as our Gods will have't; it onely stands
Our lives upon, to use our strongest hands,
Come *Menas*. *Exeunt.*

Enter Enobarbus and Lepidus.

LEPIDUS. Good Enobarbus, 'tis a worthy deed,
And shall become you well, to intreat your Captaine
To soft and gentle speech.

ENOBARBUS. I shall intreat him
To answere like himselfe: if *Cæsar* move him,
Let *Anthony* looke over *Cæsars* head,
And speake as lowd as Mars. By Jupiter,
Were I the wearer of *Anthonio's* beard,
I would not shave't to day.

LEPIDUS. Tis not a time for private stomacking.

ENOBARBUS. Every time serves for the matter that is then
borne in't.

LEPIDUS. But small to greater matters must give way.

ENOBARBUS. Not if the small come first.

LEPIDUS. Your speech is passion: but pray you stirre
No Embers up. Heere comes the Noble *Anthony*.

Enter Anthony and Ventidius.

ENOBARBUS. And yonder *Cæsar.*

Enter Cæsar, Mecenas, and Agrippa.

ANTHONY. If we compose well heere, to Parthia:
Hearke *Ventidius.*

CÆSAR. I do not know *Mecenas,* ask *Agrippa.*

LEPIDUS. Noble Friends
That which combin'd us was most great, and let not
A leaner action rend us. What's amisse,
May it be gently heard. When we debate
Our triviall difference lowd, we do commit
Murther in healing wounds. Then, Noble Partners,
The rather for I earnestly beseech,
Touch you the sowrest points with sweetest tearmes,
Nor curstnesse grow to' th' matter.

ANTHONY. Tis spoken well:
Were we before our Armes and to fight,
I should do thus.   *Flourish.*

CÆSAR. Welcome to Rome.

ANTHONY.   Thanke you.

CÆSAR.   Sit.

ANTHONY.   Sit sir.

CÆSAR.   Nay then.

ANTHONY. I learne you take things ill, which are nor so:
Or being, concerne you not.

CÆSAR. I must be laught at, if or for nothing, or a little,
Should say my selfe offended, and with you
Chiefely i' th' world. More laught at, that I should
Once name you derogately: when to sound your name
It not concern'd me.

ANTHONY. My being in Ægypt Cæsar, what was't to
    you?

CÆSAR. No more then my residing heere at Rome
Might be to you in Ægypt: yet if you there
Did practise on my state, your being in Ægypt

Might be my question.

ANTHONY.   How intend you, practis'd?

CÆSAR. You may be pleas'd to catch at mine intent,
By what did heere befall me. Your Wife and Brother
Made warres upon me, and their contestation
Was Theame for you: you were the word of warre.

ANTHONY. You do mistake your businesse, my brother
    never
Did urge me in his Act: I did inquire it,
And have my learning from some true reports
That drew their swords with you, did he not rather
Discredit my authority with yours,
And make the warres alike against my stomacke,
Having alike your cause: Of this, my Letters
Before did satisfie you. If you patch a quarrell,
As matter whole you have to take it with,
It must not be with this.

CÆSAR. You praise your selfe, by laying defects of judge-
    ment to me: but you patcht up your excuses.

ANTHONY. Not so, not so:
I know you could not lacke, I am certaine on't,
Very necessity of this thought, that I
Your partner in the cause 'gainst which he fought,
Could not with gracefull eyes attend those Warres
Which fronted mine owne peace. As for my wife,
I would you had her Spirit, in such another,
The third o' th' world is yours, which with a Snaffle,
You may pace easie, but not such a wife.

ENOBARBUS. Would we had all such wives, that the men
    might go to Warres with the women.

ANTHONY. So much uncurbable, her Garboiles (*Cæsar*)
Made out of her impatience: which not wanted
Shrodenesse of policie to: I greeving grant,
Did you too much disquiet, for that you must,
But say I could not helpe it.

CÆSAR. I wrote to you, when rioting in Alexandria you
Did pocket up my Letters: and with taunts
Did gibe my Missive out of audience.

ANTHONY. Sir, he fell upon me, ere admitted, then:
Three Kings I had newly feasted, and did want
Of what I was i' th' morning: but next day
I told him of my selfe, which was as much
As to have askt him pardon. Let this Fellow
Be nothing of our strife: if we contend,
Out of our question wipe him.

CÆSAR. You have broken the Article of your oath,
Which you shall never have tongue to charge me with.

LEPIDUS. Soft *Cæsar*.

ANTHONY. No *Lepidus*, let him speake,
The Honour is Sacred which he talkes on now,
Supposing that I lackt it: but on *Cæsar*,
The Article of my oath.

CÆSAR. To lend me Armes, and aide when I requir'd
them, the which you both denied.

ANTHONY. Neglected rather.
And then when poysoned houres had bound me up
From mine owne knowledge, as neerly as I may,
Ile play the penitent to you. But mine honesty,
Shall not make poore my greatnesse, nor my power
Worke without it. Truth is, that *Fulvia*,
To have me out of Ægypt, made Warres heere,
For which myselfe, the ignorant motive, doe
So farre aske pardon, as befits mine Honour
To stoope in such a case.

LEPIDUS.   Tis Nobly spoken.

MECENAS. If it might please you, to enforce no further
The griefes betweene ye: to forget them quite,
Were to remember that the present neede
Speakes to attone you.

LEPIDUS.   Worthy spoken *Mecenas*.

ENOBARBUS. Or if you borrow one anothers Love for the instant, you may when you heare no more words of *Pompey* returne it againe: you shall have time to wrangle in, when you have nothing else to doe.

ANTHONY. Thou art a Souldier, onely speake no more.

ENOBARBUS. That trueth should be silent, I had almost forgot.

ANTHONY. You wrong this presence, therefore speake n more.

ENOBARBUS. Go to then: your Considerate stone.

CÆSAR. I doe not much dislike the matter but
The manner of his speech: for't cannot be,
We shall remaine in friendship, our conditions
So differing in their acts. Yet if I knew,
What Hoope should hold us staunch from edge to edge
Ath' world: I would pursue it.

AGRIPPA.   Give me leave, *Cæsar.*

CÆSAR. Speake, *Agrippa.*

AGRIPPA. Thou hast a Sister by thy Mothers side, admir'd *Octavia?* Great *Marke Anthony* is now a widdower.

CÆSAR. Say not *so, Agrippa;* if *Cleopatra* heard you, your proofe were well deserved of rashnesse.

ANTHONY. I am not marryed *Cæsar:* let me heere *Agrippa* further speake.

AGRIPPA. To hold you in perpetuall amitie,
To make you Brothers, and to knit your hearts
With an un-slipping knot, take *Anthony*
Octavia to his wife: whose beauty claimes
No worse a husband then the best of men:
Whose vertue, and whose generall graces, speake
That which none else can utter. By this marriage,
All little Jelousies which now seeme great,
And all great feares, which now import their dangers,
Would then be nothing. Truths would be tales,

Where now halfe tales be truths: her love to both,
Would each to other, and all loves to both,
Draw after her. Pardon what I have spoke,
For 'tis a studied, not a present thought,
By duty ruminated.

ANTHONY.   Will *Cæsar* speake?

CÆSAR. Not till he heares how Anthony is toucht,
With what is spoke already.

ANTHONY.   What power is in *Agrippa*,
If I would say *Agrippa,* be it so,
To make this good?

CÆSAR.   The power of *Cæsar,*
And his power, unto *Octavia.*

ANTHONY.   May I never
(To this good purpose, that so fairely shewes)
Dreame of impediment: let me have thy hand
Further this act of Grace: and from this houre,
The heart of Brothers governe in our Loves,
And sway our great Designes.

CÆSAR.   There's my hand:
A Sister I bequeath you, whome no Brother
Did ever love so deerely. Let her live
To joyne our kingdomes, and our hearts, and never
Flie off our Loves againe.

LEPIDUS.   Happily, Amen.

ANTHONY. I did not thinke to draw my Sword against
    Pompey,
For he hath laid strange courtesies, and great
Of late upon me. I must thanke him onely,
Lest my remembrance, suffer ill report:
At heele of that defie him.

LEPIDUS.   Time cals upon's,
Of us must *Pompey* presently be sought,
Or else he seekes out us.

ANTHONY.   Where lies he?

CÆSAR. About the Mount-Mesena.

ANTHONY. What is his strength by land?

CÆSAR. Great, and encreasing:
But by Sea he is an absolute Master.

ANTHONY.   So is the Fame,
Would we had spoke together. Haste we for it,
Yet ere we put our selves in Armes, dispatch we
The businesse we have talkt of.

CÆSAR.   With most gladnesse,
And do invite you to my Sisters view,
Whither straight Ile lead you.

ANTHONY. Let us *Lepidus* not lacke your company.

LEPIDUS. Noble *Anthony*, not sicknesse should detaine
    me.   *Exeunt omnes.*

Manent Enobarbus, Agrippa, Mecenas.

MECENAS. Welcome from Ægypt Sir.

ENOBARBUS. Halfe the heart of *Cæsar*, worthy *Mecenas*.
    My honourable Friend *Agrippa*.

AGRIPPA. Good *Enobarbus*.

MECENAS. We have cause to be glad, that matters are so
    well digested: you stayd well by't in Egypt.

ENOBARBUS. Ay, Sir, we did sleepe day out of counte-
    naunce: and made the night light with drinking.

MECENAS. Eight Wilde-Boars rosted whole at a break-
    fast: and but twelve persons there. Is this true?

ENOBARBUS. This was but as a Flye by an Eagle: we had
    much more monstrous matter of Feast, which worthily
    deserved noting.

MECENAS. She's a most triumphant Lady, if report be
    square to her.

ENOBARBUS. When she first met *Marke Anthony*, she
    purst up his heart upon the river of *Cydnus*.

AGRIPPA. There she appear'd indeed: or my reporter de-
    vis'd well for her.

ENOBARBUS.   I will tell you,

The Barge she sat in, like a burnisht Throne
Burnt on the water: the Poope was beaten Gold,
Purple the Sailes: and so perfumed that
The Windes were Love-sicke.
With them the Oares were Silver,
Which to the tune of Flutes kept stroke and made
The water which they beate, to follow faster:
As amorous of their strokes. For her owne person,
It beggerd all description: she did lye
In her Pavillion, cloth of Gold, of Tissue,
O're-picturing that Venus, where we see
The fancie out-worke Nature. On each side her,
Stood pretty Dimpled Boyes, like smiling Cupids,
With divers colour'd Fannes whose winde did seeme,
To glove the delicate cheekes which they did coole,
And what they undid did.

AGRIPPA.   Oh rare for *Anthony*.

ENOBARBUS. Her Gentlewomen, like the Nereides,
So many Mer-maides tended her i' th' eyes,
And made their bends adornings. At the Helme,
A seeming Mer-maide steeres: The Silken Tackles
Swell with the touches of those Flower-soft hands,
That yarely frame the office. From the Barge
A strange invisible perfume hits the sense
Of the adjacent Wharfes. The Cittie cast
Her people out upon her: and *Anthony*
Enthron'd i'th' Market-place, did sit alone,
Whisling to th' ayre: which but for vacancie,
Had gone to gaze on *Cleopatra* too,
And made a gap in Nature.

AGRIPPA.   Rare Ægyptian.

ENOBARBUS. Upon her landing, *Anthony* sent to her,
Invited her to Supper: she replyed,
It should be better he became her guest:
Which she entreated, our Courteous *Anthony*:

Whom nere the word of no woman heard speake,
Being barber'd ten times o're, goes to the Feast;
And for his ordinary, paies his heart,
For what his eyes eate onely.

AGRIPPA. Royall Wench:
She made great *Cæsar* lay his Sword to bed,
He ploughed her, and she cropt.

ENOBARBUS. I saw her once
Hop forty Paces through the publicke streete,
And having lost her breath, she spoke, and panted,
That she did make defect, perfection,
And breathlesse power breath forth.

MECENAS. Now *Anthony*, must leave her utterly.

ENOBARBUS. Never, he will not:
Age cannot wither her, nor custome stale
Her infinite variety: other women cloy
The appetites they feede, but she makes hungry,
Where most she satisfies. For vilest things
Become themselves in her, that the holy Priests
Blesse her, when she is Riggish.

MECENAS. If Beauty, Wisedome, Modesty, can settle
The heart of *Anthony*, *Octavia* is
A blessed Lottery to him.

AGRIPPA. Let us go. Good *Enobarbus*, make your selfe
my guest, whilst you abide heere.

ENOBARBUS. Humbly Sir I thanke you. *Exeunt.*

Enter Anthony, Cæsar, Octavia betweene them.

ANTHONY. The world, and my great office, will
Sometimes divide me from your bosome.

OCTAVIA. All which time, before the Gods my knee shall
bowe my prayers to them for you.

ANTHONY. Goodnight Sir. My *Octavia*
Read not my blemishes in the worlds report:

I have not kept my square, but that to come
Shall all be done by th' Rule: good night deere Lady:
OCTAVIA. Good night Sir.
CÆSAR. Good night.   *Exit.*
Enter Soothsayer.
ANTHONY. Now sirrah: you do wish your selfe in Egypt?
SOOTHSAYER. Would I had never come from thence, nor
    you thither.
ANTHONY. If you can, your reason?
SOOTHSAYER. I see it in my motion: have it not in my
    tongue,
But yet hie you to Ægypt againe.
ANTHONY. Say to me, whose Fortunes shall rise higher,
Cæsars or mine?
SOOTHSAYER. *Cæsars.* Therefore (oh *Anthony*) stay not
    by his side:
Thy Dæmon (that's thy spirit which keepes thee) is
Noble, Couragious, high, unmatchable,
Whare *Cæsars* is not. But neere him thy Angell
Becomes a feare: as being o're-powr'd, and therefore
Make space enough betweene you.
ANTHONY.   Speake this no more.
SOOTHSAYER. To none but thee no more, but when to
    thee,
If thou dost play with him at any game,
Thou art sure to loose: And of that Naturall lucke,
He beates thee 'gainst the oddes. Thy Luster thickens,
When he shines by: I say againe, thy spirit
Is all affraid to governe thee neere him:
But he alway is Noble.
ANTHONY.   Get thee gone:
Say to *Ventidius* I would speake with him.   *Exit.*
He shall to Parthia, be it art or hap,
He hath spoken true. The very Dice obey him,

And in our sports my better cunning faints,
Under his chance; if we draw lots, he speeds,
His Cocks do winne the Battaile, still of mine,
When it is all to naught: and his Quailes ever
Beate mine (in hoopt) at odd's. I will to Egypt:
And though I make this marriage for my peace,
I' th' East my pleasure lies. Oh come *Ventidius*.
Enter Ventidius.
You must to Parthia, your commissions ready:
Follow me and receive't.   *Exeunt.*

Enter Lepidus, Mecenas and Agrippa.

LEPIDUS. Trouble your selfe no farther: pray you hasten generals after.

AGRIPPA. Sir, *Marke Anthony* will e'ne but kisse *Octavia,*
   and weele follow.

LEPIDUS. Till I shall see you in your Souldiers dresse,
   which will become you both: Farewell.

MECENAS. We shall, as I conceive the journey, be at the
   Mount before you *Lepidus.*

LEPIDUS. Your way is shorter, my purposes do draw me
   much about, you'le win two dayes upon me.

BOTH. Sir, good successe.

LEPIDUS. Farewell.   *Exeunt.*

Enter Cleopatra, Charmian, Iras and Alexas.

CLEOPATRA. Give me some Musicke: Musicke, moody
   foode of us that trade in love.

OMNES. The Musicke, hoa!

Enter Mardian the Eunuch.

CLEOPATRA. Let it alone, let's to Billiards: come *Charmian.*

CHARMIAN. My arme is sore, best play with *Mardian*.

CLEOPATRA. As well a woman with an Eunuch plaide, as
with a woman. Come you'le play with me Sir?

MARDIAN. As well as I can Madam.

CLEOPATRA. And when good will is shewed,
Though't come too short
The Actor may pleade pardon. Ile none now:
Give me mine Angle, weele to' th' River; there,
My Musicke playing farre off, I will betray
Tawny fine fishes, my bended hooke shall pierce
Their slimie jawes: and as I draw them up,
Ile thinke them every one an *Anthony*,
And say, ah ha; y'are caught.

CHARMIAN. Twas merry when you wager'd on your Ang-
ling, when your diver did hang a salt fish on his hooke
which he with fervencie drew up,

CLEOPATRA. That time? Oh times:
I laught him out of patience: and that night
I laught him into patience, and next morne,
Ere the ninth houre, I drunke him to his bed:
Then put my Tires and Mantels on him, whilst
I wore his Sword Philippan. Oh, from Italie!
Enter a Messenger.
Ramme thou thy fruitfull tidings in mine eares,
That long time have bin barren.

MESSENGER. Madam, Madam.

CLEOPATRA.   *Anthony's* dead,
If thou say so Villaine, thou kill'st thy Mistris:
But well and free, if thou so yeild him,
There is Gold and heere
My blewest vaines to kisse: a hand that Kings
Have lipt, and trembled kissing.

MESSENGER. First Madam, he is well.

CLEOPATRA.   Why there's more Gold.
But sirrah marke, we use

To say the dead are well: bring me to that,
The Gold I give thee, will I melt and powre
Downe thy ill uttering throate.

MESSENGER. Good Madam heare me.

CLEOPATRA.   Well, go to, I will:
But there's no goodnesse in thy face, if *Anthony*
Be free and healthfull; so tart a favour
To trumpet such good tidings. If not well,
Thou shouldst come like a Furie crown'd with Snakes,
Not like a formall man.

MESSENGER.   Wilt please you heare me?

CLEOPATRA. I have a mind to strike thee ere thou
    speake'st,
Yet if thou say *Anthony* lives, 'tis well,
Or friends with *Cæsar*, or not Captaine to him,
Ile set thee in a shower of Gold, and haile
Rich Pearles upon thee.

MESSENGER.   Madam, he's well.

CLEOPATRA.   Well sayd:

MESSENGER. And Friends with *Cæsar*.

CLEOPATRA.   Th' art an honest man.

MESSENGER. *Cæsar*, and he, are greater Friends then
    ever.

CLEOPATRA. Marke thee a Fortune from me.

MESSENGER.   But yet Madam.

CLEOPATRA. I do not like but yet, it does alay
The good precedence, fie upon but yet,
But yet is as a Jaylor to bring foorth
Some monstrous Malefactor. Prythee Friend,
Powre out the packe of matter to mine eare,
The good and bad together: he's friends with *Cæsar*,
In state of health thou saist, and thou saiest, free.

MESSENGER. Free Madam! no: I made no such report,
He's bound unto *Octavia*.

CLEOPATRA.   For what good turne?

MESSENGER. For the best i' th' bed.

CLEOPATRA. I am pale, *Charmian*.

MESSENGER. Madam, he's married to *Octavia*.

CLEOPATRA. The most infectious Pestilence upon thee.
Strikes him downe.

MESSENGER. Good Madam patience.

CLEOPATRA. What say you?
Strikes him.

Hence horrible Villaine, or Ile spurne thine eyes
Like balls before me: Ile unhaire thy head:
She hales him up and downe.
Thou shalt be whipt with Wyer, and stew'd in brine,
Smarting in lingring pickle.

MESSENGER. Gratious Madam,
I that do bring the newes, made not the match.

CLEOPATRA. Say 'tis not so, a Province I will give thee,
And make thy Fortunes proud: the blow thou had'st
Shall make thy peace, for moving me to rage,
And I will boot thee with what gift beside
Thy modesty can begge.

MESSENGER. He's married Madam.

CLEOPATRA. Rogue, thou hast liv'd too long.
Draws a knife.

MESSENGER. Nay then Ile runne:
What meane you Madam, I have made no fault.   *Exit.*

CHARMIAN. Good Madam keepe your selfe within your
selfe,
The man is innocent.

CLEOPATRA. Some Innocents scape not the thunderbolt:
Melt Egypt into Nyle; and kindled creatures
Turne all to Serpents. Call the slave againe,
Though I am mad, I will not byte him: Call?

CHARMIAN. He is afeard to come.

CLEOPATRA. I will not hurt him.
These hands do lacke Nobility, that they strike

A meaner then my selfe: since I my selfe
Have given my selfe the cause. Come hither Sir.
Enter the Messenger againe.
Though it be honest, it is never good
To bring bad newes: give to a Gratious Message
An host of tongues, but let ill tydings tell
Themselves when they be felt.

MESSENGER. I have done my duty.

CLEOPATRA.   Is he married?
I cannot hate thee worser then I do,
If thou againe say yes.

MESSENGER.   He's married, Madam.

CLEOPATRA. The gods confound thee,
Dost thou hold there still?

MESSENGER. Should I lye, Madam?

CLEOPATRA.   Oh, I would thou didst:
So halfe my Egypt were submerg'd and made
A Cesterne for scal'd Snakes. Go get thee hence,
Had'st thou *Narcissus* in thy face, to me
Thou wouldst appeare most ugly: He is married?

MESSENGER. I crave your highnesse pardon.

CLEOPATRA. He is married?

MESSENGER. Take no offence, that I would not offend
you;
To punish me for what you make me doe,
Seemes much unequall: he's married to *Octavia.*

CLEOPATRA. Oh that his fault should make a knave of
thee,
That art not what thou art sure of. Get thee hence,
The Merchandize which thou hast brought from Rome
Are all too deere for me:
Lye they upon thy hand, and be undone by em.

CHARMIAN. Good your highnesse patience.

CLEOPATRA. In praying *Anthony,* I have disprais'd
Cæsar.

CHARMIAN. Many times Madam.

CLEOPATRA. I am paid for't now: lead me from hence,
I faint, oh *Iras, Charmian:* tis no matter.
Go to the fellow, good *Alexas* bid him
Report the feature of *Octavia:* her yeares,
Her inclination, let him not leave out
The colour of her haire. Bring me word quickly.
Let him for ever goe—let him not, *Charmian,*
Though he be painted one way like a Gorgon,
The other wayes a Mars. Bid you *Alexas*
Bring me word, how tall she is: pitty me *Charmian,*
But do not speake to me. Lead me to my Chamber.

Exeunt.

*Enter Pompey, at one doore with Drum and Trumpet:
at another Cæsar, Lepidus, Anthony, Enobarbus,
Mecenas, Agrippa, Menas with Souldiers Marching.*

POMPEY. Your Hostages I have, so have you mine:
And we shall talke before we fight.

CÆSAR. Most meete that first we come to words,
And therefore have we
Our written purposes before us sent,
Which if thou hast considered, let us know,
If 't will tye up thy discontented Sword
And carry backe to Sicily much tall youth,
That else much perish heere.

POMPEY. To you all three,
The Senators alone of this great world,
Chiefe Factors for the Gods. I do not know,
Wherefore my Father should revengers want,
Having a Sonne and Friends, since *Julius Cæsar,*
Who at Philippi the good *Brutus* ghosted,
There saw you labouring for him. What was't
That mov'd pale *Cassius* to conspire? And what

Made the all-honor'd, honest Romane *Brutus,*
With the arm'd rest, Courtiers of beautious freedome,
To drench the Capitoll, but that they would
Have one man but a man, and that is it
Hath made me rigge my Navie. At whose burthen,
The anger'd Ocean fomes, with which I meant
To scourge th' ingratitude, that despightfull Rome
Cast on my Noble Father.

CÆSAR.   Take your time.

ANTHONY. Thou canst not feare us *Pompey* with thy
    sailes,
Weele speake with thee at Sea. At land thou know'st
How much we do o're-count thee.

POMPEY.   At Land indeed
Thou dost o're-count me of my fathers house.
But since the Cookoo buildes not for himselfe,
Remaine in't as thou maist.

LEPIDUS.   Be pleas'd to tell us
(For this is from the present now you talke)
The offers we have sent you.

CÆSAR.   There's the point.

ANTHONY. Which do not be entreated to,
But waigh what it is worth embrac'd.

CÆSAR. And what may follow to try a larger Fortune.

POMPEY. You have made me offer
Of Sicily, Sardinia: and I must
Rid all the Sea of Pirats. Then, to send
Measures of Wheate to Rome: this greed upon,
To part with unhackt edges, and beare backe
Our Targes undinted.

OMNES.   That's our offer.

POMPEY. Know then I came before you heere,
A man prepar'd
To take this offer. But *Marke Anthony,*
Put me to some impatience: though I loose

The praise of it by telling. You must know
When *Cæsar* and your Brother were at blowes,
Your Mother came to Sicily, and did finde
Her welcome friendly.

ANTHONY.   I have heard it *Pompey*,
And am well studied for a liberall thankes,
Which I do owe you.

POMPEY.   Let me have your hand:
I did not thinke Sir, to have met you heere.

ANTHONY. The beds i' th' East are soft, and thankes to
    you,
That call'd me timelier then my purpose hither:
For I have gained by't.

CÆSAR. Since I saw you last, ther's a change upon you.

POMPEY. Well, I know not,
What counts harsh Fortune cast's upon my face,
But in my bosome shall she never come,
To make my heart a vassaile.

LEPIDUS.   Well met heere.

POMPEY. I hope so *Lepidus,* thus we are agreed:
I crave our composition may be written
And seal'd betweene us.

CÆSAR.   That's the next to doe.

POMPEY. Weele feast each other, ere we part, and lett's
Draw lots who shall begin.

ANTHONY.   That will I *Pompey.*

POMPEY. No *Anthony* take the lot: but first or last, your
    fine Egyptian cookerie shall have the fame; I have
    heard that *Julius Cæsar,* grew fat with feasting there.

ANTHONY. You have heard much.

POMPEY. I have faire meaning Sir.

ANTHONY.   And faire words to
    them.

POMPEY. Then so much have I heard.
And I have heard *Apollodorus* carried—

ENOBARBUS. No more that: he did so.

POMPEY.   What I pray you?

ENOBARBUS. A certaine Queene to *Cæsar* in a Materice.

POMPEY. I know thee now, how far'st thou Souldier?

ENOBARBUS. Well, and well am like to doe, for I perceive
Foure Feasts are toward.

POMPEY.   Let me shake thy hand;
I never hated thee: I have seene thee fight,
When I have envied thy behaviour.

ENOBARBUS. Sir, I never lov'd you much, but I ha'
    prais'd ye
When you have well deserv'd ten times as much
As I have said you did.

POMPEY.   Injoy thy plainnesse,
It nothing ill becomes thee.
Aboord my Gally, I invite you all.
Will you leade, Lords?

ALL. Shew's the way, sir.

POMPEY. Come.

             Exeunt. Manent Enobarbus and Menas.

MENAS. Thy Father *Pompey* would ne're have made this
Treaty. You and I have knowne, sir.

ENOBARBUS. At Sea, I thinke.

MENAS. We have, Sir.

ENOBARBUS. You have done well by water.

MENAS. And you by Land.

ENOBARBUS. I will praise any man that will praise me,
    thogh it cannot be denied what I have done by Land.

MENAS. Nor what I have done by water.

ENOBARBUS. Yes some-thing you can deny for your owne
    safety: you have bin a good Theefe by Sea.

MENAS. And you by Land.

ENOBARBUS. There I deny my Land service: but give me
    your hand *Menas*, if our eyes had authority, here they
    might take two Theeves kissing.

MENAS. All mens faces are true, whatsoere their hands are.

ENOBARBUS. But there is never a faire Woman ha's a true face.

MENAS. No slander; they steale hearts.

ENOBARBUS. We came hither to fight with you.

MENAS. For my part, I am sorry it is turn'd to a Drinking. *Pompey* doth this day laugh away his Fortune.

ENOBARBUS. If he doe, sure he cannot weep 't backe againe.

MENAS. Y'have said Sir. We look'd not for *Marke Anthony* heere: pray you, is he married to *Cleopatra?*

ENOBARBUS. *Cæsars* Sister is call'd *Octavia.*

MENAS. True, Sir, she was the wife of *Caius Marcellus.*

ENOBARBUS. But she is now the wife of *Marcus Anthonius.*

MENAS. Pray y'e Sir.

ENOBARBUS. Tis true.

MENAS. Then is *Cæsar* and he for ever knit together?

ENOBARBUS. If I were bound to divine of this unity I wold not Prophesie so.

MENAS. I thinke the policy of that purpose, made more in the Marriage then the Love of the parties.

ENOBARBUS. I thinke so too. But you shall finde the band that seemes to tye their friendship together, will bee the very stranger of their Amity: *Octavia* is of a holy, cold, and still conversation.

MENAS. Who would not have his wife so?

ENOBARBUS. Not hee that himselfe is not so: which is *Marke Anthony:* he will to his Egyptian dish againe: then shall the sighes of *Octavia* blow the fire up in *Cæsar,* and (as I said before) that which is the strength of their Amity, shall prove the immediate Author of their variance. *Anthony* will use his affection where it is. Hee married but his occasion heere.

MENAS. And thus it may be. Come Sir, will you aboord? I have a health for you.

ENOBARBUS. I shall take it sir: we have us'd our Throats in Egypt.

MENAS. Come, let's a way.   *Exeunt.*

Musicke playes. Enter two or three Servants with a Bankuet.

1. Heere they'l be, man: some o' their Plants are ill rooted already; the least wind i' th' world will blow them downe.

2. *Lepidus* is high colour'd.

1. They have made him drinke Almes drinke.

2. As they pinch one another by the disposition, he cries out no more; reconciles them to his entreatie, and himselfe to' th' drinke.

1. But it raises the greater warre betweene him and his discretion.

2. Why this it is to have a name in great mens Fellowship: I had as lieve have a Reede that will doe me no service, as a Partizan I could not heave.

1. To be call'd into a huge Sphere, and not to bee seene to move in't, are the holes where eyes should bee, which pittif'lly disaster the cheekes.

A Sennet sounded. Enter Cæsar, Anthony, Pompey, Lepidus, Agrippa, Mecenas, Enobarbus, Menas, with other Captaines.

ANTHONY. Thus do they Sir: they take the flow o' th' Nyle

By certaine scale i' th' Pyramid; they know

By th' height, the lownesse, or the meane, if dearth

Or Foizon follow. The higher Nilus swels,

The more it promises; as it ebbes, the Seedsman

Upon the slime and Ooze scatters his graine,

And shortly comes to Harvest.

LEPIDUS. Y'have strange Serpents there.

ANTHONY. Ay, Lepidus.

LEPIDUS. Your Serpent of Ægypt, is bred now of your mud by the operation of the Sun: so is your Crocodile.

ANTHONY. They are so.

POMPEY. Sit, and some Wine: A health to *Lepidus.*

LEPIDUS. I am not so well as I should be:
But Ile ne're out.

ENOBARBUS. Not till you have slept: I feare me you'll bee in till then.

LEPIDUS. Nay certainly, I have heard the *Ptolemies* Pyramisis are very goodly things: without contradiction have heard that.

MENAS. *Pompey,* a word.

POMPEY. Say in mine eare, what is't.

MENAS. Forsake thy seate, I do beseech thee Captaine,
And heare me speake a word.

POMPEY. Forbeare me till anon.   *Whispers in's Eare.*
This Wine for *Lepidus.*

LEPIDUS. What manner o' thing is your Crocodile?

ANTHONY. It is shap'd sir like it selfe, and it is as broad as it hath bredth; It is just so high as it is, and mooves with its owne organs. It lives by that which nourisheth it, and the Elements once out of it, it Transmigrates.

LEPIDUS. What colour is it of?

ANTHONY. Of its owne colour too.

LEPIDUS. Tis a strange Serpent.

ANTHONY. Tis so, and the teares of it are wet.

CÆSAR. Will this description satisfie him?

ANTHONY. With the Health that *Pompey* gives him, else hee is a very Epicure.

POMPEY. Go hang sir, hang: tell me of that? Away:
Do as I bid you. Where's the Cup I call'd for?

MENAS. If for the sake of Merit thou wilt heare me,
Rise from thy stoole.

POMPEY. I thinke th'art mad: the matter?

MENAS. I have ever held my cap off to thy Fortunes.

POMPEY. Thou hast serv'd me with much faith: what's
    else to say? Be jolly Lords.

ANTHONY. These Quicke-sands *Lepidus,*
Keepe off them, for you sinke.

MENAS. Wilt thou be Lord of all the world?

POMPEY. What saist thou?

MENAS. Wilt thou be Lord of the whole world?
That's twice.

POMPEY. How should that be?

MENAS. But entertaine it, and though thou thinke mee
    poore, I am the man will give thee all the world.

POMPEY. Hast thou drunke well?

MENAS. No, *Pompey,* I have kept me from the cup.
Thou art if thou dar'st be, the earthly Jove:
What ere the Ocean pales, or skie inclippes,
Is thine, if thou wilt ha't.

POMPEY. Shew me which way?

MENAS. These three world-sharers, these Competitors,
Are in thy vessell. Let me cut the Cable;
And when we are put off, fall to their throates:
All there is thine.

POMPEY. Ah, this thou shouldst have done,
And not have spoke on't. In me tis villanie,
In thee, 't had bin good service: thou must know,
Tis not my profit that does lead mine Honour:
Mine Honour, it. Repent that ere thy tongue
Hath so betraide thine act. Being done unknowne,
I should have found it afterwards well done,
But must condemne it now: desist, and drinke.

MENAS. For this Ile never follow
Thy paul'd Fortunes more,

Who seekes and will not take, when once tis offerd,
Shall never finde it more.

POMPEY.   This health to *Lepidus*.

ANTHONY. Beare him a shore,
Ile pledge it for him, *Pompey*.

ENOBARBUS. Heere's to thee *Menas*.

MENAS. *Enobarbus*, welcome.

POMPEY. Fill till the cup be hid.

ENOBARBUS. There's a strong Fellow, *Menas*.

MENAS. Why?

ENOBARBUS. A beares the third part of the world, man:
seest not?

MENAS. The third part, then he is drunk: would it were
all, that it might go on wheeles.

ENOBARBUS. Drinke thou: encrease the Reeles.

MENAS. Come.

POMPEY. This is not yet an Alexandrian Feast.

ANTHONY. It ripens towards it: strike the Vesselles hoa.
Heere's to *Cæsar*.

CÆSAR. I could well forbear't, its monstrous labour when
I wash my braine, and it growes fouler.

ANTHONY. Be a Child o'th' time.

CÆSAR. Possesse it, Ile make answer: but I had rather
fast from all, foure dayes, then drinke so much in
one.

ENOBARBUS. Ha my brave Emperor, shall we daunce
now the Egyptian Bachanals, and celebrate our
drinke?

POMPEY. Lets ha't good Souldier.

ANTHONY. Come, let's all take hands,
Till that the conquering Wine hath steept our sense,
In soft and delicate Lethe.

ENOBARBUS.   All take hands:
Make battery to our eares with the loud Musicke,
The while, Ile place you, then the Boy shall sing.

The holding every man shall beate as loud
As his strong sides can volly.
Musicke Playes. Enobarbus places them hand in hand.

THE SONG

Come thou Monarch of the Vine,
Plumpie Bacchus with pinke eyne:
In thy Fattes our Cares be drown'd,
With thy Grapes our haires be Crown'd.
Cup us till the world go round,
Cup us till the world go round.

CÆSAR. What would you more?
Pompey goodnight. Good Brother
Let me request you off; our graver businesse
Frownes at this levitie. Gentle Lords, let's part;
You see we have burnt our cheeke. Strong *Enobarbe*
Is weaker then the Wine, and mine owne tongue
Spleets what it speakes: the wilde disguise hath almost
Antickt us all. What needs more words? goodnight.
Good *Anthony* your hand.
POMPEY.   Ile try you on the shore.
ANTHONY. And shall Sir, give's your hand.
POMPEY. Oh *Anthony,* you have my Fathers house.
But what, we are Friends.
Come downe into the Boate.
ENOBARBUS. Take heed you fall not, *Menas;* Ile not on
shore.
MENAS. No to my Cabin: these Drummes,
These Trumpets, Flutes: what!
Let Neptune heare, we bid aloud farewell
To these great Fellowes. Sound and be hang'd, sound
out.
Sound a Florish with Drummes.
ENOBARBUS. Hoo! saies a. There's my Cap.
MENAS. Hoa, Noble Captaine, come.   *Exeunt.*

Enter Ventidius as it were in a triumph, the dead body of Pacorus borne before him.

VENTIDIUS. Now darting Parthia art thou stroke, and now
Pleas'd Fortune does of *Marcus Crassus* death
Make me revenger. Beare the Kings Sonnes body
Before our Army. Thy *Pacorus Orades,*
Payes this for *Marcus Crassus.*

ROMANE.   Noble *Ventidius,*
Whilst yet with Parthian blood thy Sword is warme,
The Fugitive Parthians follow. Spurne through Media,
Mesapotamia, and the shelters, whither
The routed flie. So thy grand Captaine *Anthony*
Shall set thee on triumphant Chariots, and
Put Garlands on thy head.

VENTIDIUS.   Oh *Sillius, Sillius,*
I have done enough. A lower place, note well
May make too great an act. For learne this *Sillius,*
Better to leave undone, then by our deed
Acquire too high a Fame, when him we serve's away.
Cæsar and *Anthony,* have ever wonne
More in their officer, then person. *Sossius*
One of my place in Syria, his Lieutenant,
For quicke accumulation of renowne,
Which he atchiv'd by th' minute, lost his favour.
Who does i'th' Warres more then his Captaine can,
Becomes his Captaines Captaine: and Ambition
(The Souldiers vertue) rather makes choise of losse
Then gaine, which darkens him.
I could doe more to doe *Anthonius* good,
But 'twould offend him. And in his offence,
Should my performance perish.

ROMANE. Thou hast, *Ventidius,* that, without the which
    a Souldier and his Sword grants scarce distinction:
    thou wilt write to *Anthony?*

VENTIDIUS. Ile humbly signifie what in his name,
That magicall word of Warre, wee have effected:
How with his Banners, and his well paid rankes,
The nere-yet beaten Horse of Parthia,
We have jaded out o'th' Field.
ROMANE. Where is he now?
VENTIDIUS. He purposeth to Athens, whither with what
    hast
The waight we must convay with's, will permit:
We shall appeare before him. On there, passe along.

Exeunt.

Enter Agrippa at one doore, Enobarbus at another.
AGRIPPA. What are the Brothers parted?
ENOBARBUS. They have dispatcht with *Pompey;* he is
    gone;
The other three are Sealing. *Octavia* weepes
To part from Rome: *Cæsar* is sad, and *Lepidus*
Since *Pompey's* feast, as *Menas* sayes, is troubled
With the Greene-Sicknesse.
AGRIPPA.   Tis a Noble *Lepidus.*
ENOBARBUS. A very fine one: oh, how he loves *Cæsar.*
AGRIPPA. Nay but how deerely he adores *Mark Anthony.*
ENOBARBUS. *Cæsar?* why he's the Jupiter of men.
AGRIPPA. What's *Anthony,* the God of Jupiter?
ENOBARBUS. Spake you of *Cæsar?* Oh! the non-pareill?
AGRIPPA. Oh *Anthony,* oh thou Arabian Bird!
ENOBARBUS. Would you praise *Cæsar,* say *Cæsar,* go no
    further.
AGRIPPA. Indeed he plied them both with excellent
    praises.
ENOBARBUS. But he loves *Cæsar* best, yet he loves
    Anthony:
Hoo! Hearts, Tongues, Figure,

Scribes, Bards, Poets, cannot
Thinke, speake, cast, write, sing, number: hoo!
His love to *Anthony*. But as for *Cæsar*,
Kneele downe, kneele downe, and wonder.

AGRIPPA.   Both he loves.

ENOBARBUS. They are his Shards, and he their Beetle, so:
This is to horse: Adieu, Noble *Agrippa*.

AGRIPPA. Good Fortune worthy Souldier, and farewell.

Enter Cæsar, Antony, Lepidus, and Octavia.

ANTHONY. No farther Sir.

CÆSAR. You take from me a great part of my selfe:
Use me well in't. Sister, prove such a wife
As my thoughts make thee, and as my farthest Band
Shall passe on thy approofe: most Noble *Anthony*,
Let not the peece of Vertue which is set
Betwixt us, as the Cyment of our love
To keepe it builded, be the Ramme to batter
The Fortune of it: for better might we
Have lov'd without this meane, if on both parts
This be not cherisht.

ANTHONY. Make me not offended, in your distrust.

CÆSAR. I have said.

ANTHONY.   You shall not finde,
Though you be therein curious, the least cause
For what you seeme to feare, so the gods keepe you,
And make the hearts of Romanes serve your ends:
We will heere part.

CÆSAR. Farewell my deerest Sister, fare thee well:
The Elements be kind to thee, and make
Thy spirits all of comfort: fare thee well.

OCTAVIA. My Noble Brother.

ANTHONY. The Aprill's in her eyes, it is Loves spring,
And these the showers to bring it on: be cheerfull.

OCTAVIA. Sir, looke well to my Husbands house: and—

CÆSAR. What, *Octavia?*

OCTAVIA. Ile tell you in your eare.

ANTHONY. Her tongue will not obey her heart, nor can
Her heart informe her tongue.
The Swannes downe feather
That stands upon the Swell at full of Tide,
And neither way inclines.

ENOBARBUS. Will *Cæsar* weepe?

AGRIPPA. He ha's a cloud in's face.

ENOBARBUS. He were the worse for that were he a Horse,
so is he being a man.

AGRIPPA. Why *Enobarbus:*
When *Anthony* found *Julius Cæsar* dead,
He cryed almost to roaring. And he wept,
When at Philippi he found *Brutus* slaine.

ENOBARBUS. That year indeed, he was troubled with a
rheume;
What willingly he did confound, he wail'd,
Beleev't till I weepe too.

CÆSAR. No sweet *Octavia*,
You shall heare from me still: the time shall not
Out-go my thinking on you.

ANTHONY. Come Sir, come,
Ile wrastle with you in my strength of love:
Looke heere I have you: thus I let you go,
And give you to the gods.

CÆSAR. Adieu, be happy.

LEPIDUS. Let all the number of the Starres give light
To thy faire way.

CÆSAR. Farewell, farewell. *Kisses Octavia.*

ANTHONY. Farewell.
Trumpets sound. Exeunt.

Enter Cleopatra, Charmian, Iras, and Alexas.

CLEOPATRA. Where is the Fellow?

ALEXAS.   Halfe afeard to come.

CLEOPATRA. Go to, go to: Come hither Sir.

Enter the Messenger as before.

ALEXAS. Good Majestie, *Herod* of Jewry dare not looke upon you, but when you are well pleas'd.

CLEOPATRA. That *Herods* head, Ile have: but how? When *Anthony* is gone, through whom I might command it:

Come thou neere.

MESSENGER. Most gracious Majesty.

CLEOPATRA. Did'st thou behold *Octavia?*

MESSENGER. Ay, dread Queene.

CLEOPATRA. Where?

MESSENGER. Madam, in Rome, I lookt her in the face, and saw her led betweene her Brother and *Marke Anthony.*

CLEOPATRA. Is she as tall as me?

MESSENGER. She is not Madam.

CLEOPATRA. Didst heare her speake?

Is she shrill tongu'd or low?

MESSENGER. Madam, I heard her speake; she is low voic'd.

CLEOPATRA. That's not so good: he cannot like her long.

CHARMIAN. Like her? Oh *Isis:* tis impossible.

CLEOPATRA. I thinke so *Charmian:* dull of tongue, and dwarfish.

What Majesty is in her gate? Remember,

If ere thou look'st on Majestie.

MESSENGER. She creepes; her motion, and her station are as one:

She shewes a body, rather then a life,

A Statue, then a Breather.

CLEOPATRA.   Is this certaine?

MESSENGER. Or I have no observance.

CHARMIAN. Three in Egypt cannot make better note.

CLEOPATRA. He's very knowing; I do perceiv't,
There's nothing in her yet.
The Fellow has good judgement.

CHARMIAN. Excellent.

CLEOPATRA. Guesse at her yeares, I prythee.

MESSENGER. Madam, she was a widdow.

CLEOPATRA. Widdow? *Charmian,* hearke.

MESSENGER. And I do thinke she's thirtie.

CLEOPATRA. Bear'st thou her face in mind? is't long or round?

MESSENGER. Round, even to faultinesse.

CLEOPATRA. For the most part too, they are foolish that are so. Her haire what colour?

MESSENGER. Browne, Madam: and her forehead
As low as she would wish it.

CLEOPATRA. There's Gold for thee.
Thou must not take my former sharpenesse ill;
I will employ thee backe againe: I finde thee
Most fit for businesse. Go, make thee ready;
Our Letters are prepar'd.

CHARMIAN. A proper man.

CLEOPATRA. Indeed he is so: I repent me much
That so I harried him. Why me think's by him,
This Creature's no such thing.

CHARMIAN. Nothing Madam.

CLEOPATRA. The man hath seene some Majesty, and should know.

CHARMIAN. Hath he seene Majestie? *Isis* else defend: and serving you so long.

CLEOPATRA. I have one thing more to aske him yet good *Charmian:* but tis no matter, thou shalt bring him to me where I will write; all may be well enough.

CHARMIAN. I warrant you Madam. *Exeunt.*

Enter Anthony and Octavia.

ANTHONY. Nay, nay *Octavia*, not onely that—
That were excusable, that and thousands more
Of semblable import, but he hath wag'd
New Warres 'gainst *Pompey*, made his will, and read it,
To publike eare, spoke scantly of me,
When perforce he could not
But pay me tearmes of Honour: cold and sickly
He vented then most narrow measure: lent me,
When the best hint was given him: he had look't
Or did it from his teeth.

OCTAVIA.   Oh my good Lord,
Beleeve not all, or if you must beleeve,
Stomacke not all. A more unhappy Lady,
If this division chance, ne're stood betweene
Praying for both parts:
The good Gods will mocke me presently,
When I shall pray: oh blesse my Lord and husband,
Undo that prayer: by crying out as loud,
Oh blesse my Brother. Husband winne, winne Broth-
    er,
Prayes, and distroyes the prayer, no midway
Twixt these extreames at all.

ANTHONY.   Gentle *Octavia*,
Let your best love draw to that point which seekes
Best to preserve it: if I loose mine Honour,
I loose my selfe: better I were not yours
Then yours so branchlesse. But as you requested,
Your selfe shall go between's: the meane time Lady,
Ile raise the preparation of a Warre
Shall staine your Brother, make your soonest haste
So your desires are yours.

OCTAVIA.   Thankes to my Lord,
The Jove of Power make me most weake, most weake,

Your reconciler: Warres twixt you twaine would be,
As if the world should cleave, and that slaine men
Should solder up the Rift.

ANTHONY. When it appeares to you where this begins,
Turne your displeasure that way; for our faults
Can never be so equall, that your love
Can equally moove with them. Provide your going,
Choose your owne companie, and command what cost
Your heart has mind to.   *Exeunt.*

Enter Enobarbus, and Eros.

ENOBARBUS. How now friend *Eros?*

EROS. There's strange Newes come Sir.

ENOBARBUS. What, man?

EROS. *Cæsar* and *Lepidus* have made Warre upon *Pom-pey.*

ENOBARBUS. This is old: what is the successe?

EROS. *Cæsar* having made use of him in the warres
  'gainst *Pompey:* presently denied him rivalitie, would
  not let him partake in the glory of action, and not
  resting here, accuses him of Letters he had formerly
  wrote to *Pompey.* Upon his own appeale seizes him:
  so the poore third is up, till death enlarge his Confine.

ENOBARBUS. Then would thou hadst a paire of Chaps no
  more, and throw betweene them all the food thou
  hast, they'le grinde the other. Where's *Anthony?*

EROS. He's walking in the garden thus, and spurnes
The rush that lies before him. Cries Foole *Lepidus,*
And threats the throate of that his Officer,
That murdered *Pompey.*

ENOBARBUS.   Our great Navies rig'd.

EROS. For Italy and *Cæsar;* more, *Domitius;*
My Lord desires you presently: my Newes
I might have told hereafter.

ENOBARBUS. Twill be naught, but let it be: bring me to
   Anthony.
EROS. Come Sir.   *Exeunt*.

Enter Agrippa, Mecenas, and Cæsar.
CÆSAR. Contemning Rome, he ha's done all this, and
   more
In Alexandria: heeres the manner of it:
I'th' Market-place on a Tribunall silverd
Cleopatra and himselfe in Chaires of Gold
Were publikely enthrond: at the feet sat
Cæsarion whom they call my father's Sonne,
And all the unlawfull issue, that their lust
Since then hath made betweene them. Unto her,
He gave the stablishment of Egypt, made her
Of lower Syria, Cyprus, Lydia, absolute Queene.
MECENAS. This in the publike eye?
CÆSAR. I'th' common shew place where they exercise.
His Sonnes hither proclaimed the King of Kings:
Great Media, Parthia, and Armenia
He gave to *Alexander*. To *Ptolomy* he assign'd
Syria, Silicia, and Phœnicia: she
In th' abiliments of the Goddesse *Isis*
That day appeared, and oft before gave audience,
As tis reported, so.
MECENAS. Let Rome be thus inform'd.
AGRIPPA. Who queazie with his insolence already,
Will their good thoughts call from him.
CÆSAR. The people knowes it,
And have now receivd his accusations.
AGRIPPA. Whom does he accuse?
CÆSAR. *Cæsar*, and that having in Sicily
Sextus Pompeius spoild, we had not rated him
His part o' the Isle. Then does he say, he lent me

Some shipping unrestored. Lastly he frets
That *Lepidus* of the Triumvirate, should be depos'd;
And, being, that we detaine all his Revenue.

AGRIPPA. Sir, this should be answered.

CÆSAR. Tis done already, and his Messenger gone:
I have told him *Lepidus* was growne too cruell,
That his high Authority abus'd,
And did deserve his chance for what I have conquer'd,
I grant him part: but then in his Armenia,
And other of his conquer'd Kingdomes, I demand the
   like.

MECENAS. Hee'l never yeeld to that.

CÆSAR. Nor must not then be yeelded to in this.

Enter Octavia with her Traine.

OCTAVIA. Haile *Cæsar*, and my Lord, haile most deere
   Cæsar.

CÆSAR. That ever I should call thee Cast-away.

OCTAVIA. You have not call'd me so, nor have you cause.

CÆSAR. Why hast thou stolne upon me thus? you came
   not
Like *Cæsars* Sister: The wife of *Anthony*
Should have an Army for an Usher, and
The neighes of horse to tell of her approach,
Long ere she did appeare, The trees by'th' way
Should have borne men, and expectation fainted
Longing for what it had not. Nay, the dust
Should have ascended to the Roofe of Heaven,
Rais'd by your populous Troopes: but you are come
A Market-maid to Rome, and have prevented
The ostentation of our love; which left unshewne,
Is often left unlov'd: we should have met you
By Sea, and Land, supplying every Stage
With an augmented greeting.

OCTAVIA.   Good my Lord,
To come thus was I not constrain'd, but did it

On my free-will. My Lord *Marke Anthony,*
Hearing that you prepar'd for Warre, acquainted
My greeving eare withall: whereon I begg'd
His pardon for returne.

CÆSAR.   Which soone he granted,
Being an abstract 'tweene his Lust, and him.

OCTAVIA. Do not say so, my Lord.

CÆSAR.   I have eyes upon him.
And his affaires come to me on the wind: where is he
    now?

OCTAVIA. My Lord, in Athens.

CÆSAR. No, my most wronged Sister; *Cleopatra*
Hath nodded him to her. He hath given his Empire
Up to a Whore, who now are levying
The Kings o'th' earth for Warre. He hath assembled
Bochus the King of Lybia, *Archilaus*
Of Cappadocia, *Philadelphos* King
Of Paphlagonia: the Thracian King *Adullas,*
King *Manchus* of Arabia, King of Pont,
Herod of Jewry, *Mitridates* King
Of Comageat, *Polemen* and *Amintas,*
The Kings of Mede and Lycaonia,
With a more larger List of Scepters.

OCTAVIA.   Aye me, most wretched,
That have my heart parted betwixt two Friends
That doe afflict each other.

CÆSAR. Welcom hither; your letters did with-holde our
    breaking forth
Till we perceiv'd both how you were wrong led,
And we in negligent danger: cheere your heart.
Be you not troubled with the time which drives
O're your content, these strong necessities,
But let determin'd things to destinie
Hold unbewail'd their way. Welcome to Rome:
Nothing more deere to me. You are abus'd

Beyond the marke of thought: and the high Gods
To doe you Justice, make his Ministers
Of us, and those that love you. Best of comfort,
And ever welcome to us.

AGRIPPA.   Welcome Lady.

MECENAS. Welcome deere Madam;
Each heart in Rome does love and pitty you:
Onely th'adulterous Anthony, most large
In his abhominations, turnes you off,
And gives his potent Regiment to a Trull
That noyses it against us.

OCTAVIA.   Is it so sir?

CÆSAR. Most certaine: Sister, welcome; pray you
Be ever knowne to patience. My deer'st Sister. *Exeunt.*

Enter Cleopatra, and Enobarbus.

CLEOPATRA. I will be even with thee: doubt it not.

ENOBARBUS. But why, why, why?

CLEOPATRA. Thou hast forespoke my being in these warres,
And say'st it is not fit.

ENOBARBUS.   Well: is it, is it?

CLEOPATRA. If not, denounc'd against us, why should not we be there in person?

ENOBARBUS. Well, I could reply: if wee should serve with Horse and Mares together, the Horse were meerely lost: the Mares would beare a Soldiour and his Horse.

CLEOPATRA. What is't you say?

ENOBARBUS. Your present needs must puzle *Anthony*,
Take from his heart, take from his Braine, from's time,
What should not then be spar'd. He is already
Traduc'd for Levity, and 'tis said in Rome,
That *Photinus* an Eunuch, and your Maides

Mannage this warre.

CLEOPATRA. Sinke Rome, and their tongues rot
That speake against us. A Charge we beare i'th' Warre,
And as the president of my Kingdome will
Appeare there for a man. Speake not against it;
I will not stay behinde.

Enter Anthony and Camidius.

ENOBARBUS. Nay I have done, here comes the Emperor.

ANTHONY. Is it not strange *Camidius,*
That from Tarentum, and Brundusium,
He could so quickely cut the Ionian Sea,
And take in Toryne? You have heard on't (Sweet?)

CLEOPATRA. Celerity is never more admir'd
Then by the negligent.

ANTHONY. A good rebuke,
Which might have well becom'd the best of men
To taunt at slacknesse. *Camidius,* we,
Will fight with him by Sea.

CLEOPATRA. By Sea, what else?

CAMIDIUS. Why will my Lord do so?

ANTHONY. For that he dares us to't.

ENOBARBUS. So hath my Lord, dar'd him to single fight.

CAMIDIUS. Ay, and to wage this Battell at Pharsalia,
Where *Cæsar* fought with *Pompey.* But these offers
Which serve not for his vantage, he shakes off,
And so should you.

ENOBARBUS. Your Shippes are not well mann'd;
Your Marriners are Muliters, Reapers, people
Ingrost by swift Impresse. In *Cæsars* Fleete,
Are those, that often have 'gainst *Pompey* fought,
Their shippes are yare, yours heavy: no disgrace
Shall fall you for refusing him at Sea,
Being prepar'd for Land.

ANTHONY. By Sea, by Sea.

ENOBARBUS. Most worthy Sir, you therein throw away

The absolute Souldiership you have by Land
Distract your Armie, which doth most consist
Of Warre-markt-footemen; leave unexecuted
Your owne renowned knowledge, quite forgoe
The way which promises assurance, and
Give up your selfe meerly to chance and hazard,
From firme Security.

ANTHONY.   Ile fight at Sea.

CLEOPATRA. I have sixty Sailes, *Cæsar* none better.

ANTHONY. Our over-plus of shipping will we burne,
And with the rest full mann'd, from th' heart of Actium
Beate th' approaching *Cæsar*. But if we faile,
We then can doo't at Land.

Enter a Messenger.

Thy businesse?

MESSENGER. The newes is true, my Lord, he is discried:
Cæsar has taken Toryne.

ANTHONY. Can he be there in person? 'Tis impossible,
Strange, that his power should be so, *Camidius,*
Our nineteene Legions thou shalt hold by Land,
And our twelve thousand Horse. Wee'l to our Ship:
Away my *Thetis.*

Enter a Souldier.

                    How now worthy Souldier?

SOULDIER. Oh Noble Emperor, do not fight by Sea;
Trust not to rotten plankes: Do you misdoubt
This Sword, and these my Wounds; let th' Egyptians
And the Phœnicians go a ducking; we
Have us'd to conquer standing on the earth,
And fighting foot to foot.

ANTHONY. Well, well, away.

                    Exeunt Anthony, Cleopatra and Enobarbus.

SOULDIER. By *Hercules* I thinke I am i' th' light.

CAMIDIUS. Souldier thou art: but the whole action
     growes

Not in the power on't: so our Leaders lead,
And we are Womens men.

SOULDIER. You keep by Land the Legions and the
Horse whole, do you not?

VENTIDIUS. *Marcus Octavius, Marcus Justius,*
Publicola, and *Celius,* are for Sea:
But we keepe whole by Land. This speede of *Cæsars*
Carries beyond beleefe.

SOULDIER.   While he was yet in Rome
His power went out in such distractions,
As beguilde all Spies.

CAMIDIUS.   Who's his Lieutenant, heare you?

SOULDIER. They say, one *Towrus.*

CAMIDIUS.   Well, I know the man.

Enter a Messenger.

MESSENGER. The Emperor cals *Camidius.*

CAMIDIUS. With Newes the time's with Labour,
And throwes forth each minute, some.   *Exeunt.*

Enter Cæsar with his Army, marching.

CÆSAR. *Towrus?*

TOWRUS. My Lord.

CÆSAR. Strike not by Land.
Keepe whole, provoke not Battaile
Till we have done at Sea. Do not exceede
The Prescript of this Scroule: Our fortune lyes
Upon this jumpe.   *Exit.*

Enter Anthony, and Enobarbus.

ANTHONY. Set we our Squadrons on yond side o'th' Hill,
In eye of *Cæsar's* battaile, from which place
We may the number of the Ships behold,
And so proceed accordingly.   *Exit.*

*Camidius Marching with his Land Army one way over
the stage, and Towrus the Lieutenant of Cæsar other
way: After their going in, is heard the noise of a Sea
fight. Alarum. Enter Enobarbus.*

ENOBARBUS. Naught, naught, all naught, I can behold
   no longer:
Th' *Antoniad,* the Ægyptian Admirall,
With all their sixty flye, and turne the Rudder:
To see't, mine eyes are blasted.
Enter Scarus.

SCARUS. Gods, and Goddesses, all the whole synod of
   them!

ENOBARBUS. What's thy passion.

SCARUS. The greater Cantle of the world is lost
With very ignorance; we have kist away
Kingdomes, and Provinces.

ENOBARBUS.   How appeares the fight?

SCARUS. On our side like the Token'd Pestilence,
Where death is sure. Yon ribaudred Nagge of Ægypt,
(Whom Leprosie o're) i'th' midst o'th' fight,
When vantage like a paire of Twinnes appear'd
Both of the same, or rather ours the elder,
(The Breeze upon her) like a Cow in June,
Hoists Sailes, and flyes.

ENOBARBUS.   That I beheld:
Mine eyes did sicken at the sight, and could not
Indure a further view.

SCARUS.   She once being looft,
The Noble ruine of her Magicke, *Anthony,*
Claps on his Sea-wing, and (like a doting Mallard)
Leaving the Fight in heighth, flyes after her:
I never saw an action of such shame;
Experience, Man-hood, Honor ne're before,
Did violate so it selfe.

ENOBARBUS.   Alacke, alacke.

Enter Camidius.

CAMIDIUS. Our Fortune on the Sea is out of breath,
And sinkes most lamentably. Had our Generall
Bin what he knew himselfe, it had gone well:
Oh hee has given example for our flight,
Most grossely by his owne.

ENOBARBUS. Ay, are you thereabouts? Why then goodnight indeede.

CAMIDIUS. Toward Peloponnesus are they fled.

SCARUS. Tis easie to't,
And there I will attend what further comes.

CAMIDIUS. To *Cæsar* will I render
My Legions and my horse, six Kings already
Shew me the way of yeelding.

ENOBARBUS.   Ile yet follow
The wounded chance of *Anthony*, though my reason
Sits in the winde against me.

Enter Anthony with Attendants.

ANTHONY. Hearke, the Land bids me tread no more
upon't,
It is asham'd to beare me. Friends, come hither,
I am so lated in the world, that I
Have lost my way for ever. I have a shippe,
Laden with Gold, take that, divide it: flye,
And make your peace with *Cæsar*.

OMNES.   Fly? Not we.

ANTHONY. I have fled my selfe, and have instructed
cowards
To runne, and shew their shoulders. Friends be gone,
I have my selfe, resolv'd upon a course,
Which has no neede of you. Be gone,
My Treasure's in the Harbour. Take it: Oh,
I follow'd that I blush to looke upon,
My very haires do mutiny: for the white

Reprove the browne for rashnesse, and they them
For feare, and doting. Friends be gone, you shall
Have Letters from me to some Friends, that will
Sweepe your way for you. Pray you looke not sad.
Nor make replyes of loathnesse, take the hint
Which my dispaire proclaimes. Let them be left
Which leaves it selfe, to Sea-side straight way;
I will possesse you of that ship and Treasure.
Leave me, I pray a little: pray you now,
Nay do so: for indeede I have lost command,
Therefore I pray you, Ile see you by and by.

Sits downe.

*Enter Cleopatra led by Charmian and Iras, Eros follow-
ing.*

EROS. Nay gentle Madam, to him, comfort him.

IRAS. Do, most deere Queene.

CHARMIAN. Doe, why, what else?

CLEOPATRA. Let me sit downe: Oh *Juno.*

ANTHONY. No, no, no, no, no.

EROS. See you heere, Sir?

ANTHONY. Oh fie, fie, fie.

CHARMIAN. Madam.

IRAS. Madam, oh good Empresse.

EROS. Sir, sir.

ANTHONY. Yes my Lord, yes; he at Philippi kept
His sword e'ne like a dancer, while I strooke
The leane and wrinkled *Cassius,* and 'twas I
That the mad *Brutus* ended: he alone
Dealt on Lieutenantry, and no practise had
In the brave squares of Warre: yet now: no matter.

CLEOPATRA. Ah stand by.

EROS. The Queene my Lord, the Queene.

IRAS. Go to him, Madam, speake to him,
Hee is unqualited with very shame.

CLEOPATRA. Well then, sustaine me: Oh.

EROS. Most Noble Sir arise, the Queene approaches,
Her head's declin'd, and death will seize her, but
Your comfort makes the rescue.

ANTHONY. I have offended Reputation;
A most unnoble swerving.

EROS.   Sir, the Queene.

ANTHONY. Oh whither hast thou led me Ægypt, see
How I convey my shame, out of thine eyes,
By looking backe what I have left behinde
Stroy'd in dishonor.

CLEOPATRA.   Oh my Lord, my Lord;
Forgive my fearfull sayles, I little thought
You would have followed.

ANTHONY.   Ægypt, thou knew'st too well,
My heart was to thy Rudder tyed by th' strings,
And thou should'st stowe me after. O're my spirit
The full supremacie thou knew'st, and that
Thy becke, might from the bidding of the Gods
Command me.

CLEOPATRA.   Oh my pardon.

ANTHONY.   Now I must
To the young man send humble Treaties, dodge
And palter in the shifts of lowness, who
With halfe the bulke o' th' world plaid as I pleas'd,
Making, and marring Fortunes. You did know
How much you were my Conqueror, and that
My sword, made weake by my affection, would
Obey it on all cause.

CLEOPATRA.   Pardon, pardon.

ANTHONY. Fall not a teare I say, one of them rates
All that is wonne and lost: Give me a kisse,
Even this repayes.
We sent our Schoole master, is a come backe?
Love I am full of Lead: some Wine

Within there, and our Viands: Fortune knowes,
We scorne her most, when most the offers blowes.

Exeunt.

Enter Cæsar, Agrippa, and Dollabella, with others.
CÆSAR. Let him appeare that's com for *Anthony.*
Know you him?
DOLLABELLA.   *Cæsar,* tis his Schoolemaster:
An argument that he is pluckt, when hither
He sends so poore a Pinnion on his Wing,
Which had superfluous Kings for Messengers,
Not many Moones gone by.
Enter Ambassador from Anthony.
CÆSAR.   Approach, and speake.
AMBASSADOR. Such as I am I come from *Anthony:*
I was of late as petty to his ends,
As is the Morne-dew on the Mertle leafe
To his grand Sea.
CÆSAR.   Bee't so, declare thine office.
AMBASSADOR. Lord of his Fortunes he salutes thee, and
Requires to live in Ægypt, which not granted
He lessens his requests, and to thee sues
To let him breathe betweene the Heavens and Earth
A private man in Athens: this for him.
Next, *Cleopatra* does confesse thy greatnesse:
Submits her to thy might, and of thee craves
The Circle of the *Ptolomies* for her heyres,
Now hazarded to thy Grace.
CÆSAR.   For *Anthony,*
I have no eares to his request. The Queene,
Of Audience, nor Desire shall faile, so she
From Ægypt drive her all-disgraced Friend,
Or take his life there. This if she performe,
She shall not sue unheard. So to them both.

AMBASSADOR. Fortune pursue thee.

CÆSAR.   Bring him through the Bands:
To try thy Eloquence, now 'tis time: dispatch;
From *Anthony* winne *Cleopatra*, promise
And in our Name, when she requires, adde more
From thine invention, offers. Women are not
In their best Fortunes strong; but want will perjure
The ne're touch'd Vestall. Try thy cunning, *Thidias*,
Make thine owne Edict for thy paines, which we
Will answer as a Law.

THIDIAS.   Cæsar, I go.

CÆSAR. Observe how *Anthony* becomes his flaw,
And what thou thinkest his very Action speakes
In every power that mooves.

THIDIAS.   *Cæsar,* I shall.   *Exeunt.*

Enter Cleopatra, Enobarbus, Charmian, and Iras.

CLEOPATRA. What shall we do, *Enobarbus?*

ENOBARBUS.   Thinke, and dye.

CLEOPATRA. Is *Anthony,* or we in fault for this?

ENOBARBUS. *Anthony* onely, that would make his will
Lord of his Reason. What though you fled,
From that great face of Warre, whose severall ranges
Frighted each other? Why should he follow?
The itch of his Affection should not then
Have nickt his Captain-ship, at such a point,
When halfe to halfe the world oppos'd, he being
The meered question? Tis a shame no lesse
Then was his losse, to course your flying Flagges,
And leave his Navy gazing.

CLEOPATRA.   Prythee peace.

Enter the Ambassador, with Anthony.

ANTHONY. Is this his answer.

AMBASSADOR.   Ay, my Lord.

ANTHONY AND CLEOPATRA 245

ANTHONY. The Queene shall then have courtesie,
So she will yeeld us up.

AMBASSADOR.   He sayes so.

ANTHONY. Let her know't. To the Boy *Cæsar* send this
  grizled head, and he will fill thy wishes to the
  brimme, with Principalities.

CLEOPATRA.   That head my Lord?

ANTHONY. To him againe, tell him he weares the Rose
Of youth upon him: from which, the world should note
Something particular: His Coyne, Ships, Legions,
May be a Cowards, whose Ministers would prevaile
Under the service of a childe, as soone
As i' th' Command of *Cæsar*. I dare him therefore
To lay his gay comparisons a-part
And answer me declin'd, sword against sword,
Our selves alone; Ile write it, Follow me.

ENOBARBUS. Yes, like enough: hye-battell'd *Cæsar* will
Unstate his happinesse, and be Stag'd to' th' shew
Against a Sworder. I see mens judgements are
A parcell of their Fortunes, and things outward
Doe draw the inward quality after them
To suffer all alike, that he should dreame,
Knowing all measures, the full *Cæsar* will
Answer his emptinesse; *Cæsar* thou hast subdude
His judgement too.

Enter a Servant.

SERVANT.   A Messenger from *Cæsar*.

CLEOPATRA. What no more Ceremony? See my Women,
Against the blowne Rose may they stop their nose,
That kneel'd unto the Buds. Admit him sir.

ENOBARBUS. Mine honesty, and I, begin to square.
The Loyalty well held to Fooles, does make
Our Faith meere Folly: yet he that can endure
To follow with Allegeance a falne Lord,
Does conquer him that did his Master conquer,

And earnes a place i' th' Story.

Enter Thidias.

CLEOPATRA.   *Cæsars* will.

THIDIAS. Heare it apart.

CLEOPATRA.   None but friends: say boldly.

THIDIAS. So haply are they friends to *Anthony.*

ENOBARBUS. He needs as many (sir) as *Cæsar* has.
Or needs not us. If *Cæsar* please, our Master
Will leape to be his friend: For as you know,
Whose he is, we are, and that is *Cæsars.*

THIDIAS. So. Thus then thou most renown'd, *Cæsar*
    intreats
Not to consider in what case thou standst
Further than he is *Cæsar.*

CLEOPATRA.   Goe on, right Royall.

THIDIAS. He knowes that you embrace not *Anthony*
As you did love, but as you feared him.

CLEOPATRA.   Oh.

THIDIAS. The scarres upon your honour therefore he
Does pitty, as constrained blemishes,
Not as deserved.

CLEOPATRA.   He is a god,
And knowes what is most right. Mine honour
Was not yeelded, but conquer'd meerely.

ENOBARBUS. To be sure of that, I will aske *Anthony.*
Sir, sir, thou art so leaky
That we must leave thee thy sinking, for
Thy dearest quit thee.   *Exit Enobarbus.*

THIDIAS.   Shall I say to *Cæsar,*
What you require of him: for he partly begges
To be desir'd to give. It much would please him,
That of his fortunes you should make a staffe
To leane upon. But it would warme his spirits
To heare from me you had left *Anthony,*

And put your selfe under his shrowd, the universall
Landlord.

CLEOPATRA. What's your name?

THIDIAS. My name is Thidias.

CLEOPATRA. Most kinde Messenger,
Say to great *Cæsar* this in disputation,
I kisse his conqu'ring hand: Tell him, I am prompt
To lay my Crowne at's feet, and there to kneele.
Tell him from his all-obeying breath, I heare
The doome of Ægypt.

THIDIAS. Tis your noblest course:
Wisedome and Fortune combatting together,
If that the former dare but what it can,
No chance may shake it. Give me grace to lay
My duty on your hand.

CLEOPATRA. Your *Cæsars* Father oft,
(When he hath mus'd of taking kingdomes in)
Bestow'd his lips on that unworthy place,
As it rain'd kisses.

Enter Anthony and Enobarbus.

ANTHONY. Favours? By Jove that thunders. What **are**
thou Fellow?

THIDIAS. One that but performes
The bidding of the fullest man, and worthiest
To have command obeyde.

ENOBARBUS. You will be whipt.

ANTHONY. Approch there: ah you Kite. Now gods and
divels,
Authority melts from me of late. When I cride hoa,
Like Boyes unto a musse, Kings would start forth,
And cry your will. Have you no eares?
I am *Anthony* yet. Take hence this Jacke and whip him.

Enter a Servant.

ENOBARBUS. Tis better playing with a Lyons whelpe,

Than with an old one dying.

ANTHONY.   Moone and starres,
Whip him: wert twenty of the greatest Tributaries
That doe acknowledge *Cæsar*, should I finde them
So sawcy with the hand of she here, what's her name
Since she was *Cleopatra?* Whip him Fellowes,
Till like a Boy you see him crindge his face,
And whine aloud for mercy. Take him hence.

THIDIAS. *Marke Anthony.*

ANTHONY.   Tugge him away: being whipt,
Bring him againe, the Jacke of *Cæsars* shall
Beare us an arrant to him.   *Exeunt with Thidias.*
You were halfe blasted ere I knew you: Ha?
Have I my pillow left unprest in Rome,
Forborne the getting of a lawfull Race,
And by a Jem of Women, to be abusde
By one that lookes on Feeders?

CLEOPATRA.   Good my Lord.

ANTHONY. You have beene a boggeler ever,
But when we in our viciousnesse grew hard
(Oh misery on't) the wise gods seele our eyes
In our owne filth, drop our cleere judgements, make us
Adore our errours, laugh at's while we strut
To our confusion.

CLEOPATRA.   Oh, is't come to this?

ANTHONY. I found you as a Morsell, cold upon
Dead *Cæsars* Trencher: Nay, you were a Fragment
Of *Cneius Pompeyes*, besides what hotter houres
Unregistred in vulgar Fame, you have
Luxuriously pickt out. For I am sure,
Though you can guesse what Temperance should be,
You know not what it is.

CLEOPATRA.   Wherefore is this?

ANTHONY. To let a Fellow that will take rewards,
And say, God quit you, be familiar with

My play-fellow, your hand; this Kingly Seale,
And plighter of high hearts. O that I were
Upon the Hill of Basan, to out-roare
The horned Heard, for I have Savage cause,
And to proclaime it civilly, were like
A halter'd necke, which does the Hangman thanke,
For being yare about him. Is he whipt?

Enter a Servant with Thidias.

SERVANT. Soundly my Lord.

ANTHONY.   Cryed he? and begg'd a Pardon?

SERVANT. He did aske favour.

ANTHONY. If that thy father live, let him repent
Thou wast not made his daughter, and be thou sorry
To follow *Cæsar* in his triumph, since
Thou hast been whipt. For following him, henceforth
The white hand of a Lady Feaver thee;
Shake to looke on't. Get thee backe to *Cæsar*,
Tell him thy entertainment. looke thou say
He makes me angry with him. For he seemes
Proud and disdainfull, harping on what I am,
Not what he knew I was. He makes me angry,
And at this time most easie tis to doo't:
When my good starres, that were my former guides
Have empty left their Orbes, and shot their Fires
Into the Abisme of Hell. If he mislike
My speech and what is done, tell him he has
Hiparchus, my enfranched Bondman, whom
He may at pleasure whip, or hang, or torture,
As he shall like to quit me. Urge it thou:
Hence with thy stripes, be gone.   *Exit Thidias.*

CLEOPATRA. Have you done yet?

ANTHONY. Alacke our Terene Moone is now Eclipst.
And it portends alone the fall of *Anthony.*

CLEOPATRA. I must stay his time?

ANTHONY. To flatter *Cæsar,* would you mingle eyes

With one that tyes his poynts.

CLEOPATRA.   Not know me yet?

ANTHONY. Cold-hearted toward me?

CLEOPATRA.   Ah (Deere) if I be so,
From my cold heart, let heaven ingender haile,
And poyson it in the sourse, and the first stone
Drop in my necke: as it determines so
Dissolve my life, the next Cæsarian smile,
Till by degrees the memory of my wombe,
Together with my brave Egyptians all,
By the discandying of this pelletted storme,
Lye gravelesse, till the Flies and Gnats of Nyle
Have buried them for prey.

ANTHONY.   I am satisfied:
Cæsar sets downe in Alexandria, where
I will oppose his Fate. Our force by Land,
Hath nobly held, and sever'd Navy too
Have knit againe, and Fleet, threatning most Sea-like.
Where hast thou beene my heart? Dost thou heare
    Lady?
If from the field I shall returne once more
To kisse these lips, I will appeare in blood;
I, and my Sword, will earne my Chronicle,
Theres hope in't yet.

CLEOPATRA.   Thats my brave Lord.

ANTHONY. I will be trebble-sinewed, hearted, breath'd,
And fight maliciously: for when mine houres
Were nice and lucky, men did ransome lives
Of me for jests: But now, Ile set my teeth,
And send to darknesse all that stop me. Come,
Lets have one other gawdy night: Call to me
All my sad Captaines, fill our Bowles once more:
Lets mocke the midnight Bell.

CLEOPATRA.   It is my Birth-day:
I had thought t'have held it poore. But since my Lord

Is *Anthony* againe, I will be *Cleopatra*.

ANTHONY. We will yet doe well.

CLEOPATRA. Call all his Noble Captaines to my Lord.

ANTHONY. Doe so, wee'l speake to them,
And to night Ile force
The Wine peepe through their skarres.
Come on (my Queene)
Theres sap in't yet. The next time I doe fight
Ile make death love me: for I will contend
Even with his pestilent Sythe.   *Exeunt.*

ENOBARBUS. Now he'l out-stare the Lightning; to be
    furious
Is to be frighted out of feare, and in that moode
The Dove will pecke the Estridge; and I see still
A diminution in our Captaines braine,
Restores his heart; when valour prayes in reason,
It eates the Sword it fights with: I will seeke
Some way to leave him.   *Exeunt.*

*Enter Cæsar, Agrippa, and Mecenas with his Army,
Cæsar reading a Letter.*

CÆSAR. He cals me Boy, and chides as he had power
To beat me out of Egypt. My Messenger
He hath whipt with Rods, dares me to personall
    Combat.
Cæsar to *Anthony:* let the old Ruffian know,
I have many other wayes to dye: meane time
Laugh at this Challenge.

MECENAS.   *Cæsar* must thinke,
When one so great begins to rage, he's hunted
Even to falling. Give him no breath, but now
Make boot of his distraction: Never anger
Made good guard for it selfe.

CÆSAR.   Let our best heads know,

That to morrow, the last of many Battailes
We meane to fight. Within our Files there are,
Of those that serv'd *Marke Anthony* but late,
Enough to fetch him in. See it done,
And feast the Army, we have store to doo't,
And they have earn'd the waste. Poore *Anthony*.

Exeunt.

*Enter Anthony and Cleopatra, Enobarbus, Charmian,
Iras, Alexas, with others.*

ANTHONY. He will not fight with me, *Domitius?*

ENOBARBUS.   No?

ANTHONY. Why should he not?

ENOBARBUS. He thinks, being twenty times of better
fortune,
He is twenty men to one.

ANTHONY.   To morrow Souldier,
By Sea and Land Ile fight: or I will live,
Or bathe my dying honour in the blood,
Shall make it live againe. Woo't thou fight well.

ENOBARBUS. Ile strike, and cry, take all.

ANTHONY.   Well said, come on:
Call forth my houshold servants, lets to night
(*Enter three or foure Servitours*)
Be bounteous at our Meale. Give me thy hand,
Thou hast been rightly honest, so hast thou,
Thou, and thou, and thou: you have serv'd me well,
And Kings have beene your fellowes.

CLEOPATRA. What meanes this?

ENOBARBUS. Tis one of those odde tricks which sorrow
shoots
Out of the mind.

ANTHONY.   And thou art honest too:
I wish I could be made so many men,

And all of you clapt up together, in
An *Anthony:* that I might doe you service,
So good as you have done.

OMNES.   The gods forbid.

ANTHONY. Well, my good Fellowes, wait on me to
    night:
Scant not my Cups, and make as much of me
As when mine Empire was your Fellow too,
And suffered my command.

CLEOPATRA.   What does he meane?

ENOBARBUS. To make his Followers weepe.

ANTHONY.   Tend me to night;
May be it is the period of your duty,
Haply you shall not see me more, or if,
A mangled shadow. Perchance to morrow,
You'l serve another Master. I looke on you,
As one that takes his leave. Mine honest Friends,
I turne you not away, but like a Master
Married to your good service, stay till death:
Tend me to night two houres, I aske no more,
And the gods yeeld you for't.

ENOBARBUS.   What meane you (sir)
To give them this discomfort? Looke, you weepe,
And I an Asse am Onion-ey'd; for shame,
Transforme us not to women.

ANTHONY.   Ho, ho, ho:
Now the Witch take me, if I meant it thus.
Grace grow where those drops fall (my hearty Friends)
You take me in too dolorous a sense,
For I spake to you for your comfort, did desire you
To burne this night with Torches: know (my hearts)
I hope well of to morrow, and will lead you,
Where rather Ile expect victorious life,
Then death, and Honour. Lets to Supper, come,
And drowne consideration.   *Exeunt.*

Enter a company of Souldiers.

1 SOULDIER. Brother, good night: to morrow is the day.

2 SOULDIER. It will determine one way: Fare you well.

Heard you of nothing strange about the streets.

1. Nothing: what newes?

2. Belike tis but a Rumour, good night to you.

1. Well sir, good night.

They meet with other Souldiers.

2.   Souldiers have carefull Watch.

1. And you: Goodnight; goodnight.

They place themselves in every corner of the Stage

2. Here we, and if to morrow

Our Navy thrive, I have an absolute hope

Our Landmen will stand up.

1. Tis a brave Army, and full of purpose.

Musicke of the Hoboyes is under the Stage.

2. Peace, what noyse?

1. List, list.

2. Hearke.

1.   Musicke i'th' Ayre,

3.   Under the earth.

It signes well, does it not?

3.   No.

1. Peace I say: What should this meane?

2. Tis the god Hercules, whom *Anthony* loved,

Now leaves him.

1. Walke, lets see if other Watchmen

Doe heare what we doe?

2.   How now Masters?

                              Speake together.

OMNES. How now? how now? doe you heare this?

1. Ay, is't not strange?

3. Doe you heare Masters? Doe you heare?

1. Follow the noyse so farre as we have quarter.
Lets see how it will give off.
OMNES. Content: Tis strange.   *Exeunt.*

Enter Anthony, and Cleopatra, with others.
ANTHONY. *Eros,* mine Armour *Eros.*
CLEOPATRA.   Sleepe a little.
ANTHONY. No my Chucke, *Eros,* come mine Armour
     Eros.   *Enter Eros.*
Come good Fellow, put thine Iron on,
If Fortune be not ours to day, it is
Because we brave her. Come.
CLEOPATRA. Nay, Ile helpe too, *Anthony.*
Whats this for? Ah, let be, let be, thou art
The Armourer of my heart: False, false: This, this,
Sooth, la! Ile helpe: Thus it must be.
ANTHONY. Well, well, we shall thrive now.
Seest thou my good Fellow. Goe, put on thy defences.
EROS. Briefly sir.
CLEOPATRA. Is not this buckled well?
ANTHONY.   Rarely, rarely:
He that unbuckles this, till we doe please
To doft for our repose, shall heare a storme.
Thou fumblest *Eros,* and my Queenes a Squire
More tight at this: Dispatch. O Love,
That thou couldst see my warres to day, and knew'st
The Royall Occupation, thou shoudst see
A workeman in't.
Enter an armed souldier.
Good morrow to thee, welcome,
Thou lookst like him that knowes a warlike charge:
To businesse that we love, we rise betime,
And go too't with delight.

SOULDIER. A thousand Sir, early though't be, have on their
Rivetted trim, and at the Port expect you.
Showt. Trumpets flourish. Enter Captaines and Souldiers.
ALEXAS. The Morne is faire: Good morrow General.
ALL. Good morrow Generall.
ANTHONY.   Tis well blowne Lad:
This morning like the spirit of a youth
That meanes to be of note, begins betimes.
So, so: Come give me that, what ere becomes of me,
Fare thee well Dame, what ere become of mee,
This is a Souldiers kisse: rebukeable,
And worthy shamefull checke it were, to stand
On more Mechanicke Complement, Ile leave thee.
Now like a man of Steele, you that will fight,
Follow me close, Ile bring you too't: Adieu.   *Exeunt.*
CHARMIAN. Please you retyre to your Chamber?
CLEOPATRA.   Lead me:
He goes forth gallantly: that he and *Cæsar* might
Determine this great Warre in single fight;
Then *Anthony;* but now—Well on.   *Exeunt.*

Trumpet sound. Enter Anthony and Eros.
EROS. The Gods make this a happy day to *Anthony.*
ANTHONY. Would thou, and those thy scarres had once
     prevaild,
To make me fight at Land.
EROS.   Hadst thou done so,
The Kings that have revolted, and the Souldier
That has this morning left thee, would have still
Followed thy heeles.
ANTHONY.   Who's gone this morning?
EROS. Who? one ever neere thee: call for *Enobarbus.*

He shall not heare thee, or from *Cæsars* Campe,
Say I am none of thine.

ANTHONY. What sayest thou?

SOULDIER. Sir he is with *Cæsar*.

EROS. Sir, his Chests and Treasure he has not with him.

ANTHONY. Is he gone?

SOULDIER. Most certaine.

ANTHONY. Goe *Eros*, send his Treasure after, doe it,
Detaine no jot I charge thee: write to him,
(I will subscribe) gentle adieus, and greetings:
Say, that I wish he never find more cause
To change a Master. Oh my fortunes have
Corrupted honest men. Dispatch *Eros*. *Exit.*

Enter Agrippa, Cæsar, with Enobarbus, and Dollabella.

CÆSAR. Goe forth *Agrippa*, and begin the fight:
Our will is *Anthony* be tooke alive:
Make it so knowne.

AGRIPPA. *Cæsar*, I shall.

CÆSAR. The time of universall peace is neere,
Prove this a prosp'rous day, the three nook'd world
Shall beare the Olive freely.

Enter a Messenger.

MESSENGER. *Anthony* is come into the field.

CÆSAR. Goe charge *Agrippa*,
Plant those that have revolted in the Van,
That *Anthony* may seeme to spend his Fury
Upon himselfe. *Exeunt.*

ENOBARBUS. *Alexas* did revolt, and went to *Jewry* on
Afaires of *Anthony*: there did disswade
Great *Herod* to incline himselfe to *Cæsar*,
And leave his Master *Anthony*. For this paines,
Cæsar hath hang'd him: *Camidius* and the rest
That fell away, have entertainment, but

No honorable trust: I have done ill,
Of which I doe accuse my selfe so sorely,
That I will joy no more.
Enter a Souldier of Cæsars.
SOULDIER.   *Enobarbus, Anthony*
Hath after thee sent all thy Treasure, with
His Bounty over-plus. The Messenger
Came on my guard, and at thy Tent is now
Unloading of his Mules.
ENOBARBUS.   I give it you.
SOULDIER. Mocke not Enobarbus,
I tell you true: Best you saf't the bringer
Out of the host, I must attend mine Office,
Or would have done't my selfe. Your Emperor
Continues still a Jove.   *Exit.*
ENOBARBUS. I am alone the Villaine of the earth,
And feele I am so most. Oh *Anthony,*
Thou Mine of bounty, how wouldst thou have payed
My better service, when my turpitude
Thou dost so Crowne with Gold. This blowes my heart
If swift thought breake it not: a swifted meane
Shall out-strike thought, but thought will doo't. I feele
I fight against thee: No I will goe seeke
Some Ditch, where to dye: the foulst best fits
My latter part of life.   *Exit.*

Alarum, Drummes and Trumpets. Enter Agrippa.
AGRIPPA. Retire, we have engag'd our selves too farre:
Cæsar himselfe has worke, and our oppression
Exceeds what we expected.

Alarums. Enter Anthony, and Scarus wounded.
SCARUS. O my brave Emperor, this is fought indeed,

Had we done so at first, we had droven them home
With clowts about their head.   *Farre off.*
ANTHONY.   Thou bleedst apace.
SCARUS. I had a wound heere that was like a T,
But now tis made an H.
ANTHONY.   They doe retyre.
SCARUS. We'll beat em into Bench-holes, I have yet
Roome for six scotches more.
Enter Eros.
EROS. They are beaten Sir, and our advantage serves
For a faire victory.
SCARUS.   Let us score their backes,
And snatch em up, as we take Hares behind,
Tis sport to maul a Runner.
ANTHONY.   I will reward thee
Once for thy sprightly comfort, and ten-fold
For thy good valour. Come thee on.
SCARUS.   Ile halt after.
                                        Exeunt.

*Alarum. Enter Anthony againe in a March, Scarus, with
others.*
ANTHONY. We have beate him to his Campe: Runne one
Before, and let the Queen know of our gests: to morrow
Before the Sun shall see's, we'll spill the blood
That has to day escap'd. I thanke you all,
For doughty handed are you, and have fought
Not as you serv'd the Cause, but as't had beene
Each mans like mine: you have shewne all *Hectors;*
Enter the Citty, clip your Wives, your friends,
Tell them your feats, whilst they with joyfull teares
Wash the congealement from your wounds, and kisse
The honour'd-gashes whole.
Enter Cleopatra.

Give me thy hand,
To this great Faiery, Ile commend thy acts,
Make her thankes blesse thee. Oh thou day o'th' world,
Chaine mine arm'd necke, leape thou, Attyre and all
Through proofe of Harnesse to my part, and there
Ride on the pants triumphing.

CLEOPATRA.   Lord of Lords,
Oh infinite Vertue, comm'st thou smiling from
The worlds great snare uncaught.

ANTHONY.   My Nightingale,
We have beate them to their Beds.
What Gyrle, though gray
Do something mingle with our yonger browne, yet ha'
    we
A braine that nourishes our Nerves, and can
Get gole for gole of youth. Behold this man,
Commend unto his Lippes thy favouring hand,
Kisse it my Warriour: He hath fought to day,
As if a god in hate of Mankind, had
Destroyed in such a shape.

CLEOPATRA.   Ile give thee friend
An Armour all of gold: it was a Kings.

ANTHONY. He has deserv'd it, were it Carbunkled
Like holy Phœbus Carre. Give me thy hand,
Through *Alexandria* make a jolly March,
Beare our hackt Targets, like the men that owe them.
Had our great Palace the capacity
To Campe this host, we all would sup together,
And drinke Carowses to the next dayes Fate
Which promises Royall perill. Trumpeters
With brazen dinne blast you the Citties eare.
Make mingle with our ratling Tabourines,
That heaven and earth may strike their sounds together,
Applauding our approach.   *Exeunt.*

Enter a Centery, and his Company; Enobarbus followes.

CENTERY. If we be not reliev'd within this houre,
We must returne to' th' Court of Guard: the night
Is shiny, and they say, we shall embattaile
By'th' second houre i'th' Morne.

1 WATCH. This last day was a shrew'd one to's.

ENOBARBUS. Oh beare me witnesse night.

2. What man is this?

1.   Stand close, and list him.

ENOBARBUS. Be witnesse to me (O thou blessed Moone)
When men revolted shall upon Record
Beare hatefull memory: poore *Enobarbus* did
Before thy face repent.

CENTERY.   *Enobarbus?*

2. Peace: hearke further.

ENOBARBUS. Oh Soveraigne Mistris of true Melancholly,
The poysonous dampe of night dispunge upon me,
That life, a very Rebell to my will,
May hang no longer on me. Throw my heart
Against the flint and hardnesse of my fault,
Which being dryed with griefe, will breake to powder,
And finish all foule thoughts, Oh *Anthony*,
Nobler then my revolt is infamous,
Forgive me in thine owne particular,
But let the world ranke me in Register
A Master leaver, and a fugitive:
Oh *Anthony!* Oh *Anthony!*

1.   Lets speake to him.

CENTERY. Lets heare him, for the things he speakes
May concerne *Cæsar.*

2.   Lets doe so, but he sleepes.

CENTERY. Swoonds rather, for so bad a Prayer as his
Was never yet for sleepe.

1.   Goe we to him.

2. Awake sir, awake, speake to us.

1.   Hear you sir?

CENTERY. The hand of death hath raught him.

Drummes afarre off.

Hearke how the Drummes demurely wake the sleepers:

Let us beare him to'th' Court of Guard: he is of note:

Our houre is fully out.

2. Come on then, he may recover yet.   *Exeunt.*

Enter Anthony, and Scarus, with their Army.

ANTHONY. Their preparation is to day by Sea,

We please them not by Land.

SCARUS.   For both, my Lord.

ANTHONY. I would they'ld fight i'th' Fire, or i'th'Ayre,

Wee'ld fight there too. But this it is, our Foote

Upon the hilles adjoyning to the Citty

Shall stay with us. Order for Sea is given,

They have put forth the haven:

Where their appointment we may best discover,

And looke on their endevour.   *Exeunt.*

Enter Cæsar, and his Army.

CÆSAR. But being charg'd, we will be still by Land,

Which as I tak't we shall, for his best force

Is forth to Man his Gallies. To the Vales,

And hold our best advantage.   *Exeunt.*

                Alarum afarre off, as at a Sea-fight.

Enter Anthony, and Scarus.

ANTHONY. Yet they are not joyn'd:

Where yond Pine does stand, I shall discover all.

Ile bring thee word straight, how tis like to goe.   *Exit.*
SCARUS. Swallowes have built
In *Cleopatra's* Sailes their nests. The Auguries
Say, they know not, they cannot tell, looke grimly,
And dare not speake their knowledge. *Anthony,*
Is valiant, and dejected, and by starts
His fretted Fortunes give him hope and feare
Of what he has, and has not.
Enter Anthony.
ANTHONY.   All is lost:
This fowle Egyptian hath betrayed me:
My fleete hath yeelded to the Foe, and yonder,
They cast their Caps up, and Carowse together
Like friends long lost. Triple-turn'd Whore, tis thou
Hast sold me to this Novice, and my heart
Makes onely Warres on thee. Bid them all flye:
For when I am reveng'd upon my Charme,
I have done all. Bid them all flye, be gone.
Oh Sunne, thy uprise shall I see no more,
Fortune, and *Anthony* part heere, even heere
Doe we shake hands? All come to this? The hearts
That pannelled me at heels, to whom I gave
Their wishes, doe dis-Candy, melt their sweets
On blossoming *Cæsar:* and this Pine is barkt,
That over-topped them all. Betray'd I am.
Oh this false Soule of Egypt! this grave Charme,
Whose eye beck'd forth my Wars, and cal'd them home:
Whose bosome was my Crownet, my chiefe end,
Like a right Gypsie, hath at fast and loose
Beguild me, to the very heart of losse.
What *Eros, Eros?*
Enter Cleopatra.
                    Ah, thou Spell! Avaunt.
CLEOPATRA. Why is my Lord enrag'd against his Love?
ANTHONY. Vanish, or I shall give thee thy deserving,

And blemish *Cæsars* Triumph. Let him take thee,
And hoist thee up to th'shouting Plebeians,
Follow his Chariot, like the greatest spot
Of all thy Sex. Most Monster-like be shewne
For poor'st Diminutives, for Dolts, and let
Patient *Octavia* plough thy visage up
With her prepared nailes.　　　　*Exit Cleopatra.*
Tis well th'art gone,
If it be well to live. But better twere
Thou fellst into my fury, for one death
Might have prevented many. *Eros,* hoa?
The shirt of *Nessus* is upon me, teach me
Alcides, thou mine Ancestor, thy rage.
Let me lodge *Licas* on the hornes o'th'Moone,
And with those hands that graspt the heaviest Club,
Subdue my worthiest selfe: the Witch shall dye,
To the young Roman Boy she hath sold me, and I fall
Under this plot: she dyes for't. *Eros* hoa?

Enter Cleopatra, Charmian, Iras, Mardian.
CLEOPATRA. Helpe me my woman: Oh he is more mad
Then *Telamon* for his Shield; the Boare of Thessaly
Was never so imbost.
CHARMIAN. To th'Monument: there locke your selfe,
And send him word you are dead:
The soule and Body rive not more in parting,
Then greatnesse going off.
CLEOPATRA.　　　　　　　To'th'Monument:
Mardian, goe tell him I have slaine my selfe:
Say, that the last I spoke was *Anthony,*
And word it (prethee) pitteously. Hence *Mardian,*
And bring me how he takes my death. To th'Monument.
　　　　　　　　　　　　　　　Exeunt.

Enter Anthony, and Eros.

ANTHONY. *Eros,* thou yet beholdst me?

EROS.   Ay, Noble Lord.

ANTHONY. Sometime we see a clowd thats Dragonish,
A vapour sometime, like a Beare, or Lyon,
A toward Cittadell, a pendant Rocke,
A forked Mountaine, or blew Promontory
With Trees upon't, that nodde unto the world,
And mocke our eyes with Ayre.
Thou hast seene these signes,
They are blacke Vespers Pageants.

EROS.   Ay, my Lord.

ANTHONY. That which is now a horse, even with a
  thought
The Racke dislimes, and makes it indistinct
As water is in water.

EROS.   It does my Lord.

ANTHONY. My good Knave *Eros,* now thy Captaine is
Even such a body: heere I am *Anthony,*
Yet cannot hold this visible shape (my Knave).
I made these warres for Egypt, and the Queene,
Whose heart I thought I had, for she had mine:
Which whilst it was mine, had annext unto't
A Million moe, (now lost:) she, *Eros,* has
Packt Cards with *Cæsars,* and false plaid my Glory
Unto an Enemies triumph.
Nay, weepe not, gentle *Eros,* there is left us
Our selves to end our selves.

Enter Mardian.

Oh thy vilde Lady, she has rob'd me of my Sword.

MARDIAN. No *Anthony,*
My Mistris lov'd thee, and her Fortunes mingled
With thine intirely.

ANTHONY. Hence sawcy Eunuch: Peace! She hath be-
    traid me
And shall dye the death.
MARDIAN. Death of one person, can be paide but once,
And that she has discharg'd. What thou wouldst doe
Is done unto thy hand: the last she spake
Was *Anthony,* most Noble *Anthony:*
Then in the middst a tearing grone did breake
The name of *Anthony:* it was divided
Betweene her heart, and lips: she tendred life
Thy name so buried in her.
ANTHONY.   Dead then?
MARDIAN.   Dead.
ANTHONY. Unarme *Eros,* the long dayes taske is done,
And we must sleepe: that thou departst hence safe
Does pay thy labour richly: goe.   *Exit Mardian.*
                    Oh, plucke off:
The seven-fold shield of *Ajax* cannot keepe
The battery from my heart. Oh cleave my sides.
Heart, once be stronger then thy Continent,
Cracke thy fraile Case. Apace *Eros,* apace:
No more a Souldier: bruised peeces goe,
You have bin Nobly borne. From me awhile.   *Exit Eros.*
I will ore-take thee *Cleopatra,* and
Weepe for my pardon. So it must be, for now
All length is Torture: since the Torch is out,
Lye downe and stray no farther. Now all labour
Marres what it does: yea, very force entangles
It selfe with strength: Seale then and all is done.
Eros? I come my Queene. *Eros?* Say for me,
Where Soules doe couch on Flowers, we'll hand in hand.
And with our sprightly Port make the Ghostes gaze:
Dido, and her *Æneas* shall want Troopes,
And all the haunt be ours. Come *Eros, Eros.*
Enter Eros.

EROS. What would my Lord?

ANTHONY.   Since *Cleopatra* dyed,
I have liv'd in such dishonor, that the gods
Detest my basenesse. I, that with my Sword,
Quarter'd the World, and ore greene Neptunes backe
With Ships, made Citties; condemne my selfe, to lacke
The Courage of a Woman, lesse Noble minde
Then she which by her death, our *Cæsar* telles
I am Conqueror of my selfe. Thou art sworne *Eros,*
That when the exigent should come, which now
Is come indeed: When I should see behind me
Th'inevitable prosecution of disgrace and horror,
That on my command, thou then wouldst kill me.
Doo't, the time is come: thou strikst not me,
Tis *Cæsar* thou defeat'st. Put colour in thy cheeke.

EROS. The gods with-hold me.
Shall I doe that which all the Parthian Darts,
(Though Enemy) lost ayme, and could not.

ANTHONY.   *Eros,*
Wouldst thou be window'd in great Rome, and see
Thy Master thus with pleacht Armes, bending downe
His corrigible necke, his face subdu'de
To penetrative shame; whilst the wheeld seate
Of fortunate *Cæsar* drawne before him, branded
His basenesse that ensued.

EROS.   I would not see't.

ANTHONY. Come then: for with a wound I must be cur'd.
Draw that thy honest Sword which thou hast worne
Most usefull for thy Country.

EROS.   Oh sir, pardon me.

ANTHONY. When I did make thee free, sworst thou not
    then
To doe this when I bad thee? Doe it at once,
Or thy precedent Services are all
But accidents unpurpos'd. Draw, and come.

EROS. Turne from me then that Noble countenance,
Wherein the worship of the whole world lyes.
ANTHONY. Loe thee!
EROS. My sword is drawne.
ANTHONY.   Then let it doe at once
The thing why thou hast drawne it.
EROS.   My deere Master,
My Captaine, and my Emperor, let me say
Before I strike this bloody stroke, farewell.
ANTHONY. Tis said man, and farewell.
EROS. Farewell great Chiefe. Shall I strike now?
ANTHONY. Now *Eros.*
EROS. Why there then: *Killes himselfe.*
Thus I doe escape the sorrow of *Anthonies* death.
ANTHONY. Thrice-Nobler then my selfe,
Thou teachest me: Oh valiant *Eros,* what
I should, and thou couldst not. My Queene and *Eros*
Have by their brave instruction got upon me
A Noblenesse in Record. But I will be
A Bride-groome in my death, and run into't
As to a Lovers bed. Come then, and *Eros,*
Thy Master dyes thy Scholler: to doe thus
I learnt of thee. How, not dead? not dead?
The Guard, how? oh dispatch me.
Enter Decretas and Guards.
1 GUARD. Whats the noise?
ANTHONY. I have done my worke ill friends:
Oh make an end of what I have begun.
2. The Starre is falne.
1. And time is at his Period.
ALL.   Alas, and woe.
ANTHONY. Let him that loves me, strike me dead.
1.   Not I.
2. Nor I.
3. Nor any one.   *Exeunt.*

DECRETAS. Thy death and fortunes bid thy followers flye
This sword but shewne to *Cæsar* with this tydings,
Shall enter me with him.
Enter Diomedes.
DIOMEDES. Wheres *Anthony?*
DECRETAS.   There *Diomed* there.
DIOMEDES. Lives he: wilt thou not answer man?
ANTHONY. Art thou there *Diomed?*
Draw thy sword, and give me,
Sufficing strokes for death.
DIOMEDES.   Most absolute Lord:
My Mistris *Cleopatra* sent me to thee.
ANTHONY. When did shee send thee?
DIOMEDES.   Now my Lord.
ANTHONY.   Where is she?
DIOMEDES. Lockt in her Monument: she had a Prophesy-
    ing feare
Of what hath come to passe: for when she saw
(Which never shall be found) you did suspect
She had dispos'd with *Cæsar,* and that your rage
Would not be purg'd, she sent you word she was dead:
But fearing since how it might worke, hath sent
Me to proclaime the truth, and I am come
I dread, too late.
ANTHONY. Too late good *Diomed:* call my Guard I pre-
    thee.
DIOMEDES. What hoa: the Emperors Guard.
The Guard, what hoa? Come, your Lord calles.
Enter 4 or 5 of the Guard of Anthony.
ANTHONY. Beare me good Friends where *Cleopatra*
    bides;
Tis the last service that I shall command you.
1. Woe, woe are we sir, you may not live to weare
All your true Followers out.
ALL.   Most heavy day.

ANTHONY. Nay good my fellowes, doe not please sharp
    fate
To grace it with your sorrowes. Bid that welcome
Which comes to punish us, and we punish it
Seeming to beare it lightly. Take me up,
I have led you oft, carry me now good friends,
And have my thanks for all.   *Exeunt bearing Anthony.*

*Enter Cleopatra, and her Maides aloft, with Charmian,
and Iras.*
CLEOPATRA. Oh *Charmian,* I will never goe from hence.
CHARMIAN. Be comforted deere Madam.
CLEOPATRA.   No, I will not:
All strange and terrible events are welcome,
But comforts we despise; our size of sorrow
Proportion'd to our cause, must be as great
As that which makes it.
Enter Diomedes.   How now? is he dead?
DIOMEDES. His deaths upon him, but not dead.
Looke out o'th' other side your Monument,
His Guard have brought him hither.
Enter Anthony, and the Guard.
CLEOPATRA.   Oh Sunne,
Burne the great Sphere thou mov'st in, darkling stand
The varrying shore o'th'world. O *Anthony, Anthony, An-
thony*
Helpe *Charmian,* helpe *Iras* helpe: helpe friends
Below, lets draw him hither.
ANTHONY.   Peace,
Not *Caesars* Valour hath orethrowne *Anthony,*
But *Anthonies* hath Triumpht on it selfe.
CLEOPATRA. So it should be,
That none but *Anthony* should conquer *Anthony,*
But woe tis so.

ANTHONY. I am dying Ægypt, dying: onely
I heere importune death a-while, untill
Of many thousand kisses the poore last
I lay upon thy lippes.

CLEOPATRA.   I dare not Deere,
Deere my Lord pardon: I dare not
Lest I be taken: not th'Imperious shew
Of the full-fortun'd *Cæsar,* ever shall
Be brooch'd with me, if Knife, Drugges, Serpents have
Edge, sting, or operation, I am safe:
Your Wife *Octavia,* with her modest eyes,
And still conclusion, shall acquire no honor
Demuring upon me: but, come, come *Anthony;*
Helpe me my women, we must draw thee up:
Assist good friends.

ANTHONY.   Oh quicke, or I am gone.

CLEOPATRA. Heeres sport indeed:
How heavy weighes my Lord?
Our strength is all gone into heavinesse,
That makes the waight. Had I great *Juno's* power,
The strong wing'd Mercury should fetch thee up,
And set thee by Joves side. Yet come a little:
Wishers were ever Fooles. Oh come, come, come.
They heave Anthony aloft to Cleopatra.
And welcome, welcome. Dye when thou hast liv'd,
Quicken with kissing: had my lippes that power,
Thus would I wear them out.

ALL.   A heavy sight.

ANTHONY. I am dying Ægypt, dying.
Give me some Wine, and let me speake a little.

CLEOPATRA. No, let me speake, and let me rayle so hye,
That the false Huswife Fortune, breake her Wheele,
Provok'd by my offence.

ANTHONY.   One word (sweet Queene)
Of *Cæsar* seeke your honor, with your safety. Oh.

CLEOPATRA. They doe not goe together.

ANTHONY.   Gentle heare me,
None about *Cæsar* trust, but *Proculeius*.

CLEOPATRA. My Resolution, and my hands, Ile trust,
None about *Cæsar*.

ANTHONY. The miserable change now at my end,
Lament nor sorrow at: but please your thoughts
In feeding them with those my former Fortunes
Wherein I lived. The greatest Prince o'th' world,
The Noblest: and doe now not basely dye,
Not Cowardly put off my Helmet to
My Countryman. A Roman, by a Roman
Valiantly vanquish'd. Now my spirit is going,
I can no more.

CLEOPATRA.   Noblest of men, woo't dye?
Hast thou no care of me? Shall I abide
In this dull world, which in thy absence is
No better then a Stye? Oh see, my women,
The Crowne o'th' earth doth melt. My Lord?
Oh wither'd is the Garland of the Warre,
The Souldiers pole is falne: young Boyes and Gyrles
Are levell now with men: The oddes is gone,
And there is nothing left remarkeable
Beneath the visiting Moone.

CHARMIAN.   Oh quitnesse, Lady.

IRAS. Shes dead too, our Sovereaigne.

CHARMIAN.   Lady.

IRAS.   Madam.

CHARMIAN. Oh Madam, Madam, Madam.

IRAS. Royall Egypt: Empresse.

CHARMIAN. Peace, peace, *Iras*.

CLEOPATRA. No more but e'en a Woman, and commanded
By such poore passion, as the Maid that Milkes,

And does the meanest chares. It were for me,
To throw my Scepter at the injurious gods,
To tell them that this World did equall theirs
Till they had stolne our Jewell. Alls but naught:
Patience is sottish, and impatience does
Become a Dogge thats mad: then is it sinne,
To rush into the secret house of death,
Ere death dare come to us? How doe you Women?
What, what good cheere? Why how now *Charmian?*
My Noble Gyrles? Ah women, women! Looke
Our Lampe is spent, its out. Good sirs, take heart,
Wee'll bury him: And then, whats brave, what Noble,
Lets doo't after the high Roman fashion,
And make death proud to take us. Come, away,
This case of that huge Spirit now is cold.
Ah women, women! Come, we have no friend
But Resolution, and the briefest end.

                    Exeunt, bearing off Anthonies body.

*Enter Cæsar, Agrippa, Dollabella, Menas, with his
Counsell of Warre.*
CÆSAR. Goe to him *Dolabella,* bid him yeeld,
Being so frustrate, tell him,
He mockes the pawses that he makes.
DOLABELLA.   *Cæsar,* I shall.
Enter Decretas with the sword of Anthony.
CÆSAR. Wherefore is that? and what art thou that dar'st
Appeare thus to us?
DECRETAS.   I am call'd *Decretas.*
Marke Anthony I serv'd, who best was worthy
Best to be serv'd: whilst he stood up, and spoke
He was my Master, and I wore my life
To spend upon his haters. If thou please

To take me to thee, as I as was to him,
Ile be to *Cæsar:* if thou pleasest not, I yeild thee up my
    life.

CÆSAR. What ist thou sayst?

DECRETAS. I say (Oh *Cæsar*) *Anthony* is dead.

CÆSAR. The breaking of so great a thing, should make
A greater cracke. The round World
Should have shooke Lyons into civill streets,
And Citizens to their dennes. The death of *Anthony*
Is not a single doome; in the name lay
A moity of the world.

DECRETAS.   He is dead *Cæsar,*
Not by a publike minister of Justice,
Nor by a hyred Knife, but that selfe-hand
Which writ his honour in the Acts it did,
Hath with the Courage which the heart did lend it,
Splitted the heart. This is his Sword,
I robb'd his wound of it: behold it staind
With his most Noble blood.

CÆSAR.   Looke you sad friends,
The gods rebuke me, but it is a Tydings
To wash the eyes of Kings.

DOLABELLA.   And strange it is,
That Nature must compell us to lament
Our most persisted deeds.

MECENAS. His taints and honors, way equall with him.

DOLABELLA. A Rarer spirit never
Did steere humanity: but you gods will give us
Some faults to make us men. *Cæsar* is touch'd.

MECENAS. When such a spacious Mirror's set before him,
He needes must see himselfe.

CÆSAR.   Oh *Anthony,*
I have followed thee to this, but we doe launch
Diseases in our Bodies. I must perforce
Have shewne to thee such a declining day,

Or looke on thine: we could not stall together,
In the whole world. But yet let me lament
With teares as Soveraigne as the blood of hearts,
That thou my brother, my Competitor,
In top of all designes; my Mate in Empire,
Friend and Companion in the front of Warre,
The Arme of mine owne Body, and the heart
Where mine his thoughts did kindle; that our Starres
Unreconciliable, should divide our equalnesse to this.
Heare me good friends,
But I will tell you at some meeter Season,
The businesse of this man lookes out of him,
Wee'll heare him what he sayes.

Enter an Ægyptian.

Whence are you?

ÆGYPTIAN. A poore Ægyptian yet, the Queene my Mistris
Confin'd in all, she has her Monument
Of thy intents, desires, instruction,
That she preparedly may frame her selfe
To th'way shees forc'd to.

CÆSAR.   Bid her have good heart:
She soone shall know of us, by some of ours,
How honorable, and how kindly We
Determine for her. For *Cæsar* cannot leave to be ungentle.

ÆGYPTIAN. So the gods preserve thee.   *Exit.*

CÆSAR. Come hither *Proculeius,* Goe and say
We purpose her no shame: give her what comforts
The quality of her passion shall require;
Lest in her greatnesse, by some mortall stroke
She doe defeate us. For her life in Rome,
Would be eternall in our Triumph: goe,
And with your speediest bring us what she sayes,
And how you find of her.

PROCULEIUS.   *Cæsar* I shall.

Exit Proculeius.

CÆSAR. Gallus, goe you along: wheres *Dolabella,* to
   second *Proculeius?*

ALL. *Dolabella!*

CÆSAR. Let him alone: for I remember now
How hes imployd: he shall in time be ready.
Goe with me to my Tent, where you shall see
How hardly I was drawne into this Warre;
How calme and gentle I proceeded still
In all my Writings. Goe with me, and see
What I can shew in this.   *Exeunt.*

Enter Cleopatra, Charmian, Iras, and Mardian.

CLEOPATRA. My desolation does begin to make
A better life: Tis paltry to be *Cæsar:*
Not being fortune, hes but fortunes knave,
A minister of her will: and it is great
To doe that thing that ends all other deeds,
Which shackles accidents, and bolts up change;
Which sleepes, and never pallats more the dung,
The beggers Nurse, and *Cæsars.*

Enter Proculeius.

PROCULEIUS. *Cæsar* sends greeting to the Queene of
   Egypt,
And bids thee study on what faire demands
Thou mean'st to have him grant thee.

CLEOPATRA.   Whats thy name?

PROCULEIUS. My name is *Proculeius.*

CLEOPATRA.   *Anthony*
Did tell me of you, bad me trust you, but
I doe not greatly care to be deceiv'd
That have no use for trusting. If your Master
Would have a Queene his begger, you must tell him,

That Majesty to keepe *decorum,* must
No lesse begge then a Kingdome: if he please
To give me conquer'd Egypt for my Sonne,
He gives me so much of mine owne, as I
Will kneele to him with thankes.

PROCULEIUS.   Be of good cheere:
Y'are falne into a Princely hand; feare nothing:
Make your full reference freely to my Lord,
Who is so full of Grace, that it flowes over
On all that neede. Let me report to him
Your sweet dependancy, and you shall find
A Conqueror that will pray in ayde for kindnesse,
Where he for grace is kneel'd too.

CLEOPATRA.   Pray you tell him,
I am his Fortunes Vassall, and I send him
The greatnesse he has got. I hourely learne
A Doctrine of Obedience, and would gladly
Looke him i'th' Face.

PROCULEIUS. This Ile report (deere Lady).
Have comfort, for I know your plight is pittied
Of him that caus'd it.

GALLUS. You see how easily she may be surpriz'd:
Guard her till *Cæsar* come.

IRAS. Royall Queene.

CHARMIAN. Oh *Cleopatra,* thou art taken Queene.

CLEOPATRA. Quicke, quicke, good hands.

PROCULEIUS.   Hold worthy Lady, hold:
Doe not your selfe such wrong, who are in this
Reliev'd, but not betraid.

CLEOPATRA. What of death too that rids our dogs of
    languish?

PROCULEIUS. *Cleopatra,* doe not abuse my Masters
    bounty, by
Th'undoing of your selfe: Let the world see
His Noblenesse well acted, which your death

Will never let come forth.

CLEOPATRA.   Where art thou death?
Come hither come; Come, come, and take a Queene
Worth many Babes and Beggers.

PROCULEIUS.   Oh temperance Lady.

CLEOPATRA. Sir, I will eate no meate, Ile not drinke sir,
If idle talke will once be necessary
Ile not sleepe neither. This mortall house Ile ruine,
Doe *Cæsar* what he can. Know sir, that I
Will not waite pinnion'd at your Masters Court,
Nor once be chastic'd with the sober eye
Of dull *Octavia*. Shall they hoyst me up,
And shew me to the showting Varlotry
Of censuring Rome? Rather a ditch in Egypt
Be gentle grave unto me; rather on Nylus mudde
Lay me starke-nak'd, and let the water-Flies
Blow me into abhorring; rather make
My Countries hygh pyramides my Gibbet,
And hang me up in Chaines.

PROCULEIUS.   You doe extend
These thoughts of horror further then you shall
Find cause in *Cæsar*.

Enter Dolabella.

DOLABELLA.   *Proculeius,*
What thou hast done, thy Master *Cæsar* knowes,
And he hath sent for thee: as for the Queene,
Ile take her to my Guard.

PROCULEIUS.   So *Dolabella,*
It shall content me best: be gentle to her,
To *Cæsar* I will speake, what you shall please,
If youll imploy me to him.   *Exit Proculeius.*

CLEOPATRA.   Say, I would dye.

DOLABELLA. Most Noble Empresse, you have heard of
  me.

CLEOPATRA. I cannot tell.

DOLABELLA.   Assuredly you know me.

CLEOPATRA. No matter sir, what I have heard or
  knowne:

You laugh when Boyes or Women tell their Dreames,

Ist not your tricke?

DOLABELLA.   I understand not, Madam.

CLEOPATRA. I dreampt there was an Emperor *Anthony*.

Oh such another sleepe, that I might see

But such another man.

DOLABELLA.   If it might please ye.

CLEOPATRA. His face was as the heavens, and therein
  stucke

A Sunne and Moone, which kept their course, and
  lighted

The little O, th'earth.

DOLABELLA.   Most Soveraigne Creature.

CLEOPATRA. His legges bestrid the Ocean, his rear'd
  arme

Crested the world: his voyce was propertied

As all the tuned Spheres, and that to friends:

But when he meant to quaile, and shake the Orbe,

He was as ratling Thunder. For his bounty,

There was no winter in't. An *Anthony* it was,

That grew the more by reaping: his delights

Were Dolphin-like, they shew'd his backe above

The Element they liv'd in; in his Livery

Walk'd Crownes and Crownets: Realmes and Islands

As plates dropt from his pocket.

DOLABELLA.   *Cleopatra*.

CLEOPATRA. Thinke you there was, or might be such a
  man

As this I dreampt of?

DOLABELLA.   Gentle Madam, no.

CLEOPATRA. You Lye up to the hearing of the gods:

But if there be, nor ever were one such

Its past the size of dreaming: Nature wants stuffe
To vye strange formes with fancy, yet t'imagine
An *Anthony* were Natures piece 'gainst Fancy,
Condemning shadowes quite.

DOLABELLA.   Heare me, good Madam:
Your losse is as your selfe, great; and you beare it
As answering to the waight: would I might never
Ore-take pursu'de successe: but I doe feele
By the rebound of yours, a griefe that suites
My very heart at roote.

CLEOPATRA.   I thanke you sir:
Know you what *Cæsar* meanes to doe with me?

DOLABELLA. I am loath to tell you what, I would you
    knew.

CLEOPATRA. Nay pray you sir.

DOLABELLA.   Though he be honorable.

CLEOPATRA. He'll leade me then in Triumph?

DOLABELLA. Madam he will, I knowt.

Enter Proculeius, Cæsar, Gallus, Mecenas,
and others of his Traine.

ALL. Make way there, *Cæsar*.

CÆSAR. Which is the Queene of Egypt.

DOLABELLA. It is the Emperor, Madam.

Cleopatra kneeles.

CÆSAR. Arise, you shall not kneele:
I pray you rise, rise Egypt.

CLEOPATRA. Sir, the gods will have it thus;
My Master and my Lord I much obey.

CÆSAR. Take to you no hard thoughts,
The Record of what injuries you did us,
Though written in our flesh, we shall remember
As things but done by chance.

CLEOPATRA.   Sole Sir o'th'world,
I cannot project mine owne cause so well
To make it cleare, but doe confesse I have

Beene laden with like frailties, which before
Have often sham'd our Sex.

CÆSAR.   *Cleopatra* know,
We will extenuate rather then inforce:
If you apply your selfe to our intents,
Which towards you are most gentle, you shall finde
A benefit in this change, but if you seeke
To lay on me a Cruelty, by taking
Anthonies course, you shall bereave your selfe
Of my good purposes, and put your children
To that destruction which Ile guard them from,
If thereon you relye. Ile take my leave.

CLEOPATRA. And may through all the world: tis yours,
     and we
Your Scutcheons, and your signes of Conquest shall
Hang in what place you please. Here my good Lord.

CÆSAR. You shall advise me in all for *Cleopatra*.

CLEOPATRA. This is the briefe: of Money, Plate, and
     Jewels
I am possest of, tis exactly valewed,
Not petty things admitted. Wheres *Seleucus?*

SELEUCUS. Heere Madam.

CLEOPATRA. This is my Treasurer, let him speake (my
     Lord)
Upon his perill, that I have reserv'd
To my selfe nothing. Speake the truth *Seleucus.*

SELEUCUS. Madam I had rather seele my lippes,
Then to my perill speake that which is not.

CLEOPATRA. What have I kept backe?

SELEUCUS. Enough to purchase what you have made
     known.

CÆSAR. Nay blush not *Cleopatra,* I approve
Your Wisedome in the deed.

CLEOPATRA.   See *Cæsar:* Oh behold,
How pompe is followed: Mine will now be yours,

And should we shift estates, yours would be mine.
The ingratitude of this *Seleucus* does
Even make me wilde. Oh Slave, of no more trust
Then love thats hyr'd? What goest thou backe, thou
    shalt
Goe backe I warrant thee: but Ile catch thine eyes
Though they had wings: Slave, soule-lesse, Villaine,
    Dog,
O rarely base!
CÆSAR.   Good Queene, let us intreat you.
CLEOPATRA. O *Cæsar,* what a wounding shame is this,
That thou vouchsafing heere to visit me,
Doing the honor of thy Lordlinesse
To one so meeke, that mine owne Servant should
Parcell the summe of my disgraces, by
Addition of his Envy! Say (good *Cæsar*)
That I some Lady-trifles have reserv'd,
Immoment toyes, things of such Dignity
As we greet moderne friends withall, and say
Some Nobler token I have kept apart
For *Livia* and *Octavia,* to induce
Their mediation; must I be unfolded
With one that I have bred: the gods! it smites me
Beneath the fall I have. Prethee goe hence,
Or I shall shew the Cynders of my spirits
Through th'Ashes of my chance: Wer't thou a man,
Thou wouldst have mercy on me.
CÆSAR.   Forbeare *Seleucus.*
CLEOPATRA. Be it knowne, that we the greatest are mis-
    thought
For things that others doe: and when we fall,
We answer others merits, in our name
Are therefore to be pittied.
CÆSAR.   *Cleopatra,*
Not what you have reserv'd, nor what acknowledg'd

Put we i'th'Roll of Conquest: still be't yours,
Bestow it at your pleasure, and beleeve
Cæsar's no Merchant, to make prize with you
Of things that Merchants sold. Therefore be cheer'd:
Make not your thoughts your prisons: No deere Queen,
For we intend so to dispose you, as
Your selfe shall give us counsell: Feede, and sleepe:
Our care and pitty is so much upon you,
That we remaine your friend, and so adieu.

CLEOPATRA. My Master, and my Lord.

CÆSAR. Not so. Adieu.   *Exeunt Cæsar, and his Traine.*

CLEOPATRA. He words me Gyrles, he words me,
That I should not be Noble to my selfe.
But hearke thee *Charmian.*

IRAS. Finish good Lady, the bright day is done,
And we are for the darke.

CLEOPATRA.   Hye thee againe.
I have spoke already, and it is provided;
Goe put it to the haste.

CHARMIAN. Madam, I will.

Enter Dolabella.

DOLABELLA. Where's the Queene?

CHARMIAN.   Behold sir.

CLEOPATRA.   *Dolabella.*

DOLABELLA. Madam, as thereto sworne, by your com-
    mand
(Which my love makes Religion to obey)
I tell you this: *Cæsar* through Syria
Intends his journey, and within three dayes,
You with your Children will he send before,
Make your best use of this. I have perform'd
Your pleasure, and my promise.

CLEOPATRA. *Dolabella,* I shall remaine your debter.

DOLABELLA. I your Servant:
Adieu good Queene, I must attend on *Cæsar.*   *Exit.*

CLEOPATRA. Farewell, and thankes.
Now *Iras,* what think'st thou?
Thou, an Egyptian Puppet shalt be shewne
In Rome as well as I: Mechanicke Slaves
With greazy Aprons, Rules, and Hammers shall
Uplift us to the view. In their thicke breathes,
Ranke of grosse dyet, shall we be enclowded,
And forc'd to drinke their vapour.
IRAS.   The gods forbid.
CLEOPATRA. Nay, tis most certaine *Iras*: sawcy Lictors
Will catch at us like Strumpets, and scald Rimers
Ballad us out a Tune. The quicke Comedians
Extemporally will stage us, and present
Our Alexandria Revels: *Anthony*
Shall be brought drunken forth, and I shall see
Some squeaking *Cleopatra* boy my greatnesse
I'th'posture of a Whore.
IRAS.   O the good gods!
CLEOPATRA. Nay thats certaine.
IRAS. Ile never see't; for I am sure my Nailes
Are stronger then mine eyes.
CLEOPATRA. Why thats the way to foole their prepara-
    tion,
And conquer their most absurd intents.
Enter Charmian.
Now *Charmian.*
Shew me my Women like a Queene: Goe fetch
My best Attyres. I am againe for *Cidrus*
To meet *Marke Anthony.* Sirra *Iras,* goe
(Now Noble *Charmian,* wee'l dispatch indeed,)
And when thou hast done this chare, Ile give thee leave
To play till Doomesday: bring our Crowne, and all.
A noyse within.
Wherefore's this noyse?
Enter a Guardsman.

GUARDSMAN. Here is a rurall Fellow,
That will not be deny'd your Highnesse presence,
He brings you Figges.

CLEOPATRA. Let him come in.   *Exit Guardsman.*
How poore an Instrument
May doe a Noble deed: he brings me liberty:
My Resolution's plac'd, and I have nothing
Of woman in me: Now from head to foot
I am Marble constant: now the fleeting Moone
No Planet is of mine.

Enter Guardsman and Clowne.

GUARDSMAN.   This is the Man.

CLEOPATRA. Avoyd and leave him.   *Exit Guardsman.*
Hast thou the pretty worme of Nylus there,
That kils and paines not?

CLOWN. Truely I have him: but I would not be the
    partie that should desire you to touch him, for his
    byting is immortall: those that doe dye of it, doe sel-
    dome or never recover.

CLEOPATRA. Remember'st thou any that have dyed on't?

CLOWN. Very many men and women too. I heard of
    one of them no longer than yesterday, a very honest
    woman, but something given to lye, as a woman
    should not doe, but in the way of honesty, how she
    dyed of the byting of it, what paine she felt: Truely,
    she makes a very good report o' th' worme: but he
    that will beleeve all that they say, shall never be
    saved by halfe that they doe: but this is most fallible,
    the Worme's an odde Worme.

CLEOPATRA. Get thee hence, farewell.

CLOWN. I wish you all joy of the Worme.

CLEOPATRA. Farewell.

CLOWN. You must thinke this (looke you) that the
Worme will doe his kinde.

CLEOPATRA. Ay, Ay, farewell.

CLOWN. Looke you, the Worme is not to be trusted, but
in the keeping of wise people: for indeed, there is no
goodnesse in the Worme.

CLEOPATRA. Take no care, it shall be heeded.

CLOWN. Very good: give it nothing I pray you, for it is
not worth the feeding.

CLEOPATRA. Will it eate me?

CLOWN. You must not thinke I am so simple, but I
know the divell himselfe will not eate a woman: I
know, that a woman is a dish for the gods, if the
divell dresse her not. But truely, these same whorson
Divels doe the gods great harme in their women: for
in every ten that they make, the divels marre five.

CLEOPATRA. Well, get thee gone, farewell.

CLOWN. Yes forsooth, I wish you joy o'th'worme. *Exit.*

CLEOPATRA. Give me my Robe, put on my Crowne, I
have
Immortall longings in me. Now no more
The juyce of Egypts Grape shall moyst this lip.
Yare, yare, good *Iras* quicke: me thinkes I heare
Anthony call: I see him rowse himself
To praise my Noble Act. I heare him mocke
The lucke of *Cæsar,* which the gods give men
To excuse their after wrath. Husband, I come:
Now to that name, my courage prove my Title.
I am Fire, and Ayre; my other Elements
I give to baser life. So, have you done?
Come then, and take the last warmth of my lippes.
Farewell kinde *Charmian, Iras,* long farewell.
[*Kisses them. Iras falls and dies.*]
Have I the Aspicke in my lips? Dost fall?
If thou, and Nature can so gently part,
The stroke of death is as a Lovers pinch,
Which hurts, and is desir'd. Dost thou lie still?
If thus thou vanishest, thou tell'st the world,

It is not worth leave taking.

CHARMIAN. Dissolve thicke Cloud, and Raine, that I may say,

The gods themselves doe weepe.

CLEOPATRA.   This proves me base:
If she first meete the curled *Anthony,*
Hee'l make demand of her, and spend that kisse
Which is my heaven to have. Come thou mortall wretch,
With thy sharpe teeth this knot intrinsicate,
Of life at once untie: Poore venemous Foole,
Be angry and dispatch. Oh couldst thou speake,
That I might heare thee call great *Cæsar* Asse, un-
    policied.

CHARMIAN. Oh Easterne starre.

CLEOPATRA.   Peace, peace:
Dost thou not see my Baby at my breast,
That suckes the Nurse asleepe.

CHARMIAN.   O breake! O breake!

CLEOPATRA. As sweet as Balme, as soft as Ayre, as
    gentle.

O *Anthony!* Nay I will take thee too.

What should I stay—   *Dyes.*

CHARMIAN. In this wilde world? So fare thee well:
Now boast thee Death, in thy possession lies
A Lasse unparalell'd. Downy Windowes cloze.
And golden Phœbus never be beheld
Of eyes againe so Royall: your Crownes away,
Ile mend it, and then play—

Enter the Guard rustling in, and Dolabella.

1 GUARD. Wheres the Queene?

CHARMIAN.   Speake softly, wake her not.

1. *Cæsar* hath sent—

CHARMIAN.   Too slow a Messenger.

Oh come apace, dispatch, I partly feele thee.

1. Approach hoa,

All's not well: *Cæsars* beguilde.

2. Theres *Dolabella* sent from *Cæsar:* call him.

1. What worke is here *Charmian?*

Is this well done?

CHARMIAN. It is well done, and fitting for a Princesse

Descended of so many Royall Kings.

Ah Souldier.   *Charmian dyes.*

Enter Dolabella.

DOLABELLA. How goes it here?

2 GUARD. All dead.

DOLABELLA. *Cæsar*, thy thoughts

Touch their effects in this: thy selfe art comming

To see perform'd the dreaded Act which thou

So sought'st to hinder.

Enter Cæsar and all his Traine, marching.

ALL. A way there, a way for *Cæsar*.

DOLABELLA. Oh Sir, you are too sure an Augurer:

That you did feare, is done.

CÆSAR.   Bravest at the last,

She levell'd at our purposes, and being Royall

Tooke her owne way: the manner of their deaths?

I doe not see them bleed.

DOLABELLA.   Who was last with them?

1 GUARD. A simple countryman, that brought her Figs:

This was his Basket.

CÆSAR.   Poyson'd then.

1 GUARD.   Oh *Cæsar:*

This *Charmian* liv'd but now, she stood and spake:

I found her trimming up the Diadem

On her dead Mistris; tremblingly she stood,

And on the sodaine dropt.

CÆSAR.   Oh noble weakenesse:

If they had swallow'd poyson, twould appeare.

By externall swelling: but she lookes like sleepe,

As she would catch another *Anthony*

In her strong toyle of Grace.

DOLABELLA.   Here on her brest,
There is a vent of blood, and something blowne,
The like is on her Arme.

1 GUARD.   This is an Aspickes traile
And these Fig-leaves have slime upon them such
As th'Aspicke leaves upon the Caves of Nyle.

CÆSAR. Most probable
That so she dyed: for her Physitian tels me
She hath pursu'd Conclusions infinite
Of easie wayes to dye. Take up her bed,
And beare her Women from the Monument,
She shall be buried by her *Anthony.*
No Grave upon the earth shall clip in it
A paire so famous: high events as these
Strike those that make them: and their story is
No lesse in pitty, than his glory which
Brought them to be lamented. Our Army shall
In solemne shew, attend this Funerall,
And then to Rome. Come *Dolabella,* see
High Order, in this great Solemnity.   *Exeunt omnes.*

FROM *The Two Noble Kinsmen*

(*Sometimes ascribed to Shakespeare*)

Here they kneel.

PALAMON. Hail Sovereign Queen of secrets, who hast
   power
To call the fiercest Tyrant from his rage;
And weep unto a Girl; that hast the might
Even with an eye-glance, to choak *Marsis* Drum
And turn th' allarm to whispers, that canst make
A Cripple florish with his Crutch, and cure him

Before *Apollo;* that may'st force the King
To be his subjects vassal, and induce
Stale gravity to [daunce], the pould Batchelor
Whose youth like wanton boys through Bonfires
Have skipt thy flame, at seventy, thou canst catch
And make him to the scorn of his hoarse throat
Abuse young lays of Love; what godlike power
Hast thou not power upon? To *Phoebus* thou
Add'st flames, hotter than his the heavenly fires
Did scorch his mortal Son, thine him; the huntress
All moist and cold, some say, began to throw
Her Bow away, and sigh: take to thy grace
Me thy vow'd Soldier, who do bear thy yoak
As 'twere a wreath of Roses, yet is heavier
Than Lead it self, stings more than Nettles;
I have never been foul-mouth'd against thy Law,
Ne'er reveal'd secret, for I knew none; would not
Had I ken'd all that were; I never practis'd
Upon mans wife, nor would the Libels read
Of liberal wits: I never at great feasts
Sought to betray a beauty, but have blush'd
At simpring Sirs that did: I have been harsh
To large Confessors, and have hotly ask'd 'em
If they had Mothers, I had one, a woman,
And women 't were they wrong'd. I knew a man
Of eighty winters, this I told them, who
A Lass of fourteen brided, 'twas thy power
To put life into dust, the aged Cramp
Had screw'd his square foot round,
The Gout had knit his fingers into knots,
Torturing Convulsions from his globy eies,
Had almost drawn their spheres, that what was life
In him seem'd torture: this Anatomie
Had by his young fair [pheare] a Boy, and I
Believ'd it was his, for she swore it was,

And who would not believe her? brief I am
To those that prate, and have done, no Companion;
To those that boast and have not, a defyer;
To those that would and cannot, a Rejoycer.
Yea him I do not love, that tells close offices
The foulest way, nor names concealments in
The boldest language, such a one I am,
And vow that lover never yet made sigh
Truer than I. Oh then most soft sweet goddess
Give me the victory of this question, which
Is true loves merit, and bless me with a sign
Of thy great pleasure.
Here Musick is heard, Doves are seen to flutter, they fall
again upon their faces, then on their knees.
Oh thou that from eleven to ninety reign'st
In mortal bosoms, whose Chase is this world
And we in Herds thy Game; I give thee thanks
For this fair Token, which being laid unto
Mine innocent true heart, arms in assurance   *They bow.*
My body to this business; Let us rise
And bow before the goddess: Time comes on.
Exeunt. Still Musick of Records.

(Act V, scene *i*)

John Webster

(c.1580–1638)

All the Flowers of the Spring

FROM *The Devil's Law-Case*

All the Flowers of the Spring
Meet to perfume our burying:
These have but their growing prime,
And man does flourish but his time.
Survey our progresse from our birth,
We are set, we grow, we turne to earth.
Courts adieu, and all delights,
All bewitching appetites;
Sweetest Breath, and clearest eye,
Like perfumes goe out and dye;
And consequently this is done,
As shadowes wait upon the Sunne.
Vaine the ambition of Kings,
Who seeke by trophies and dead things,
To leave a living name behind,
And weave but nets to catch the wind.

Call for the Robin-Red-brest

FROM *The White Divel*

Call for the Robin-Red-brest and the wren,
Since ore shadie groves they hover,
And with leaves and flowres doe cover
The friendlesse bodies of unburied men.
Call unto his funerall Dole
The Ante, the field-mouse, and the mole
To reare him hillockes, that shall keepe him warme,
And (when gay tombes are rob'd) sustaine no harme,
But keepe the wolfe far thence, that's foe to men,
For with his nailes hee'l dig them up agen.
Let holie Church receive him duly,
Since hee payd the Church tithes truly.

FROM *The White Divel*

Padua. Brachiano's palace

Characters: Vittoria, a Venetian Lady, first married to Camillo, and afterwards to Brachiano; Flamineo, secretary to Brachiano; Zanche, a Moor, servant to Vittoria; Lodovico, an Italian count, but decayed; Gasparo, Flamineo's friend, dependent of the Duke of Florence.

VITTORIA. What, are you drop't?
FLAMINEO. I am mixt with Earth already. As you are
  Noble
Performe your vowes, and bravely follow mee.

VITTORIA. Whither—to hell?

ZANCHE.   To most assured damnation.

VITTORIA. O thou most cursed devill.

ZANCHE.   Thou art caught—

VITTORIA. In thine owne Engine, I tread the fire out
That would have bene my ruine.

FLAMINEO. Will you be perjur'd? what a religious oath
    was Stix that the Gods never durst sweare by and
    violate; ô that wee had such an oath to minister, and
    to be so well kept in our Courts of Justice.

VITTORIA. Thinke whither thou art going.

ZANCHE.   And remember
What villanies thou hast acted.

VITTORIA.   This thy death
Shall make me like a blazing ominous starre,
Looke up and tremble.

FLAMINEO.   O I am caught with a springe!

VITTORIA. You see the Fox comes many times short
    home,
'Tis here prov'd true.

FLAMINEO.   Kild with a couple of braches.

VITTORIA. No fitter offring for the infernall furies
Then one in whom they raign'd while hee was living.

FLAMINEO. O the waies darke and horrid! I cannot see,
Shall I have no company?

VITTORIA.   O yes thy sinnes,
Do runne before thee to fetch fire from hell,
To light thee thither.

FLAMINEO.   O I smell soote,
Most stinking soote, the chimneis a-fire,
My liver's purboil'd like scotch holly-bread;
There's a plumber laying pipes in my guts, it scalds;
Wilt thou out-live mee?

ZANCHE.   Yes, and drive a stake
Thorough thy body; for we'le give it out,

Thou didst this volence upon thy selfe.

FLAMINEO. O cunning Devils! now I have tri'd your love,
And doubled all your reaches. I am not wounded:
Flamineo riseth.

The pistols held no bullets: 'twas a plot
To prove your kindnesse to mee; and I live
To punish your ingratitude—I knew
One time or other you would finde a way
To give me a strong potion—ô Men
That lye upon your death-beds, and are haunted
With howling wives, neere trust them, they'le re-marry
Ere the worme peirce your winding sheete: ere the
Spider
Make a thinne curtaine for your Epitaphes.

How cunning you were to discharge! Do you practise
at the Artillery yard? Trust a woman? never, never;
Brachiano bee my precedent: we lay our soules to
pawne to the Devill for a little pleasure, and a woman
makes the bill of sale. That ever man should marry!
For one *Hypermnestra* that sav'd her Lord and husband, forty nine of her sisters cut their husbands
throates all in one night. There was a shole of vertuous horse-leeches. Here are two other Instruments.

Enter Lodovico, Gasparo, disguised.

VITTORIA. Helpe, helpe!

FLAMINEO. What noise is that? hah? falce keies i'th'
Court.

LODOVICO. We have brought you a Maske.

FLAMINEO.   A matachine it seemes,
By your drawne swords. Church-men turn'd revellers!

GASPARO. *Isabella, Isabella!*

LODOVICO. Doe you know us now?

FLAMINEO.   *Lodovico* and *Gasparo!*

LODOVICO. Yes and that Moore the Duke gave pention to
Was the great Duke of Florence.

VITTORIA.   O wee are lost.

FLAMINEO. You shall not take Justice from forth my
    hands,
O let me kill her.——Ile cut my safty
Through your coates of steele: Fate's a Spaniell,
Wee cannot beat it from us: what remaines now?
Let all that doe ill, take this precedent:
Man may his Fate foresee, but not prevent.
And of all Axiomes this shall winne the prise,
'Tis better to be fortunate then wise.

GASPARO. Bind him to the pillar.

VITTORIA.   O your gentle pitty:
I have seene a black-bird that would sooner fly
To a mans bosome, then to stay the gripe
Of the feirce Sparrow-hawke.

GASPARO.   Your hope deceives you.

VITTORIA. If Florence be i' th' Court, would hee would
    kill mee!

GASPARO. Foole! Princes give rewards with their owne
    hands,
But death or punishment by the handes of others.

LODOVICO. Sirha you once did strike mee, Ile strike you
Into the Center.

FLAMINEO. Thou'lt doe it like a hangeman; a base
    hangeman;
Not like a noble fellow, for thou seest
I cannot strike againe.

LODOVICO.   Dost laugh?

FLAMINEO. Wouldst have me dye, as I was borne, in
    whining?

GASPARO. Recommend your selfe to heaven.

FLAMINEO. Noe I will carry mine owne commendations
    thither.

LODOVICO. Oh could I kill you forty times a day
And us't foure yeere together; 'tweare too little:

Nought greev's but that you are too few to feede
The famine of our vengeance. What dost thinke on?
FLAMINEO. Nothing; of nothing: leave thy idle questions,
I am i'th' way to study a long silence,
To prate were idle, I remember nothing.
Thers nothing of so infinit vexation
As mans owne thoughts.
LODOVICO.   O thou glorious strumpet,
Could I devide thy breath from this pure aire
When't leaves thy body, I would sucke it up
And breath't upon some dunghill.
VITTORIA.   You, my Deathsman!
Me thinkes thou doest not looke horrid enough,
Thou hast too good a face to be a hangeman,
If thou be, doe thy office in right forme;
Fall downe upon thy knees and aske forgivenesse.
LODOVICO. O thou hast bin a most prodigious comet,
But Ile cut off your traine: kill the Moore first.
VITTORIA. You shall not kill her first; behould my breast,
I will be waited on in death; my servant
Shall never go before mee.
GASPARO.   Are you so brave?
VITTORIA. Yes I shall wellcome death
As Princes doe some great Embassadors;
Ile meete thy weapon halfe way.
LODOVICO.   Thou dost tremble,
Mee thinkes feare should dissolve thee into ayre.
VITTORIA. O thou art deceiv'd, I am too true a woman:
Conceit can never kill me: Ile tell thee what,
I will not in my death shed one base teare,
Or if looke pale, for want of blood, not feare.
GASPARO. Thou art my taske, blacke fury.
ZANCHE.   I have blood
As red as either of theirs; wilt drinke some?
'Tis good for the falling sicknesse: I am proud

Death cannot alter my complexion,
For I shall neere looke pale.

LODOVICO.   Strike, strike,
With a Joint motion.

VITTORIA.   'Twas a manly blow,
The next thou giv'st, murder some sucking Infant,
And then thou wilt be famous.

FLAMINEO.   O what blade is't?
A Toledo, or an English Fox?
I ever thought a Cutler should distinguish
The cause of my death, rather then a Doctor.
Search my wound deeper: tent it with the steele
That made it.

VITTORIA.   O my greatest sinne lay in my blood.
Now my blood paies for't.

FLAMINEO.   Th'art a noble sister,
I love thee now; if woeman doe breed man,
Shee ought to teach him manhood: Fare thee well.
Know many glorious woemen that are fam'd
For masculine vertue, have bin vitious,
Onely a happier silence did betyde them.
Shee hath no faults, who hath the art to hide them.

VITTORIA. My soule, like to a ship in a blacke storme,
Is driven I know not whither.

FLAMINEO.   Then cast ancor.
"Prosperity doth bewitch men seeming cleere,
But seas doe laugh, shew white, when Rocks are neere.
Wee cease to greive, cease to be fortunes slaves,
Nay cease to dye by dying." Art thou gonne
And thou so neare the bottome? falce reporte
Which saies that woemen vie with the nine Muses
For nine tough durable lives: I doe not looke
Who went before, nor who shall follow mee;
Noe, at my selfe I will begin and end.
"While we looke up to heaven wee confound

Knowledge with knowledge." ô I am in a mist.

VITTORIA. "O happy they that never saw the Court,

Nor ever knew great Man but by report." *Vittoria dyes.*

FLAMINEO. I recover like a spent taper, for a flash

And instantly go out.

Let all that belong to Great men remember th'ould
   wives tradition, to be like the Lyons i' th' Tower on
   Candlemas day, to mourne if the Sunne shine, for
   feare of the pittifull reminder of winter to come.

'Tis well yet there's some goodnesse in my death,

My life was a blacke charnell: I have caught

An everlasting could. I have lost my voice

Most irrecoverably: Farewell glorious villaines,

"This busie trade of life appeares most vaine,

Since rest breeds rest, where all seeke paine by paine."

Let no harsh flattering Bels resound my knell,

Strike thunder, and strike lowde to my farewell.   *Dyes.*

(*Act V, scene vi, lines 120–276*)

FROM *The Dutchesse of Malfy*

Amalfi. The Palace of the Dutchesse.

Enter Dutchesse and Cariola.

DUTCHESSE. What hideous noyse was that?

CARIOLA. 'Tis the wild consort

Of Mad-men (Lady) which your Tyrant brother

Hath plac'd about your lodging: This tyranny,

I thinke was never practis'd till this howre.

DUTCHESSE. Indeed I thanke him: nothing but noyce,
   and folly

Can keepe me in my right wits, whereas reason

And silence, make me starke mad: Sit downe,

Discourse to me some dismall Tragedy.

CARIOLA. O 'twill encrease your mellancholly.

DUTCHESSE. Thou art deceiv'd,

To heare of greater griefe, would lessen mine—

This is a prison?

CARIOLA. Yes, but you shall live

To shake this durance off.

DUTCHESSE. Thou art a foole,

The Robin red-brest, and the Nightingale,

Never live long in cages.

CARIOLA. Pray drie your eyes.

What thinke you of, Madam?

DUTCHESSE. Of nothing:

When I muse thus, I sleepe.

CARIOLA. Like a mad-man, with your eyes open?

DUTCHESSE. Do'st thou thinke we shall know one another,

In th' other world?

CARIOLA. Yes, out of question.

DUTCHESSE. O that it were possible we might

But hold some two dayes conference with the dead,

From them, I should learne somewhat, I am sure

I never shall know here: I'll tell thee a miracle—

I am not mad yet, to my cause of sorrow.

Th' heaven ore my head, seemes made of molten brasse,

The earth of flaming sulphure, yet I am not mad:

I am acquainted with sad misery,

As the tan'd galley-slave is with his Oare,

Necessity makes me suffer constantly,

And custome makes it easie—who do I looke like now?

CARIOLA. Like to your picture in the gallery,

A deale of life in shew, but none in practise:

Or rather like some reverend monument

Whose ruines are even pittied.

DUTCHESSE. Very proper:

And Fortune seemes onely to have her eie-sight,
To behold my Tragedy:
How now, what noyce is that?
Enter Servant.
SERVANT. I am come to tell you,
Your brother hath entended you some sport:
A great Physitian, when the Pope was sicke
Of a deepe mellancholly, presented him
With severall sorts of mad-men, which wilde object
(Being full of change, and sport,) forc'd him to laugh,
And so th' impost-hume broke: the selfe same cure,
The Duke intends on you.
DUTCHESSE. Let them come in.
SERVANT. There's a mad Lawyer, and a secular Priest,
A Doctor that hath forfeited his wits
By jealousie: an Astrologian,
That in his workes, sayd such a day o'th' moneth
Should be the day of doome; and fayling of't,
Ran mad: an English Taylor, crais'd i'th' braine,
With the studdy of new fashion: a gentleman usher
Quite beside himselfe, with care to keepe in minde,
The number of his Ladies salutations,
Or "how do you," she employ'd him in each morning:
A Farmer too, (an excellent knave in graine)
Mad, 'cause he was hindred transportation,
And let one Broaker (that's mad) loose to these,
You'ld thinke the divell were among them.
DUTCHESSE. Sit *Cariola:* let them loose when you please,
For I am chain'd to endure all your tyranny.
*Here (by a Mad-man) this song is sung, to a dismall
kind of Musique.*

    O let us howle, some heavy note,
       some deadly-dogged howle,
    Sounding, as from the threatning throat,
       of beastes, and fatall fowle.

As Ravens, Schrich-owles, Bulls, and Beares,
    we'll bell, and bawle our parts,
Till yerk-some noyce have cloy'd your eares,
    and corasiv'd your hearts.
At last when as our quire wants breath,
    our bodies being blest,
We'll sing like Swans, to welcome death,
    and die in love and rest.

1 MAD-MAN (ASTROLOGER). Doomes-day not come. yet?
I'll draw it neerer by a perspective, or make a glasse,
that shall set all the world on fire upon an instant: I
cannot sleepe, my pillow is stuff't with a littour of
Porcupines.

2 MAD-MAN (LAWYER). Hell is a meere glasse-house,
where the divells are continually blowing up womens
soules, on hollow yrons, and the fire never goes out.

3 MAD-MAN (PRIEST). I will lie with every woman in my
parish the tenth night: I will tithe them over, like
hay-cockes.

4 MAD-MAN (DOCTOR). Shall my Pothecary out-go me,
because I am a Cuck-old? I have found out his ro-
guery: he makes allom of his wives urin, and sells it
to Puritaines, that have sore throates with over-strayn-
ing.

1. I have skill in Harroldry.

2. Hast?

1. You do give for your creast a wood-cockes head, with
the Braines pickt out on't, you are a very ancient
Gentleman.

3. Greeke is turn'd Turke, we are onely to be sav'd by
the Helvetian translation.

1. Come on Sir, I will lay the law to you.

2. Oh, rather lay a corazive—the law will eate to the
bone.

3. He that drinkes but to satisfie nature is damn'd.

4. If I had my glasse here, I would shew a sight should make all the women here call me mad Doctor.

1. What's he, a rope-maker?

2. No, no, no, a snufling knave, that while he shewes the tombes, will have his hand in a wenches placket.

3. Woe to the Caroach, that brought home my wife from the Masque, at three a clocke in the morning, it had a large Feather-bed in it.

4. I have paired the divells nayles forty times, roasted them in Ravens egges, and cur'd agues with them.

3. Get me three hundred milch bats, to make possets, to procure sleepe.

4. All the Colledge may throw their caps at me, I have made a Soape-boyler costive, it was my master-peece:

Here the Daunce consisting of 8 Mad-men, with musicke answerable thereunto, after which, Bosola (like an old man) enters.

DUTCHESSE. Is he mad too?

SERVANT. 'Pray question him: I'll leave you.

BOSOLA. I am come to make thy tombe.

DUTCHESSE. Hah, my tombe?

Thou speak'st, as if I lay upon my death bed,

Gasping for breath: do'st thou perceive me sicke?

BOSOLA. Yes, and the more dangerously, since thy sick-nesse is insensible.

DUTCHESSE. Thou art not mad sure, do'st know me?

BOSOLA. Yes.

DUTCHESSE. Who am I?

BOSOLA. Thou art a box of worme-seede, at best, but a salvatory of greene mummey: what's this flesh? a little cruded milke, phantasticall puffe-paste: our bodies are weaker then those paper prisons boyes use to keepe flies in: more contemptible: since ours is to preserve earth-wormes: didst thou ever see a Larke in

a cage? such is the soule in the body: this world is
like her little turfe of grasse, and the Heaven ore our
heades, like her looking glasse, onely gives us a miserable knowledge of the small compasse of our prison.

DUTCHESSE. Am not I, thy Dutchesse?

BOSOLA. Thou art some great woman sure, for riot begins
to sit on thy fore-head (clad in gray haires) twenty
yeares sooner, then on a merry milkemaydes. Thou
sleep'st worse, then if a mouse should be forc'd to
take up her lodging in a cats eare: a little infant, that
breedes its teeth, should it lie with thee, would crie
out, as if thou were the more unquiet bed-fellow.

DUTCHESSE. I am Dutchesse of *Malfy* still.

BOSOLA. That makes thy sleepes so broken:
"Glories (like glowe-wormes) afarre off, shine bright,
But look'd too neere, have neither heate, nor light."

DUTCHESSE. Thou art very plaine.

BOSOLA. My trade is to flatter the dead, not the living—
I am a tombe-maker.

DUTCHESSE. And thou com'st to make my tombe?

BOSOLA. Yes.

DUTCHESSE. Let me be a little merry—
Of what stuffe wilt thou make it?

BOSOLA. Nay, resolve me first, of what fashion?

DUTCHESSE. Why, do we grow phantasticall in our death-
bed?
Do we affect fashion in the grave?

BOSOLA. Most ambitiously: Princes images on their
tombes
Do not lie, as they were wont, seeming to pray
Up to heaven: but with their hands under their cheekes,
(As if they died of the tooth-ache)—they are not carved
With their eies fix'd upon the starres; but as
Their mindes were wholy bent upon the world,
The selfe-same way they seeme to turne their faces.

DUTCHESSE. Let me know fully therefore the effect
Of this thy dismall preparation,
This talke, fit for a charnell?
BOSOLA. Now, I shall—
Enter Executioners with a Coffin, Cords, and a Bell.
Here is a present from your Princely brothers,
And may it arrive wel-come, for it brings
Last benefit, last sorrow.
DUTCHESSE. Let me see it—
I have so much obedience, in my blood,
I wish it in ther veines, to do them good.
BOSOLA. This is your last presence Chamber.
CARIOLA. O my sweete Lady.
DUTCHESSE. Peace, it affrights not me.
BOSOLA. I am the common Bell-man,
That usually is sent to condemn'd persons
The night before they suffer:
DUTCHESSE. Even now thou said'st,
Thou wast a tombe-maker?
BOSOLA. 'Twas to bring you
By degrees to mortification: Listen.
Hearke, now every thing is still—
The Schritch-Owle, and the whistler shrill,
Call upon our Dame, aloud,
And bid her quickly don her shrowd:
Much you had of Land and rent,
Your length in clay's now competent.
A long war disturb'd your minde,
Here your perfect peace is sign'd—
Of what is't fooles make such vaine keeping?
Sin their conception, their birth, weeping:
Their life, a generall mist of error,
Their death, a hideous storme of terror—
Strew your haire, with powders sweete:
Don cleane linnen, bath your feete,

And (the foule feend more to checke)
A crucifixe let blesse your necke,
'Tis now full tide, 'tweene night, and day,
End your groane, and come away.

CARIOLA. Hence villaines, tyrants, murderers: alas!
What will you do with my Lady? call for helpe.

DUTCHESSE. To whom, to our next neighbours? they are
    mad-folkes.

BOSOLA. Remoove that noyse.

DUTCHESSE. Farwell *Cariola*,
In my last will, I have not much to give—
A many hungry guests have fed upon me,
Thine will be a poore reversion.

CARIOLA. I will die with her.

DUTCHESSE. I pray-thee looke thou giv'st my little boy
Some sirrop, for his cold, and let the girle
Say her prayers, ere she sleepe. Now what you please,
What death?

BOSOLA. Strangling, here are your Executioners.

DUTCHESSE. I forgive them:
The apoplexie, cathar, or cough o'th' loongs,
Would do as much as they do.

BOSOLA. Doth not death fright you?

DUTCHESSE. Who would be afraid on't?
Knowing to meete such excellent company
In th' other world.

BOSOLA. Yet, me thinkes,
The manner of your death should much afflict you,
This cord should terrifie you?

DUTCHESSE.   Not a whit—
What would it pleasure me, to have my throate cut
With diamonds? or to be smothered
With Cassia? or to be shot to death, with pearles?
I know death hath ten thousand severall doores
For men, to take their *Exits:* and 'tis found

They go on such strange geometricall hinges,
You may open them both wayes: any way, (for heaven
    sake)
So I were out of your whispering: Tell my brothers,
That I perceive death, (now I am well awake)
Best guift is, they can give, or I can take—
I would faine put off my last womans-fault,
I'ld not be tedious to you.
EXECUTIONER. We are ready.
DUTCHESSE. Dispose my breath, how please you, but
    my body
Bestow upon my women, will you?
EXECUTIONER.   Yes.
DUTCHESSE. Pull, and pull strongly, for your able
    strength,
Must pull downe heaven upon me:
Yet stay, heaven gates are not so highly arch'd
As Princes pallaces—they that enter there
Must go upon their knees: Come violent death,
Serve for *Mandragora,* to make me sleepe;
Go tell my brothers, when I am laid out,
They then may feede in quiet.
They strangle her.
BOSOLA. Where's the waiting woman?
Fetch her: Some other strangle the children:
Looke you, there sleepes your mistris.
CARIOLA. Oh you are damn'd
Perpetually for this: My turne is next,
Is't not so ordered?
BOSOLA.   Yes, and I am glad
You are so well prepar'd for't.
CARIOLA. You are deceiv'd Sir,
I am not prepar'd for't, I will not die,
I will first come to my answere; and know
How I have offended.

BOSOLA.   Come, dispatch her:
You kept her counsell, now you shall keepe ours.

CARIOLA. I will not die, I must not, I am contracted
To a young Gentle-man.

EXECUTIONER. Here's your wedding Ring.

CARIOLA. Let me but speake with the Duke: I'll discover
Treason to his person.

BOSOLA. Delayes: throttle-her.

EXECUTIONER. She bites: and scratches:

CARIOLA. If you kill me now
I am damn'd: I have not bin at Confession
This two yeeres:

BOSOLA.   When!

CARIOLA. I am quicke with child.

BOSOLA.   Why then,
Your credit's sav'd: beare her into th' next roome:
They strangle her, and bear her away. Enter Ferdinand.
Let this lie still.

FERDINAND.   Is she dead?

BOSOLA. Shee is what
You'll'd have her: But here begin your pitty—
Shewes the children strangled.
Alas, how have these offended?

FERDINAND.   The death
Of young Wolffes, is never to be pittied.

BOSOLA. Fix your eye here:

FERDINAND.   Constantly.

BOSOLA. Doe you not weepe?
Other sinnes onely speake; Murther shreikes out:
The Element of water moistens the Earth,
But blood flies upwards, and bedewes the Heavens.

FERDINAND. Cover her face: Mine eyes dazell: she di'd
    yong.

BOSOLA. I thinke not so: her infelicitie
Seem'd to have yeeres too many.

FERDINAND. She, and I were Twinnes:
And should I die this instant, I had liv'd
Her Time to a Mynute.
BOSOLA. It seemes she was borne first:
You have bloodely approv'd the auncient truth,
That kindred commonly doe worse agree
Then remote strangers.
FERDINAND. Let me see her face againe;
Why didst not thou pitty her? what an excellent
Honest man might'st thou have bin
If thou hadst borne her to some Sanctuary!
Or (bold in a good cause) oppos'd thy selfe
With thy advanced sword above thy head,
Betweene her Innocence, and my Revenge!
I bad thee, when I was distracted of my wits,
Goe kill my dearest friend, and thou hast don't.
For let me but examine well the cause;
What was the meanenes of her match to me?
Onely I must confesse, I had a hope
(Had she continu'd widow) to have gain'd
An infinite masse of Treasure by her death:
And that was the mayne cause; her Marriage—
That drew a streame of gall quite through my heart;
For thee, (as we observe in Tragedies
That a good Actor many times is curss'd
For playing a villaines part) I hate thee for't:
And (for my sake) say thou hast done much ill, well:
BOSOLA. Let me quicken your memory: for I perceive
You are falling into ingratitude: I challenge
The reward due to my service.
FERDINAND. I'll tell thee,
What I'll give thee—
BOSOLA.   Doe:
FERDINAND. I'll give thee a pardon
For this murther:

BOSOLA. Hah?

FERDINAND.   Yes: and 'tis
The largest bounty I can studie to doe thee.
By what authority did'st thou execute
This bloody sentence?

BOSOLA.   By yours—

FERDINAND. Mine? was I her Judge?
Did any ceremoniall forme of Law,
Doombe her to not-Being? did a compleat Jury
Deliver her conviction up i'th' Court?
Where shalt thou find this judgement registerd
Unlesse in hell? See: like a bloody foole
Th' hast forfeyted thy life, and thou shalt die for't.

BOSOLA. The Office of Justice is perverted quite
When one Thiefe hangs another: who shall dare
To reveale this?

FERDINAND.   Oh, I'll tell thee:
The Wolfe shall finde her Grave, and scrape it up:
Not to devoure the corpes, but to discover
The horrid murther.

BOSOLA. You; not I, shall quake for't.

FERDINAND. Leave me:

BOSOLA. I will first receive my Pention.

FERDINAND. You are a villaine:

BOSOLA. When your Ingratitude
Is Judge, I am so.

FERDINAND.   O horror!
That not the feare of him, which bindes the divels
Can prescribe man obedience.
Never looke upon me more.

BOSOLA.   Why fare thee well:
Your brother, and your selfe, are worthy men;
You have a paire of hearts, are hollow Graves,
Rotten, and rotting others: and your vengeance,

(Like two chain'd bullets) still goes arme in arme—
You may be Brothers: for treason, like the plague,
Doth take much in a blood: I stand like one
That long hath ta'ne a sweet, and golden dreame.
I am angry with my selfe, now that I wake.

FERDINAND. Get thee into some unknowne part o'th'
    world
That I may never see thee.

BOSOLA.   Let me know
Wherefore I should be thus neglected? sir,
I serv'd your tyranny: and rather strove,
To satisfie your selfe, then all the world;
And though I loath'd the evill, yet I lov'd
You that did councell it: and rather sought
To appeare a true servant, then an honest man.

FERDINAND. I'll goe hunt the Badger, by Owle-light:
'Tis a deed of darkenesse.   *Exit.*

BOSOLA. He's much distracted: Off my painted
    honour!—
While with vaine hopes, our faculties we tyre,
We seeme to sweate in yce, and freeze in fire;
What would I doe, were this to doe againe?
I would not change my peace of conscience
For all the wealth of Europe: She stirres; here's life:
Returne (faire soule) from darkenes, and lead mine
Out of this sencible Hell: She's warme, she breathes:
Upon thy pale lips I will melt my heart
To store them with fresh colour: who's there?
Some cordiall drinke! Alas! I dare not call:
So, pitty would destroy pitty: her Eye opes,
And heaven in it seems to ope, (that late was shut)
To take me up to mercy.

DUTCHESSE. *Antonio.*

BOSOLA. Yes (Madam) he is living,

The dead bodies you saw, were but faign'd statues;
He's reconcil'd to your brothers: the Pope hath wrought
The attonement.

DUTCHESSE.   Mercy!   *She dies.*

BOSOLA. Oh, she's gone againe: there the cords of life
    broake:
Oh sacred Innocence, that sweetely sleepes
On Turtles feathers: whil'st a guilty conscience
Is a blacke Register, wherein is writ
All our good deeds, and bad: a Perspective
That showes us hell; that we cannot be suffer'd!
To doe good when we have a mind to it!
This is manly sorrow:
These teares, I am very certaine, never grew
In my Mothers Milke. My estate is suncke below
The degree of feare: where were these penitent foun-
    taines,
While she was living?
Oh, they were frozen up: here is a sight
As direfull to my soule, as is the sword
Unto a wretch hath slaine his father: Come,
I'll beare thee hence,
And execute thy last will; that's deliver
Thy body to the reverend dispose
Of some good women: that the cruell tyrant
Shall not denie me: Then I'll poast to *Millaine,*
Where somewhat I will speedily enact
Worth my dejection.   (Act *IV*, scene *ii*

Milan. Part of the fortifications of the city.

*Enter Antonio and Delio. There is an Echo, from the
Dutchesse's grave.*

DELIO. Yond's the Cardinall's window: This fortification

Grew from the ruines of an aunctient Abbey:
And to yond side o'th' river, lies a wall
(Peece of a Cloyster) which in my opinion
Gives the best Eccho, that you ever heard;
So hollow, and so dismall, and withall
So plaine in the destinction of our words,
That many have supposde it is a Spirit
That answeres.
ANTONIO. I doe love these aunctient ruynes:
We never tread upon them, but we set
Our foote upon some reverend History.
And questionles, here in this open Court
(Which now lies naked to the injuries
Of stormy weather) some men lye Enterr'd
Lov'd the Church so well, and gave so largely to't,
They thought it should have canopide their Bones
Till Doombes-day: But all things have their end:
Churches, and Citties (which have diseases like to men)
Must have like death that we have.
ECCHO. *Like death that we have.*
DELIO. Now the *Eccho* hath caught you:
ANTONIO. It groan'd (me thought) and gave
A very deadly Accent?
ECCHO. *Deadly Accent.*
DELIO. I told you 'twas a pretty one: You may make it
A Huntes-man, or a Faulconer, a Musitian,
Or a Thing of Sorrow.
ECCHO. *A Thing of Sorrow.*
ANTONIO. Ay sure: that suites it best.
ECCHO. *That suites it best.*
ANTONIO. 'Tis very like my wifes voyce.
ECCHO. *Ay, wifes-voyce.*
DELIO. Come: let's walke farther from't:
I would not have you go to th' *Cardinalls* to-night:
Doe not.

ECCHO. *Doe not.*

DELIO. Wisdome doth not more moderate wasting Sorrow

Then time: take time for't: be mindfull of thy safety.

ECCHO. *Be mindfull of thy safety.*

ANTONIO. Necessitie compells me:

Make scruteny throughout the passages

Of your owne life; you'll find it impossible

To flye your fate.

ECCHO. *O flye your fate.*

DELIO. Harke: the dead stones seeme to have pitty on
you

And give you good counsell.

ANTONIO. *Eccho,* I will not talke with thee;

For thou art a dead Thing.

ECCHO. *Thou art a dead Thing.*

ANTONIO. My Dutchesse is asleepe now,

And her litle-Ones, I hope sweetly: oh Heaven

Shall I never see her more?

ECCHO. *Never see her more:*

ANTONIO. I mark'd not one repetition of the *Eccho*

But that: and on the sudden, a cleare light

Presented me a face folded in sorrow.

DELIO. Your fancy; meerely.

ANTONIO. Come: I'll be out of this Ague;

For to live thus, is not indeed to live:

It is a mockery, and abuse of life—

I will not henceforth save my selfe by halves,

Loose all, or nothing.

DELIO. Your owne vertue save you!

I'll fetch your eldest sonne; and second you:

It may be that the sight of his owne blood

Spred in so sweet a figure, may beget

The more compassion.

ANTONIO. How ever, fare you well:
Though in our miseries, Fortune have a part,
Yet, in our noble suffrings, she hath none—
Contempt of paine, that we may call our owne.

(*Act V, scene iii*)

Ben Jonson

(1572–1637)

FROM *The Poetaster*

OVID, JR. O sacred *poesie*, thou spirit of artes,
The soule of science, and the queene of soules,
What prophane violence, almost sacriledge,
Hath here beene offered thy divinities!
That thine owne guiltlesse povertie should arme
Prodigious ignorance to wound thee thus!
For thence, is all their force of argument
Drawne forth against thee; or from the abuse
Of thy great powers in adultrate braines:
When, would men learne but to distinguish spirits,
And set true difference twixt those jaded wits
That runne a broken pase for common hire,
And the high raptures of a happy *Muse*,
Borne on the wings of her immortall thought,
That kickes at earth with a disdainefull heele,
And beats at heaven gates with her bright hooves;
They would not then with such distorted faces,
And desp'rate censures stab at *poesie*.
They would admire bright knowledge, and their minds
Should ne're descend on so unworthy objects,
As gold, or titles: they would dread farre more,
To be thought ignorant, then be knowne poore.
"The time was once, when wit drown'd wealth: but
   now,

316

Your onely barbarisme is t'have wit, and want.
No matter now in vertue who excells,
He, that hath coine, hath all perfection else."

(Act I, scene ii)

CÆSAR. There is no bountie to be shew'd to such,
As have no reall goodnesse: Bountie is
A spice of vertue: and what vertuous act
Can take effect on them, that have no power
Of equall habitude to apprehend it,
But live in worship of that idoll, vice,
As if there were no vertue, but in shade
Of strong imagination, meerely enforc't?
This shewes, their knowledge is meere ignorance;
Their farre-fetcht dignitie of soule, a phansy;
And all their square pretext of gravitie
A meere vaine glorie: hence, away with 'hem.
I will preferre for knowledge, none, but such
As rule their lives by it, and can becalme
All sea of humour, with the marble *trident*
Of their strong spirits: Others fight below
With gnats, and shaddowes, others nothing know.

(Act III, scene vi)

The Vision of Delight

[A MASQUE.]

Presented at Court in Christmas, 1617.

The Scene—A Street in perspective of faire building discovered.

Delight is seene to come as afarre off, accompanied with

Grace, Love, Harmonie, Revell, Sport, Laughter. Wonder following. Delight spake in song (stylo recitativo).

> Let us play, and dance, and sing,
>   Let us now turne every sort
> O' the pleasures of the Spring,
>   To the graces of a Court.

From ayre, from cloud, from dreams, from toyes,
  To sounds, to sence, to love, to joyes;
Let your shewes be new, as strange,
  Let them oft and sweetly varie;
Let them haste so to their change,
  As the Seers may not tarrie;
Too long to 'expect the pleasing'st sight
  Doth take away from the delight.

Here the first Anti-maske enter'd. A she Monster delivered of sixe Burratines, that dance with six Pantalones, which done, Delight, spoke againe.

> Yet heare what your delight doth pray:
>   All sowre and sullen looks away,
>   That are the servants of the day;
>   Our sports are of the humorous night,
>   Who feeds the stars that give her light,
>   And useth (then her wont) more bright,
>   To help the vision of *Delight*.

Here the Night rises, and tooke her Chariot bespangled with starres. Delight, proceeds.

> See, see her Scepter, and her Crowne
>   Are all of flame, and from her gowne
>   A traine of light comes waving down.
> This night in dew she will not steepe
>   The braine, nor locke the sence in sleepe;
>   But all awake with *Phantomes* keepe,
>   And those to make *Delight* more deep.

By this time the Night, and Moone being both risen;
Night hovering over the place, sung.

> Breake, *Phant'sie,* from thy cave of cloud,
>   And spread thy purple wings;
> Now all thy figures are allow'd,
>   And various shapes of things:
> Create of ayrie formes, a streame;
>   It must have bloud, and naught of fleame,
> And though it be a waking dreame;

>   THE QUIRE
>   Yet let it like an odour rise
>   To all the Sences here,
>   And fall like sleep upon their eies,
>   Or musick in their eare.

The Scene here changed to Cloud, and Phant'sie break-
ing forth, spake.

Bright Night, I obey thee, and am come at thy call,
But it is no one dreame that can please these all;
Wherefore I would know what Dreames would delight
        'em;
For never was Phant'sie more loth to affright 'em.
And Phant'sie, I tell you, has dreams that have wings,
And dreams that have honey, and dreams that have
        stings;
Dreames of the maker, and Dreames of the teller,
Dreames of the kitchin, and Dreames of the Cellar:
Some that are tall, and some that are Dwarffes,
Some that are halter'd, and some that weare scarffes;
Some that are proper, and signifie o' thing,
And some another, and some that are nothing:
For say the French Verdingale, and the French hood
Were here to dispute; must it be understood,
A feather, for a wispe, were a fit moderator?

Your Ostrich, beleeve it, 's no faithfull translator
Of perfect Utopian; And then 'twere an od-piece
To see the conclusion peepe forth at a cod-piece.
    The politique pudding hath still his two ends,
Tho' the bellows, and the bag-pipe were nev'r so good
        friends:
And who can report what offence it would be
For the Squirrell to see a Dog clime a tree?
If a Dreame should come in now, to make you afeard,
With a Windmill on his head, and bells at his beard;
Would you streight weare your spectacles, here, at your
        toes,
And your boots o' your browes, and your spurs o' your
        nose?
Your Whale he will swallow a hogs-head for a pill;
But the maker o' the mouse-trap, is he that hath skill.
And the nature of the Onion, is to draw teares,
As well as the Mustard; peace, pitchers have eares,
And Shitlecocks wings; these things, doe not mind 'em.
If the Bell have any sides, the clapper will find 'em:
There's twice so much musicke in beating the tabor,
As i' the Stock-fish, and somewhat lesse labour.
Yet all this while, no proportion is boasted
'Twixt an egge, and an Oxe, though both have been
        rosted,
For grant the most Barbers can play o' the Citterne,
Is it requisite a Lawyer should plead to a Ghitterne?
    You will say now, the Morris-bells were but bribes
To make the heele forget that ev'r it had kibes;
I say, let the wine make nev'r so good jelly,
The conscience o' the bottle, is much i' the belly:
For why? doe but take common Councell i' your way,
And tell me who'le then set a bottle of hay
Before the old Usurer, and to his horse
A slice of salt-butter, perverting the course

Of civill societie? Open that gap,
And out skip your fleas, foure and twenty at a clap,
With a chaine and a trundle-bed following at th'heeles,
And will they not cry then, the world runs a wheeles:
As for example, a belly, and no face,
With the bill of a Shoveler, may here come in place;
The haunches of a Drum, with the feet of a pot,
And the tayle of a Kentishman to it; why not?
Yet would I take the stars to be cruell,
If the Crab, and the Ropemaker ever fight duell,
On any dependance, be it right, be it wrong.
But mum; a thread may be drawne out too long.

*Here the second Anti-masque of Phantasmes came forth,
which danced, Phant'sie proceeded.*

Why, this, you will say, was phantasticall now,
As the Cocke, and the Bull, the Whale, and the Cow;
   But vanish away, I have change to present you,
And such as (I hope) will more truly content you:
   Behold the gold-haired *Houre* descending here,
That keepes the gate of Heaven, and turnes the yeare,
   Alreadie with her sight, how she doth cheare,
And makes another face of things appeare.

*Here one of the Houres descending, the whole Scene
changed to the Bower of Zephyrus, whilst Peace sung,
as followeth.*

   Why looke you so, and all turne dumbe!
      To see the opener of the New-yeare come?
   My presence rather should invite,
      And ayd, and urge, and call to your delight.
   The many pleasures that I bring
      Are all of youth, of heate, of life, and spring,
   And were prepard to warme your blood,
      Not fixe it thus as if you Statues stood.

THE QUIRE

We see, we heare, we feele, we taste,
We smell the change in every flowre,
We onely wish that all could last,
And be as new still as the houre.

The Song ended, Wonder spake.

Wonder must speake, or breake; what is this? Growes
The wealth of Nature here, or Art? It showes
As if *Favonius,* father of the Spring,
Who, in the verdant Meads, doth reigne sole king,
Had rowsd him here, and shooke his feathers, wet
With purple-swelling Nectar? and had let
The sweet and fruitfull dew fall on the ground
To force out all the flowers that might be found?
   Or a *Minerva* with her needle had
Th'enamourd earth with all her riches clad,
And made the downie *Zephire* as he flew
Still to be followd with the Springs best hue?
   The gaudie Peacocke boasts not in his traine,
So many lights and shadowes, nor the raine—
Resolving *Iris,* when the Sun doth court her,
Nor purple Phesant while his Aunt doth sport her
To heare him crow; and with a pearched pride
Wave his dis-coloured necke, and purple side.
   I have not seene the place could more surprize,
It looks (me thinkes) like one of natures eyes,
Of her whole bodie set in art? Behold!
How the blew Binde-weed doth it selfe infold
With Honey-suckle, and both these intwine
Themselves with Bryonie, and Jessamine,
To cast a kinde and odoriferous shade!

PHANT'SIE

How better then they are, are all things made
By *Wonder!* But a while refresh thine eye,
Ile put thee to thy oftner, what, and why?

*Here (to a loud musicke) the Bower opens, and the
Maskers discovered, as the glories of the Spring. Wonder
againe spake.*

Thou wilt indeed; what better change appeares?
Whence is it that the ayre so sudden cleares,
And all things in a moment turne so milde?
Whose breath or beames, have got proud earth with
        child,
Of all the treasure that great Nature's worth,
And makes her every minute to bring forth?
How comes it Winter is so quite forc't hence,
And lockt up under ground? that every sence
Hath severall objects? Trees have got their heads,
The fields their coats? that now the shining Meads
Doe boast the *Paunce,* the *Lillie,* and the *Rose;*
And every flower doth laugh as *Zephire* blowes?
That Seas are now more even then the Land?
The Rivers runne as smoothed by his hand;
Onely their heads are crisped by his stroake:
How plaies the Yeareling with his brow scarce broke
Now in the open Grasse? and frisking Lambs
Make wanton Salts about their drie-suckt Dams;
Who to repaire their bags doe rob the fields?
    How is't each bough a severall musicke yeilds?
The lusty *Throstle,* early *Nightingale*
Accord in tune, though varie in their tale?
The chirping *Swallow* cald forth by the Sun,
And crested *Larke* doth his division run?
The yellow *Bees,* the ayre with murmure fill?

The *Finches* caroll, and the *Turtles* bill?
Whose power is this? what God?

PHANT'SIE

Behold a King
Whose presence maketh this perpetuall *Spring*,
The glories of which Spring grow in that Bower,
And are the marks and beauties of his power.

To which the Quire answered.

'Tis he, 'tis he, and no power els,
That makes all this what *Phant'sie* tels;
    The founts, the flowers, the birds, the bees,
The heards, the flocks, the grasse, the trees,
Do all confesse him; but most *These*
Who call him lord of the foure Seas,
King of the lesse and greater Iles,
And all those happy when he smiles.
    Advance, his favour calls you to advance,
And do your (this nights) homage in a dance.

*Here they danced their entry, after which they sung
againe.*

Againe, againe; you cannot be
Of such a true delight too free,
    Which who once saw would ever see;
And if they could the object prize,
Would while it lasts not thinke to rise,
    But wish their bodies all were eyes.

They Danc'd their maine Dance, after which they sung.

In curious knots and mazes so
The Spring at first was taught to go;
And *Zephire*, when he came to wooe
His *Flora*, had their motions too,

And thence did *Venus* learne to lead
Th' *Idalian* Braules, and so to tread
As if the wind, not she did walke;
Nor prest a flower, nor bow'd a stalke.

*They Danc'd with Ladies, and the whole Revells fol-
lowed; after which Aurora appeared (the Night and
Moone descended) and this Epilogue followed.*

AURORA

I was not wearier where I lay
By frozen *Tythons* side to night;
Then I am willing now to stay,
And be a part of your delight.
    But I am urged by the Day,
Against my will, to bid you come away.

THE QUIRE

They yeild to Time, and so must all.
As Night to sport, Day doth to action call,
    Which they the rather doe obey,
Because the Morne, with Roses strew's the way.

Here they Danc'd their going off, and Ended.

Song

FROM *Cynthia's Revells*

Slow, slow, fresh fount, keepe time with my salt teares;
    Yet slower, yet, ô faintly gentle springs:
List to the heavy part the musique beares,
        "Woe weepes out her division, when shee sings.
            Droupe hearbs, and flowres;
            Fall griefe in showres;

Our beauties are not ours":
                              O, I could still
(Like melting snow upon some craggie hill,)
        drop, drop, drop, drop,
Since natures pride is, now, a wither'd daffodill.

The Hymne

FROM *Cynthia's Revells*

Queene, and *Huntress,* chaste, and faire,
Now the Sunne is laid to sleepe,
Seated in thy silver chaire,
State in wonted manner keepe:
  Hesperus intreats thy light,
  Goddesse, excellently bright.

Earth, let not thy envious shade
Dare it selfe to interpose;
Cynthias shining orbe was made
Heaven to cleere, when day did close:
  Blesse us then with wished sight,
  Goddesse, excellently bright.

Lay thy bow of pearle apart,
And thy cristall-shining quiver;
Give unto the flying hart
Space to breathe, how short soever:
  Thou that mak'st a day of night,
  Goddesse, excellently bright.

Karolin's Song

FROM *The Sad Shepherd*

Though I am young, and cannot tell,
    Either what Death, or Love is well,
Yet I have heard, they both beare darts,
    And both doe ayme at humane hearts:
And then againe, I have beene told
    Love wounds with heat, as Death with cold;
So that I feare, they doe but bring
    Extreames to touch, and meane one thing.

As in a ruine, we it call
    One thing to be blowne up, or fall;
Or to our end, like way may have,
    By a flash of lightning, or a wave:
So Loves inflamed shaft, or brand,
    May kill as soone as Deaths cold hand;
Except Loves fires the vertue have
    To fright the frost out of the grave.

On My First Sonne

Farewell, thou child of my right hand, and joy;
    My sinne was too much hope of thee, lov'd boy,
Seven yeeres tho'wert lent to me, and I thee pay,
    Exacted by thy fate, on the just day.
O, could I loose all father, now. For why
    Will man lament the state he should envie?
To have so soone scap'd worlds, and fleshes rage,

And, if no other miserie, yet age?
Rest in soft peace, and, ask'd, say here doth lye
BEN. JONSON his best piece of *poetrie*.
For whose sake, hence-forth, all his vowes be such,
As what he loves may never like too much.

Epitaph on S[alomon] P[avy] a Child of Q. El[izabeths] Chapel

Weepe with me all you that read
    This little storie:
And know, for whom a teare you shed,
    Death's selfe is sorry.
'Twas a child, that so did thrive
    In grace, and feature,
As *Heaven* and *Nature* seem'd to strive
    Which own'd the creature.
Yeeres he numbred scarce thirteene
    When *Fates* turn'd cruell,
Yet three fill'd *Zodiackes* had he beene
    The stages jewell;
And did act (what now we mone)
    Old men so duely,
As, sooth, the *Parcæ* thought him one,
    He plai'd so truely.
So, by error, to his fate
    They all consented;
But viewing him since (alas, too late)
    They have repented.
And have sought (to give new birth)
    In bathes to steepe him;
But, being so much too good for earth,
    Heaven vowes to keepe him.

Song: To Celia

Drinke to me, onely, with thine eyes,
   And I will pledge with mine;
Or leave a kisse but in the cup,
   And Ile not looke for wine.
The thirst, that from the soule doth rise,
   Doth aske a drinke divine:
But might I of JOVE's *Nectar* sup,
   I would not change for thine.

I sent thee, late, a rosie wreath,
   Not so much honoring thee,
As giving it a hope, that there
   It could not withered bee.
But thou thereon did'st onely breath,
   And sent'st it backe to mee:
Since when it growes, and smells, I sweare,
   Not of it selfe, but thee.

Inviting a Friend to Supper

Tonight, grave sir, both my poore house, and I
   Doe equally desire your companie:
Not that we thinke us worthy such a ghest,
   But that your worth will dignifie our feast,
With those that come; whose grace may make that
   seeme
   Something, which, else, could hope for no esteeme.
It is the faire acceptance, Sir, creates
   The entertaynment perfect: not the cates.

Yet shall you have, to rectifie your palate,
    An olive, capers, or some better sallade
Ushring the mutton; with a short-leg'd hen,
    If we can get her, full of egs, and then,
Limons, and wine for sauce: to these, a coney
    Is not to be despair'd of, for our money;
And, though fowle, now, be scarce, yet there are clarkes,
    The skie not falling, thinke we may have larkes.
Ile tell you of more, and lye, so you will come:
    Of partrich, pheasant, wood-cock, of which some
May yet be there; and godwit, if we can:
    Knat, raile, and ruffe too. How so ere, my man
Shall reade a piece of VIRGIL, TACITUS,
    LIVIE, or of some better booke to us,
Of which wee'll speake our minds, amidst our meate;
    And Ile professe no verses to repeate:
To this, if ought appeare, which I not know of,
    That will the pastrie, not my paper, show of.
Digestive cheese, and fruit there sure will bee;
    But that, which most doth take my *Muse,* and mee,
Is a pure cup of rich *Canary*-wine,
    Which is the *Mermaids,* now, but shall be mine:
Of which had HORACE, or ANACREON tasted,
    Their lives, as doe their lines, till now had lasted.
Tabacco, Nectar, or the *Thespian* spring,
    Are all but LUTHERS beere, to this I sing.
Of this we will sup free, but moderately,
    And we will have no *Pooly',* or *Parrot* by;
Nor shall our cups make any guiltie men:
    But, at our parting, we will be, as when
We innocently met. No simple word,
    That shall be utter'd at our mirthfull boord,
Shall make us sad next morning: or affright
    The libertie, that wee'll enjoy to night.

To Penshurst

Thou art not, PENSHURST, built to envious show,
　　Of touch, or marble; nor canst boast a row
Of polish'd pillars, or a roofe of gold:
　　Thou hast no lantherne, whereof tales are told;
Or stayre, or courts; but stand'st an ancient pile,
　　And these grudg'd at, art reverenc'd the while.
Thou joy'st in better markes, of soyle, of ayre,
　　Of wood, of water: therein thou art faire.
Thou hast thy walkes for health, as well as sport:
　　Thy *Mount,* to which the *Dryads* doe resort,
Where PAN, and BACCHUS their high feasts have made,
Beneath the broad beech, and the chest-nut shade;
That taller tree, which of a nut was set,
　　At his great birth, where all the Muses met.
There, in the writhed barke, are cut the names
　　Of many a SYLVANE, taken with his flames.
And thence, the ruddy *Satyres* often provoke
　　The lighter *Faunes,* to reach thy *Ladies oke.*
Thy copp's, too, nam'd of GAMAGE, thou hast there,
　　That never failes to serve thee season'd deere,
When thou would'st feast, or exercise thy friends.
　　The lower land, that to the river bends,
Thy sheepe, thy bullocks, kine, and calves doe feed:
　　The middle grounds thy mares, and horses breed.
Each banke doth yeeld thee coneyes; and the topps
　　Fertile of Wood, ASHORE, and SYDNEY's copp's
To crowne thy open table, doth provide
　　The purpled pheasant, with the speckled side:
The painted patrich lyes in every field,
　　And, for thy messe, is willing to be kill'd.

And if the high-swolne *Medway* faile thy dish,
   Thou hast thy ponds, that pay thee tribute fish,
Fat, aged carps, that runne into thy net.
   And pikes, now weary their owne kinde to eat,
As loth, the second draught, or cast to stay,
   Officiously, at first, themselves betray.
Bright eeles, that emulate them, and leape on land,
   Before the fisher, or into his hand.
Then hath thy orchard fruit, thy garden flowers,
   Fresh as the ayre, and new as are the houres.
The earely cherry, with the later plum,
   Fig, grape, and quince, each in his time doth come:
The blushing apricot, and woolly peach
   Hang on thy walls, that every child may reach.
And though thy walls be of the countrey stone,
   They'are rear'd with no mans ruine, no mans grone,
There's none, that dwell about them, wish them downe;
   But all come in, the farmer, and the clowne:
And no one empty-handed, to salute
   Thy lord, and lady, though they have no sute.
Some bring a capon, some a rurall cake,
   Some nuts, some apples; some that thinke they make
The better cheeses, bring 'hem; or else send
   By their ripe daughters, whom they would commend
This way to husbands; and whose baskets beare
   An embleme of themselves, in plum, or peare.
But what can this (more then expresse their love)
   Adde to thy free provisions, farre above
The neede of such? whose liberall boord doth flow,
   With all, that hospitalitie doth know!
Where comes no guest, but is allow'd to eate,
   Without his feare, and of thy lords owne meate:
Where the same beere, and bread, and selfe-same wine,
   That is his Lordships, shall be also mine.
And I not faine to sit (as some, this day,

At great mens tables) and yet dine away.
Here no man tells my cups; nor, standing by,
    A waiter, doth my gluttony envy:
But gives me what I call, and lets me eate,
    He knowes, below, he shall finde plentie of meate,
Thy tables hoord not up for the next day,
    Nor, when I take my lodging, need I pray
For fire, or lights, or livorie: all is there;
    As if thou, then, wert mine, or I raign'd here:
There's nothing I can wish, for which I stay.
    That found King JAMES, when hunting late, this way,
With his brave sonne, the Prince, they saw thy fires
    Shine bright on every harth as the desires
Of thy *Penates* had beene set on flame,
    To entertayne them; or the countrey came,
With all their zeale, to warme their welcome here.
    What (great, I will not say, but) sodayne cheare
Did'st thou, then, make 'hem! and what praise was
        heap'd
    On thy good lady, then! who, therein, reap'd
The just reward of her high huswifery;
    To have her linnen, plate, and all things nigh,
When shee was farre: and not a roome, but drest,
    As if it had expected such a guest!
These, PENSHURST, are thy praise, and yet not all.
    Thy lady's noble, fruitfull, chaste withall.
His children thy great lord may call his owne:
    A fortune, in this age, but rarely knowne.
They are, and have beene taught religion: Thence
    Their gentler spirits have suck'd innocence.
Each morne, and even, they are taught to pray,
    With the whole houshold, and may, every day,
Reade, in their vertuous parents noble parts,
    The mysteries of manners, armes, and arts.
Now, PENSHURST, they that will proportion thee

With other edifices, when they see
Those proud, ambitious heaps, and nothing else,
 May say, their lords have built, but thy lord dwells.

FROM *A Celebration of Charis*

HIS EXCUSE FOR LOVING

Let it not your wonder move,
Lesse your laughter; that I love.
Though I now write fiftie yeares,
I have had, and have my Peeres;
Poëts, though divine, are men:
Some have lov'd as old agen.
And it is not alwayes face,
Clothes, or Fortune gives the grace;
Or the feature, or the youth:
But the Language, and the Truth,
With the Ardor, and the Passion,
Gives the Lover weight, and fashion.
If you then will read the Storie,
First, prepare you to be sorie,
That you never knew till now,
Either whom to love, or how:
But be glad, as soone with me,
When you know, that this is she,
Of whose Beautie it was sung,
She shall make the old man young,
Keepe the middle age at stay,
And let nothing high decay,
Till she be the reason why,
All the world for love may die.

HER TRIUMPH

See the Chariot at hand here of Love,
   Wherein my Lady rideth!
Each that drawes, is a Swan, or a Dove,
   And well the Carre Love guideth.
As she goes, all hearts doe duty
               Unto her beauty;
And enamour'd, doe wish, so they might
               But enjoy such a sight,
That they still were to run by her side,
Thorough Swords, thorough Seas, whether she would
   ride.

Doe but looke on her eyes, they doe light
   All that Loves world compriseth!
Doe but looke on her Haire, it is bright
   As Loves starre when it riseth!
Doe but marke, her forehead's smoother
               Then words that sooth her!
And from her arched browes, such a grace
               Sheds it selfe through the face,
   As alone there triumphs to the life
All the Gaine, all the Good, of the Elements strife.

Have you seene but a bright Lillie grow,
   Before rude hands have touch'd it?
Ha' you mark'd but the fall o' the Snow
   Before the soyle hath smutch'd it?
Ha' you felt the wooll o' the Bever?
               Or Swans Downe ever?
Or have smelt o' the bud o' the Brier?
               Or the Nard in the fire?
   Or have tasted the bag of the Bee?
O so white! O so soft! O so sweet is she!

BEGGING ANOTHER, ON COLOUR
OF MENDING THE FORMER

For *Loves*-sake, kisse me once againe,
   I long, and should not beg in vaine,
     Here's none to spie, or see:
       Why doe you doubt, or stay?
   I'le taste as lightly as the Bee,
That doth but touch his flower, and flies away.
   Once more, and (faith) I will be gone,
   Can he that loves, aske lesse then one?
     Nay, you may erre in this,
      And all your bountie wrong:
   This could be call'd but halfe a kisse.
What w'are but once to doe, we should doe long.
   I will but mend the last, and tell
   Where, how it would have relish'd well;
     Joyne lip to lip, and try:
      Each suck others breath.
   And whilst our tongues perplexed lie,
Let who thinke us dead, or wish our death.

The Dreame

   Or Scorne, or pittie on me take,
   I must the true Relation make,
     I am undone to night;
    Love is a subtile Dreame disguis'd,
    Hath both my heart and me surpriz'd,
  Whom never yet he durst attempt t' awake;
  Nor will he tell me for whose sake
        He did me the Delight,
         Or Spight,

But leaves me to inquire,
In all my wild desire,
  Of sleepe againe, who was his Aid,
  And sleepe so guiltie and afraid,
As since he dares not come within my sight.

My Picture Left in Scotland

I now thinke, LOVE is rather deafe, then blind,
  For else it could not be,
    That she,
Whom I adore so much, should so slight me,
  And cast my love behind:
I'm sure my language to her, was as sweet
  And every close did meet
  In sentence, of as subtile feet,
    As hath the youngest Hee,
  That sits in shadow of *Apollo's* tree.
  Oh, but my conscious feares,
    That flie my thoughts betweene,
    Tell me that she hath seene
  My hundreds of gray haires,
  Told seven and fortie yeares.
Read so much wast, as she cannot imbrace
My mountaine belly, and my rockie face,
And all these through her eyes, have stopt her eares.

An Ode: To Himselfe

Where do'st thou carelesse lie,
    Buried in ease and sloth?
Knowledge, that sleepes, doth die;
And this Securitie,
    It is the common Moath,
That eats on wits, and Arts, and oft destroyes them both.

Are all th' *Aonian* springs
    Dri'd up? lyes *Thespia* wast?
Doth *Clarius* Harp want strings,
That not a Nymph now sings?
    Or droop they as disgrac't,
To see their Seats and Bowers by chattring Pies defac't?

If hence thy silence be,
    As 'tis too just a cause;
Let this thought quicken thee,
Minds that are great and free,
    Should not on fortune pause,
'Tis crowne enough to vertue still, her owne applause.

What though the greedie Frie
    Be taken with false Baytes
Of worded Balladrie,
And thinke it Poësie?
    They die with their conceits,
And only pitious scorne, upon their folly waites.

Then take in hand thy Lyre,
    Strike in thy proper straine,
With *Japhets* lyne, aspire
Sols Chariot for new fire,

To give the world againe:
Who aided him, will thee, the issue of *Joves* braine.

And since our Daintie age,
Cannot indure reproofe,
Make not thy selfe a Page,
To that strumpet the Stage,
But sing high and aloofe,
Safe from the wolves black jaw, and the dull Asses
hoofe.

A Fit of Rime Against Rime

Rime, the rack of finest wits,
That expresseth but by fits,
True Conceipt,
Spoyling Senses of their Treasure,
Cosening Judgement with a measure,
But false weight.
Wresting words, from their true calling;
Propping Verse, for feare of falling
To the ground.
Joynting Syllabes, drowning Letters,
Fastning Vowells, as with fetters
They were bound!
Soone as lazie thou wert knowne,
All good Poëtrie hence was flowne,
And Art banish'd.
For a thousand yeares together,
All *Parnassus* Greene did wither,
And wit vanish'd.
Pegasus did flie away,
At the Wells no Muse did stay,

But bewailed
So to see the Fountaine drie,
And *Apollo's* Musique die,
    All light failed!
Starveling rimes did fill the Stage,
Not a Poët in an Age,
    Worth a crowning.
Not a worke deserving Baies,
Nor a lyne deserving praise,
    Pallas frowning.
Greeke was free from Rimes infection,
Happy Greeke, by this protection,
    Was not spoyled.
Whilst the Latin, Queene of Tongues,
Is not yet free from Rimes wrongs,
    But rests foiled.
Scarce the Hill againe doth flourish,
Scarce the world a Wit doth nourish,
    To restore
Phoebus to his Crowne againe;
And the Muses to their braine:
    As before.
Vulgar Languages that want
Words, and sweetnesse, and be scant
    Of true measure,
Tyran Rime hath so abused,
That they long since have refused
    Other ceasure.
He that first invented thee,
May his joynts tormented bee,
    Cramp'd for ever;
Still may Syllabes jarre with time,
Stil may reason warre with rime,
    Resting never.
May his Sense, when it would meet

The cold tumor in his feet,
　　　　　　Grow unsounder.
And his Title be long foole,
That in rearing such a Schoole,
　　　　　　Was the founder.

An *Elegie*

Let me be what I am, as *Virgil* cold;
　As *Horace* fat; or as *Anacreon* old;
No Poets verses yet did ever move,
　Whose Readers did not thinke he was in love.
Who shall forbid me then in Rithme to bee
　As light, and active as the youngest hee
That from the Muses fountaines doth indorse
　His lynes, and hourely sits the Poets horse?
Put on my Ivy Garland, let me see
　Who frownes, who jealous is, who taxeth me.
Fathers, and Husband, I doe claime a right
　In all that is call'd lovely: take my sight
Sooner then my affection from the faire.
　No face, no hand, proportion, line, or Ayre
Of beautie; but the Muse hath interest in:
　There is not worne that lace, purle, knot or pin,
But is the Poëts matter: And he must,
　When he is furious, love, although not lust.
Be then content, your Daughters and your Wives,
　(If they be faire and worth it) have their lives
Made longer by our praises. Or, if not,
　Wish, you had fowle ones, and deformed got;
Curst in their Cradles, or there chang'd by Elves,
　So to be sure you doe injoy your selves.
Yet keepe those up in sackcloth too, or lether,

For Silke will draw some sneaking Songster thither.
It is a ryming Age, and Verses swarme
   At every stall; The Cittie Cap's a charme.
But I who love, and have liv'd twentie yeare
   Where I may handle Silke, as free, and neere,
As any Mercer; or the whale-bone man
   That quilts those bodies, I have leave to span:
Have eaten with the Beauties, and the wits
   And braveries of Court, and felt their fits
Of love, and hate: and came so nigh to know
   Whether their faces were their owne, or no:
It is not likely I should now looke downe
   Upon a Velvet Petticote, or a Gowne,
Whose like I have knowne the Taylors Wife put on
   To doe her Husbands rites in, e're 'twere gone
Home to the Customer: his Letcherie
   Being, the best clothes still to præoccupie.
Put a Coach-mare in Tissue, must I horse
   Her presently? Or leape thy Wife of force,
When by thy sordid bountie she hath on
   A Gowne of that, was the Caparison?
So I might dote upon thy Chaires, and Stooles
   That are like cloath'd: must I be of those foole
Of race accompted, that no passion have
   But when thy Wife (as thou conceiv'st) is brave?
Then ope thy wardrobe, thinke me that poore Groome
   That from the Foot-man, when he was become
An Officer there, did make most solemne love,
   To ev'ry Petticote he brush'd, and Glove
He did lay up, and would adore the shooe,
   Or slipper was left off, and kisse it too,
Court every hanging Gowne, and after that,
   Lift up some one, and doe, I tell not what.
Thou didst tell me; and wert o're-joy'd to peepe
   In at a hole, and see these Actions creepe

From the poore wretch, which though he play'd in
    prose,
  He would have done in verse, with any of those
Wrung on the Withers, by Lord Loves despight,
  Had he'had the facultie to reade, and write!
Such Songsters there are store of; witnesse he
  That chanc'd the lace, laid on a Smock, to see,
And straight-way spent a Sonnet; with that other
  That (in pure Madrigall) unto his Mother
Commended the French-hood, and Scarlet gowne
  The Lady Mayresse pass'd in through the Towne,
Unto the Spittle Sermon. O, what strange
  Varietie of Silkes were on th' Exchange!
Or in Moore-fields, this other night! sings one,
  Another answers, "Lasse, those Silkes are none,"
In smiling *L'envoye,* as he would deride
  Any Comparison had with his Cheap-side.
And vouches both the Pageant, and the Day,
  When not the Shops, but windowes doe display
The Stuffes, the Velvets, Plushes, Fringes, Lace,
  And all the originall riots of the place.
Let the poore fooles enjoy their follies, love
  A Goat in Velvet; or some block could move
Under that cover; an old Mid-wives hat!
  Or a Close-stoole so cas'd! or any fat
Bawd, in a Velvet scabberd! I envy
  None of their pleasures! nor will aske thee, why
Thou art jealous of thy Wifes, or Daughters Case:
  More then of eithers manners, wit, or face!

To the Immortall Memorie, and Friendship of That Noble Paire, Sir Lucius Cary, and Sir H. Morison

THE TURNE

Brave Infant of *Saguntum,* cleare
Thy comming forth in that great yeare,
When the Prodigious *Hannibal* did crowne
His rage, with razing your immortall Towne.
Thou, looking then about,
E're thou wert halfe got out,
Wise child, did'st hastily returne,
And mad'st thy Mothers wombe thine urne.
How summ'd a circle didst thou leave man-kind
Of deepest lore, could we the Center find!

THE COUNTER-TURNE

Did wiser Nature draw thee back,
From out the horrour of that sack?
Where shame, faith, honour, and regard of right
Lay trampled on; the deeds of death, and night,
Urg'd, hurried forth, and horld
Upon th'affrighted world:
Sword, fire, and famine, with fell fury met;
And all on utmost ruine set;
As, could they but lifes miseries fore-see,
No doubt all Infants would returne like thee.

THE STAND

For, what is life, if measur'd by the space,
Not by the act?
Or masked man, if valu'd by his face,

Above his fact?
Here's one out-liv'd his Peeres,
And told forth fourescore yeares;
He vexed time, and busied the whole State;
Troubled both foes, and friends;
But ever to no ends:
What did this Stirrer, but die late?
How well at twentie had he falne, or stood!
For three of his foure-score, he did no good.

THE TURNE

Hee entred well, by vertuous parts,
Got up and thriv'd with honest arts:
He purchas'd friends, and fame, and honours then,
And had his noble name advanc'd with men:
But weary of that flight,
Hee stoop'd in all mens sight
To sordid flatteries, acts of strife,
And sunke in that dead sea of life
So deep, as he did then death's waters sup;
But that the Corke of Title boy'd him up.

THE COUNTER-TURNE

Alas, but *Morison* fell young:
Hee never fell, thou fall'st my tongue.
Hee stood, a Souldier to the last right end,
A perfect Patriot, and a noble friend,
But most, a vertuous Sonne.
All Offices were done
By him, so ample, full, and round,
In weight, in measure, number, sound,
As though his age imperfect might appeare,
His life was of Humanitie the Spheare.

THE STAND

Goe now, and tell out dayes summ'd up with feares,
And make them yeares;

Produce thy masse of miseries on the Stage,
To swell thine age;
Repeat of things a throng,
To shew thou hast beene long,
Not liv'd; for Life doth her great actions spell,
But what was done and wrought
In season, and so brought
To light: her measures are, how well
Each syllab'e answer'd, and was form'd, how
     faire;
These make the lines of life, and that's her ayre.

THE TURNE

It is not growing like a tree
In bulke, doth make man better bee;
Or standing long an Oake, three hundred yeare,
To fall a logge at last, dry, bald, and seare:
A Lillie of a Day,
Is fairer farre, in May,
Although it fall, and die that night;
It was the Plant, and flowre of light.
In small proportions, we just beautie see:
And in short measures, life may perfect bee.

THE COUNTER-TURNE

Call, noble *Lucius,* then for Wine,
And let thy lookes with gladnesse shine:
Accept this garland, plant it on thy head,
And thinke, nay know, thy *Morison's* not dead.
Hee leap'd the present age,
Possest with holy rage,
To see that bright eternall Day:
Of which we *Priests,* and *Poëts* say
Such truths, as we expect for happy men,
And there he lives with memorie; and *Ben.*

THE STAND

Jonson, who sung this of him, e're he went
Himselfe to rest,
Or taste a part of that full joy he meant
To have exprest,
In this bright *Asterisme:*
Where it were friendships schisme,
(Were not his *Lucius* long with us to tarry)
To separate these twi-
Lights, the *Dioscuri;*
And keepe the one halfe from his *Harry.*
But fate doth so alternate the designe,
Whilst that in heav'n, this light on earth must shine.

THE TURNE

And shine as you exalted are;
Two names of friendship, but one Starre:
Of hearts the union. And those not by chance
Made, or indentur'd, or leas'd out to 'advance
The profits for a time.
No pleasures vaine did chime,
Of rimes, or ryots, at your feasts,
Orgies of drinke, or fain'd protests:
But simple love of greatnesse, and of good;
That knits brave minds, and manners, more than blood.

THE COUNTER-TURNE

This made you first to know the Why
You lik'd, then after, to apply
That liking; and approach so one the tother,
Till either grew a portion of the other:
Each stiled by his end,
The Copie of his friend.
You liv'd to be the great surnames,
And titles, by which all made claimes

Unto the Vertue. Nothing perfect done,
But as a CARY, or a MORISON.

THE STAND

And such a force the faire example had,
As they that saw
The good, and durst not practise it, were glad
That such a Law
Was left yet to Man-kind;
Where they might read, and find
Friendship, in deed, was written, not in words:
And with the heart, not pen,
Of two so early men,
Whose lines her rowles were, and records.
Who, e're the first downe bloomed on the chin,
Had sow'd these fruits, and got the harvest in.

To the Memory of My Beloved, the Author Mr. William Shakespeare: and What He Hath Left Us

To draw no envy (*Shakespeare*) on thy name,
    Am I thus ample to thy Booke, and Fame:
While I confesse thy writings to be such,
    As neither *Man,* nor *Muse,* can praise too much.
'Tis true, and all mens suffrage. But these wayes
    Were not the paths I meant unto thy praise:
For seeliest Ignorance on these may light,
    Which, when it sounds at best, but eccho's right;
Or blinde Affection, which doth ne're advance
    The truth, but gropes, and urgeth all by chance;
Or crafty Malice, might pretend this praise,
    And thinke to ruine, where it seem'd to raise.

These are, as some infamous Baud, or Whore,
   Should praise a Matron. What could hurt her
      more?
But thou art proofe against them, and indeed
   Above th'll fortune of them, or the need.
I, therefore will begin. Soule of the Age!
   The applause! delight! the wonder of our Stage!
My Shakespeare, rise; I will not lodge thee by
   Chaucer, or *Spenser,* or bid *Beaumont* lye
A little further, to make thee a roome:
   Thou art a Moniment, without a tombe,
And art alive still, while thy Booke doth live,
   And we have wits to read, and praise to give.
That I not mixe thee so, my braine excuses;
   I meane with great, but disproportion'd *Muses:*
For, if I thought my judgement were of yeeres,
   I should commit thee surely with thy peeres,
And tell, how farre thou dist our *Lily* out-shine,
   Or sporting *Kid,* or *Marlowes* mighty line.
And though thou hadst small *Latine,* and lesse *Greeke,*
   From thence to honour thee, I would not seeke
For names; but call forth thund'ring *Aeschilus,*
   Euripides, and *Sophocles* to us,
Paccuvius, Accius, him of Cordova dead
   To life againe, to heare thy Buskin tread,
And shake a Stage: Or, when thy Sockes were on,
   Leave thee alone, for the comparison
Of all, that insolent *Greece,* or haughtie *Rome*
   Sent forth, or since did from their ashes come.
Triúmph, my *Britaine,* thou hast one to showe,
   To whom all Scenes of *Europe* homage owe.
He was not of an age, but for all time!
   And all the *Muses* still were in their prime,
When like *Apollo* he came forth to warme
   Our eares, or like a *Mercury* to charme!

Nature her selfe was proud of his designes,
    And joy'd to weare the dressing of his lines!
Which were so richly spun, and woven so fit,
    As, since, she will vouchsafe no other Wit.
The merry *Greeke*, tart *Aristophanes*,
    Neat *Terence*, witty *Plautus*, now not please;
But antiquated, and deserted lye
    As they were not of Natures family.
Yet must I not give Nature all: Thy Art,
    My gentle *Shakespeare*, must enjoy a part.
For though the Poets matter, Nature be,
    His Art doth give the fashion. And, that he,
Who casts to write a living line, must sweat,
    (Such as thine are) and strike the second heat
Upon the *Muses* anvile: turne the same,
    (And himselfe with it) that he thinkes to frame;
Or for the lawrell, he may gaine a scorne,
    For a good *Poet's* made, as well as borne.
And such wert thou. Looke how the fathers face
    Lives in his issue, even so, the race
Of *Shakespeares* minde, and manners brightly shines
    In his well torned, and true-filed lines:
In each of which, he seemes to shake a Lance,
    As brandish't at the eyes of Ignorance.
Sweet Swan of *Avon!* what a sight it were
    To see thee in our waters yet appeare,
And make those flights upon the bankes of *Thames*,
    That so did take *Eliza*, and our *James!*
But stay, I see thee in the *Hemisphere*
    Advanc'd, and make a Constellation there!
Shine forth, thou Starre of *Poets*, and with rage,
    Or influence, chide, or cheere the drooping Stage;
Which, since thy flight from hence, hath mourn'd like
    night,
    And despaires day, but for thy Volumes light.

FROM *The Alchemist*

MAMMON. Come on, sir. Now, you set your foot on shore
In *novo orbe;* Here's the rich *Peru:*
And there within, sir, are the golden mines,
Great *Salomon's Ophir!* He was sayling to't,
Three yeeres, but we have reach't it in ten months.
This is the day, wherein, to all my friends,
I will pronounce the happy word, *be rich.*
This day, you shall be *spectatissimi.*
You shall no more deale with the hollow die,
Or the fraile card. No more be at charge of keeping
The livery-punke, for the young heire, that must
Seale, at all houres, in his shirt. No more
If he denie, ha' him beaten to't, as he is
That brings him the commoditie. No more
Shall thirst of satten, or the covetous hunger
Of velvet entrailes, for a rude-spun cloke,
To be displaid at *Madame Augusta's,* make
The sonnes of *sword,* and *hazzard* fall before
The golden calfe, and on their knees, whole nights,
Commit idolatrie with wine, and trumpets:
Or goe a feasting, after drum and ensigne.
No more of this. You shall start up yong *Vice-royes,*
And have your punques, and punquettes, my *Surly.*
And unto thee, I speake it first, *be rich.*
Where is my *Subtle,* there? Within hough?
(*Voice within.*)   Sir.
Hee'll come to you, by and by.
MAMMON.   That's his fire-drake,
His lungs, his *Zephyrus,* he that puffes his coales,
Till he firke nature up, in her owne center.

You are not faithfull, sir. This night, I'll change
All, that is mettall, in thy house, to gold.
And, early in the morning, will I send
To all the plumbers, and the pewterers,
And buy their tin, and lead up: and to *Lothbury*,
For all the copper.

SURLY.   What, and turne that too?

MAMMON. Yes, and I'll purchase *Devonshire*, and
        Cornwaile,
And make them perfect *Indies!* You admire now?

SURLY. No faith.

MAMMON.   But when you see th' effects of the
        great med'cine!
Of which one part projected on a hundred
Of *Mercurie*, or *Venus*, or the *Moone*,
Shall turne it, to as many of the *Sunne;*
Nay, to a thousand, so *ad infinitum:*
You will beleeve me.

SURLY.   Yes, when I see't, I will.
But, if my eyes doe cossen me so (and I
Giving 'hem no occasion) sure, I'll have
A whore, shall pisse 'hem out, next day.

MAMMON.   Ha! Why?
Doe you thinke, I fable with you? I assure you,
He that has once the *flower of the sunne*,
The perfect *ruby*, which we call *elixir*,
Not onely can doe that, but by it's vertue,
Can confer honour, love, respect, long life,
Give safetie, valure: yea, and victorie,
To whom he will. In eight, and twentie dayes,
I'll make an old man, of fourescore, a childe.

SURLY. No doubt, hee's that alreadie.

MAMMON.   Nay, I meane,
Restore his yeeres, renew him, like an eagle,
To the fifth age; make him get sonnes, and daughters,

Yong giants; as our *Philosophers* have done
(The antient *Patriarkes* afore the floud)
But taking, once a weeke, on a knives point,
The quantitie of a graine of mustard, of it:
Become stout *Marses,* and beget yong *Cupids.*

SURLY. The decay'd *Vestall's* of *Pickt-hatch* would thanke you,
That keepe the fire a-live, there.

MAMMON.   'Tis the secret
Of nature, naturiz'd 'gainst all infections,
Cures all diseases, comming of all causes,
A month's griefe, in a day; a yeeres, in twelve:
And, of what age soever, in a month.
Past all the doses, of your drugging Doctors.
I'll undertake, withall, to fright the plague
Out o' the kingdome, in three months.

SURLY.   And I'll
Be bound, the players shall sing your praises, then.
Without their poets.

MAMMON.   Sir, I'll doo't. Meanetime,
I'll give away so much, unto my man,
Shall serve th'whole citie, with preservative,
Weekely, each house his dose, and at the rate—

SURLY. As he that built the water-worke, do's with water?

MAMMON. You are incredulous.

SURLY.   Faith, I have a humor,
I would not willingly be gull'd. Your *stone*
Cannot transmute me.

MAMMON.   *Pertinax, Surly,*
Will you beleeve antiquitie? recordes?
I'll shew you a booke, where *Moses,* and his sister,
And *Salomon* have written, of the art;
I, and a treatise penn'd by Adam.

SURLY.   How!

MAMMON. O' the *Philosophers stone,* and in high-*Dutch.*

SURLY. Did *Adam* write, sir, in high-*Dutch?*

MAMMON.   He did:
Which proves it was the primitive tongue.

SURLY.   What paper?

MAMMON. On cedar board.

SURLY.   O that, indeed (they say)
Will last 'gainst wormes.

MAMMON.   'Tis like your *Irish* wood,
'Gainst cob-webs. I have a peece of *Jasons* fleece, too,
Which was no other, then a booke of *alchemie,*
Writ in large sheepe-skin, a good fat ram-vellam.
Such was *Pythagora's* thigh, *Pandora's* tub;
And, all that fable of *Medeas* charmes,
The manner of our worke: The Bulls, our fornace,
Still breathing fire; our *argent-vive,* the Dragon:
The Dragons teeth, *mercury* sublimate,
That keepes the whitenesse, hardnesse, and the biting;
And they are gather'd, into *Jason's* helme,
(Th' *alembeke*) and then sow'd in *Mars* his field,
And, thence, sublim'd so often, till they are fix'd.
Both this, th' *Hesperian* garden, *Cadmus* storie,
Jove's shower, the boone of *Midas, Argus* eyes,
Boccace his *Demogorgon,* thousands more,
All abstract riddles of our *stone.* How now?
Enter Face
Doe wee succeed? Is our day come? and hold's it?

FACE. The evening will set red, upon you, sir;
You have colour for it, crimson: the red *ferment*
Has done his office. Three houres hence, prepare you
To see projection.

MAMMON.   *Pertinax,* my *Surly,*
Againe, I say to thee, aloud: *be rich.*
This day, thou shalt have ingots: and, to morrow,
Give lords th'affront. Is it, my *Zephyrus,* right?

Blushes the *bolts-head?*

FACE.   Like a wench with child, sir,
That were, but now, discover'd to her master.

MAMMON. Excellent wittie *Lungs!* My onely care is,
Where to get stuffe, inough now, to project on,
This towne will not halfe serve me.

FACE.   No, sir? Buy
The covering of o' churches.

MAMMON.   That's true.

FACE.   Yes.
Let 'hem stand bare, as doe their auditorie.
Or cap 'hem, new, with shingles.

MAMMON.   No, good thatch:
Thatch will lie light upo' the rafters, *Lungs.*
Lungs, I will manumit thee, from the fornace;
I will restore thee thy complexion, *Puffe,*
Lost in the embers; and repaire this braine,
Hurt wi' the fume o' the mettalls.

FACE.   I have blowne, sir,
Hard, for your worship; throwne by many a coale,
When 'twas not beech; weigh'd those I put in, just,
To keepe your heat, still even; These bleard-eyes
Have wak'd, to reade your severall colours, sir,
Of the *pale citron,* the *greene lyon,* the *crow,*
The *peacocks taile,* the *plumed swan.*

MAMMON.   And, lastly,
Thou hast descryed the *flower,* the *sanguis agni?*

FACE. Yes, sir.

MAMMON.   Where's master?

FACE.   At's praiers, sir, he,
Good man, hee's doing his devotions,
For the successe.

MAMMON.   *Lungs,* I will set a period,
To all thy labours: Thou shalt be the master
Of my *seraglia.*

FACE.　　　　　　Good, sir.

MAMMON.　　　　　　　　But doe you heare?
I'll geld you, *Lungs.*

FACE.　　　　　　　Yes, sir.

MAMMON.　　　　　　　　　For I doe meane
To have a list of wives, and concubines,
Equall with *Salomon;* who had the *stone*
Alike, with me: and I will make me, a back
With the *elixir,* that shall be as tough
As *Hercules,* to encounter fiftie a night.
Th'art sure, thou saw'st it *bloud?*

FACE.　　　　　　　　　Both *bloud,* and *spirit,* sir.

MAMMON. I will have all my beds, blowne up; not stuft:
Downe is too hard. And then, mine oval roome,
Fill'd with such pictures, as *Tiberius* tooke
From *Elephantis:* and dull *Aretine*
But coldly imitated. Then, my glasses,
Cut in more subtill angles, to disperse,
And multiply the figures, as I walke
Naked between my *succubæ.* My mists
I'le have of perfume, vapor'd 'bout the roome,
To loose our selves in; and my baths, like pits
To fall into: from whence, we will come forth,
And rowle us drie in gossamour, and roses.
(Is it arriv'd at *ruby?*)— Where I spie
A wealthy citizen, or rich lawyer,
Have a sublim'd pure wife, unto that fellow
I'll send a thousand pound, to be my cuckold.

FACE. And I shall carry it?

MAMMON.　　　　　　　No. I'll ha' no bawds,
But fathers, and mothers. They will doe it best.
Best of all others. And, my flatterers
Shall be the pure, and gravest of Divines,
That I can get for money. My mere fooles,

Eloquent burgesses, and then my poets
The same that writ so subtly of the *fart*,
Whom I will entertaine, still, for that subject.
The few, that would give out themselves, to be
Court, and towne-stallions, and, each where, belye
Ladies, who are knowne most innocent, for them;
Those will I begge, to make me *eunuchs* of:
And they shall fan me with ten estrich tailes
A piece, made in a plume, to gather wind.
We will be brave, *Puffe*, now we ha' the *med'cine*.
My meat, shall all come in, in *Indian* shells,
Dishes of agate, set in gold, and studded
With emeralds, saphyres, hiacynths, and rubies.
The tongues of carpes, dormise, and camels heeles,
Boil'd i' the spirit of *Sol*, and dissolv'd pearle,
(*Apicius* diet, 'gainst the *epilepsie*)
And I will eate these broaths, with spoones of amber,
Headed with diamant, and carbuncle.
My foot-boy shall eate phesants, calverd salmons,
Knots, godwits, lamprey's: I my selfe will have
The beards of barbels, serv'd, in stead of sallades;
Oild mushromes; and the swelling unctuous paps
Of a fat pregnant sow, newly cut off,
Drest with an exquisite, and poynant sauce;
For which, Ile say unto my cooke, there's gold,
Goe forth, and be a knight.

FACE.   Sir, I'll goe looke
A little, how it heightens.

MAMMON.   Doe. My shirts
I'll have of taffata-sarsnet, soft, and light
As cob-webs; and for all my other rayment
It shall be such, as might provoke the *Persian*;
Were he to teach the world riot, a new.
My gloves of fishes, and birds-skins, perfum'd

With gummes of *paradise*, and easterne aire—
SURLY. And do'you thinke, to have the *stone*, with this?
MAMMON. No, I doe thinke, t'have all this, with the
   stone.

(Act II, *scenes i–ii*)

John Fletcher

(1579–1625)

and

Francis Beaumont

(1584–1616)

Songs from the Plays

<small>FROM</small> *The Tragedy of Valentinian*

Heare ye Ladies that despise
  What the mighty Love has done,
Feare examples, and be wise,
  Faire *Calisto* was a Nun,
Laeda sayling on the streame,
  To deceive the hopes of man,
Love accounting but a dream,
  Doted on a silver Swan,
Danae in a Brazen Tower,
  Where no love was, lov'd a Showre.

Heare ye Ladies that are coy,
  What the mighty Love can doe,
Feare the fiercenesse of the Boy,
  The chaste Moon he makes to wooe:
Vesta kindling holy fires,
  Circled round about with spies,

Never dreaming loose desires,
   Doting at the Altar dies.
     Ilion in a short hour higher
     He can build, and once more fire.

FROM *The Bloody Brother*

Take, oh take those Lips away
   That so sweetly were forsworn,
And those Eyes, like break of day,
   Lights that do mislead the Morn,
But my Kisses bring again,
   Seals of Love, though seal'd in vain.

Hide, oh hide those hills of Snow,
   Which thy frozen Blossom bears,
On whose tops the Pinks that grow
   Are of those that *April* wears,
But first set my poor Heart free,
   Bound in those Ivy Chains by thee.

FROM *Henry the Eighth*

Orpheus with his Lute made Trees,
And the Mountaine tops that freeze,
Bow themselves when he did sing.
To his Musicke, Plants and Flowers
Ever spring; as Sunne and Showres,
There had been a lasting Spring.
Every thing that heard him play,
Even the Billowes of the Sea,
Hung their heads, and then lay by.
In sweet Musicke is such Art,
Killing care, and griefe of heart,
Fall asleepe, or hearing dye.

FROM *The Tragedy of Valentinian*

Care charming sleep, thou easer of all woes,
Brother to death, sweetly thy self dispose
On this afflicted Prince, fall like a Cloud
In gentle showres, give nothing that is lowd,
Or painfull to his slumbers; easie, sweet,
And as a purling stream, thou son of night,
Passe by his troubled senses; sing his pain
Like hollow murmuring Winde, or silver Raine,
Into this Prince gently, Oh, gently slide,
And kisse him into slumbers like a Bride.

FROM *The Nice Valour*

Hence all you vaine Delights,
As short as are the nights,
    Wherein you spend your folly,
Ther's nought in this life, sweet,
If man were wise to see't,
    But only Melancholy,
    Oh sweetest Melancholy.
Welcome folded Armes, and fixed Eyes,
A sigh that piercing mortifies,
A look that's fast'ned to the ground,
A tongue chain'd up without a sound.

Fountaine heads, and pathlesse Groves,
Places which pale passion loves:
Moon-light walkes, when all the fowles
Are warmly hous'd, save Bats and Owles;
    A mid-night Bell, a parting groane,
    These are the sounds we feed upon;

Then stretch our bones in a still gloomy valley,
Nothing so daintie sweet, as lovely Melancholy.

FROM *Love's Cure*

Turn, turn thy beauteous face away,
How pale and sickly looks the day,
　　In emulation of thy brighter beams!
Oh envious light, fly, fly, begone,
Come night, and peece two breasts as one;
　　When what love does, we will repeat in dreams.
Yet (thy eyes open) who can day hence fright,
Let but their lids fall, and it will be night.

FROM *Women Pleas'd*

O faire sweet face, O eyes celestiall bright,
Twin-stars in Heaven that now adorn the night;
O fruitfull lips, where Cherries ever grow,
And Damask cheeks, where all sweet beauties blow;
O thou from head to foot divinely faire,
Cupid's most cunning Nets made of that haire,
And as he weaves himselfe for curious eyes;
O me, O me, I am caught my selfe, he cryes:
Sweet rest about thee sweet and golden sleepe,
Soft peacefull thoughts, your hourly watches keep,
While I in wonder sing this sacrifice,
To beauty sacred, and those Angell-eyes.

Thomas Middleton

(1580–1627)

FROM *The Changeling*

DEFLORES. What makes your lip so strange? This must
   not be betwixt us.

BEATRICE. The man talks wildly.

DEFLORES. Come kisse me with a zeal now.

BEATRICE. Heaven I doubt him.

DEFLORES. I will not stand so long to beg 'em shortly.

BEATRICE. Take heed *Deflores* of forgetfulness, 'twill
   soon betray us.

DEFLORES. Take you heed first;
Faith y'are grown much forgetfull, y'are to blame in't.

BEATRICE. He's bold, and I am blam'd for't.

DEFLORES. I have eas'd you of your trouble, think on't,
   I'me in pain,
And must be eas'd of you; 'tis a charity,
Justice invites your blood to understand me.

BEATRICE. I dare not.

DEFLORES. Quickly.

BEATRICE. Oh I never shall, speak it yet further of that
   I may lose
What has been spoken, and no sound remain on't.
I would not hear so much offence again for such another
   deed.

DEFLORES. Soft, Lady, soft; the last is not yet paid for,
   oh this act
Has put me into spirit; I was as greedy on't

363

As the parcht earth of moisture, when the clouds weep.
Did you not mark, I wrought my self into't.
Nay sued, and kneel'd for't: Why was all that pains
    took?
You see I have thrown contempt upon your gold,
Not that I want it, for I doe piteously,
In order I will come unto't, and make use on't,
But 'twas not held so pretious to begin with;
For I place wealth after the heels of pleasure,
And were I not resolv'd in my belief
That thy virginity were perfect in thee,
I should but take my recompence with grudging,
As if I had but halfe my hopes I agreed for.
BEATRICE. Why 'tis impossible thou canst be so wicked,
Or shelter such a cunning cruelty,
To make his death the murderer of my honor.
Thy language is so bold and vitious,
I cannot see which way I can forgive it with any mod-
    esty.
DEFLORES. Push, you forget your selfe, a woman dipt in
    blood, and talk of modesty.
BEATRICE. O misery of sin! would I had been bound
Perpetually unto my living hate
In that *Piracquo*, then to hear these words.
Think but upon the distance that Creation
Set 'twixt thy blood and mine, and keep thee there.
DEFLORES. Look but into your conscience, read me
    there,
'Tis a true Book, you'l find me there your equall:
Push, flye not to your birth, but settle you
In what the act has made you, y'are no more now,
You must forget your parentage to me,
Y'are the deeds creature, by that name
You lost your first condition, and I challenge you,

As peace and innocency has turn'd you out,
And made you one with me.
BEATRICE. With thee, foul villain?
DEFLORES. Yes, my fair murdress; Do you urge me?
Though thou writ'st maid, thou whore in thy affection,
'Twas chang'd from thy first love, and that's a kind
Of whoredome in thy heart, and he's chang'd now,
To bring thy second on thy *Alsemero*,
Whom 'by all sweets that ever darkness tasted,
If I enjoy thee not thou ne're enjoyst,
I'le blast the hopes and joyes of marriage,
I'le confess all, my life I rate at nothing.
BEATRICE. *Deflores.*
DEFLORES. I shall rest from all lovers plagues then,
I live in pain now: that shooting eye
Will burn my heart to cinders.
BEATRICE. O sir, hear me.
DEFLORES. She that in life and love refuses me,
In death and shame my partner she shall be.
BEATRICE. Stay, hear me once for all, I make thee master
Of all the wealth I have in gold and jewels,
Let me go poor unto my bed with honor,
And I am rich in all things.
DEFLORES. Let this silence thee,
The wealth of all *Valentia* shall not buy my pleasure
  from me,
Can you weep Fate from its determin'd purpose?
So soon may weep me.
BEATRICE. Vengeance begins;
Murder I see is followed by more sins.
Was my creation in the womb so curst,
It must ingender with a Viper first?
DEFLORES. Come, rise, and shrowd your blushes in my
  bosome,

Silence is one of pleasures best receipts:
Thy peace is wrought for ever in this yeelding.
'Lasse how the Turtle pants! Thou'lt love anon,
What thou so fear'st, and faintst to venture on.   *Exeunt.*

(Act III, scene *iv*)

Enter Deflores bringing in Beatrice.

DEFLORES. Here we are, if you have any more
To say to us, speak quickly, I shall not,
Give you the hearing else, I am so stout yet,
And so I think that broken rib of mankind.

VERMANDERO. An Host of enemies entred my Citadell,
Could not amaze like this, *Joanna, Beatrice, Joanna.*

BEATRICE. O come not neer me sir, I shall defile you,
I am that of your blood was taken from you
For your better health, look no more upon't,
But cast it to the ground regardlessly,
Let the common shewer take it from distinction,
Beneath the starres, upon yon Meteor
Ever hang my fate, 'mongst things corruptible,
I ne're could pluck it from him, my loathing
Was Prophet to the rest, but ne're believ'd
Mine honour fell with him, and now my life.
Alsemero, I am a stranger to your bed,
Your bed was coz'ned on the nuptiall night,
For which your false-bride died.

ALFEMERO. *Diaphanta?*

DEFLORES. Yes, and the while I coupled with your mate
At barly-break; now we are left in hell.

VERMANDERO. We are all there, it circumscribes here.

DEFLORES. I lov'd this woman in spite of her heart,
Her love I earn'd out of *Piracquos* murder.

TOMASO. Ha, my brothers murtherer.

DEFLORES. Yes, and her honors prize
Was my reward, I thank life for nothing
But that pleasure, it was so sweet to me,
That I have drunk up all, left none behinde,
For any man to pledge me.

(Act V, scene iii)

Cyril Tourneur

(1575?–1626)

FROM The Revenger's Tragedy

Enter Vindice, with the skull of his love drest up in Tires.

VINDICE. Madame, his grace will not be absent long.
Secret? nere doubt us Madame? twill be worth
Three velvet gownes to your Ladyship—knowne?
Few Ladies respect that? disgrace, a poore thin shell,
Tis the best grace you have to do it well,
Ile save your hand that labour, ile unmaske you?
HIPPOLITO. Why brother, brother.
VINDICE. Art thou beguild now? tut, a Lady can,
At such all hid, beguile a wiser man,
Have I not fitted the old surfetter
With a quaint piece of beauty, age and bare bone
Are ere allied in action; here's an eye,
Able to tempt a great man—so serve God,
A prety hanging lip, that has forgot now to dissemble
Me thinkes this mouth should make a swearer tremble,
A drunckard claspe his teeth, and not undo 'em.
Heres a cheeke keepes her colour let the wind go
    whistle,
Spout Raine, we feare thee not, be hot or cold
Alls one with us; and is not he absur'd,
Whose fortunes are upon their faces set,
That fear no other God but winde and wet.
HIPPOLITO. Brother y'ave spoke that right,

Is this the forme that living shone so bright?
VINDICE. The very same,
And now me thinkes I could e'en chide my selfe,
For doating on her beauty, tho her death
Shall be revenged after no common action;
Dos the Silke-worme expend her yellow labours
For thee? for thee dos she undoe herselfe?
Are Lord-ships sold to maintaine Lady-ships
For the poore benefit of a bewitching minute?
Why dos yon fellow falsify hie-waies
And put his life betweene the Judges lippes,
To refine such a thing, keepes horse and men
To beate their valours for her?
Surely wee're all mad people, and they
Whome we thinke are, are not, we mistake those,
Tis we are mad in sense, they but in clothes.
HIPPOLITO. Faith and in clothes too we, give us our due.
VINDICE. Dos every proud and selfe-affecting Dame
Camphire her face for this? and grieve her Maker
In sinfull baths of milke,—when many an infant starves,
For her superfluous out-side, all for this?
Who now bids twenty pound a night, prepares
Musick, perfumes, and sweete-meates, all are husht,
Thou maist lie chast now! it were fine me thinkes:
To have thee seene at Revells, forgetfull feasts,
And uncleane Brothells; sure twould fright the sinner
And make him a good coward, put a Reveller,
Out off his Antick amble
And cloye an Epicure with empty dishes?
Here might a scornefull and ambitious woman,
Looke through and through her selfe—see Ladies, with
     false formes,
You deceive men, but cannot deceive wormes.
Now to my tragick businesse, looke you brother,
I have not fashiond this onely—for show

And useless property, no, it shall beare a part
E'en in its owne Revenge. This very skull,
Whose Mistris the Duke poysoned, with this drug
The mortall curse of the earth; shall be revengd
In the like straine, and kisses his lippes to death,
As much as the dumbe thing can, he shall feele:
What fayles in poyson, weele supply in steele.

HIPPOLITO. Brother I do applaud thy constant vengeance,
The quaintnesse of thy malice above thought.

VINDICE. So tis layde on: now come and welcome Duke,
I have her for thee, I protest it brother:
Me thinkes she makes almost as faire a sine
As some old gentlewoman in a Periwig?
Hide thy face now for shame, thou hadst neede have a
Maske now
Tis vaine when beauty flowes, but when it fleetes
This would become graves better then the streetes.

HIPPOLITO. You have my voice in that; harke, the
Duke's come.

VINDICE. Peace, let's observe what company he brings,
And how he dos absent e'm, for you knowe
Heele wish all private,—brother fall you back a little,
With the bony Lady.

HIPPOLITO.   That I will.

VINDICE. So, so,—now nine years vengeance crowde
into a minute!

(Act III, scene v)

John Ford

(1586–1640?)

Can you paint a thought?

FROM *The Broken Heart*

Can you paint a thought? or number
Every fancy in a slumber?
Can you count soft minutes roving
From a dyals point by moving?
Can you graspe a sigh? or lastly,
Rob a Virgins honour chastly?
  No, ô no; yet you may
    Sooner doe both that and this,
    This and that, and never misse,
  Then by any praise display
    Beauties beauty, such a glory
    As beyond all Fate, all Story,
      All armes, all arts,
      All loves, all hearts,
    Greater then those, or they,
    Doe, shall, and must obey.

Oh no more, no more, too late

FROM *The Broken Heart*

Oh no more, no more, too late
Sighes are spent; the burning Tapers
Of a life as chast as Fate,

Pure as are unwritten papers,
        Are burnt out: no heat, no light
        Now remaines, 'tis ever night.
Love is dead, let lovers eyes,
        Lock'd in endlesse dreames,
        Th'extremes of all extremes,
Ope' no more, for now Love dyes,
        Now Love dyes, implying
Loves Martyrs must be ever, every dying.

FROM *The Broken Heart*

BASSANES. Beasts onely capable of sense, enjoy
The benefit of food and ease with thankfulnesse;
Such silly creatures, with a grudging kicke not
Against the portion Nature hath bestow'd;
But men endow'd with reason and the use
Of reason, to distinguish from the chaffe
Of abject scarscity, the Quintescence,
Soule, and Elixar of the Earths abundance,
The treasures of the Sea, the Ayre, nay heaven
Repining at these glories of creation,
Are verier beasts than beasts; and of those beasts
The worst am I; I, who was made a Monarch
Of what a heart could wish, for a chast wife,
Endeavour'd what in me lay, to pull downe
That Temple built for adoration onely,
And level't in the dust of causelesse scandall:
But to redeeme a sacrilege so impious,
Humility shall powre before the deities:
I have incenst a largenesse of more patience
Then their displeased Altars can require:
No tempests of commotion shall disquiet
The calmes of my composure.

                                        (Act IV, scene ii)

FROM *The Lovers Melancholy*

MELEANDER. If thou canst wake with me, forget to eate,
Renounce the thought of Greatnesse; tread on Fate;
Sigh out a lamentable tale of things
Done long agoe, and ill done; and when sighes
Are wearied, piece up what remaines behind,
With weeping eyes, and hearts that bleed to death:
Thou shalt be a companion fit for me,
And we will sit together like true friends,
And never be devided. With what greedinesse
Doe I hug my afflictions? there's no mirth
Which is not truly season'd with some madnesse.

(Act IV, scene ii)

EROCLEA. Minutes are numbred by the fall of Sands;
As by an houre-glasse, the span of time
Doth waste us to our graves, and we looke on it.
An age of pleasures revel'd out, comes home
At last, and ends in sorrow, but the life
Weary of ryot, numbers every Sand,
Wayling in sighes, untill the last drop downe,
So to conclude calamity in rest.

(Act IV, scene iii)

John Donne

(1572–1631)

The Good-Morrow

I wonder by my troth, what thou, and I
Did, till we lov'd? were we not wean'd till then?
But suck'd on countrey pleasures, childishly?
Or snorted we in the seaven sleepers den?
T'was so; But this, all pleasures fancies bee.
If ever any beauty I did see,
Which I desir'd, and got, 'twas but a dreame of thee.

And now good morrow to our waking soules,
Which watch not one another out of feare;
For love, all love of other sights controules,
And makes one little roome, an every where.
Let sea-discoverers to new worlds have gone,
Let Maps to other, worlds on worlds have showne,
Let us possesse one world, each hath one, and is one.

My face is thine eye, thine in mine appeares,
And true plaine hearts doe in the faces rest,
Where can we finde two better hemispheares
Without sharpe North, without declining West?
What ever dyes, was not mixt equally;
If our two loves be one, or, thou and I
Love so alike, that none doe slacken, none can die.

The Sunne Rising

Busie old foole, unruly Sunne,
   Why dost thou thus,
Through windowes, and through curtaines call on us?
Must to thy motions lovers seasons run?
   Sawcy pedantique wretch, goe chide
   Late schoole boyes, and sowre prentices,
  Goe tell Court-huntsmen, that the King will ride,
  Call countrey ants to harvest offices;
Love, all alike, no season knowes, nor clyme,
Nor houres, dayes, moneths, which are the rags of time.

   Thy beames, so reverend, and strong
   Why shouldst thou thinke?
I could eclipse and cloud them with a winke,
But that I would not lose her sight so long:
   If her eyes have not blinded thine,
   Looke, and to-morrow late, tell mee,
  Whether both the'India's of spice and Myne
  Be where thou leftst them, or lie here with mee.
Aske for those Kings whom thou saw'st yesterday,
And thou shalt heare, All here in one bed lay.

   She'is all States, and all Princes, I,
   Nothing else is.
Princes doe but play us; compar'd to this,
All honor's mimique; All wealth alchimie.
   Thou sunne art halfe as happy'as wee,
   In that the world's contracted thus;
  Thine age askes ease, and since thy duties bee
  To warme the world, that's done in warming us
Shine here to us, and thou art every where;
This bed thy center is, these walls, thy spheare.

Song

Goe, and catche a falling starre,
  Get with child a mandrake roote,
Tell me, where all past yeares are,
  Or who cleft the Divels foot,
Teach me to heare Mermaides singing,
  Or to keep off envies stinging,
        And finde
        What winde
Serves to advance an honest minde.

If thou beest borne to strange sights,
  Things invisible to see,
Ride ten thousand daies and nights,
  Till age snow white haires on thee,
Thou, when thou retorn'st, wilt tell mee
All strange wonders that befell thee,
        And sweare
        No where
Lives a woman true, and faire.

If thou findst one, let mee know,
  Such a Pilgrimage were sweet;
Yet doe not, I would not goe,
  Though at next doore wee might meet,
Though shee were true, when you met her,
And last, till you write your letter,
        Yet shee
        Will bee
False, ere I come, to two, or three.

Song

Sweetest love, I do not goe,
　For wearinesse of thee,
Nor in hope the world can show
　A fitter Love for mee;
　　But since that I
Must dye at last, 'tis best,
To use my selfe in jest
　Thus by fain'd deaths to dye;

Yesternight the Sunne went hence,
　And yet is here to day,
He hath no desire nor sense,
　Nor halfe so short a way:
　　Then feare not mee,
But beleeve that I shall make
Speedier journeyes, since I take
　More wings and spurres than hee.

O how feeble is mans power,
　That if good fortune fall,
Cannot adde another houre,
　Nor a lost houre recall!
　　But come bad chance,
And wee joyne to'it our strength,
And wee teach it art and length,
　It selfe o'r us to'advance.

When thou sigh'st, thou sigh'st not winde,
　But sigh'st my soule away,
When thou weep'st, unkindly kinde,
　My lifes blood doth decay.

It cannot bee
That thou lov'st mee, as thou say'st,
If in thine my life thou waste,
    That art the best of mee.

Let not thy divining heart
    Forethinke me any ill,
Destiny may take thy part,
    And may thy feares fulfill;
        But thinke that wee
Are but turn'd aside to sleepe;
They who one another keepe
    Alive, ne'r parted bee.

Lovers Infinitenesse

If yet I have not all thy love,
Deare, I shall never have it all,
I cannot breath one other sigh, to move,
Nor can intreat one other teare to fall,
And all my treasure, which should purchase thee,
Sighs, teares, and oathes, and letters I have spent.
Yet no more can be due to mee,
Then at the bargaine made was ment,
If then thy gift of love were partiall,
That some to mee, some should to others fall,
    Deare, I shall never have Thee All.

Or if then thou gavest mee all,
All was but All, which thou hadst then;
But if in thy heart, since, there be or shall,
New love created bee, by other men,
Which have their stocks intire, and can in teares,
In sighs, in oathes, and letters outbid mee,

This new love may beget new feares,
For, this love was not vowed by thee.
And yet it was, thy gift being generall,
The ground, thy heart is mine, what ever shall
   Grow there, deare, I should have it all.

Yet I would not have all yet,
Hee that hath all can have no more,
And since my love doth every day admit
New growth, thou shouldst have new rewards in store;
Thou canst not every day give me thy heart,
If thou canst give it, then thou never gavest it:
Loves riddles are, that though thy heart depart,
It stayes at home, and thou with losing savest it:
But wee will have a way more liberall,
Then changing hearts, to joyne them, so wee shall
   Be one, and one anothers All.

A Nocturnall upon S. Lucies Day, Being the Shortest Day

Tis the yeares midnight, and it is the dayes,
Lucies, who scarce seaven houres herself unmaskes,
  The Sunne is spent, and now his flasks
  Send forth light squibs, no constant rayes;
    The worlds whole sap is sunke:
The generall balme th'hydroptique earth hath drunk,
Whither, as to the beds-feet, life is shrunke,
Dead and enterr'd; yet all these seeme to laugh,
Compar'd with mee, who am their Epitaph.

Study me then, you who shall lovers bee
At the next world, that is, at the next Spring:
  For I am every dead thing,

   In whom love wrought new Alchimie.
      For his art did expresse
A quintessence even from nothingnesse,
From dull privations, and leane emptinesse:
He ruin'd mee, and I am re-begot
Of absence, darknesse, death; things which are not.

All others, from all things, draw all that's good,
Life, soule, forme, spirit, whence they beeing have;
   I, by loves limbecke, am the grave
   Of all, that's nothing. Oft a flood
      Have wee two wept, and so
Drownd the whole world, us two; oft did we grow
To be two Chaosses, when we did show
Care to ought else; and often absences
Withdrew our soules, and made us carcasses.

But I am by her death, (which word wrongs her)
Of the first nothing, the Elixer grown;
   Were I a man, that I were one,
   I needs must know; I should preferre,
      If I were any beast,
Some ends, some means: Yea plants, yea stones detest,
And love; All, all some properties invest;
If I an ordinary nothing were,
As shadow, a light, and body must be here.

But I am None; nor will my Sunne renew.
You lovers, for whose sake, the lesser Sunne
   At this time to the Goat is runne
   To fetch new lust, and give it you,
      Enjoy your summer all;
Since shee enjoyes her long nights festivall,
Let mee prepare towards her, and let mee call
This houre her Vigill, and her Eve, since this
Both the yeares, and the dayes deep midnight is.

A Valediction: Forbidding Mourning

As virtuous men passe mildly away,
   And whisper to their soules, to goe,
Whilst some of their sad friends doe say,
   The breath goes now, and some say, no:

So let us melt, and make no noise,
   No teare-floods, nor sigh-tempests move,
T'were prophanation of our joyes
   To tell the layetie our love.

Moving of th'earth brings harmes and feares,
   Men reckon what it did and meant,
But trepidation of the spheares,
   Though greater farre, is innocent.

Dull sublunary lovers love
   (Whose soule is sense) cannot admit
Absence, because it doth remove
   Those things which elemented it.

But we by a love, so much refin'd,
   That our selves know not what it is,
Inter-assured of the mind,
   Care lesse, eyes, lips, and hands to misse.

Our two soules therefore, which are one,
   Though I must goe, endure not yet
A breach, but an expansion,
   Like gold to ayery thinnesse beate.

If they be two, they are two so
   As stiffe twin compasses are two,

Thy soule the fixt foot, makes no show
   To move, but doth, if th' other doe.

And though it in the center sit,
   Yet when the other far doth rome,
It leanes, and hearkens after it,
   And growes erect, as that comes home.

Such wilt thou be to mee, who must
   Like th'other foot, obliquely runne;
Thy firmnes drawes my circle just,
   And makes me end, where I begunne.

The Canonization

For Godsake hold your tongue, and let me love,
   Or chide my palsie, or my gout,
My five gray haires, or ruin'd fortune flout,
   With wealth your state, your minde with Arts
      improve,
     Take you a course, get you a place,
     Observe his honour, or his grace,
Or the Kings reall, or his stamped face
   Contemplate, what you will, approve,
   So you will let me love.

Alas, alas, who's injur'd by my love?
   What merchants ships have my sighs drown'd?
Who saies my teares have overflow'd his ground?
   When did my colds a forward spring remove?
     When did the heats which my veines fill
     Adde one more to the plaguie Bill?
Soldiers finde warres, and Lawyers finde out still
   Litigious men, which quarrels move,
   Though she and I do love.

Call us what you will, wee are made such by love;
  Call her one, mee another flye,
We'are Tapers too, and at our owne cost die,
  And wee in us finde the'Eagle and the Dove.
    The Phœnix riddle hath more wit
    By us, we two being one, are it.
So to one neutrall thing both sexes fit,
  Wee dye and rise the same, and prove
  Mysterious by this love.

Wee can dye by it, if not live by love,
  And if unfit for tombes and hearse
Our legend bee, it will be fit for verse;
  And if no peece of Chronicle wee prove,
    We'll build in sonnets pretty roomes;
    As well a well wrought urne becomes
The greatest ashes, as halfe-acre tombes,
  And by these hymnes, all shall approve
  Us *Canoniz'd* for Love:

And thus invoke us; You whom reverend love
  Made one anothers hermitage;
You, to whom love was peace, that now is rage;
  Who did the whole worlds soule contract, and drove
    Into the glasses of your eyes
    (So made such mirrors, and such spies,
That they did all to you epitomize,)
  Countries, Townes, Courts: Beg from above
  A patterne of your love!

The Funerall

Who ever comes to shroud me, do not harme
        Nor question much
That subtile wreath of haire, which crowns my arme;

The mystery, the signe you must not touch,
    For'tis my outward Soule,
Viceroy to that, which then to heaven being gone,
    Will leave this to controule,
And keep these limbes, her Provinces, from dissolution.

For if the sinewie thread my braine lets fall
    Through every part,
Can tye those parts, and make mee one of all;
These haires which upward grew, and strength and art
    Have from a better braine,
Can better do'it; Except she meant that I
    By this should know my pain,
As prisoners then are manacled, when they'are con-
    demn'd to die.

What ere shee meant by'it, bury it with me,
    For since I am
Loves martyr, it might breed idolatrie,
If into others hands these Reliques came;
    As 'twas humility
To afford to it all that a Soule can doe,
    So, 'tis some bravery,
That since you would save none of mee, I bury some
    of you.

The Relique

When my grave is broke up againe
Some second ghest to entertaine,
    (For graves have learn'd that woman-head
    To be to more than one a Bed)
    And he that digs it, spies
A bracelet of bright haire about the bone,
    Will he not let'us alone,

And thinke that there a loving couple lies,
Who thought that this device might be some way
To make their soules, at the last busie day,
Meet at this grave, and make a little stay?

   If this fall in a time, or land,
   Where mis-devotion doth command,
   Then, he that digges us up, will bring
   Us, to the Bishop, and the King,
    To make us Reliques; then
Thou shalt be a Mary Magdalen, and I
   A something else thereby;
All women shall adore us, and some men;
And since at such time, miracles are sought,
I would have that age by this paper taught
What miracles wee harmlesse lovers wrought.

   First, we lov'd well and faithfully,
   Yet knew not what wee lov'd, nor why,
   Difference of sex no more wee knew,
   Than our Guardian Angells doe;
    Comming and going, wee
Perchance might kisse, but not between those meales;
   Our hands ne'r toucht the seales,
Which nature, injur'd by late law, sets free:
These miracles wee did; but now alas,
All measure, and all language, I should passe,
Should I tell what a miracle shee was.

A Jeat Ring Sent

  Thou art not so black, as my heart,
 Nor halfe so brittle, as her heart, thou art;
What would'st thou say? shall both our properties by
  thee bee spoke,

Nothing more endlesse, nothing sooner broke?
    Marriage rings are not of this stuffe;
Oh, why should ought lesse precious, or lesse tough
Figure our loves? Except in thy name thou have bid it
        say,
    I'am cheap, and nought but fashion, fling me'away.

    Yet stay with mee since thou art come,
    Circle this fingers top, which did'st her thombe.
Be justly proud, and gladly safe, that thou dost dwell
    with me,
    She that, Oh, broke her faith, would soon breake
    thee.

Twicknam Garden

Blasted with sighs, and surrounded with teares,
    Hither I come to seeke the spring,
    And at mine eyes, and at mine eares,
Receive such balmes, as else cure every thing;
    But O, selfe traytor, I do bring
The spider love, which transubstantiates all,
    And can convert Manna to gall,
And that this place may thoroughly be thought
    True Paradise, I have the serpent brought.

'Twere wholsomer for mee, that winter did
    Benight the glory of this place,
    And that a grave frost did forbid
These trees to laugh, and mocke mee to my face;
    But that I may not this disgrace
Indure, nor yet leave loving, Love let mee
    Some senslesse peece of this place bee;
Make me a mandrake, so I may groane here,
    Or a stone fountaine weeping out my yeare.

Hither with christall vyals, lovers come,
    And take my teares, which are loves wine,
    And try your mistresse Teares at home,
For all are false, that tast not just like mine;
    Alas, hearts do not in eyes shine,
Nor can you more judge womans thoughts by teares,
    Than by her shadow, what she weares.
O perverse sexe, where none is true but shee,
    Who's therefore true, because her truth kills mee.

The Extasie

Where, like a pillow on a bed,
    A Pregnant banke swel'd up, to rest
The violets reclining head,
    Sat we two, one anothers best.
Our hands were firmely cimented
    With a fast balme, which thence did spring,
Our eye-beames twisted, and did thred
    Our eyes, upon one double string;
So to'entergraft our hands, as yet
    Was all the meanes to make us one,
And pictures in our eyes to get
    Was all our propagation.
As 'twixt two equall Armies, Fate
    Suspends uncertaine victorie,
Our soules, (which to advance their state,
    Were gone out,) hung 'twixt her, and mee.
And whil'st our soules negotiate there,
    Wee like sepulchrall statues lay;
All day, the same our postures were,
    And wee said nothing, all the day.
If any, so by love refin'd,

That he soules language understood,
And by good love were growen all minde,
   Within convenient distance stood,
He (though he knew not which soul spake,
   Because both meant, both spake the same)
Might thence a new concoction take,
   And part farre purer than he came.
This Extasie doth unperplex
   (We said) and tell us what we love,
Wee see by this, it was not sexe,
   Wee see, we saw not what did move:
But as all severall soules containe
   Mixture of things, they know not what,
Love, these mixt soules, doth mixe againe,
   And makes both one, each this and that.
A single violet transplant,
   The strength, the colour, and the size,
(All which before was poore, and scant,)
   Redoubles still, and multiplies.
When love, with one another so
   Interinanimates two soules,
That abler soule, which thence doth flow,
   Defects of lonelinesse controules.
Wee then, who are this new soule, know,
   Of what we are compos'd, and made,
For, th'Atomies of which we grow,
   Are soules, whom no change can invade.
But O alas, so long, so farre
   Our bodies why doe wee forbeare?
They are ours, though they are not wee, Wee are
   The intelligences, they the spheares.
We owe them thankes, because they thus,
   Did us, to us, at first convay,
Yeelded their forces, sense, to us,
   Nor are drosse to us, but allay.

On man heavens influence workes not so,
    But that it first imprints the ayre,
Soe soule into the soule may flow,
    Though it to body first repaire.
As our blood labours to beget
    Spirits, as like soules as it can,
Because such fingers need to knit
    That subtile knot, which makes us man:
So must pure lovers soules descend
    T'affections, and to faculties,
Which sense may reach and apprehend,
    Else a great Prince in prison lies.
To'our bodies turne wee then, that so
    Weake men on love reveal'd may looke;
Loves mysteries in soules doe grow,
    But yet the body is his booke.
And if some lover, such as wee,
    Have heard this dialogue of one,
Let him still marke us, he shall see
    Small change, when we'are to bodies gone.

The Autumnall

No *Spring*, nor *Summer* Beauty hath such grace,
    As I have seen in one *Autumnall* face.
Yong *Beauties* force our love, and that's a *Rape*,
    This doth but *counsaile,* yet you cannot scape.
If t'were a *shame* to love, here t'were no *shame,*
    Affection here takes *Reverences* name.
Were her first yeares the *Golden Age;* That's true,
    But now shee's *gold* oft tried, and ever new.
That was her torrid and inflaming time,
    This is her tolerable *Tropique clyme.*

Faire eyes, who askes more heate then comes from
    hence,
  He in a fever wishes pestilence.
Call not these wrinkles, *graves;* If graves they were,
  They were *Loves graves;* for else he is no where.
Yet lies not Love *dead* here, but here doth sit
  Vow'd to this trench, like an *Anachorit.*
And here, till hers, which must be his *death,* come,
  He doth not digge a *Grave,* but build a *Tombe.*
Here dwells he, though he sojourne ev'ry where,
  In *Progresse,* yet his standing house is here.
Here, where still *Evening* is; not *noone,* nor *night;*
  Where no *voluptuousnesse,* yet all *delight.*
In all her words, unto all hearers fit,
  You may at *Revels,* you at *Counsaile,* sit.
This is loves timber, youth his under-wood;
  There he, as wine in *June,* enrages blood,
Which then comes seasonabliest, when our tast
  And appetite to other things, is past.
Xerxes strange *Lydian* love, the *Platane* tree,
  Was lov'd for age, none being so large as shee,
Or else because, being yong, nature did blesse
  Her youth with ages glory, *Barrennesse.*
If we love things long sought, *Age* is a thing
  Which we are fifty yeares in compassing.
If transitory things, which soone decay,
  Age must be lovelyest at the latest day.
But name not *Winter-faces,* whose skin's slacke;
  Lanke, as an unthrifts purse; but a soules sacke;
Whose *Eyes* seeke light within, for all here's shade;
  Whose *mouthes* are holes, rather worne out, then
    made;
Whose every tooth to a severall place is gone,
  To vexe their soules at *Resurrection;*
Name not these living *Deaths-heads* unto mee,

For these, not *Ancient*, but *Antique* be.
I hate extreames; yet I had rather stay
With *Tombs,* then *Cradles,* to weare out a day.
Since such loves naturall lation is, may still
My love descend, and journey downe the hill,
Not panting after growing beauties, so,
I shall ebbe out with them, who home-ward goe.

On His Mistris

By our first strange and fatall interview,
By all desires which thereof did ensue,
By our long starving hopes, by that remorse
Which my words masculine perswasive force
Begot in thee, and by the memory
Of hurts, which spies and rivals threatned me,
I calmly beg: But by thy fathers wrath,
By all paines, which want and divorcement hath,
I conjure thee, and all the oathes which I
And thou have sworne to seale joynt constancy,
Here I unsweare, and overswear them thus,
Thou shalt not love by wayes so dangerous.
Temper, ô faire Love, loves impetuous rage,
Be my true Mistris still, not my faign'd Page;
I'll goe, and, by thy kinde leave, leave behinde
Thee, onely worthy to nurse in my minde,
Thirst to come backe; ô if thou die before,
My soule from other lands to thee shall soare.
Thy (else Almighty) beautie cannot move
Rage from the Seas, nor thy love teach them love,
Nor tame wilde Boreas harshnesse; Thou hast reade
How roughly hee in peeces shivered
Faire Orithea, whom he swore he lov'd.

Fall ill or good, 'tis madnesse to have prov'd
Dangers unurg'd; Feed on this flattery,
That absent Lovers one in th'other be.
Dissemble nothing, not a boy, nor change
Thy bodies habite, nor mindes; bee not strange
To thy selfe onely; All will spie in thy face
A blushing womanly discovering grace;
Richly cloath'd Apes, are call'd Apes, and as soone
Ecclips'd as bright we call the Moone the Moone.
Men of France, changeable Camelions,
Spittles of diseases, shops of fashions,
Loves fuellers, and the rightest company
Of Players, which upon the worlds stage be,
Will quickly know thee, and no lesse, alas!
Th'indifferent Italian, as we passe
His warme land, well content to thinke thee Page,
Will hunt thee with such lust, and hideous rage,
As *Lots* faire guests were vext. But none of these
Nor spungy hydroptique Dutch shall thee displease,
If thou stay here. O stay here, for, for thee
England is onely a worthy Gallerie,
To walke in expectation, till from thence
Our greatest King call thee to his presence.
When I am gone, dreame me some happinesse,
Nor let thy lookes our long hid love confesse,
Nor praise, nor dispraise me, nor blesse nor curse
Openly loves force, nor in bed fright thy Nurse
With midnights startings, crying out, oh, oh
Nurse, ô my love is slaine, I saw him goe
O'r the white Alpes alone; I saw him I,
Assail'd, fight, taken, stabb'd, bleed, fall, and die.
Augure me better chance, except dread *Jove*
Thinke it enough for me to'have had thy love.

Satire, III

Kinde pitty chokes my spleene; brave scorn forbids
Those teares to issue which swell my eye-lids;
I must not laugh, nor weepe sinnes, and be wise,
Can railing then cure these worne maladies?
Is not our Mistresse faire Religion,
As worthy of all our Soules devotion,
As vertue was to the first blinded age?
Are not heavens joyes as valiant to asswage
Lusts, as earths honour was to them? Alas,
As wee do them in meanes, shall they surpasse
Us in the end, and shall thy fathers spirit
Meete blinde Philosophers in heaven, whose merit
Of strict life may be imputed faith, and heare
Thee, whom hee taught so easie wayes and neare
To follow, damn'd? O if thou dar'st, feare this;
This feare great courage, and high valour is.
Dar'st thou ayd mutinous Dutch, and dar'st thou lay
Thee in ships woodden Sepulchers, a prey
To leaders rage, to stormes, to shot, to dearth?
Dar'st thou dive seas, and dungeons of the earth?
Hast thou couragious fire to thaw the ice
Of frozen North discoveries? and thrise
Colder than Salamanders, like divine
Children in th'oven, fires of Spaine, and the line,
Whose countries limbecks to our bodies bee,
Canst thou for gaine beare? and must every hee
Which cryes not, Goddesse, to thy Mistresse, draw,
Or eate thy poysonous words? courage of straw!
O desperate coward, wilt thou seeme bold, and
To thy foes and his (who made thee to stand

Sentinell in his worlds garrison) thus yeeld,
And for the forbidden warres, leave th'appointed field?
Know thy foes: The foule Devill (whom thou
Strivest to please,) for hate, not love, would allow
Thee faine, his whole Realme to be quit; and as
The worlds all parts wither away and passe,
So the worlds selfe, thy other lov'd foe, is
In her decrepit wayne, and thou loving this,
Dost love a withered and worne strumpet; last,
Flesh (it selfes death) and joyes which flesh can taste,
Thou lovest; and thy faire goodly soule, which doth
Give this flesh power to taste joy, thou dost loath.
Seeke true religion. O where? Mirreus
Thinking her unhous'd here, and fled from us,
Seekes her at Rome; there, because hee doth know
That shee was there a thousand yeares agoe,
He loves her ragges so, as wee here obey
The statecloth where the Prince sate yesterday.
Crantz to such brave Loves will not be inthrall'd,
But loves her onely, who at Geneva is call'd
Religion, plaine, simple, sullen, yong,
Contemptuous, yet unhansome; As among
Lecherous humors, there is one that judges
No wenches wholsome, but course country drudges.
Graius stayes still at home here, and because
Some Preachers, vile ambitious bauds, and lawes
Still new like fashions, bid him thinke that shee
Which dwels with us, is onely perfect, hee
Imbraceth her, whom his Godfathers will
Tender to him, being tender, as Wards still
Take such wives as their Guardians offer, or
Pay valewes. Carelesse Phrygius doth abhorre
All, because all cannot be good, as one
Knowing some women whores, dares marry none.
Gracious loves all as one, and thinkes that so

As women do in divers countries goe
In divers habits, yet are still one kinde,
So doth, so is Religion; and this blind-
nesse too much light breeds; but unmoved thou
Of force must one, and forc'd but one allow;
And the right; aske thy father which is shee,
Let him aske his; though truth and falsehood bee
Neare twins, yet truth a little elder is;
Be busie to seeke her, beleeve mee this,
Hee's not of none, nor worst, that seekes the best.
To adore, or scorne an image, or protest,
May all be bad; doubt wisely; in strange way
To stand inquiring right, is not to stray;
To sleepe, or runne wrong, is. On a huge hill,
Cragged, and steep, Truth stands, and hee that will
Reach her, about must, and about must goe;
And what the hills suddennes resists, winne so;
Yet strive so, that before age, deaths twilight,
Thy Soule rest, for none can worke in that night.
To will, implyes delay, therefore now doe:
Hard deeds, the bodies paines; hard knowledge too
The mindes indeavours reach, and mysteries
Are like the Sunne, dazling, yet plaine to all eyes.
Keepe the truth which thou hast found; men do not stand
In so ill case here, that God hath with his hand
Sign'd Kings blanck-charters to kill whom they hate,
Nor are they Vicars, but hangman to Fate.
Foole and wretch, wilt thou let thy Soule be tyed
To mans lawes, by which she shall not be tryed
At the last day? Oh, will it then boot thee
To say a Philip, or a Gregory,
A Harry, or a Martin taught thee this?
Is not this excuse for mere contraries,
Equally strong? cannot both sides say so?
That thou mayest rightly obey power, her bounds know;

Those past, her nature, and name is chang'd; to be
Then humble to her is idolatrie.
As streames are, Power is; those blest flowers that dwell
At the rough streames calme head, thrive and do well,
But having left their roots, and themselves given
To the streames tyrannous rage, alas are driven
Through mills, and rockes, and woods, and at last, almost
Consum'd in going, in the sea are lost:
So perish Soules, which more chuse mens unjust
Power from God claym'd, than God himselfe to trust.

FROM *The Progresse of the Soule*

It quickned next a toyfull Ape, and so
Gamesome it was, that it might freely goe
From tent to tent, and with the children play.
His organs now so like theirs hee doth finde,
That why he cannot laugh, and speake his minde,
He wonders. Much with all, most he doth stay
With Adams fift daughter *Siphatecia*,
Doth gaze on her, and, where she passeth, passe,
Gathers her fruits, and tumbles on the grasse,
    And wisest of that kinde, the first true lover was.

He was the first that more desir'd to have
One than another; first that ere did crave
Love by mute signes, and had no power to speake;
First that could make love faces, or could doe
The valters sombersalts, or us'd to wooe
With hoiting gambolls, his owne bones to breake
To make his mistresse merry; or to wreake
Her anger on himselfe. Sinnes against kinde

They easily doe, that can let feed their minde
  With outward beauty; beauty they in boyes and
    beasts do find.

By this misled, too low things men have prov'd,
And too high; beasts and angels have beene lov'd.
This Ape, though else through-vaine, in this was wise,
He reach'd at things too high, but open way
There was, and he knew not she would say nay;
His toyes prevaile not, likelier meanes he tries,
He gazeth on her face with teare-shot eyes,
And up lifts subtly with his russet pawe
Her kidskinne apron without feare or awe
  Of Nature; Nature hath no gaole, though shee hath
    law.

First she was silly and knew not what he ment.
That vertue, by his touches, chaft and spent,
Succeeds an itchie warmth, that melts her quite;
She knew not first, nowe cares not what he doth,
And willing halfe and more, more than halfe loth,
She neither puls nor pushes, but outright
Now cries, and now repents; when *Tethlemite*
Her brother, enterd, and a great stone threw
After the Ape, who, thus prevented, flew.
  This house thus batter'd downe, the Soule possest a
    new.

(Stanzas 46–49)

Holy Sonnets

Thou hast made me, And shall thy worke decay?
Repaire me now, for now mine end doth haste,
I runne to death, and death meets me as fast,

And all my pleasures are like yesterday;
I dare not move my dimme eyes any way,
Despaire behind, and death before doth cast
Such terrour, and my feeble flesh doth waste
By sinne in it, which it t'wards hell doth weigh;
Onely thou art above, and when towards thee
By thy leave I can looke, I rise againe;
But our old subtle foe so tempteth me,
That not one houre my selfe I can sustaine;
Thy Grace may wing me to prevent his art,
And thou like Adamant draw mine iron heart.

(i)

At the round earths imagin'd corners, blow
Your trumpets, Angells, and arise, arise
From death, you numberlesse infinities
Of soules, and to your scattred bodies goe,
All whom the flood did, and fire shall o'erthrow,
All whom warre, dearth, age, agues, tyrannies,
Despaire, law, chance, hath slaine, and you whose eyes,
Shall behold God, and never tast deaths woe.
But let them sleepe, Lord, and mee mourne a space,
For, if above all these, my sinnes abound,
'Tis late to aske abundance of thy grace,
When wee are there; here on this lowly ground,
Teach mee how to repent; for that's as good
As if thou'hadst seal'd my pardon, with thy blood.

(vii)

If poysonous mineralls, and if that tree,
Whose fruit threw death on else immortall us,
If lecherous goats, if serpents envious

Cannot be damn'd; Alas; why should I bee?
Why should intent or reason, borne in mee,
Make sinnes, else equall, in mee more heinous?
And mercy being easie, and glorious
To God; in his sterne wrath, why threatens hee?
But who am I, that dare dispute with thee
O God? Oh! of thine onely worthy blood,
And my teares, make a heavenly Lethean flood,
And drowne in it my sinnes black memorie;
That thou remember them, some claime as debt,
I thinke it mercy if thou wilt forget.

(ix)

Death be not proud, though some have called thee
Mighty and dreadfull, for, thou art not soe,
For, those, whom thou think'st, thou dost overthrow,
Die not, poore death, nor yet canst thou kill mee.
From rest and sleepe, which but thy pictures bee,
Much pleasure, then from thee, much more must flow,
And soonest our best men with thee doe goe,
Rest of their bones, and soules deliverie.
Thou art slave to Fate, Chance, kings, and desperate
    men,
And dost with poyson, warre, and sicknesse dwell,
And poppie, or charmes can make us sleepe as well,
And better than thy stroake; why swell'st thou then?
One short sleepe past, wee wake eternally,
And death shall be no more; death, thou shalt die.

(x)

Why are wee by all creatures waited on?
Why doe the prodigall elements supply
Life and food to mee, being more pure than I,

Simple, and further from corruption?
Why brook'st thou, ignorant horse, subjection?
Why dost thou bull, and bore so seelily
Dissemble weaknesse, and by'one mans stroke die,
Whose whole kinde, you might swallow and feed upon?
Weaker I am, woe is mee, and worse then you,
You have not sinn'd, nor need be timorous.
But wonder at a greater wonder, for to us
Created nature doth these things subdue,
But their Creator, whom sin, nor nature tyed,
For us, his Creatures, and his foes, hath dyed.

(*xii*)

Batter my heart, three person'd God; for, you
As yet but knocke, breathe, shine, and seeke to mend;
That I may rise, and stand, o'erthrow mee,'and bend
Your force, to breake, blowe, burn and make me new.
I, like an usurpt towne, to'another due,
Labour to'admit you, but Oh, to no end,
Reason your viceroy in mee, mee should defend,
But is captiv'd, and proves weake or untrue.
Yet dearely'I love you,'and would be loved faine,
But am bethroth'd unto your enemie:
Divorce mee,'untie, or breake that knot againe,
Take mee to you, imprison mee, for I
Except you'enthrall mee, never shall be free,
Nor ever chast, except you ravish mee.

(*xiv*)

Oh, to vex me, contraryes meet in one:
Inconstancy unnaturally hath begott
A constant habit; that when I would not
I change in vowes, and in devotione.

As humorous in my contritione
As my prophane Love, and as soone forgott:
As ridlingly distemper'd, cold and hott,
As praying, as mute; as infinite, as none.
I durst not view heaven yesterday; and to day
In prayers, and flattering speaches I court God:
To morrow I quake with true feare of his rod.
So my devout fitts come and go away
Like a fantastique Ague: save that here
Those are my best dayes, when I shake with feare.

(*xix*)

The Litanie

THE FATHER

Father of Heaven, and him, by whom
It, and us for it, and all else, for us
  Thou madest, and govern'st ever, come
And re-create mee, now growne ruinous:
     My heart is by dejection, clay,
      And by selfe-murder, red.
From this red earth, O Father, purge away
All vicious tinctures, that new fashioned
I may rise up from death, before I'm dead.

THE SONNE

  O Sonne of God, who seeing two things,
Sinne, and death crept in, which were never made,
  By bearing one, tryed'st with what stings
The other could thine heritage invade;
     O be thou nail'd unto my heart,
      And crucified againe,
Part not from it, though it from thee would part,
But let it be, by applying so thy paine,
Drown'd in thy blood, and in thy passion slaine.

THE HOLY GHOST

O Holy Ghost, whose temple I
Am, but of mudde walls, and condensed dust,
   And being sacrilegiously
Halfe wasted with youths fires, of pride and lust,
       Must with new stormes be weatherbeat;
       Double in my heart thy flame,
Which let devout sad teares intend; and let
(Through this glasse lanthorne, flesh, do suffer maime)
Fire, Sacrifice, Priest, Altar be the same.

THE TRINITY

O Blessed glorious Trinity,
Bones to Philosophy, but milke to faith,
   Which, as wise serpents, diversly
Most slipperinesse, yet most entanglings hath,
       As you distinguish'd undistinct
       By power, love, knowledge bee,
Give mee a such selfe different instinct
Of these; let all mee elemented bee,
Of power, to love, to know, you unnumbred three.

THE VIRGIN MARY

For that faire blessed Mother-maid,
Whose flesh redeem'd us; that she-Cherubin,
   Which unlock'd Paradise, and made
One claime for innocence, and disseiz'd sinne,
       Whose wombe was a strange heav'n, for there
       God cloath'd himselfe, and grew,
Our zealous thankes wee poure. As her deeds were
Our helpes, so are her prayers; nor can she sue
In vaine, who hath such titles unto you.

THE ANGELS

And since this life our nonage is,
And wee in Wardship to thine Angels be,

Native in heavens faire Palaces,
Where we shall be but denizen'd by thee,
    As th'earth conceiving by the Sunne,
    Yeelds faire diversitie,
Yet never knowes which course that light doth run,
So let mee study, that mine actions bee
Worthy their sight, though blinde in how they see.

THE PATRIARCHES

And let thy Patriarches Desire
(Those great Grandfathers of thy Church, which saw
    More in the cloud, than wee in fire,
Whom Nature clear'd more, then us Grace and Law,
    And now in Heaven still pray, that wee
    May use our new helpes right,)
Be satisfy'd, and fructifie in mee;
Let not my minde be blinder by more light
Nor Faith, by Reason added, lose her sight.

THE PROPHETS

Thy Eagle-sighted Prophets too,
Which were thy Churches Organs, and did sound
    That harmony, which made of two
One law, and did unite, but not confound;
    Those heavenly Poëts which did see
    Thy will, and it expresse
In rythmique feet, in common pray for mee,
That I by them excuse not my excesse
In seeking secrets, or Poëtiquenesse.

THE APOSTLES

And thy illustrious Zodiacke
Of twelve Apostles, which ingirt this All,
    (From whom whosoever do not take
Their light, to darke deep pits, throw downe, and fall,)
    As through their prayers, thou'hast let mee know

That their bookes are divine;
May they pray still, and be heard, that I goe
Th'old broad way in applying; O decline
Mee, when my comment would make thy word mine.

THE MARTYRS

And since thou so desirously
Did'st long to die, that long before thou could'st,
And long since thou no more couldst dye,
Thou in thy scatter'd mystique body wouldst
In Abel dye, and ever since
In thine; let their blood come
To begge for us, a discreet patience
Of death, or of worse life: for Oh, to some
Not to be Martyrs, is a martyrdome.

THE CONFESSORS

Therefore with thee triumpheth there
A Virgin Squadron of white Confessors,
Whose bloods betroth'd, not marryed were,
Tender'd, not taken by those Ravishers:
They know, and pray, that wee may know,
In every Christian
Hourly tempestuous persecutions grow;
Tentations martyr us alive; A man
Is to himselfe a Dioclesian.

THE VIRGINS

The cold white snowie Nunnery,
Which, as thy mother, their high Abbesse, sent
Their bodies backe againe to thee,
As thou hadst lent them, cleane and innocent,
Though they have not obtain'd of thee,
That or thy Church, or I,
Should keep, as they, our first integrity;
Divorce thou sinne in us, or bid it die,
And call chast widowhead Virginitie.

THE DOCTORS

Thy sacred Academie above
Of Doctors, whose paines have unclasp'd, and taught
  Both bookes of life to us (for love
To know thy Scriptures tells us, we are wrote
    In thy other booke) pray for us there
    That what they have misdone
Or mis-said, wee to that may not adhere;
Their zeale may be our sinne. Lord let us runne
Meane waies, and call them stars, but not the Sunne.

And whil'st this universall Quire,
That Church in triumph, this in warfare here,
  Warm'd with one all-partaking fire
Of love, that none be lost, which cost thee deare,
    Prayes ceaslesly, 'and thou hearken too,
    (Since to be gratious
Our taske is treble, to pray, beare, and doe)
Heare this prayer Lord: O Lord deliver us
From trusting in those prayers, though powr'd out thus.

From being anxious, or secure,
Dead clods of sadnesse, or light squibs of mirth,
  From thinking, that great courts immure
All, or no happinesse, or that this earth
    Is only for our prison fram'd,
    Or that thou art covetous
To them thou lovest, or that they are maim'd
From reaching this worlds sweet, who seek thee thus,
With all their might, Good Lord deliver us.

From needing danger, to bee good,
From owing thee yesterdaies teares to day,
  From trusting so much to thy blood,
That in that hope, wee wound our soule away,

From bribing thee with Almes, to excuse
    Some sinne more burdenous,
From light affecting, in religion, newes,
From thinking us all soule, neglecting thus
Our mutuall duties, Lord deliver us.

    From tempting Satan to tempt us,
By our connivence, or slack companie,
    From measuring ill by vitious,
Neglecting to choake sins spawne, Vanitie,
        From indiscreet humilitie,
        Which might be scandalous,
And cast reproach on Christianitie,
From being spies, or to spies pervious,
From thirst, or scorne of fame, deliver us.

    Deliver us for thy descent
Into the Virgin, whose wombe was a place
    Of middle kind; and thou being sent
To'ungratious us, staid'st at her full of grace;
        And through thy poore birth, where first thou
        Glorifiedst Povertie,
And yet soone after riches didst allow,
By accepting Kings gifts in the Epiphanie,
Deliver, and make us, to both waies free.

    And through that bitter agonie,
Which is still the agonie of pious wits,
    Disputing what distorted thee,
And interrupted evennesse, with fits;
        And through thy free confession
        Though thereby they were then
Made blind, so that thou might'st from them have
        gone,
Good Lord deliver us, and teach us when
Wee may not, and we may blinde unjust men.

Through thy submitting all, to blowes
Thy face, thy clothes to spoile; thy fame to scorne,
   All waies, which rage, or Justice knowes,
And by which thou could'st shew, that thou wast born;
     And through thy gallant humblenesse
     Which thou in death did'st shew,
Dying before thy soule they could expresse,
Deliver us from death, by dying so,
To this world, ere this world doe bid us goe.

   When senses, which thy souldiers are,
Wee arme against thee, and they fight for sinne,
   When want, sent but to tame, doth warre
And worke despaire a breach to enter in,
     When plenty, Gods image, and seale
     Makes us Idolatrous,
And love it, not him, whom it should reveale,
When wee are mov'd to seeme religious
Only to vent wit, Lord deliver us.

   In Churches, when the'infirmitie
Of him which speakes, diminishes the Word,
   When Magistrates doe mis-apply
To us, as we judge, lay or ghostly sword,
     When plague, which is thine Angell, raignes,
     Or wars, thy Champions, swaie,
When Heresie, thy second deluge, gaines;
In th'houre of death, th'Eve of last judgement day,
Deliver us from the sinister way.

   Heare us, O heare us Lord; to thee
A sinner is more musique, when he prayes,
   Than spheares, or Angells praises bee,
In Panegyrique Allelujaes;
     Heare us, for till thou heare us, Lord
     We know not what to say;

Thine eare to'our sighes, teares, thoughts gives voice
          and word.
O Thou who Satan heard'st in Jobs sicke day,
Heare thy selfe now, for thou in us dost pray.

   That wee may change to evennesse
This intermitting aguish Pietie;
   That snatching cramps of wickednesse
And Apoplexies of fast sin, may die;
      That musique of thy promises,
      Not threats in Thunder may
Awaken us to our just offices;
What in thy booke, thou dost, or creatures say,
That we may heare, Lord heare us, when wee pray.

   That our eares sicknesse wee may cure,
And rectifie those Labyrinths aright,
   That wee, by harkning, not procure
Our praise, nor others dispraise so invite,
      That wee get not a slipperinesse,
      And senslesly decline,
From hearing bold wits jeast at Kings excesse,
To'admit the like of majestie divine,
That we may locke our eares, Lord open thine.

   That living law, the Magistrate,
Which to give us, and make us physicke, doth
   Our vices often aggravate,
That Preachers taxing sinne, before her growth,
      That Satan, and invenom'd men
      Which well, if we starve, dine,
When they doe most accuse us, may see then
Us, to amendment, heare them; thee decline:
That we may open our eares, Lord lock thine.

   That learning, thine Ambassador,
From thine allegeance wee never tempt,

That beauty, paradises flower
For physicke made, from poyson be exempt,
That wit, borne apt high good to doe,
By dwelling lazily
On Natures nothing, be not nothing too,
That our affections kill us not, nor dye,
Heare us, weake ecchoes, O thou eare, and cry.

Sonne of God heare us, and since thou
By taking our blood, owest it us againe,
Gaine to thy self, or us allow;
And let not both us and thy selfe be slaine;
O Lambe of God, which took'st our sinne
Which could not stick to thee,
O let it not returne to us againe,
But Patient and Physition being free,
As sinne is nothing, let it no where be.

Goodfriday, 1613. Riding Westward

Let mans Soule be a Spheare, and then, in this,
The intelligence that moves, devotion is,
And as the other Spheares, by being growne
Subject to forraigne motions, lose their owne,
And being by others hurried every day,
Scarce in a yeare their naturall forme obey:
Pleasure or businesse, so, our Soules admit
For their first mover, and are whirld by it.
Hence is't, that I am carryed towards the West
This day, when my Soules forme bends toward the East.
There I should see a Sunne, by rising set,
And by that setting endlesse day beget;

But that Christ on this Crosse, did rise and fall,
Sinne had eternally benighted all.
Yet dare I'almost be glad, I do not see
That spectacle of too much weight for mee.
Who sees Gods face, that is selfe life, must dye;
What a death were it then to see God dye?
It made his owne Lieutenant Nature shrinke,
It made his footstoole crack, and the Sunne winke.
Could I behold those hands which span the Poles,
And turne all spheares at once, peirc'd with those holes?
Could I behold that endlesse height which is
Zenith to us, and our Antipodes,
Humbled below us? or that blood which is
The seat of all our Soules, if not of his,
Made durt of dust, or that flesh which was worne
By God, for his apparell, rag'd, and torne?
If on these things I durst not looke, durst I
Upon his miserable mother cast mine eye,
Who was Gods partner here, and furnish'd thus
Halfe of that Sacrifice, which ransom'd us?
Though these things, as I ride, be from mine eye,
They'are present yet unto my memory,
For that looks towards them; and thou look'st towards
    mee,
O Saviour, as thou hang'st upon the tree;
I turne my backe to thee, but to receive
Corrections, till thy mercies bid thee leave.
O thinke mee worth thine anger, punish mee,
Burne off my rusts, and my deformity,
Restore thine Image, so much, by thy grace,
That thou may'st know mee, and I'll turne my face.

Hymne to God My God, in My Sicknesse

Since I am comming to that Holy roome,
   Where, with thy Quire of Saints for evermore,
I shall be made thy Musique; As I come
   I tune the Instrument here at the dore,
   And what I must doe then, thinke here before.

Whilst my Physitians by their love are growne
   Cosmographers, and I their Mapp, who lie
Flat on this bed, that by them may be showne
   That this is my South-west discoverie
   Per fretum febris, by these streights to die,

I joy, that in these straits, I see my West;
   For, though theire currants yeeld returne to none,
What shall my West hurt me? As West and East
   In all flatt Maps (and I am one) are one,
   So death doth touch the Resurrection.

Is the Pacifique Sea my home? Or are
   The Easterne riches? Is *Jerusalem?*
Anyan, and *Magellan,* and *Gibraltare,*
   All streights, and none but streights, are wayes to
     them,
   Whether where *Japhet* dwelt, or *Cham,* or *Sem.*

We thinke that *Paradise* and *Calvarie,*
   Christs Crosse, and *Adams* tree, stood in one place;
Looke Lord, and finde both *Adams* met in me;
   As the first *Adams* sweat surrounds my face,
   May the last *Adams* blood my soule embrace.

So, in his purple wrapp'd receive mee Lord,
   By these his thornes give me his other Crowne;

And as to others soules I preach'd thy word,
  Be this my Text, my Sermon to mine owne,
  Therfore that he may raise the Lord throws down.

A Hymne to God the Father

Wilt thou forgive that sinne where I begunne,
  Which was my sin, though it were done before?
Wilt thou forgive that sinne; through which I runne,
  And do run still: though still I do deplore?
    When thou hast done, thou hast not done,
      For I have more.

Wilt thou forgive that sinne which I have wonne
  Others to sinne? and, made my sinne their doore?
Wilt thou forgive that sinne which I did shunne
  A yeare, or two: but wallowed in, a score?
    When thou hast done, thou hast not done,
      For I have more.

I have a sinne of feare, that when I have spunne
  My last thred, I shall perish on the shore;
But sweare by thy selfe, that at my death thy sonne
  Shall shine as he shines now, and heretofore;
    And, having done that, Thou haste done,
      I feare no more.

Lord Herbert of Cherbury

(1583–1648)

To His Watch, When He Could Not Sleep

Uncessant Minutes, whil'st you move you tell
   The time that tells our life, which though it run
   Never so fast or farr, you'r new begun
Short steps shall overtake; for though life well

May scape his own Account, it shall not yours,
   You are Death's Auditors, that both divide
And summ what ere that life inspir'd endures
   Past a beginning, and through you we bide

The doom of Fate, whose unrecall'd Decree
   You date, bring, execute; making what's new
   Ill and good, old, for as we die in you,
You die in Time, Time in Eternity.

Madrigal

How should I love my best?
What though my love unto that height be grown,
   That taking joy in you alone
     I utterly this world detest,
Should I not love it yet as th'only place
   Where Beauty hath his perfect grace,
     And is possest?

413

But I beauties despise,
You, universal beauty seem to me,
        Giving and shewing form and degree
        To all the rest, in your fair eyes,
Yet should I not love them as parts whereon
        Your beauty, their perfection
        And top, doth rise?

But ev'n my self I hate,
So far my love is from the least delight
        That at my very self I spite,
        Sensless of any happy state,
Yet may I not with justest reason fear
        How hating hers, I truly her
        Can celebrate?

This unresolved still
Although world, life, nay what is fair beside
        I cannot for your sake abide,
        Methinks I love not to my fill,
Yet if a greater love you can devise,
        In loving you some otherwise,
        Believe't, I will.

Elegy over a Tomb

Must I then see, alas! eternal night
        Sitting upon those fairest eyes,
And closing all those beams, which once did rise
        So radiant and bright,
That light and heat in them to us did prove
        Knowledge and Love?

Oh, if you did delight no more to stay
    Upon this low and earthly stage
But rather chose an endless heritage,
    Tell us at least, we pray,
Where all the beauties that those ashes ow'd
    Are now bestow'd?

Doth the Sun now his light with yours renew?
    Have Waves the curling of your hair?
Did you restore unto the Sky and Air,
    The red, and white, and blew?
Have you vouchsafed to flowrs since your death
    That sweetest breath?

Had not Heav'ns Lights else in their houses slept,
    Or to some private life retir'd?
Must not the Sky and Air have else conspir'd,
    And in their Regions wept?
Must not each flower else the earth could breed
    Have been a weed?

But thus enrich'd may we not yield some cause
    Why they themselves lament no more?
That must have changed the course they held before,
    And broke their proper Laws,
Had not your beauties giv'n this second birth
    To Heaven and Earth?

Tell us, for Oracles must still ascend,
    For those that crave them at your tomb:
Tell us, where are those beauties now become,
    And what they now intend:
Tell us, alas, that cannot tell our grief,
    Or hope relief.

Sonnet

Innumerable Beauties, thou white haire
   Spredde forth like to a Region of the Aire,
Curld like a sea, and like Ethereall fire
   Dost from thy vitall principles aspire
To bee the highest Element of faire,
   From thy proud heights, thou so commandst desire
That when it would presume, it grows, dispare,
   And from it selfe a Vengeance, doth require,
While absolute in that thy brave command
   Knittinge each haire, into an awfull frowne
Like to an Hoste of Lightninges, thou dost stand
   To ruine all that fall not prostrate doune
   While to the humble like a beamy Croune
Thou seemest wreathed, by some immortall Hande.

Echo to a Rock

Thou heaven-threat'ning Rock, gentler then she!
     Since of my pain
  Thou still more sensible wilt be,
Only when thou giv'st leave but to complain.
       Echo Complain.

But thou dost answer too, although in vain
  Thou answer'st when thou canst no pity show.
          Echo Oh.
    What canst thou speak and pity too?
    Then yet a further favour do,

And tell if of my griefs I any end shall know.

Echo No.

Sure she will pity him that loves her so truly.

Echo You ly.

Vile Rock, thou now grow'st so unruly,

That had'st thou life as thou hast voice,

Thou should'st dye at my foot.

Echo Dye at my foot.

Thou canst not make me do't,

Unless thou leave it to my choice,

Who thy hard sentence shall fulfill,

When thou shalt say, I dye to please her only will.

Echo I will.

When she comes hither, then, I pray thee, tell,

Thou art my Monument, and this my last farewell.

Echo Well.

William Drummond
of Hawthornden

(1585–1649)

Madrigal

Like the *Idalian* Queene
Her Haire about her Eyne,
With Necke and Brests ripe Apples to be seene,
At first Glance of the *Morne*
In *Cyprus* Gardens gathering those faire Flowrs
Which of her Bloud were borne,
I saw, but fainting saw, my Paramours.
The *Graces* naked danc'd about the Place,
The *Winds* and *Trees* amaz'd
With Silence on Her gaz'd,
The Flowrs did smile, like those upon her Face,
And as their Aspine Stalkes those fingers band,
(That Shee might read my Case)
A *Hyacinth* I wisht mee in her Hand.

Iölas' Epitaph

Here deare *Iölas* lies,
Who whilst hee liv'd in Beautie did surpasse
That Boy, whose heavenly Eyes

418

Brought *Cypris* from above,
Or him till Death who look'd in watrie Glasse,
Even Judge the God of Love:
And if the Nymphe once held of him so deare,
Dorine the faire, would heere but shed one Teare,
Thou shouldst (in *Natures* Scorne)
A purple Flowre see of this Marble borne.

For the Magdalene

These Eyes (deare Lord) once Brandons of Desire,
Fraile Scouts betraying what they had to keepe,
Which their owne heart, then others set on fire,
Their traitrous blacke before thee heere out-weepe:
These Lockes, of blushing deedes the faire attire,
Smooth-frizled Waves, sad Shelfes which shadow deepe,
Soule-stinging Serpents in gilt curles which creepe,
To touch thy sacred Feete doe now aspire.
In Seas of Care behold a sinking Barke,
By windes of sharpe Remorse unto thee driven
O let mee not expos'd be Ruines marke,
My faults confest (Lord) say they are forgiven.
   Thus sigh'd to Jesus the Bethanian faire,
   His teare-wet Feet still drying with her Haire.

To Sir W. A.

Though I have twice beene at the Doores of *Death*,
And twice found shoote those Gates which ever mourne,
This but a lightning is, Truce tane to Breath,
For late borne Sorrowes augure fleete returne.

Amidst thy sacred Cares, and courtlie Toyles,
Alexis, when thou shalt heare wandring Fame
Tell, *Death* hath triumph'd o're my mortall Spoyles,
And that on Earth I am but a sad Name;

If thou e're helde mee deare, by all our Love,
By all that Blisse, those Joyes Heaven heere us gave,
I conjure Thee, and by the Maides of *Jove,*
To grave this short Remembrance on my Grave.
    Heere *Damon* lyes, whose Songes did some-time
      grace
    The murmuring *Eske,* may Roses shade the place.

Madrigal

The Beautie, and the Life,
Of *Lifes,* and *Beauties* fairest Paragon,
(O Teares! O Griefe!) hang at a feeble Thread,
To which pale *Atropos* had set her Knife,
The Soule with many a Grone
Had left each outward Part,
And now did take his last Leave of the Heart,
Nought else did want, save *Death,* even to be dead:
When the afflicting Band about her Bed
    (Seeing so faire him come in Lips, Cheekes, Eyes)
    Cried, *ah!* and can *Death enter Paradise?*

Regrat

    In this Worlds raging sea
    Where many Sillas barke,
    Where many Syrens are,

Save, and not cast away,
Hee onlye saves his barge
With too much ware who doth it not o'recharge;
Or when huge stormes arise,
And waves menace the skies,
Gives what he got with no deploring show,
And doth againe in seas his burthen throw.

William Browne

(c.1591–c.1643)

On the Countess Dowager of Pembroke

Underneath this sable Herse
Lies the subject of all Verse;
Sidney's sister, Pembroke's mother:
Death, ere thou hast slaine another,
Faire, and learn'd, and good as she,
Time shall throw a dart at thee.

Marble piles let no man raise
To her name, for after-dayes:
Some kind woman borne as she,
Reading this, (like Niobe)
Shall turne Marble, and become
Both her mourner and her tombe.

Henry King

(1592–1669)

The Exequy

Accept thou Shrine of my dead Saint,
Insteed of Dirges this complaint;
And for sweet flowres to crown thy hearse,
Receive a strew of weeping verse
From thy griev'd friend, whom thou might'st see
Quite melted into tears for thee.

   Dear loss! since thy untimely fate
My task hath been to meditate
On thee, on thee: thou art the book,
The library whereon I look
Though almost blind. For thee (lov'd clay)
I languish out not live the day,
Using no other exercise
But what I practise with mine eyes:
By which wet glasses I find out
How lazily time creeps about
To one that mourns: this, onely this
My exercise and bus'ness is:
So I compute the weary houres
With sighs dissolved into showres.

   Nor wonder if my time go thus
Backward and most preposterous;
Thou hast benighted me, thy set
This Eve of blackness did beget,

Who was't my day, (though overcast
Before thou had'st thy Noon-tide past)
And I remember must in tears,
Thou scarce had'st seen so many years
As Day tells houres. By thy cleer Sun
My love and fortune first did run;
But thou wilt never more appear
Folded within my Hemisphear,
Since both thy light and motion
Like a fled Star is fall'n and gon,
And twixt me and my soules dear wish
The earth now interposed is,
With such a strange eclipse doth make
As ne're was read in Almanake.

I could allow thee for a time
To darken me and my sad Clime,
Were it a month, a year, or ten,
I would thy exile live till then;
And all that space my mirth adjourn,
So thou wouldst promise to return;
And putting off thy ashy shrowd
At length disperse this sorrows cloud.

But woe is me! the longest date
Too narrow is to calculate
These empty hopes: never shall I
Be so much blest as to descry
A glimpse of thee, till that day come
Which shall the earth to cinders doome,
And a fierce Feaver must calcine
The body of this world like thine,
(My Little World!) that fit of fire
Once off, our bodies shall aspire
To our soules bliss: then we shall rise,
And view our selves with cleerer eyes

In that calm Region, where no night
Can hide us from each others sight.

    Mean time, thou hast her earth: much good
May my harm do thee. Since it stood
With Heavens will I might not call
Her longer mine, I give thee all
My short-liv'd right and interest
In her, whom living I lov'd best:
With a most free and bounteous grief,
I give thee what I could not keep.
Be kind to her, and prethee look
Thou write into thy Dooms-day book
Each parcell of this Rarity
Which in thy Casket shrin'd doth ly:
See that thou make thy reck'ning streight,
And yield her back again by weight;
For thou must audit on thy trust
Each graine and atome of this dust,
As thou wilt answer *Him* that lent,
Not gave thee my dear Monument.

    So close the ground, and 'bout her shade
Black curtains draw, my *Bride* is laid.

    Sleep on my *Love* in thy cold bed
Never to be disquieted!
My last good night! Thou wilt not wake
Till I thy fate shall overtake:
Till age, or grief, or sickness must
Marry my body to that dust
It so much loves; and fill the room
My heart keeps empty in thy Tomb.
Stay for me there; I will not faile
To meet thee in that hallow Vale.
And think not much of my delay;

I am already on the way,
And follow thee with all the speed
Desire can make, or sorrows breed.
Each minute is a short degree,
And ev'ry houre a step towards thee.
At night when I betake to rest,
Next morn I rise neerer my West
Of life, almost by eight houres saile,
Then when sleep breath'd his drowsie gale.

Thus from the Sun my Bottom stears,
And my dayes Compass downward bears:
Nor labour I to stemme the tide
Through which to *Thee* I swiftly glide.

'Tis true, with shame and grief I yield,
Thou like the *Vann* first took'st the field,
And gotten hast the victory
In thus adventuring to dy
Before me, whose more years might crave
A just precedence in the grave.
But heark! My pulse like a soft Drum
Beats my approach, tells *Thee* I come;
And slow howere my marches be,
I shall at last sit down by *Thee*.

The thought of this bids me go on,
And wait my dissolution
With hope and comfort. *Dear* (forgive
The crime) I am content to live
Divided, with but half a heart,
Till we shall meet and never part.

James Shirley

(1596–1666)

Dirge

FROM *The Contention of Ajax and Ulysses*

The glories of our blood and state,
  Are shadows, not substantial things,
There is no armour against fate,
  Death lays his icy hand on Kings,
      Scepter and crown,
      Must tumble down,
And in the dust be equal made,
With the poor crooked sithe and spade.

Some men with swords may reap the field,
  And plant fresh laurels where they kill,
But their strong nerves at last must yield,
  They tame but one another still;
      Early or late,
      They stoop to fate,
And must give up their murmuring breath,
When they pale Captives creep to death.

The Garlands wither on your brow,
  Then boast no more your mighty deeds,
Upon Deaths purple Altar now,
  See where the Victor-victim bleeds,
      Your heads must come,
      To the cool Tomb,

Onely the actions of the just
Smell sweet, and blossom in their dust.

Song

FROM *The Imposture*

You Virgins that did late despair
    To keep your wealth from cruell men,
Tie up in silk your careles hair,
    Soft peace is come agen.

Now Lovers eyes may gently shoot
    A flame that wo'not kill:
The Drum was angry, but the Lute
    Shall wisper what you will.

Sing *Io, Io,* for his sake,
    Who hath restor'd your drooping heads,
With choice of sweetest flowers make
    A garden where he treads.

Whilst we whole groves of Laurel bring,
    A petty triumph to his brow,
Who is the Master of our Spring,
    And all the bloom we owe.

William Strode

(1602?–1645)

On Westwall Downes

When Westwall Downes I gan to tread,
Where cleanely wynds the greene did sweepe,
Methought a landskipp there was spread,
Here a bush and there a sheepe:
   The pleated wrinkles of the face
   Of wave-swolne earth did lend such grace,
   As shadowings in Imag'ry
   Which both deceive and please the eye.

The sheepe sometymes did tread the maze
By often wynding in and in,
And sometymes round about they trace
Which milkmaydes call a Fairie ring:
   Such semicircles have they runne,
   Such lynes acrosse so trymly spunne
   That sheppeards learne whenere they please
   A new Geometry with ease.

The slender food upon the downe
Is allwayes even, allwayes bare,
Which neither spring nor winter's frowne
Can ought improve or ought impayre:
   Such is the barren Eunuches chynne,
   Which thus doth evermore begynne
   With tender downe to be orecast
   Which never comes to haire at last.

Here and there twoe hilly crests
Amiddst them hugg a pleasant greene,
And these are like twoe swelling breasts
That close a tender fall betweene.
　　Here would I sleepe, or read, or pray
　　From early morne till flight of day:
　　But harke! a sheepe-bell calls mee upp,
　　Like Oxford colledge bells, to supp.

A Devonshire Song

Thou ne're wutt riddle, neighbour Jan
　　Where ich a late ha been-a?
Why ich ha been at Plymoth, Man,
　　The leeke was yet ne're zeen-a.
Zutch streetes, zutch men, zutch hugeous zeas,
　　Zutch things with guns there tumbling,
Thy zelfe leeke me thoudst blesse to see,
　　Zutch overmonstrous grumbling.

The towne orelaid with shindle stone
　　Doth glissen like the skee-a:
Brave shopps stand ope, and all yeare long
　　I thinke a Faire there bee-a:
A many gallant man there goth
　　In gold that zaw the King-a;
The King zome zweare himzelfe was there,
　　A man or zome zutch thing-a.

Voole thou that hast no water past,
　　But thicka in the Moore-a,
To zee the zea would be agast,
　　It doth zoe rage and roar-a:

Zoe zalt it tasts thy tongue will thinke
  The vier is in the water;
It is zoe wide noe lande is spide,
  Looke ne're zoe long thereafter.

The Water vrom the Element
  None can dezeave cha vore-a,
It semmeth low, yet all consent
  Tis higher than the Moore-a.
Tis strang how looking down the Cliffe
  Men looke mere upward rather;
If these same Eene had it not zeen
  Chud scarce beleeve my Vather.

Amid the water woodden birds,
  And vlying houses zwimme-a,
All vull of goods as ich have heard
  And men up to the brimm-a:
They venter to another world
  Desiring to conquier-a,
Vow which their guns, vowle develish ons,
  Doe dunder and spitt vier-a.

Good neighbour Tom, how farre is that?
  This meazell towne chill leave-a;
Chill mope noe longer here, that's vlatt
  To watch a Sheepe or Sheare-a:
Though it as varre as London be,
  Which ten mile ich imagin,
Chill thither hie for this place I
  Doe take in greate indulgin.

On His Mistress

(Attributed to Strode)

Gaze not on swans in whose soft breast
A full hatcht beauty seems to rest,
Nor snow which falling from the sky
Hovers in its virginity.

Gaze not on roses though new blown
Grac'd with a fresh complexion,
Nor lilly which no subtle bee
Hath rob'd by kissing chemistry.

Gaze not on that pure milky way
Where night vies splendour with the day,
Nor pearls whose silver walls confine
The riches of an Indian mine:

For if my emperesse appears
Swans moultring dy, snows melt to tears,
Roses do blush and hang their heads
Pale lillyes shrink into their beds;

The milky way rides past to shrowd
Its baffled glory in a clowd,
And pearls do climb unto her eare
To hang themselves for envy there.

So have I seene stars big with light,
Proud lanthorns to the moon-ey'd night,
Which when Sol's rays were once display'd
Sunk in their sockets and decay'd.

Aurelian Townshend

(c.1583–c.1651)

Though regions farr devided

Though regions farr devided
  And tedious tracts of tyme,
By my missfortune guided,
  Make absence thought a cryme;
Though wee were set a sunder
  As far, as East from West,
Love still would worke this wonder,
  Thou shouldst be in my breast.

How slow alasse are paces,
  Compar'd to thoughts that flye
In moment back to places,
  Whole ages scarce descry.
The body must have pauses;
  The mynde requires noe rest;
Love needs no second causes
  To guide thee to my breast.

Accept in that poore dwelling,
  But welcome, nothing great,
With pride noe turretts swelling,
  But lowly as the seate;
Wher, though not much delighted,
  In peace thou mayst be blest,
Unfeasted yet unfrighted
  By rivalls, in my breast.

433

But this is not the dyett,
　　That doeth for glory strive;
Poore beawties seeke in quiet
　　To keepe one heart alive.
The price of his ambition,
　　That lookes for such a guest,
Is hopelesse of fruition
　　To beate an empty breast.

See then my last lamenting,
　　Upon a cliffe I'le sitt,
Rock Constancy presenting,
　　Till I grow part of itt;
My teares a quicksand feeding,
　　Wher on noe foote can rest,
My sighs a tempest breeding
　　About my stony breast.

Those armes, wherin wide open
　　Loves fleete was wont to putt,
Shall layd acrosse betoken
　　That havens mouth is shutt.
Myne eyes noe light shall cherish
　　For shipps att sea distrest,
But darkeling let them perish
　　Or splitt against my breast.

Yet if I can discover
　　When thyne before itt rides,
To shew I was thy lover
　　I'le smooth my rugged sides,
And soe much better measure
　　Afford thee then the rest,
Thou shalt have noe displeasure
　　By knocking att my breast.

A *Dialogue Betwixt Time and a Pilgrime*

PILGRIME. Aged man, that mowes these fields.

TIME. Pilgrime speak, what is thy will?

PILGRIME. Whose soile is this that such sweet Pasture
    yields?
  Or who are thou whose Foot stand never still?
    Or where am I? TIME. In love.
          PILGRIME. His Lordship lies above.

TIME. Yes and below, and round about
  Where in all sorts of flow'rs are growing
Which as the early Spring puts out,
  Time fals as fast as mowing.

PILGRIME. If thou art Time, these Flow'rs have Lives,
  And then I fear,
Under some Lilly she I love
  May now be growing there.

TIME. And in some Thistle or some spyre of grasse,
My syth thy stalk before hers come may passe.

PILGRIME. Wilt thou provide it may. TIME. No.
          PILGRIME. Alleage the cause.

TIME. Because Time cannot alter but obey Fates laws.

CHORUS. Then happy those whom Fate, that is the
    stronger,
Together twists their threads, and yet draws hers the
    longer.

Sir Richard Fanshawe

(1608–1666)

A Rose

(*After Góngora*)

Blowne in the Morning, thou shalt fade ere Noone:
   What bootes a Life which in such hast forsakes thee?
   Th'art wondrous frolick being to dye so soon:
   And passing proud a little colour makes thee.

If thee thy brittle beauty so deceives,
   Know then the thing that swells thee is thy bane;
   For the same beauty doth in bloody leaves
   The sentence of thy early death containe.

Some Clownes course Lungs will poison thy sweet flow'r,
   If by the careless Plough thou shalt be torne:
   And many *Herods* lye in wait each how'r
   To murther thee as soon as thou art borne,

Nay, force thy Bud to blow; their Tyrant breath
Anticipating Life, to hasten death.

William Cartwright

(1611–1643)

No Platonique Love

Tell me no more of Minds embracing Minds,
    And hearts exchang'd for hearts;
That Spirits Spirits meet, as Winds do winds,
    And mix their subt'lest parts;
That two unbodi'd Essences may kiss,
And then like Angels, twist and feel one Bliss.

I was that silly thing that once was wrought
    To Practise this thin Love;
I climb'd from Sex to Soul, from Soul to Thought;
    But thinking there to move,
Headlong I rowl'd from Thought to Soul, and then
From Soul I lighted at the Sex agen.

As some strict down-look'd Men pretend to fast,
    Who yet in Closets Eat;
So Lovers who profess they Spirits taste,
    Feed yet on grosser meat;
I know they boast they Soules to Soules Convey,
Howe'r they meet, the Body is the Way.

Come, I will undeceive thee, they that tread
    Those vain Aëriall waies,
Are like young Heyrs and Alchymists misled
    To waste their Wealth and Daies,
For searching thus to be for ever Rich,
They only find a Med'cine for the Itch.

George Herbert
(1593–1633)

The Sacrifice

Oh all ye, who passe by, whose eyes and minde
To worldly things are sharp, but to me blinde;
To me, who took eyes that I might you finde:
                   Was ever grief like mine?

The Princes of my people make a head
Against their Maker: they do wish me dead,
Who cannot wish, except I give them bread:
                   Was ever grief like mine?

Without me each one, who doth now me brave,
Had to this day been an Egyptian slave.
They use that power against me, which I gave:
                   Was ever grief like mine?

Mine own Apostle, who the bag did beare,
Though he had all I had, did not forbeare
To sell me also, and to put me there:
                   Was ever grief like mine?

For thirtie pence he did my death devise,
Who at three hundred did the ointment prize,
Not half so sweet as my sweet sacrifice:
                   Was ever grief like mine?

Therefore my soul melts, and my hearts deare treasure
Drops bloud (the onely beads) my words to measure:

438

O let this cup passe, if it be thy pleasure:
                              Was ever grief like mine?

These drops being temper'd with a sinners tears
A Balsome are for both the Hemispheres:
Curing all wounds, but mine; all, but my fears:
                              Was ever grief like mine?

Yet my Disciples sleep: I cannot gain
One houre of watching; but their drowsie brain
Comforts not me, and doth my doctrine stain:
                              Was ever grief like mine?

Arise, arise, they come. Look how they runne!
Alas! what haste they make to be undone!
How with their lanterns do they seek the sunne!
                              Was ever grief like mine?

With clubs and staves they seek me, as a thief,
Who am the Way and Truth, the true relief;
Most true to those, who are my greatest grief:
                              Was ever grief like mine?

Judas, dost thou betray me with a kisse?
Canst thou finde hell about my lips? and misse
Of life, just at the gates of life and blisse?
                              Was ever grief like mine?

See, they lay hold on me, not with the hands
Of faith, but furie: yet at their commands
I suffer binding, who have loos'd their bands:
                              Was ever grief like mine?

All my Disciples flie; fear puts a barre
Betwixt my friends and me. They leave the starre,
That brought the wise men of the East from farre.
                              Was ever grief like mine?

Then from one ruler to another bound
They leade me; urging, that it was not sound
What I taught: Comments would the text confound.
                    Was ever grief like mine?

The Priest and rulers all false witness seek
'Gainst him, who seeks not life, but is the meek
And readie Paschal Lambe of this great week:
                    Was ever grief like mine?

Then they accuse me of great blasphemie,
That I did thrust into the Deitie,
Who never thought that any robberie:
                    Was ever grief like mine?

Some said, that I the Temple to the floore
In three dayes raz'd, and raised as before.
Why, he that built the world can do much more:
                    Was ever grief like mine?

Then they condemne me all with that same breath,
Which I do give them daily, unto death.
Thus *Adam* my first breathing rendereth:
                    Was ever grief like mine?

They binde, and leade me unto *Herod:* he
Sends me to *Pilate.* This makes them agree;
But yet their friendship is my enmitie:
                    Was ever grief like mine?

Herod and all his bands do set me light,
Who teach all hands to warre, fingers to fight,
And onely am the Lord of Hosts and might:
                    Was ever grief like mine?

Herod in judgement sits, while I do stand;
Examines me with a censorious hand:
I him obey, who all things else command:
                    Was ever grief like mine?

The *Jews* accuse me with despitefulnesse;
And vying malice with my gentlenesse,
Pick quarrels with their onely happinesse:
>   Was ever grief like mine?

I answer nothing, but with patience prove
If stonie hearts will melt with gentle love.
But who does hawk at eagles with a dove?
>   Was ever grief like mine?

My silence rather doth augment their crie;
My dove doth back into my bosome flie,
Because the raging waters still are high:
>   Was ever grief like mine?

Heark how they crie aloud still, *Crucifie.*
It is not fit he live a day, they crie,
Who cannot live lesse then eternally:
>   Was ever grief like mine?

Pilate, a stranger, holdeth off; but they,
Mine owne deare people, cry, *Away, away,*
With noises confused frighting the day:
>   Was ever grief like mine?

Yet still they shout, and crie, and stop their eares,
Putting my life among their sinnes and fears,
And therefore wish *my bloud on them and theirs:*
>   Was ever grief like mine?

See how spite cankers things. These words aright
Used, and wished, are the whole worlds light:
But hony is their gall, brightnesse their night:
>   Was ever grief like mine?

They choose a murderer, and all agree
In him to do themselves a courtesie:
For it was their own case who killed me:
>   Was ever grief like mine?

And a seditious murderer he was:
But I the Prince of peace; peace that doth passe
All understanding, more then heav'n doth glasse:
                Was ever grief like mine?

Why, Cæsar is their onely King, not I:
He clave the stonie rock, when they were drie;
But surely not their hearts, as I well trie:
                Was ever grief like mine?

Ah! how they scourge me! yet my tendernesse
Doubles each lash: and yet their bitternesse
Windes up my grief to a mysteriousnesse:
                Was ever grief like mine?

They buffet him, and box him as they list,
Who grasps the earth and heaven with his fist,
And never yet, whom he would punish, miss'd:
                Was ever grief like mine?

Behold, they spit on me in scornfull wise,
Who by my spittle gave the blinde man eies,
Leaving his blindnesse to my enemies:
                Was ever grief like mine?

My face they cover, though it be divine.
As *Moses* face was vailed, so is mine,
Lest on their double-dark souls either shine:
                Was ever grief like mine?

Servants and abjects flout me; they are wittie:
Now prophesie who strikes thee, is their dittie.
So they in me denie themselves all pitie:
                Was ever grief like mine?

And now I am deliver'd unto death,
Which each one calls for so with utmost breath,
That he before me well nigh suffereth:
                Was ever grief like mine?

Weep not, deare friends, since I for both have wept
When all my tears were bloud, the while you slept:
Your tears for your own fortunes should be kept:
                    Was ever grief like mine?

The souldiers lead me to the Common Hall;
There they deride me, they abuse me all:
Yet for twelve heav'nly legions I could call:
                    Was ever grief like mine?

Then with a scarlet robe they me aray;
Which shews my bloud to be the onely way
And cordiall left to repair mans decay:
                    Was ever grief like mine?

Then on my head a crown of thorns I wear:
For these are all the grapes *Sion* doth bear,
Though I my vine planted and watred there:
                    Was ever grief like mine?

So sits the earths great curse in *Adams* fall
Upon my head: so I remove it all
From th' earth unto my brows, and bear the thrall:
                    Was ever grief like mine?

Then with the reed they gave to me before,
They strike my head, the rock from whence all store
Of heav'nly blessings issue evermore:
                    Was ever grief like mine?

They bow their knees to me, and cry, *Hail king:*
What ever scoffes and scornfulnesse can bring,
I am the floore, the sink, where they it fling:
                    Was ever grief like mine?

Yet since mans scepters are as frail as reeds,
And thorny all their crowns, bloudie their weeds;
I, who am Truth, turn into truth their deeds:
                    Was ever grief like mine?

The souldiers also spit upon that face,
Which Angels did desire to have the grace,
And Prophets, once to see, but found no place:
                    Was ever grief like mine?

Thus trimmed, forth they bring me to the rout,
Who *Crucifie him,* crie with one strong shout.
God holds his peace at man, and man cries out:
                    Was ever grief like mine?

They leade me in once more, and putting then
Mine own clothes on, they leade me out agen.
Whom devils flie, thus is he toss'd of men:
                    Was ever grief like mine?

And now wearie of sport, glad to ingrosse
All spite in one, counting my life their losse,
They carrie me to my most bitter crosse:
                    Was ever grief like mine?

My crosse I bear my self, untill I faint:
Then Simon bears it for me by constraint,
The decreed burden of each mortall Saint:
                    Was ever grief like mine?

O all ye who passe by, behold and see;
Man stole the fruit, but I must climbe the tree;
The tree of life to all, but onely me:
                    Was ever grief like mine?

Lo, here I hang, charg'd with a world of sinne,
The greater world o' th' two; for that came in
By words, but this by sorrow I must win:
                    Was ever grief like mine?

Such sorrow as, if sinfull man could feel,
Or feel his part, he would not cease to kneel,
Till all were melted, though he were all steel:
                    Was ever grief like mine?

But, *O my God, my God!* why leav'st thou me,
The sonne, in whom thou dost delight to be?
My God, my God—

                    Never was grief like mine.

Shame tears my soul, my bodie many a wound;
Sharp nails pierce this, but sharper that confound;
Reproches, which are free, while I am bound,

                    Was ever grief like mine?

Now heal thy self, Physician; now come down.
Alas! I did so, when I left my crown
And fathers smile for you, to feel his frown:

                    Was ever grief like mine?

In healing not my self, there doth consist
All that salvation, which ye now resist;
Your safetie in my sicknesse doth subsist:

                    Was ever grief like mine?

Betwixt two theeves I spend my utmost breath,
As he that for some robberie suffereth.
Alas! what have I stollen from you? Death.

                    Was ever grief like mine?

A king my title is, prefixt on high;
Yet by my subjects am condemn'd to die
A servile death in servile companie:

                    Was ever grief like mine?

They give me vineger mingled with gall,
But more with malice: yet, when they did call,
With Manna, Angels food, I fed them all:

                    Was ever grief like mine?

They part my garments, and by lot dispose
My coat, the type of love, which once cur'd those
Who sought for help, never malicious foes:

                    Was ever grief like mine?

Nay, after death their spite shall further go;
For they will pierce my side, I full well know;
That as sinne came, so Sacraments might flow:
> Was ever grief like mine?

But now I die; now all is finished.
My wo, mans weal: and now I bow my head.
Onely let others say, when I am dead,
> Never was grief like mine.

Easter-Wings

Lord, who createdst man in wealth and store,
Though foolishly he lost the same,
Decaying more and more,
Till he became
Most poore:
With thee
O let me rise
As larks, harmoniously,
And sing this day thy victories:
Then shall the fall further the flight in me.

My tender age in sorrow did beginne:
And still with sicknesses and shame
Thou didst so punish sinne,
That I became
Most thinne.
With thee
Let me combine
And feel this day thy victorie:
For, if I imp my wing on thine,
Affliction shall advance the flight in me.

Holy Baptisme

Since, Lord, to thee
A narrow way and little gate
Is all the passage, on my infancie
Thou didst lay hold, and antedate
My faith in me.

O let me still
Write thee great God, and me a childe:
Let me be soft and supple to thy will,
Small to my self, to others milde,
Behither ill.

Although by stealth
My flesh get on, yet let her sister
My soul bid nothing, but preserve her wealth:
The growth of flesh is but a blister;
Childhood is health.

Prayer

Prayer the Churches banquet, Angels age,
    Gods breath in man returning to his birth,
    The soul in paraphrase, heart in pilgrimage,
The Christian plummet sounding heav'n and earth;
Engine against th' Almightie, sinners towre,
    Reversed thunder, Christ-side-piercing spear,
    The six-daies world transposing in an houre,
A kinde of tune, which all things heare and fear;

Softnesse, and peace, and joy, and love, and blisse,
    Exalted Manna, gladnesse of the best,
    Heaven in ordinarie, man well drest,
The milkie way, the bird of Paradise,
    Church-bels beyond the starres heard, the souls
      bloud,
    The land of spices; something understood.

The Temper

How should I praise thee, Lord! how should my rymes
    Gladly engrave thy love in steel,
      If what my soul doth feel sometimes,
        My soul might ever feel!

Although there were some fourtie heav'ns, or more,
    Sometimes I peere above them all;
    Sometimes I hardly reach a score,
      Sometimes to hell I fall.

O rack me not to such a vast extent;
    Those distances belong to thee:
    The world's too little for thy tent,
      A grave too big for me.

Wilt thou meet arms with man, that thou dost stretch
    A crumme of dust from heav'n to hell?
    Will great God measure with a wretch?
      Shall he thy stature spell?

O let me, when thy roof my soul hath hid,
    O let me roost and nestle there:
    Then of a sinner thou art rid,
      And I of hope and fear.

Yet take thy way; for sure thy way is best:
　　Stretch or contract me, thy poore debter:
　　This is but tuning of my breast,
　　　　To make the musick better.

Whether I flie with angels, fall with dust,
　　Thy hands made both, and I am there:
　　Thy power and love, my love and trust
　　　　Make one place ev'ry where.

Jordan

Who sayes that fictions onely and false hair
Become a verse? Is there in truth no beautie?
Is all good structure in a winding stair?
May no lines passe, except they do their dutie
　　Not to a true, but painted chair?

Is it no verse, except enchanted groves
And sudden arbours shadow course-spunne lines?
Must purling streams refresh a lovers loves?
Must all be vail'd, while he that reades, divines,
　　Catching the sense at two removes?

Shepherds are honest people; let them sing:
Riddle who list, for me, and pull for Prime:
I envie no mans nightingale or spring;
Nor let them punish me with losse of rime,
　　Who plainly say, *My God, My King*.

The Rose

Presse me not to take more pleasure
   In this world of sugred lies,
And to use a larger measure
   Then my strict, yet welcome size.

First, there is no pleasure here:
   Colour'd griefs indeed there are,
Blushing woes, that look as cleare
   As if they could beautie spare.

Or if such deceits there be,
   Such delights I meant to say;
There are no such things to me,
   Who have pass'd my right away.

But I will not much oppose
   Unto what you now advise:
Onely take this gentle rose,
   And therein my answer lies.

What is fairer than a rose?
   What is sweeter? yet it purgeth,
Purgings enmitie disclose,
   Enmitie forbearance urgeth.

If then all that worldings prize
   Be contracted to a rose;
Sweetly there indeed it lies,
   But it biteth in the close.

So this flower doth judge and sentence
   Worldly joyes to be a scourge:

For they all produce repentance,
  And repentance is a purge.

But I health, not physick choose:
  Onely though I you oppose,
Say that fairly I refuse,
  For my answer is a rose.

The Quidditie

My God, a verse is not a crown,
No point of honour, or gay suit,
No hawk, or banquet, or renown,
Nor a good sword, nor yet a lute:

It cannot vault, or dance, or play;
It never was in *France* or *Spain;*
Nor can it entertain the day
With my great stable or demain:

It is no office, art, or news,
Nor the Exchange, or busie Hall;
But it is that which while I use
I am with thee, and *most take all.*

Deniall

When my devotions could not pierce
  Thy silent eares;
Then was my heart broken, as was my verse:
  My breast was full of fears
    And disorder:

My bent thoughts, like a brittle bow,
　　　　Did flie asunder:
Each took his way; some would to pleasures go,
　　　Some to the warres and thunder
　　　　　Of alarms.

As good go any where, they say,
　　　　As to benumme
Both knees and heart, in crying night and day,
　　　Come, come, my God, O come,
　　　　But no hearing.

O that thou shouldst give dust a tongue
　　　　To crie to thee,
And then not heare it crying! all day long
　　　My heart was in my knee,
　　　　　But no hearing.

Therefore my soul lay out of sight,
　　　　Untun'd, unstrung:
My feeble spirit, unable to look right,
　　　Like a nipt blossome, hung
　　　　　Discontented.

O cheer and tune my heartlesse breast,
　　　　Deferre no time;
That so thy favours granting my request,
　　　They and my minde may chime,
　　　　And mend my ryme.

Sighs and Grones

　　　　　O do not use me
After my sinnes! look not on my desert,
But on thy glorie! then thou wilt reform

And not refuse me: for thou onely art
The mightie God, but I a sillie worm;
           O do not bruise me!

           O do not urge me!
For what account can thy ill steward make?
I have abus'd thy stock, destroy'd thy woods,
Suckt all thy magazens: my head did ake,
Till it found out how to consume thy goods:
           O do not scourge me!

           O do not blinde me!
I have deserv'd that an Egyptian night
Should thicken all my powers; because my lust
Hath still sow'd fig-leaves to exclude thy light:
But I am frailtie, and already dust;
           O do not grind me!

           O do not fill me
With the turn'd viall of thy bitter wrath!
For thou hast other vessels full of bloud,
A part whereof my Saviour empti'd hath,
Ev'n unto death: since he di'd for my good,
           O do not kill me!

           But O reprieve me!
For thou hast life and death at thy command;
Thou art both *Judge* and *Saviour, feast* and *rod,*
Cordiall and *Corrosive:* put not thy hand
Into the bitter box; but O my God,
           My God, relieve me!

The Pearl

(*Matthew 13:45*)

I know the wayes of Learning; both the head
And pipes that feed the presse, and make it runne;
What reason hath from nature borrowed,
Or of it self, like a good huswife, spunne
In laws and policie; what the starres conspire,
What willing nature speaks, what forc'd by fire;
Both th' old discoveries, and the new-found seas,
The stock and surplus, cause and historie:
All these stand open, or I have the keyes:
            Yet I love thee.

I know the wayes of Honour, what maintains
The quick returns of courtesie and wit:
In vies of favours whether partie gains,
When glorie swells the heart, and moldeth it
To all expressions both of hand and eye,
Which on the world a true-love-knot may tie,
And bear the bundle, wheresoe're it goes:
How many drammes of spirit there must be
To sell my life unto my friends or foes:
            Yet I love thee.

I know the wayes of Pleasure, the sweet strains,
The lullings and the relishes of it;
The propositions of hot bloud and brains;
What mirth and musick mean; what love and wit
Have done these twentie hundred yeares, and more:
I know the projects of unbridled store:
My stuffe is flesh, not brasse; my senses live,
And grumble oft, that they have more in me

Then he that curbs them, being but one to five:
              Yet I love thee.

I know all these, and have them in my hand:
Therefore not sealed, but with open eyes
I flie to thee, and fully understand
Both the main sale, and the commodities;
And at what rate and price I have thy love;
With all the circumstances that may move:
Yet through these labyrinths, not my groveling wit,
But thy silk twist let down from heav'n to me,
Did both conduct and teach me, how by it
              To climbe to thee.

Man

              My God, I heard this day,
That none doth build a stately habitation,
       But he that means to dwell therein.
       What house more stately hath there been,
Or can be, then is Man? to whose creation
              All things are in decay.

       For Man is ev'ry thing,
And more: He is a tree, yet bears more fruit;
       A beast, yet is, or should be more:
       Reason and speech we onely bring.
Parrats may thank us, if they are not mute,
              They go upon the score.

       Man is all symmetrie,
Full of proportions, one limbe to another,
       And all to all the world besides:
       Each part may call the furthest, brother:

For head with foot hath private amitie,
    And both with moons and tides.

    Nothing hath got so farre,
But Man hath caught and kept it, as his prey.
    His eyes dismount the highest starre:
    He is in little all the sphere.
Herbs gladly cure our flesh; because that they
    Find their acquaintance there.

    For us the windes do blow,
The earth doth rest, heav'n move, and fountains flow.
    Nothing we see, but means our good,
    As our delight, or as our treasure:
The whole is, either our cupboard of food,
    Or cabinet of pleasure.

    The starres have us to bed;
Night draws the curtain, which the sunne withdraws;
    Musick and light attend our head.
    All things unto our flesh are kinde
In their descent and being; to our minde
    In their ascent and cause.

    Each thing is full of dutie:
Waters united are our navigation;
    Distinguished, our habitation;
    Below, our drink; above, our meat;
Both are our cleanlinesse. Hath one such beautie?
    Then how are all things neat?

    More servants wait on Man,
Then he'l take notice of: in ev'ry path
    He treads down that which doth befriend him,
    When sicknesse makes him pale and wan.
Oh mightie love! Man is one world, and hath
    Another to attend him.

Since then, my God, thou hast
So brave a Palace built; O dwell in it,
    That it may dwell with thee at last!
    Till then, afford us so much wit;
That, as the world serves us, we may serve thee,
        And both thy servants be.

Miserie

    Lord, let the Angels praise thy name.
Man is a foolish thing, a foolish thing,
    Folly and Sinne play all his game.
His house still burns, and yet he still doth sing,
        Man is but grasse,
        He knows it, fill the glasse.

    How canst thou brook his foolishnesse?
Why, he'l not lose a cup of drink for thee:
    Bid him but temper his excesse;
Not he: he knows where he can better be,
        As he will swear,
        Then to serve thee in fear.

    What strange pollutions doth he wed,
And make his own? as if none knew but he.
    No man shall beat into his head,
That thou within his curtains drawn canst see:
        They are of cloth,
        Where never yet came moth.

    The best of men, turn but thy hand
For one poore minute, stumble at a pinne:
    They would not have their actions scann'd,

Nor any sorrow tell them that they sinne,
        Though it be small,
        And measure not their fall.

    They quarrell thee, and would give over
The bargain made to serve thee: but thy love
    Holds them unto it, and doth cover
Their follies with the wing of thy milde Dove,
        Not suff'ring those
        Who would, to be thy foes.

    My God, Man cannot praise thy name:
Thou art all brightnesse, perfect puritie;
    The sunne holds down his head for shame,
Dead with eclipses, when we speak of thee:
        How shall infection
        Presume on thy perfection?

    As dirtie hands foul all they touch,
And those things most, which are most pure and fine:
    So our clay hearts, ev'n when we crouch
To sing thy praises, make them lesse divine.
        Yet either this,
        Or none, thy portion is.

    Man cannot serve thee; let him go,
And serve the swine: there, there is his delight:
    He doth not like this vertue, no;
Give him his dirt to wallow in all night:
        These Preachers make
        His head to shoot and ake.

    Oh foolish man! where are thine eyes?
How hast thou lost them in a croud of cares?
    Thou pull'st the rug, and wilt not rise,
No, not to purchase the whole pack of starres:
        There let them shine,
        Thou must go sleep, or dine.

The bird that sees a daintie bowre
Made in the tree, where she was wont to sit,
   Wonders and sings, but not his power
Who made the arbour: this exceeds her wit.
       But Man doth know
       The spring, whence all things flow:

And yet, as though he knew it not,
His knowledge winks, and lets his humours reigne;
   They make his life a constant blot,
And all the bloud of God to run in vain.
       Ah wretch! what verse
       Can thy strange wayes rehearse?

Indeed at first Man was a treasure,
A box of jewels, shop of rarities,
   A ring, whose posie was, *My pleasure;*
He was a garden in a Paradise:
       Glorie and grace
       Did crown his heart and face.

But sinne hath fool'd him. Now he is
A lump of flesh, without a foot or wing
   To raise him to a glimpse of blisse:
A sick toss'd vessel, dashing on each thing;
       Nay, his own shelf:
       My God, I mean my self.

Hope

I gave to Hope a watch of mine: but he
       An anchor gave to me.
Then an old prayer-book I did present:
       And he an optick sent.

With that I gave a viall full of tears:
    But he a few green eares.
Ah Loyterer! I'le no more, no more I'le bring:
    I did expect a ring.

Artillerie

As I one ev'ning sat before my cell,
Me thoughts a starre did shoot into my lap.
I rose, and shook my clothes, as knowing well,
That from small fires comes oft no small mishap.
  When suddenly I heard one say,
  Do as thou usest, disobey,
  Expell good motions from thy breast,
Which have the face of fire, but end in rest.

I, who had heard of musick in the spheres,
But not of speech in starres, began to muse:
But turning to my God, whose ministers
The starres and all things are; If I refuse,
  Dread Lord, said I, so oft my good;
  Then I refuse not ev'n with bloud
  To wash away my stubborn thought:
For I will do or suffer what I ought.

But I have also starres and shooters too,
Born where thy servants both artilleries use.
My tears and prayers night and day do wooe,
And work up to thee; yet thou dost refuse.
  Not but I am (I must say still)
  Much more oblig'd to do thy will,
  Then thou to grant mine: but because
Thy promise now hath ev'n set thee thy laws.

Then we are shooters both, and thou dost deigne
To enter combate with us, and contest
With thine own clay. But I would parley fain:
Shunne not my arrows, and behold my breast.
    Yet if thou shunnest, I am thine:
    I must be so, if I am mine.
    There is no articling with thee:
I am but finite, yet thine infinitely.

The Collar

I struck the board, and cry'd, No more.
          I will abroad.
    What? shall I ever sigh and pine?
My lines and life are free; free as the rode,
    Loose as the winde, as large as store.
        Shall I be still in suit?
Have I no harvest but a thorn
To let me bloud, and not restore
What I have lost with cordiall fruit?
        Sure there was wine
Before my sighs did drie it: there was corn
    Before my tears did drown it.
    Is the yeare onely lost to me?
        Have I no bayes to crown it?
No flowers, no garlands gay? all blasted?
        All wasted?
Not so, my heart: but there is fruit,
        And thou hast hands.
Recover all thy sigh-blown age
On double pleasures: leave thy cold dispute
Of what is fit, and not. Forsake thy cage,
        Thy rope of sands,

Which pettie thoughts have made, and made to thee
    Good cable, to enforce and draw,
        And be thy law,
    While thou didst wink and wouldst not see.
        Away; take heed:
        I will abroad.
Call in thy deaths head there: tie up thy fears.
        He that forbears
    To suit and serve his need,
      Deserves his load.
But as I rav'd and grew more fierce and wilde
      At every word,
  Me thought I heard one calling, *Child!*
    And I reply'd *My Lord.*

Clasping of Hands

Lord, thou art mine, and I am thine,
If mine I am: and thine much more,
Then I or ought, or can be mine.
Yet to be thine, doth me restore;
So that again I now am mine,
And with advantage mine the more,
Since this being mine, brings with it thine,
And thou with me dost thee restore.
    If I without thee would be mine,
    I neither should be mine nor thine.

Lord, I am thine, and thou art mine:
So mine thou art, that something more
I may presume thee mine, then thine.
For thou didst suffer to restore
Not thee, but me, and to be mine,

And with advantage mine the more,
Since thou in death wast none of thine,
Yet then as mine didst me restore.
    O be mine still! still make me thine!
    Or rather make no Thine and Mine!

The Flower

How fresh, O Lord, how sweet and clean
Are thy returns! ev'n as the flowers in spring;
    To which, besides their own demean,
The late-past frosts tributes of pleasure bring.
        Grief melts away
        Like snow in May,
As if there were no such cold thing.

Who would have thought my shrivel'd heart
Could have recover'd greennesse? It was gone
    Quite under ground; as flowers depart
To see their mother-root, when they have blown;
        Where they together
        All the hard weather,
Dead to the world, keep house unknown.

These are thy wonders, Lord of power,
Killing and quickning, bringing down to hell
    And up to heaven in an houre;
Making a chiming of a passing-bell.
        We say amisse,
        This or that is:
Thy word is all, if we could spell.

O that I once past changing were,
Fast in thy Paradise, where no flower can wither!

Many a spring I shoot up fair,
Offring at heav'n, growing and groning thither:
Nor doth my flower
Want a spring-showre,
My sinnes and I joining together.

But while I grow in a straight line,
Still upwards bent, as if heav'n were mine own,
Thy anger comes, and I decline:
What frost to that? what pole is not the zone,
Where all things burn,
When thou dost turn,
And the least frown of thine is shown?

And now in age I bud again,
After so many deaths I live and write;
I once more smell the dew and rain,
And relish versing: O my onely light,
It cannot be
That I am he
On whom thy tempests fell all night.

These are thy wonders, Lord of love,
To make us see we are but flowers that glide:
Which when we once can finde and prove,
Thou hast a garden for us, where to bide.
Who would be more,
Swelling through store,
Forfeit their Paradise by their pride.

Love

Love bade me welcome: yet my soul drew back,
Guiltie of dust and sinne.
But quick-ey'd Love, observing me grow slack

From my first entrance in,
Drew nearer to me, sweetly questioning,
If I lack'd any thing.

A guest, I answer'd, worthy to be here:
Love said, You shall be he.
I the unkinde, ungratefull? Ah my deare,
I cannot look on thee.
Love took my hand, and smiling did reply,
Who made the eyes but I?

Truth Lord, but I have marr'd them: let my shame
Go where it doth deserve.
And know you not, sayes Love, who bore the blame?
My deare, then I will serve.
You must sit down, sayes Love, and taste my meat:
So I did sit and eat.

Richard Crashaw

(1613?–1649)

In the Holy Nativity of Our Lord God

A HYMN SUNG AS BY THE SHEPHEARDS

CHORUS. Come we shepheards whose blest Sight
　　Hath mett love's Noon in Nature's night;
　　　Come lift we up our loftyer Song
And wake the SUN that lyes too long.

To all our world of well-stoln joy
　　He slept; and dream't of no such thing.
While we found out Heavn's fairer ey
　　And Kis't the Cradle of our KING.
Tell him He rises now, too late
To show us ought worth looking at.

Tell him we now can show Him more
　　Than He e're show'd to mortall Sight;
Then he Himselfe e're saw before;
　　Which to be seen needes not His light.
Tell him, Tityrus, where th'hast been
Tell him, Thyrsis, what th'hast seen.

TITYRUS. Gloomy night embrac't the Place
　　Where The Noble Infant lay.
The BABE look't up and shew'd his Face;
　　In spite of Darknes, it was DAY.
It was THY day, SWEET! and did rise
Not from the EAST, but from thine EYES.

CHORUS. It was THY day, SWEET, etc.

THYRSIS. WINTER chidde aloud; and sent
 The angry North to wage his warres.
The North forgott his feirce Intent;
 And left perfumes in stead of scarres.
By those sweet eyes' persuasive powrs
Where he mean't frost, he scatter'd flowrs.

CHORUS. By those sweet eyes', etc.

BOTH. We saw thee in thy baulmy Nest,
 Young dawn of our æternall DAY!
We saw thine eyes break from their EASTE
 And chase the trembling shades away.
We saw thee; and we blest the sight
We saw thee by thine own sweet light.

TITYRUS. Poor WORLD (said I.) what wilt thou doe
 To entertain this starry STRANGER?
Is this the best thou canst bestow?
 A cold, and not too cleanly, manger?
Contend, ye powres of heav'n and earth.
To fitt a bed for this huge birthe.

CHORUS. Contend ye powres, etc.

THYRSIS. Proud world, said I; cease your contest
 And let the MIGHTY BABE alone.
The Phænix builds the Phænix' nest.
 Love's architecture is his own.
The BABE whose birth embraves this morn,
Made his own bed e're he was born.

CHORUS. The BABE whose, etc.

TITYRUS. I saw the curl'd drops, soft and slow,
 Come hovering o're the place's head;
Offring their whitest sheets of snow

To furnish the fair INFANT's bed
Forbear, sayd I; be not too bold.
Your fleece is white but t's too cold.

CHORUS. Forbear, sayd I, etc.

THYRSIS. I saw the obsequious SERAPHIMS
    Their rosy fleece of fire bestow.
For well they now can spare their wings
    Since HEAVN itself lyes here below.
Well done, sayd I: but are you sure
Your down so warm, will passe for pure?

CHORUS. Well done, sayd I, etc.

TITYRUS. No no, your KING's not yet to seeke
    Where to repose his Royall HEAD
See see, how soon his new-bloom'd CHEEK
    Twixt's mother's brests is gone to bed.
Sweet choise, sayd we! no way but so
Not to ly cold, yet sleep in snow.

CHORUS. Sweet choise, sayd we, etc.

BOTH. We saw thee in thy baulmy nest,
    Bright dawn of our æternall Day!
We saw thine eyes break from their EAST
    And chase the trembling shades away.
We saw thee: and we blest the sight.
We saw thee, by thine own sweet light.

CHORUS. We saw thee, etc.

FULL CHORUS. Wellcome, all WONDERS in one sight!
    Æternity shutt in a span.
Sommer in Winter. Day in Night.
    Heaven in earth, and GOD in MAN.
Great little one! whose all-embracing birth
Lifts earth to heaven, stoopes heav'n to earth.

Wellcome, though nor to gold nor silk.
　　To more then Cæsar's birthright is;
Two sister-seas of Virgin-Milk,
　　With many a rarely-temper'd kisse
That breathes at once both MAID and MOTHER,
Warmes in the one, cooles in the other.

Wellcome, though not to those gay flyes.
　　Guilded i'th' Beames of earthly kings;
Slippery soules in smiling eyes;
　　But to poor Shepheards, home-spun things:
Whose Wealth's their flock; whose witt, to be
　　Well read in their simplicity.
Yet when young April's husband showrs
　　Shall blesse the fruitfull Maja's bed
We'l bring the First-born of her flowrs
　　To kisse thy FEET and crown thy HEAD.
To thee, dread lamb! whose love must keep
　　The shepheards, more then they the sheep.
To THEE, meek Majesty! soft KING
　　Of simple GRACES and sweet LOVES.
Each of us his lamb will bring
　　Each his pair of sylver Doves;
Till burnt at last in fire of Thy fair eyes,
　　Our selves become our own best SACRIFICE.

In the Glorious Epiphanie of Our Lord God

The Three Kings

1 KINGE. Bright BABE! Whose awfull beautyes make
The morn incurr a sweet mistake;
2 KINGE. For whom the'officious heavns devise
To disinheritt the sun's rise,

3 KINGE. Delicately to displace
The Day, and plant it fairer in thy face;
1. O thou born KING of loves,
> 2. Of lights,
> 3. Of joyes!

CHORUS. Look up, sweet BABE, look up and see
> For love of Thee
> Thus farr from home
> The EAST is come

To seek her self in thy sweet Eyes
1. We, who strangely went astray,
> Lost in a bright
> Meridian night,
2. A Darkenes made of too much day,
> 3. Becken'd from farr
> By thy fair starr,

Lo at last have found our way.
CHORUS. To THEE, thou DAY of night! thou east of west!
Lo we at last have found the way.
To thee, the world's great universal east.
The Generall and indifferent DAY.
1. All-circling point. All centring sphear.
The world's one, round, Æternall year.
2. Whose full and all-unwrinkled face
Nor sinks nor swells with time or place;
3. But every where and every while
Is One Consistent solid smile;
> 1. Not vext and tost
> 2. 'Twixt spring and frost,
3. Nor by alternate shredds of light
Sordidly shifting hands with shades and night.
CHORUS. O little all! in thy embrace
The world lyes warm, and likes his place.
Nor does his full Globe fail to be
Kist on Both his cheeks by Thee.

Time is too narrow for thy YEAR
Nor makes the whole WORLD thy half-sphear.
      1. To Thee, to Thee
      From him we flee
2. From HIM, whom by a more illustrious ly,
The blindnes of the world did call the eye;
3. To HIM, who by These mortall clouds hast made
Thy self our sun, though thine own shade.
1. Farewell, the world's false light.
        Farewell, the white
        Ægypt! a long farewell to thee
        Bright IDOL; black IDOLATRY.
The dire face of inferior DARKNES, kis't
And courted in the pompous mask of a more specious
           mist.
       2. Farewell, farewell
       The proud and misplac't gates of hell,
       Pertch't, in the morning's way
And double-guilded as the doores of DAY.
The deep hypocrisy of DEATH and NIGHT
More desperately dark, Because more bright.
       3. Welcome, the world's sure Way!
       HEAVN's wholsom ray.
       CHORUS. Wellcome to us; and we
       (SWEET) to our selves, in THEE.
1. The deathles HEIR of all thy FATHER's day!
       2. Decently Born.
Embosom'd in a much more ROSY MORN,
The Blushes of thy All-unblemish't mother.
       3. No more that other
       Aurora shall sett ope
Her ruby casements, or hereafter hope
       From mortall eyes
To meet Religious welcomes at her rise.
CHORUS. We (Pretious ones!) in you have won

A gentler MORN, a juster sun.

1. His superficiall Beames sun-burn't our skin;
       2. But left within
3. The night and winter still of death and sin.
CHORUS. Thy softer yet more certaine DARTS
Spare our eyes, but peirce our HARTS.
1. Therefore with His proud persian spoiles
2. We court thy more concerning smiles.
       3. Therfore with his Disgrace
We guild the humble cheek of this chast place;
CHORUS. And at thy FEET powr forth his FACE.
1. The doating nations now no more
Shall any day but THINE adore.
2. Nor (much lesse) shall they leave these eyes
For cheap Ægyptian Deityes.
3. In whatsoe're more Sacred shape
Of Ram, He-goat, or reverend ape,
Those beauteous ravishers opprest so sore
The too-hard-tempted nations.
       1. Never more
By wanton heyfer shall be worn
2. A Garland, or a guilded horn.
The altar-stall'd ox, fatt OSYRIS now
       With his fair sister cow,
3. Shall kick the clouds no more; But lean and tame,
CHORUS. See his horn'd face, and dy for shame.
And MITHRA now shall be no name.
1. No longer shall the immodest lust
Of Adulterous GODLES dust
2. Fly in the face of heav'n; As if it were
The poor world's Fault that he is fair.
3. Nor with perverse loves and Religious RAPES
Revenge thy Bountyes in their beauteous shapes;
And punish Best Things worst; Because they stood
Guilty of being much for them too Good.

1. Proud sons of death! that durst compell
Heav'n it self to find them hell;
2. And by strange witt of madnes wrest
From this world's EAST the other's WEST.
3. All-Idolizing wormes! that thus could crowd
And urge Their sun into thy cloud;
Forcing his sometimes eclips'd face to be
A long deliquium to the light of thee.
CHORUS. Alas with how much heavyer shade
The shamefac't lamp hung down his head
          For that one eclipse he made
          Then all those he suffered!
1. For this he look't so bigg; and every morn
With a red face confes't this scorn.
Or hiding his vex't cheeks in a hir'd mist
Kept them from being so unkindly kis't.
2. It was for this the day did rise
          So oft with blubber'd eyes.
For this the evening wept; and we ne're knew
          But call'd it deaw.
          3. This dayly wrong
Silenc't the morning-sons, and damp't their song
CHORUS. Nor was't our deafnes, but our sins, that thus
Long made th'Harmonious orbes all mute to us
          1. Time has a day in store
          When this so proudly poor
And self-oppressed spark, that has so long
By the love-sick world bin made
Not so much their sun as SHADE,
Weary of this Glorious wrong
From them and from himself shall flee
For shelter to the shadow of thy TREE;
CHORUS. Proud to have gain'd this pretious losse
And chang'd his false crown for thy CROSSE.
2. That dark Day's clear doom shall define

Whose is the Master FIRE, which sun should shine.
That sable Judgment-seat shall by new lawes
Decide and settle the Great cause
            Of controverted light,
CHORUS. And natur's wrongs rejoyce to doe thee Right.
3. That forfeiture of noon to night shall pay
All the idolatrous thefts done by this night of day;
And the Great Penitent presse his own pale lipps
With an elaborate love-eclipse
            To which the low world's lawes
            Shall lend no cause
CHORUS. Save those domestick which he borrowes
From our sins and his own sorrowes.
1. Three sad hour's sackcloth then shall show to us
His penance, as our fault, conspicuous.
2. And he more needfully and nobly prove
The nation's terror now then erst their love.
3. Their hated loves changd into wholsom feares,
CHORUS. The shutting of his eye shall open Theirs.
1. As by a fair-ey'd fallacy of day
Miss-ledde before they lost their way,
So shall they, by the seasonable fright
Of an unseasonable night,
Loosing it once again, stumble'on true LIGHT
2. And as before his too-bright eye
Was Their more blind idolatry,
So his officious blindnes now shall be
Their black, but faithfull perspective of thee;
            3. His new prodigious night,
Their new and admirable light;
The supernatural DAWN of Thy pure day.
            While wondring they
(The happy converts now of him
Whom they compell'd before to be their sin)
            Shall henceforth see

To kisse him only as their rod
Whom so long courted as GOD,
CHORUS. And their best use of him they worship't be
To learn of Him at lest, to worship Thee.
1. It was their Weaknes woo'd his beauty;
        But it shall be
Their wisdome now, as well as duty,
To'injoy his Blott; and as a large black letter
Use it to spell Thy beautyes better;
And make the night it self their torch to thee.
2. By the oblique ambush of this close night
        Couch't in that conscious shade
The right-ey'd Areopagite
Shall with a vigorous guesse invade
And catche thy quick reflex; and sharply see
        On this dark Ground
        To descant THEE.
3. O prize of the rich SPIRIT! with what feirce chase
        Of his strong soul, shall he
        Leap at thy lofty FACE,
And seize the swift Flash, in rebound
From this obsequious cloud;
        Once call'd a sun;
        Till dearly thus undone,
CHORUS. Till thus triumphantly tam'd (o ye two
Twinne SUNNES!) and taught now to negotiate you.
1. Thus shall that reverend child of light,
2. By being scholler first of that new night,
Come forth Great master of the mystick day;
3. And teach obscure MANKIND a more close way
By the frugall negative light
Of a most wise and well-abused Night
To read more legible thine originall Ray,
CHORUS. And make our Darknes serve THY day;
Maintaining 'twixt thy world and ours

A commerce of contrary powres,
     A mutuall trade
     'Twixt sun and SHADE,
By confederat BLACK and WHITE
Borrowing day and lending night.
1. Thus we, who when with all the noble powres
That (at thy cost) are call'd, not vainly, ours
     We vow to make brave way
Upwards, and presse on for the pure intelligentiall Prey;
     2. At lest to play
     The amorous Spyes
And peep and proffer at thy sparkling Throne;
3. In stead of bringing in the blissfull PRIZE
     And fastening on Thine eyes,
     Forfeit our own
     And nothing gain
But more Ambitious losse, at lest of brain;
CHORUS. Now by abased liddes shall learn to be
Eagles; and shutt our eyes that we may see.

THE CLOSE

Therfore to THEE and thine Auspitious ray
     (Dread sweet!) lo thus
     At lest by us,
The delegated EYE of DAY
Does first his scepter, then HIMSELF in solemne Tribute
     pay.
     Thus he undresses
     His sacred unshorn tresses;
At thy adored FEET, thus, he layes down
     1. His gorgeous tire
     Of flame and fire,
2. His glittering Robe, 3. his sparkling CROWN,
1. His GOLD, 2. his MIRRH, 3. his FRANKINCENCE,

CHORUS. To which He now has no pretence.
For being show'd by this day's light, how farr
He is from sun enough to make THY starr,
His best ambition now, is but to be
Somthing a brighter SHADOW [sweet] of thee.
Or on heavn's azure forhead high to stand
Thy golden index; with a duteous Hand
Pointing us Home to our own sun
The world's and his HYPERION.

A *Hymn to the Name and Honor* of the Admirable Sainte Teresa

Love, thou art Absolute sole lord
Of LIFE and DEATH. To prove the word,
Wee'l now appeal to none of all
Those thy old Souldiers, Great and tall,
Ripe Men of Martyrdom, that could reach down
With strong armes, their triumphant crown;
Such as could with lusty breath
Speak lowd into the face of death
Their Great LORD's glorious name, to none
Of those whose spatious Bosomes spread a throne
For LOVE at larg to fill: spare blood and sweat;
And see him take a private seat,
Making his mansion in the mild
And milky soul of a soft child.
    Scarse has she learn't to lisp the name
Of Martyr; yet she thinks it shame
Life should so long play with that breath
Which spent can buy so brave a death.
She never undertook to know
What death with love should have to doe;

Nor has she e're yet understood
Why to show love, she should shed blood
Yet though she cannot tell you why,
She can LOVE, and she can DY.

Scarse has she Blood enough to make
A guilty sword blush for her sake;
Yet has she'a HEART dares hope to prove
How much lesse strong is DEATH then LOVE.

Be love but there; let poor six yeares
Be pos'd with the maturest Feares
Man trembles at, you straight shall find
LOVE knowes no nonage, nor the MIND.
'Tis LOVE, not YEARES or LIMBS that can
Make the Martyr, or the man.

LOVE touch't her HEART, and lo it beates
High, and burnes with such brave heates;
Such thirsts to dy, as dares drink up,
A thousand cold deaths in one cup.
Good reason. For she breathes All fire.
Her weake brest heaves with strong desire
Of what she may with fruitles wishes
Seek for amongst her MOTHER's kisses.

Since 'tis not to be had at home
She'll travail to a Martyrdom.
No home for hers confesses she
But where she may a Martyr be.

She'l to the Moores; And trade with them,
For this unvalued Diadem.
She'l offer them her dearest Breath,
With CHRIST's Name in't, in change for death.
She'l bargain with them; and will give
Them GOD; teach them how to live
In him: or, if they this deny,
For him she'l teach them how to DY.
So shall she leave amongst them sown

Her LORD's BLOOD; or at lest her own.
    Farewell, then, all the world! Adieu.
TERESA is no more for you.
Farewell, all pleasures, sports, and joyes,
(Never till now esteemed toyes)
Farewell what ever deare may bee,
MOTHER's armes or FATHER's knee
Farewell house, and farewell home!
SHE's for the Moores, and MARTYRDOM.

    SWEET, not so fast! lo thy fair Spouse
Whom thou seekst with no swift vowes,
Calls thee back, and bidds thee come
T'embrace a milder MARTYRDOM.

    Blest powres forbid, Thy tender life
Should bleed upon a barborous knife;
Or some base hand have power to race
Thy Brest's chast cabinet, and uncase
A soul kept there so sweet, ô no;
Wise heavn will never have it so
THOU art love's victime; and must dy
A death more mysticall and high.
Into love's armes thou shalt let fall
A still-surviving funerall.
His is the DART must make the DEATH
Whose stroke shall tast thy hallow'd breath;
A Dart thrice dip't in that rich flame
Which writes thy spouse's radiant Name
Upon the roof of Heav'n; where ay
It shines, and with a soveraign ray
Beates bright upon the burning faces
Of soules which in that name's sweet graces
Find everlasting smiles. So rare,
So spirituall, pure, and fair
Must be th'immortall instrument
Upon whose choice point shall be sent

A life so lov'd; And that there be
Fitt executioners for Thee,
The fair'st and first-born sons of fire
Blest SERAPHIM, shall leave their quire
And turn love's souldiers, upon THEE
To exercise their archerie.
    O how oft shalt thou complain
Of a sweet and subtle PAIN.
Of intolerable JOYES;
Of a DEATH, in which who dyes
Loves his death, and dyes again.
And would for ever so be slain.
And lives, and dyes; and knowes not why
To live, But that he thus may never leave to DY.
    How kindly will thy gentle HEART
Kisse the sweetly-killing DART!
And close in his embraces keep
Those delicious Wounds, that weep
Balsom to heal themselves with. Thus
When These thy DEATHS, so numerous,
Shall all at last dy into one,
And melt thy Soul's sweet mansion;
Like a soft lump of incense, hasted
By too hott a fire, and wasted
Into perfuming clouds, so fast
Shalt thou exhale to Heavn at last
In a resolving SIGH, and then
O what? Ask not the Tongues of men.
Angells cannot tell, suffice,
Thy selfe shall feel thine own full joyes
And hold them fast for ever. There
So soon as thou shalt first appear,
The MOON of maiden starrs, thy white
MISTRESSE, attended by such bright
Soules as thy shining self, shall come

And in her first rankes make thee room;
Where 'mongst her snowy family
Immortall wellcomes wait for thee.
   O what delight, when reveal'd LIFE shall stand
And teach thy lipps heav'n with his hand;
On which thou now maist to thy wishes
Heap up thy consecrated kisses.
What joyes shall seize thy soul, when she
Bending her blessed eyes on thee
(Those second Smiles of Heav'n) shall dart
Her mild rayes through thy melting heart!
   Angels, thy old friends, there shall greet thee
Glad at their own home now to meet thee.
   All thy good WORKES which went before
And waited for thee, at the door,
Shall own thee there; and all in one
Weave a constellation
Of CROWNS, with which the KING thy spouse
Shall build up thy triumphant browes.
   All thy old woes shall now smile on thee
And thy paines sitt bright upon thee
All thy sorrows here shall shine,
All thy SUFFRINGS be divine.
TEARES shall take comfort, and turn gemms
And WRONGS repent to Diademms.
Ev'n thy DEATHS shall live; and new
Dresse the soul that erst they slew.
Thy wounds shall blush to such bright scarres
As keep account of the LAMB's warres.
   Those rare WORKES where thou shalt leave writt,
Love's noble history, with witt
Taught thee by none but him, while here
They feed our soules, shall cloth THINE there.
Each heavnly word by whose hid flame
Our hard Hearts shall strike fire, the same

Shall flourish on thy browes. And be
Both fire to us and flame to thee;
Whose light shall live bright in thy FACE
By glory, in our hearts by grace.
    Thou shalt look round about, and see
Thousands of crown'd Soules throng to be
Themselves thy crown. Sons of thy vowes
The virgin-births with which thy soveraign spouse
Made fruitfull thy fair soul, goe now
And with them all about thee bow
To Him, put on (hee'l say) put on
(My rosy love) That thy rich zone
Sparkling with the sacred flames
Of thousand soules, whose happy names
Heav'n keeps upon thy score. (Thy bright
Life brought them first to kisse the light
That kindled them to starrs.) And so
Thou with the LAMB, thy lord, shalt goe;
And whereso'ere he setts his white
Stepps, walk with HIM those wayes of light
Which who in death would live to see,
Must learn in life to dy like thee.

The Flaming Heart

UPON THE BOOK AND PICTURE OF THE
SERAPHICALL SAINT TERESA (AS SHE
IS USUALLY EXPRESSED WITH
SERAPHIM BISIDE HER)

Well meaning readers! you that come as freinds
And catch the pretious name this peice pretends;
Make not too much hast to' admire

That fir-cheek't fallacy of fire.
That is a SERAPHIM, they say
And this the great TERESIA.
Readers, be rul'd by me; and make
Here a well-plac't and wise mistake
You must transpose the picture quite,
And spell it wrong to read it right;
Read HIM for her, and her for him;
And call the SAINT the SERAPHIM.

 Painter, what didst thou understand
To put her dart into his hand!
See, even the yeares and size of him
Showes this the mother SERAPHIM.
This is the mistresse flame; and duteous he
Her happy fire-works, here, comes down to see.
O most poor-spirited of men!
Had thy cold Pencil kist her PEN
Thou couldst not so unkindly err
To show us This faint shade for HER
Why man, this speakes pure mortall frame;
And mockes with female FROST love's manly flame.
One would suspect thou meant'st to paint
Some weak, inferiour, woman saint.
But had thy pale-fac't purple took
Fire from the burning cheeks of that bright Booke
Thou wouldst on her have heap't up all
That could be found SERAPHICALL;
What e're this youth of fire weares fair,
Rosy fingers, radiant hair,
Glowing cheek, and glistering wings,
All those fair and flagrant things,
But before all, that fiery DART
Had fill'd the Hand of this great HEART.

 Doe then as equall right requires,
Since HIS the blushes be, and her's the fires,

Resume and rectify thy rude design;
Undresse thy Seraphim into MINE.
Redeem this injury of thy art;
Give HIM the vail, give her the dart.

   Give Him the vail; that he may cover
The Red cheeks of a rivall'd lover.
Asham'd that our world, now, can show
Nests of new Seraphims here below.

   Give her the DART for it is she
(Fair youth) shootes both thy shaft and THEE
Say, all ye wise and well-peirc't hearts
That live and dy amidst her darts,
What is't your tastfull spirits doe prove
In that rare life of Her, and love?
Say and bear wittnes. Sends she not
A SERAPHIM at every shott?
What magazins of immortall *Armes* there shine!
Heavn's great artillery in each love-spun line.
Give then the dart to her who gives the flame;
Give him the veil, who kindly takes the shame.

   But if it be the frequent fate
Of worst faults to be fortunate;
If all 's præscription; and proud wrong
Hearkens not to an humble song;
For all the gallantry of him,
Give me the suffring SERAPHIM.
His be the bravery of all those Bright things,
The glowing cheekes, the glistering wings;
The Rosy hand, the radiant DART;
Leave HER alone THE FLAMING HEART.

   Leave her that; and thou shalt leave her
Not one loose shaft but love's whole quiver.
For in love's feild was never found
A nobler weapon then a *Wound*.
Love's passives are his activ'st part.

The wounded is the wounding heart.
O HEART! The æquall poise of love's both parts
Bigge alike with wounds and darts.
Live in these conquering leaves; live all the same;
And walk through all tongues one triumphant FLAME
Live here, great HEART; and love and dy and kill;
And bleed and wound; and yeild and conquer still.
Let this immortall life where it comes
Walk in a crowd of loves and MARTYRDOMES.
Let mystick DEATHS wait on't; and wise soules be
The love-slain wittnesses of this life of thee.
O sweet incendiary! shew here thy art,
Upon this carcasse of a hard, cold, hart,
Let all thy scatter'd shafts of light, that play
Among the leaves of thy larg Books of day,
Combin'd against this BREST at once break in
And take away from me my self and sin,
This gratious Robbery shall thy bounty be;
And my best fortunes such fair spoiles of me.
O thou undanted daughter of desires!
By all thy dowr of LIGHTS and FIRES;
By all the eagle in thee, all the dove;
By all thy lives and deaths of love;
By thy larg draughts of intellectuall day,
And by thy thirsts of love more large then they;
By all thy brim-fill'd Bowles of feirce desire
By thy last Morning's draught of liquid fire;
By the full kingdome of that finall kisse
That seiz'd thy parting Soul, and seal'd thee his;
By all the heav'ns thou hast in him
(Fair sister of the SERAPHIM!)
By all of HIM we have in THEE;
Leave nothing of my SELF in me.
Let me so read thy life, that I
Unto all life of mine may dy.

Wishes

TO HIS (SUPPOSED) MISTRESSE

Who ere shee bee,
That not impossible shee
That shall comand my heart and mee;

Where ere shee lye,
Lock't up from mortall Eye,
In shady leaves of Destiny:

Till that ripe Birth
Of studied fate stand forth,
And teach her faire steps to our Earth;

Till that Divine
Idæa, take a shrine
Of Chrystall flesh, through which to shine:

Meet you her my wishes,
Bespeake her to my blisses,
And bee yee call'd my absent kisses.

I wish her Beauty,
That owes not all his Duty
To gaudy Tire, or glistring shoo-ty.

Something more than
Taffata or Tissew can,
Or rampant feather, or rich fan.

More then the spoyle
Of shop, or silkewormes Toyle
Or a bought blush, or a set smile.

A face thats best
By its owne beauty drest,
And can alone commend the rest.

A face made up
Out of no other shop,
Then what natures white hand sets ope.

A cheeke where Youth,
And Blood, with Pen of Truth
Write, what the Reader sweetly ru'th.

A Cheeke where growes
More then a Morning Rose:
Which to no Boxe his being owes.

Lipps, where all Day
A lovers kisse may play,
Yet carry nothing thence away.

Lookes that oppresse
Their richest Tires but dresse
And cloath their simplest Nakednesse.

Eyes, that displaces
The Neighbour Diamond, and out faces
That Sunshine by their owne sweet Graces.

Tresses, that weare
Jewells, but to declare
How much themselves more pretious are.

Whose native Ray,
Can tame the wanton Day
Of Gems, that in their bright shades play.

Each Ruby there,
Or Pearle that dare appeare,
Bee its owne blush, bee its owne Teare.

A well tam'd Heart,
For whose more noble smart,
Love may bee long chusing a Dart.

Eyes, that bestow
Full quivers on loves Bow;
Yet pay lesse Arrowes then they owe.

Smiles, that can warme
The blood, yet teach a charme,
That Chastity shall take no harme.

Blushes, that bin
The burnish of no sin
Nor flames of ought too hot within.

Joyes, that confesse,
Vertue their Mistresse,
And have no other head to dresse.

Feares, fond and flight,
As the coy Brides, when Night
First does the longing lover right.

Teares, quickly fled,
And vaine, as those are shed
For a dying Maydenhead.

Dayes, that need borrow,
No part of their good Morrow,
From a fore spent night of sorrow.

Dayes, that in spight
Of Darkenesse, by the Light
Of a cleere mind are Day all Night.

Nights, sweet as they,
Made short by lovers play,
Yet long by th'absence of the Day.

Life, that dares send
A challenge to his end,
And when it comes say *Welcome Friend*.

Sydnæan showers
Of sweet discourse, whose powers
Can Crowne old Winters head with flowers,

Soft silken Houres,
Open sunnes; shady Bowers,
Bove all; Nothing within that lowres.

What ere Delight
Can make Dayes forehead bright;
Or give Downe to the Wings of Night.

In her whole frame,
Have Nature all the Name,
Art and ornament the shame.

Her flattery,
Picture and Poesy,
Her counsell her owne vertue bee.

I wish, her store
Of worth, may leave her poore
Of wishes; And I wish—No more.

Now if Time knowes
That her whose radiant Browes,
Weave them a Garland of my vowes;

Her whose just Bayes,
My future hopes can raise,
A trophie to her present praise;

Her that dares bee,
What these Lines wish to see:
I seeke no further, it is shee.

'Tis shee, and heere
Lo I uncloath and cleare,
My wishes cloudy Character.

May shee enjoy it,
Whose merit dare apply it,
But Modesty dares still deny it.

Such worth as this is,
Shall fixe my flying wishes,
And determine them to kisses.

Let her full Glory,
My fancyes, fly before yee,
Bee ye my fictions; But her story.

Henry Vaughan

(1622–1695)

The Retreate

Happy those early dayes! when I
Shin'd in my Angell-infancy.
Before I understood this place
Appointed for my second race,
Or taught my soul to fancy ought
But a white, Celestiall thought,
When yet I had not walkt above
A mile, or two, from my first love,
And looking back (at that short space,)
Could see a glimpse of his bright-face;
When on some *gilded Cloud,* or *flowre*
My gazing soul would dwell an houre,
And in those weaker glories spy
Some shadows of eternity;
Before I taught my tongue to wound
My Conscience with a sinfull sound,
Or had the black art to dispence
A sev'rall sinne to ev'ry sence,
But felt through all this fleshly dresse
Bright *shootes* of everlastingnesse.
 O how I long to travell back
And tread again that ancient track!
That I might once more reach that plaine,
Where first I left my glorious traine,
From whence th' Inlightned spirit sees

That shady City of Palme trees;
But (ah!) my soul with too much stay
Is drunk, and staggers in the way.
Some men a forward motion love,
But I by backward steps would move,
And when this dust falls to the urn
In that state I came return.

The World

I saw Eternity the other night
Like a great *Ring* of pure and endless light,
   All calm, as it was bright,
And round beneath it, Time in hours, days, years
     Driv'n by the spheres
Like a vast shadow mov'd, In which the world
   And all her train were hurl'd;
The doting Lover in his queintest strain
     Did their Complain,
Neer him, his Lute, his fancy, and his flights,
     Wits sour delights,
With gloves, and knots the silly snares of pleasure
     Yet his dear Treasure
All scatter'd lay, while he his eys did pour
     Upon a flowr.

The darksome States-man hung with weights and woe
Like a thick midnight-fog mov'd there so slow
   He did nor stay, nor go;
Condemning thoughts (like sad Ecclipses) scowl
     Upon his soul,
And Clouds of crying witnesses without
   Pursued him with one shout.

Yet dig'd the Mole, and lest his ways be found
    Workt under ground,
Where he did Clutch his prey, but one did see
    That policie,
Churches and altars fed him, Perjuries
    Were gnats and flies,
It rain'd about him bloud and tears, but he
    Drank them as free.

The fearfull miser on a heap of rust
Sate pining all his life there, did scarce trust
    His own hands with the dust,
Yet would not place one peece above, but lives
    In feare of theeves.
Thousands there were as frantick as himself
    And hug'd each one his pelf,
The down-right Epicure plac'd heav'n in sense
    And scornd pretence
While others slipt into a wide Excesse
    Said little lesse;
The weaker sort slight, triviall wares Inslave
    Who think them brave,
And poor, despised truth sate Counting by
    Their victory.

Yet some, who all this while did weep and sing,
And sing, and weep, soar'd up into the *Ring*.
    But most would use no wing.
O fools (said I,) thus to prefer dark night
    Before true light,
To live in grots, and caves, and hate the day
    Because it shews the way,
The way which from this dead and dark abode
    Leads up to God,
A way where you might tread the Sun, and be
    More bright than he.

But as I did their madnes so discusse
    One whisper'd thus,
This Ring the Bride-groome did for none provide
    But for his bride.

Man

    Weighing the stedfastness and state
Of some mean things which here below reside,
Where birds like watchful Clocks the noiseless date
    And Intercourse of times divide,
Where Bees at night get home and hive, and flowrs
      Early, aswel as late,
Rise with the Sun, and set in the same bowrs;

    I would (said I) my God would give
The staidness of these things to man! for these
To his divine appointments ever cleave,
    And no new business breaks their peace;
The birds nor sow, nor reap, yet sup and dine,
      The flowres without clothes live,
Yet *Solomon* was never drest so fine.

    Man hath still either toyes, or Care,
He hath no root, nor to one place is ty'd,
But ever restless and Irregular
    About this Earth doth run and ride,
He knows he hath a home, but scarce knows where,
      He sayes it is so far
That he hath quite forgot how to go there.

    He knocks at all doors, strays and roams,
Nay hath not so much wit as some stones have
Which in the darkest nights point to their homes,

By some hid sense their Maker gave;
Man is the shuttle, to whose winding quest
    And passage through these looms
God order'd motion, but ordain'd no rest.

They are all gone into the world of light

They are all gone into the world of light!
    And I alone sit lingring here;
Their very memory is fair and bright,
    And my sad thoughts doth clear.

It glows and glitters in my cloudy brest
    Like stars upon some gloomy grove,
Or those faint beams in which this hill is drest,
    After the Sun's remove.

I see them walking in an Air of glory,
    Whose light doth trample on my days:
My days, which are at best but dull and hoary,
    Meer glimering and decays.

O holy hope! and high humility,
    High as the Heavens above!
These are your walks, and you have shew'd them me
    To kindle my cold love,

Dear, beauteous death! the Jewel of the Just,
    Shining no where, but in the dark;
What mysteries do lie beyond thy dust;
    Could man outlook that mark!

He that hath found some fledg'd birds nest, may know
    At first sight, if the bird be flown;

But what fair Well, or Grove he sings in now,
    That is to him unknown.

And yet, as Angels in some brighter dreams
    Call to the soul, when man doth sleep:
So some strange thoughts transcend our wonted theams,
    And into glory peep.

If a star confin'd into a Tomb
    Her captive flames must needs burn there;
But when the hand that lockt her up, gives room,
    She'l shine through all the sphære.

O Father of eternal life, and all
    Created glories under thee!
Resume thy spirit from this world of thrall
    Into true liberty.

Either disperse these mists, which blot and fill
    My perspective (still) as they pass,
Or else remove me hence unto that hill.
    Where I shall need no glass.

The Water-Fall

With what deep murmurs through times silent stealth
Doth thy transparent, cool and watry wealth
    Here flowing fall,
    And chide, and call,
As if his liquid, loose Retinue staid
Lingring, and were of this steep place afraid,
    The common pass
    Where, clear as glass,
    All must descend
    Not to an end:

But quickned by this deep and rocky grave,
Rise to a longer course more bright and brave.

Dear stream! dear bank, where often I
Have sate, and pleas'd my pensive eye,
Why, since each drop of thy quick store
Runs thither, whence it flow'd before,
Should poor souls fear a shade or night,
Who came (sure) from a sea of light?
Or since those drops are all sent back
So sure to thee, that none doth lack,
Why should frail flesh doubt any more
That what God takes, hee'l not restore?
O useful Element and clear!
My sacred wash and cleanser here,
My first consigner unto those
Fountains of life, where the Lamb goes?
What sublime truths, and wholesome themes,
Lodge in thy mystical, deep streams!
Such as dull man can never finde
Unless that Spirit lead his minde,
Which first upon thy face did move,
And hatch'd all with his quickning love.
As this loud brooks incessant fall
In streaming rings restagnates all,
Which reach by course the bank, and then
Are no more seen, just so pass men.
O my invisible estate,
My glorious liberty, still late!
Thou art the Channel my soul seeks,
Not this with Cataracts and Creeks.

The Bird

Hither thou com'st: the busie wind all night
Blew through thy lodging, where thy own warm wing
Thy pillow was. Many a sullen storm
(For which course man seems much the fitter born,)
      Rain'd on thy bed
      And harmless head.

And now as fresh and chearful as the light
Thy little heart in early hymns doth sing
Unto that *Providence,* whose unseen arm
Cu⌐b'd them, and cloath'd thee well and warm.
      All things that be, praise him; and had
      Their lesson taught them, when first made.

So hills and valleys into singing break,
And though poor stones have neither speech nor tongue,
While active winds and streams both run and speak,
Yet stones are deep in admiration.
Thus Praise and Prayer here beneath the Sun
Make lesser mornings, when the great are done.

For each inclosed Spirit is a star
    Inlightning his own little sphære,
Whose light, though fetcht and borrowed from far,
    Both mornings makes, and evenings there.

But as these Birds of light make a land glad,
Chirping their solemn Matins on each tree:
So in the shades of night some dark fowls be,
Whose heavy notes make all that hear them, sad.

    The Turtle then in Palm-trees mourns,
      While Owls and Satyrs howl;

The pleasant Land to brimstone turns
And all her streams grow foul.

Brightness and mirth, and love and faith, all flye,
Till the Day-spring breaks forth again from high.

The Night

(*John* 2:3)

Through that pure *Virgin-shrine*,
That sacred vail drawn o'r thy glorious noon
That men might look and live as Glo-worms shine,
And face the Moon:
Wise *Nicodemus* saw such light
As made him know his God by night.

Most blest believer he!
Who in that land of darkness and blinde eyes
Thy long expected healing wings could see,
When thou didst rise,
And what can never more be done,
Did at mid-night speak with the Sun!

O who will tell me, where
He found thee at that dead and silent hour!
What hallow'd solitary ground did bear
So rare a flower,
Within whose sacred leafs did lie
The fulness of the Deity.

No mercy-seat of gold,
No dead and dusty *Cherub*, nor carv'd stone,
But his own living works did my Lord hold
And lodge alone;

Where *trees* and *herbs* did watch and peep
And wonder, while the *Jews* did sleep.

Dear night! this worlds defeat;
The stop to busie fools; cares check and curb;
The day of Spirits; my souls calm retreat
  Which none disturb!
 Christs progress, and his prayer time;
 The hours to which high Heaven doth chime.

Gods silent, searching flight:
When my Lords head is fill'd with dew, and all
His locks are wet with the clear drops of night;
  His still, soft call;
 His knocking time; The souls dumb watch,
 When Spirits their fair kinred catch.

Were all my loud, evil days
Calm and unhaunted as is thy dark Tent,
Whose peace but by some *Angels* wing or voice
  Is seldom rent;
 Then I in Heaven all the long year
 Would keep, and never wander here.

But living where the Sun
Doth all things wake, and where all mix and tyre
Themselves and others, I consent and run
  To ev'ry myre,
 And by this worlds ill-guiding light,
 Erre more then I can do by night.

There is in God (some say)
A deep, but dazling darkness; As men here
Say it is late and dusky, because they
  See not all clear;
 O for that night! where I in him
 Might live invisible and dim.

The Queer

O tell me whence that joy doth spring
Whose diet is divine and fair,
Which wears heaven, like a bridal ring,
And tramples on doubts and despair?

Whose Eastern traffique deals in bright
And boundless Empyrean themes,
Mountains of spice, Day-stars and light,
Green trees of life, and living streams?

Tell me, O tell who did thee bring
And here, without my knowledge, plac'd,
Till thou didst grow and get a wing,
A wing with eyes, and eyes that taste?

Sure, *holyness* the *Magnet* is,
And *Love* the *Lure,* that woos thee down;
Which makes the high transcendent bliss
Of knowing thee, so rarely known.

The Revival

Unfold, unfold! take in his light,
Who makes thy Cares more short than night.
The Joys, which with his *Day-star* rise,
He deals to all, but drowsy Eyes:
And what the men of this world miss,
Some *drops* and *dews* of future bliss.
　　Hark! how his *winds* have chang'd their *note,*

And with warm *whispers* call thee out.
The *frosts* are past, the *storms* are gone:
And backward *life* at last comes on.
The lofty *groves* in express Joyes
Reply unto the *Turtles* voice,
And here in *dust* and *dirt,* O here
The *Lilies* of his love appear!

Thomas Traherne

(1636–1674)

Eden

A learned and a happy Ignorance
        Divided me
      From all the Vanity,
From all the Sloth, Care, Sorrow, that advance
   The Madness and the Misery
Of Men. No Error, no Distraction, I
Saw cloud the Earth, or over-cast the Sky.

I knew not that there was a Serpent's Sting,
       Whose Poyson shed
      On Men, did overspread
The World: Nor did I dream of such a thing
   As Sin, in which Mankind lay dead.
They all were brisk and living Things to me,
Yea pure, and full of Immortality.

Joy, Pleasure, Beauty, Kindness, charming Lov,
       Sleep, Life, and Light,
      Peace, Melody, my Sight
Mine Ears and Heart did fill and freely mov;
   All that I saw did me delight:
The *Universe* was then a *World* of Treasure
To me an Universal World of Pleasure.

Unwelcom Penitence I then thought not on;
       Vain costly Toys,

503

Swearing and roaring Boys,
Shops, Markets, Taverns, Coaches, were unknown,
　　So all things were that drown my Joys:
No Thorns choakt-up my Path, nor hid the face
Of Bliss and Glory, nor eclypst my place.

Only what Adam in his first Estate
　　　　Did I behold;
　　　Hard Silver and dry Gold
As yet lay under-ground: My happy Fate
　　Was more acquainted with the old
And innocent Delights which he did see
In his Original Simplicity

Those things which first his *Eden* did adorn,
　　　　My Infancy
　　　Did crown: Simplicity
Was my Protection when I first was born.
　　Mine Eys those Treasures first did see
Which God first made: The first Effects of Lov
My first Enjoyments upon Earth did prov.

And were so Great, and so Divine, so Pure,
　　　　So fair and sweet,
　　　So tru; when I did meet
Them here at first, they did my Soul allure,
　　And drew away mine Infant-feet
Quite from the Works of Men, that I might see
The glorious Wonders of the DEITY.

The Preparative

My Body being dead, my Limbs unknown;
　　　Before I skill'd to prize
　　　Those living Stars, mine Eys;
Before or Tongue or Cheeks I call'd mine own,

Before I knew these Hands were mine,
Or that my Sinews did my Members join;
   When neither Nostril, foot, nor Ear,
As yet could be discern'd, or did appear;
      I was within
A House I knew not, newly cloath'd with Skin.

Then was my Soul my only All to me,
      A living endless Ey,
      Scarce bounded with the Sky,
Whose Power, and Act, and Essence was to see:
   I was an inward Sphere of Light,
Or an interminable Orb of Sight,
   Exceeding that which makes the Days,
A *vital* Sun that shed abroad his Rays:
         All Life, all Sense,
A naked, simple, pure Intelligence.

I then no Thirst nor Hunger did perceiv;
      No dire Necessity
      Nor Want was known to me:
Without disturbance then I did receiv
   The tru Ideas of all Things,
The Hony did enjoy without the Stings.
   A meditating inward Ey
Gazing at Quiet did within me ly,
         And all things fair
Delighted me that was to be their Heir.

For *Sight* inherits Beauty; *Hearing,* Sounds;
      The *Nostril,* sweet Perfumes,
      All Tastes have secret Rooms
Within the *Tongue;* the *Touching* feeleth Wounds
   Of Pain or Pleasure; and yet I
Forgat the rest, and was all Sight or Ey,
   Unbody'd and devoid of Care,

Just as in Hev'n the Holy Angels are:
    For simple Sense
Is Lord of all created Excellence.

Being thus prepar'd for all Felicity;
    Not prepossest with Dross,
    Nor basely glued to gross
And dull Materials that might ruin me,
    Nor fetter'd by an Iron Fate,
By vain Affections in my earthy State,
    To any thing that should seduce
My Sense, or els bereav it of its Use;
    I was as free
As if there were nor Sin nor Misery.

Pure nativ Powers that Corruption loath,
    Did, like the fairest Glass
    Or, spotless polisht Brass,
Themselvs soon in their Object's Image cloath:
    Divine Impressions, when they came,
Did quickly enter and my Soul enflame.
    'Tis not the Object, but the Light,
That maketh Hev'n: 'Tis a clearer Sight.
    Felicity
Appears to none but them that purely see.

A disentangled and a naked Sense,
    A Mind that's unpossest,
    A disengaged Breast,
A quick unprejudic'd Intelligence
    Acquainted with the Golden Mean,
An eeven Spirit, quiet, and serene,
    Is that where Wisdom's Excellence
And Pleasure keep their Court of Residence.
    My Soul get free,
And then thou may'st possess Felicity.

Christendom

When first mine Infant-Ear
  Of *Christendom* did hear,
I much admir'd what kind of Place or Thing
  It was of which the Folk did talk:
  What Coast, what Region, what therin
  Did mov, or might be seen to walk.
        My great Desire
        Like ardent fire
Did long to know what Things did ly behind
That *Mystic Name,* to which mine Ey was blind.

  Som Depth it did conceal,
    Which till it did reveal
Its self to me, no Quiet, Peace, or Rest,
  Could I by any Means attain;
  My earnest Thoughts did me molest
  Till som one should the thing explain:
        I thought it was
        A Glorious Place,
Where Souls might dwell in all Delight and Bliss;
So thought, yet fear'd that I the Truth might miss:

  Among ten thousand things,
    Gold, Silver, Cherub's Wings,
Pearls, Rubies, Diamonds, a Church with Spires,
  Masks, Stages, Games and Plays,
  That then might suit my yong Desires,
  Feathers, and Farthings, Holidays,
        Cards, Musick, Dice,
        So much in price;

A *City* did before mine Eys present
Its self, wherin there reigned sweet Content.

    A Town beyond the Seas
      Whose Prospect much did pleas,
And to my Soul so sweetly raise Delight
   As if a long expected Joy,
    Shut up in that transforming Sight,
   Would into me its Self convey;
       And Blessedness
       I there possess,
As if that City stood on my own Ground,
And all the Profit mine which there was found.

    Whatever Force me led,
      My Spirit sweetly fed
On these Conceits; That 'twas a City strange
   Wherin I saw no gallant Inns,
    No Markets, New or Old Exchange,
    No Childish Trifles, useles Things;
       Nor any Bound
       That Town surround;
But as if all its Streets ev'n endless were;
Without or Gate or Wall it did appear.

    Things Native sweetly grew,
      Which there mine Ey did view,
Plain, simple, cheap, on either side the Street,
   Which was exceeding fair and wide;
   Sweet Mansions there mine Eys did meet;
   Green Trees the shaded Doors did hide:
       My chiefest Joys
       Were Girls and Boys
That in those Streets still up and down did play,
Which crown'd the Town with constant Holiday.

A sprightly pleasant Time,
(Ev'n Summer in its prime)
Did gild the Trees, the Houses, Children, Skies,
And made the City all divine;
It ravished my wondring Eys
To see the Sun so brightly shine:
        The Heat and Light
        Seem'd in my sight
With such a dazling Lustre shed on them,
As made me think 'twas th' *New Jerusalem.*

Beneath the lofty Trees
I saw, of all Degrees,
Folk calmly sitting in their doors; while som
Did standing with them kindly talk,
Som smile, som sing, or what was don
Observ, while others by did walk;
        They view'd the Boys
        And Girls, their Joys,
The Streets adorning with their Angel-faces,
Themselvs diverting in those pleasant Places.

The Streets like Lanes did seem,
Not pav'd with Stones, but green,
Which with red Clay did partly mixt appear;
'Twas Holy Ground of great Esteem;
The Springs choice Liveries did wear
Of verdant Grass that grew between
        The purling Streams,
        Which golden Beams
Of Light did varnish, coming from the Sun
By which to distant Realms was Service don.

In fresh and cooler Rooms
Retir'd they dine: Perfumes
They wanted not, having the pleasant Shade,

And Peace to bless their House within,
By sprinkled Waters cooler made,
For those incarnat Cherubin.
This happy Place,
With all the Grace
The Joy and Beauty which did it beseem,
Did ravish me and highten my Esteem.

That here to rais Desire
All Objects do conspire,
Peeple in Years, and Yong enough to play,
Their Streets of Houses, common Peace,
In one continued Holy day
Whose gladsom Mirth shall never cease:
Since these becom
My *Christendom,*
What learn I more than that *Jerusalem*
Is *mine,* as 'tis *my Maker's,* choicest Gem.

Before I was aware
Truth did to me appear,
And represented to my Virgin-Eys
Th' unthought of Joys and Treasures
Wherin my Bliss and Glory lies;
My God's Delight, (which givs me Measure)
His Turtle Dov,
Is Peace and Lov
In Towns: for holy Children, Maids, and Men
Make up the King of Glory's Diadem.

On *Christmas-Day*

Shall Dumpish Melancholy spoil my Joys
While Angels sing
And Mortals ring

My Lord and Savior's Prais!
Awake from Sloth, for that alone destroys,
'Tis Sin defiles, 'tis Sloth puts out thy Joys.
   See how they run from place to place,
   And seek for Ornaments of Grace;
   Their Houses deckt with sprightly Green,
   In Winter makes a Summer seen;
     They Bays and Holly bring
      As if 'twere Spring!

Shake off thy Sloth, my drouzy Soul, awake;
     With Angels sing
     Unto thy King,
   And pleasant Musick make;
Thy Lute, thy Harp, or els thy Heart-strings take,
And with thy Musick let thy Sense awake.
   See how each one the other calls
   To fix his Ivy on the walls,
   Transplanted there it seems to grow
   As if it rooted were below:
     Thus He, who is thy King,
     Makes Winter, Spring.

Shall Houses clad in Summer-Liveries
     His Praises sing
     And laud thy King,
   And wilt not thou arise?
Forsake thy Bed, and grow (my Soul) more wise,
Attire thy self in cheerful Liveries:
   Let pleasant Branches still be seen
   Adorning thee, both quick and green;
   And, which with Glory better suits,
   Be laden all the Year with Fruits;
     Inserted into Him,
      For ever spring.

'Tis He that Life and Spirit doth infuse:
   Let ev'ry thing
   The Praises sing
  Of *Christ* the King of Jews;
Who makes things green, and with a Spring infuse
A Season which to see it doth not use:
 Old Winter's Frost and hoary hair,
 With Garland's crowned, Bays doth wear;
 The nipping Frost of Wrath b'ing gon,
 To Him the Manger made a Throne,
  Du Praises let us sing,
   Winter and Spring.

See how, their Bodies clad with finer Cloaths,
   They now begin
   His Prais to sing
  Who purchas'd their Repose:
Wherby their inward Joy they do disclose;
Their Dress alludes to better Works than those:
 His gayer Weeds and finer Band,
 New Suit and Hat, into his hand
 The Plow-man takes; his neatest Shoos,
 And warmer Glovs, he means to use:
  And shall not I, my King
   Thy Praises sing

See how their Breath doth smoak, and how they haste
   His Prais to sing
   With Cherubim;
  They scarce a Break-fast taste;
But throu the Streets, lest precious Time should waste,
When Service doth begin, to Church they haste.
 And shall not I, Lord, com to Thee,
 The Beauty of thy Temple see?
 Thy Name with Joy I will confess,
 Clad in my Savior's Righteousness;

    'Mong all thy Servants sing
        To Thee my King.

'Twas thou that gav'st us Caus for fine Attires;
        Ev'n thou, O King,
        As in the Spring,
    Dost warm us with thy fires
Of Lov: Thy Blood hath bought us new Desires;
Thy Righteousness doth cloath with new Attires.
    Both fresh and fine let me appear
    This Day divine, to close the Year;
    Among the rest let me be seen
    A living Branch and always green,
        Think it a pleasant thing
        Thy Prais to sing.

At break of Day, O how the Bells did ring!
        To thee, my King,
        The Bells did ring;
        To thee the Angels sing:
Thy Goodness did produce this other Spring,
For this it is they make the Bells to ring:
    The sounding Bells do throu the Air
    Proclaim thy Welcom far and near;
    While I alone with Thee inherit
    All these Joys, beyond my Merit.
        Who would not always sing
        To such a King?

I all these Joys, abov my Merit, see
        By Thee, my King,
        To whom I sing,
        Entire convey'd to me.
My Treasure, Lord, thou mak'st the Peeple be
That I with pleasure might thy Servants see.
    Ev'n in their rude external ways

They do set forth my Savior's Prais,
And minister a Light to me;
While I by them do hear to Thee
    Praises, my Lord and King,
        Whole Churches ring.

Hark how remoter Parishes do sound!
        Far off they ring
        For thee, my King,
    Ev'n round about the Town:
The Churches scatter'd over all the Ground
Serv for thy Prais, who art with Glory crown'd.
    This City is an Engin great
    That makes my Pleasure more compleat;
    The Sword, the Mace, the Magistrate,
    To honor Thee attend in State;
        The whole Assembly sings;
        The Minster rings.

Right *Apprehension*

Giv but to things their tru Esteem,
And those which now so vile and worthless seem
    Will so much fill and pleas the Mind,
That we shall there the only Riches find.
        How wise was I
        In Infancy!
    I then saw in the clearest Light;
But corrupt Custom is a second Night.

    Custom; that must a Trophy be
When Wisdom shall compleat her Victory:
    For Trades, Opinions, Errors, are
False Lights, but yet receiv'd to set off Ware

More false: We're sold
    For worthless Gold.
Diana was a Goddess made
That Silver-Smiths might have the better Trade.

  But giv to Things their tru Esteem,
And then what's magnify'd most vile will seem:
   What commonly's despis'd will be
The truest and the greatest Rarity.
      What Men should prize
      They all despise;
  The best Enjoiments are abus'd;
The Only Wealth by Madmen is refus'd.

  A Globe of Earth is better far
Than if it were a Globe of Gold: A Star
   Much brighter than a precious Stone:
The Sun more Glorious than a Costly Throne;
      His warming Beam,
      A living Stream
  Of liquid Pearl, that from a Spring
Waters the Earth, is a most precious thing.

  What Newness once suggested to,
Now clearer Reason doth improv, my View:
   By Novelty my Soul was taught
At first; but now Reality my Thought
      Inspires: And I
      Perspicuously
  Each way instructed am; by Sense
Experience, Reason, and Intelligence.

  A Globe of Gold must Barren be,
Untill'd and Useless: We should neither see
   Trees, Flowers, Grass, or Corn
Such a Metalline Massy Globe adorn:
      As Splendor blinds,

So Hardness binds;
No Fruitfulness it can produce;
A Golden World can't be of any Use.

Ah me! This World is more divine:
The Wisdom of a God in this doth shine.
What ails Mankind to be so cross?
The Useful Earth they count vile Dirt and Dross
And neither prize
Its Qualities,
Nor Donor's Lov. I fain would know
How or why Men God's Goodness disallow.

The Earth's rare ductile Soil,
Which duly yields unto the Plow-man's Toil,
Its fertile Nature, givs Offence;
And its Improvment by the Influence
Of Hev'n; For, these
Do not well pleas,
Becaus they do upbraid Mens hardned Hearts,
And each of them an Evidence imparts

Against the Owner; whose Design
It is that Nothing be reputed fine,
Nor held for any Excellence,
Of which he hath not in himself the Sense.
He too well knows
That no Fruit grows
In him, Obdurat Wretch, who yields
Obedience to Hev'n, less than the Fields:

But being, like his loved Gold,
Stiff, barren, and impen'trable; tho told
He should be otherwise: He is
Uncapable of any hev'nly Bliss.
His Gold and he
Do well agree;

For he's a formal Hypocrite,
Like *that* Unfruitful, yet on th' outside bright.

Ah! Happy Infant! Wealthy Heir!
How blessed did the Hev'n and Earth appear
     Before thou knew'st there was a thing
Call'd Gold! Barren of Good; of Ill the Spring
          Beyond Compare!
          Most quiet were
Those Infant-Days, when I did see
Wisdom and Wealth couch'd in Simplicity.

Shadows in the Water

In unexperienc'd Infancy
Many a sweet Mistake doth ly:
Mistake, tho false, intending tru;
A *Seeming* somwhat more than *View;*
     That doth instruct the Mind
     In Things that ly behind,
And many Secrets to us show
Which afterwards we com to know.

Thus did I by the Water's brink
Another World beneath me think;
And while the lofty spacious Skies
Reversed there abus'd mine Eys,
     I fancy'd other Feet
     Came mine to touch or meet;
As by som Puddle I did play
Another World within it lay.

Beneath the Water Peeple drown'd,
Yet with another Hev'n crown'd,

In spacious Regions seem'd to go
As freely moving to and fro:
    In bright and open Space
    I saw their very face;
Eys, Hands, and Feet they had like mine;
Another Sun did with them shine.

'Twas strange that Peeple there should walk,
And yet I could not hear them talk:
That throu a little watry Chink,
Which one dry Ox·or Horse might drink,
    We other Worlds should see,
    Yet not admitted be;
And other Confines there behold
Of Light and Darkness, Heat and Cold.

I call'd them oft, but call'd in vain;
No Speeches we could entertain:
Yet did I there expect to find
Som other World, to pleas my Mind.
    I plainly saw by these
    A new *Antipodes,*
Whom, tho they were so plainly seen,
A Film kept off that stood between.

By walking Men's reversed Feet
I chanc'd another World to meet;
Tho it did not to View exceed
A Phantasm, 'tis a World indeed,
    Where Skies beneath us shine,
    And Earth by Art divine
Another face presents below,
Where Peeple's feet against Ours go.

Within the Regions of the Air,
Compass'd about with Hev'ns fair,
Great Tracts of Land there may be found

Enricht with Fields and fertil Ground;
    Where many num'rous Hosts,
    In those far distant Coasts,
For other great and glorious Ends,
Inhabit, my yet unknown Friends.

O ye that stand upon the Brink,
Whom I so near me, throu the Chink,
With Wonder see: What Faces there,
Whose Feet, whose Bodies, do ye wear?
    I my Companions see
    In You, another Me.
They seemed Others, but are We;
Our second Selvs those Shadows be.

Look how far off those lower Skies
Extend themselves! scarce with mine Eys
I can them reach. O ye my Friends,
What *Secret* borders on those Ends?
    Are lofty Hevens hurl'd
    'Bout your inferior World?
Are ye the Representatives
Of other Peopl's distant Lives?

Of all the Play-mates which I knew
That here I do the Image view
In other Selvs; what can it mean?
But that below the purling Stream
    Som unknown Joys there be
    Laid up in Store for me;
To which I shall, when that thin Skin
Is broken, be admitted in.

Hosanna

No more shall Walls, no more shall Walls confine
That glorious Soul which in my Flesh doth shine:
    No more shall Walls of Clay or Mud,
      Nor Ceilings made of Wood,
    Nor Crystal Windows, bound my Sight,
    But rather shall admit Delight.
      The Skies that seem to bound
        My Joys and Treasures,
      Of more endearing Pleasures
      Themselvs becom a Ground:
While from the Center to the utmost Sphere
My Goods are multiplied evry where.

The Deity, the Deity to me
Doth All things giv, and make me clearly see
    The Moon and Stars, the Air and Sun
      Into my Chamber com:
    The Seas and Rivers hither flow,
    Yea, here the Trees of *Eden* grow,
      The Fowls and Fishes stand,
        Kings and their Thrones,
      As 'twere, at my Command;
      God's Wealth, His Holy Ones,
The Ages too, and Angels all conspire:
While I, that I the Center am, admire.

No more, No more shall Clouds eclyps my Treasures,
Nor viler Shades obscure my highest Pleasures;
    No more shall earthen Husks confine
      My Blessings which do shine

Within the Skies, or els *abov:*
Both Worlds one Heven made by Lov,
   In common happy I
     With Angels walk
   And there my Joys espy;
   With God himself I talk;
Wondring with Ravishment all Things to see
Such *Reall* Joys, so truly *Mine,* to be.

No more shall Trunks and Dishes be my Store,
Nor Ropes of Pearl, nor Chains of Golden Ore;
   As if such Beings yet were not,
     They all shall be forgot.
   No such in Eden did appear,
   No such in Heven: Heven here
     Would be, were those remov'd;
       The Sons of Men
   Liv in Jerusalem,
   Had they not Baubles lov'd.
These Clouds dispers'd, the Hevens clear I see:
Wealth new-invented, *mine* shall never be.

Transcendent Objects doth my God provide,
In such convenient Order all contriv'd,
   That All things in their proper place
     My Soul doth best embrace,
   Extends its Arms beyond the Seas,
   Abov the Hevens its self can pleas,
     With God enthron'd may reign:
       Like sprightly Streams
     My Thoughts on Things remain;
     Ev'n as som vital Beams
They reach to, shine on, quicken Things, and make
Them truly Usefull; while I *All* partake.

For Me the World created was by Lov;
For Me the Skies, the Seas, the Sun, do mov;

The Earth for Me doth stable stand;
   For Me each fruitful Land,
For Me the very Angels God made *His,*
And *my* Companions in Bliss;
    His Laws command all Men
      That they lov Me,
    Under a Penalty
    Severe, in case they miss:
His Laws require His Creatures all to prais
His Name, and when they do 't be most my Joys.

Abraham Cowley

(1618–1667)

Beauty

Beauty, thou wild fantastick Ape,
Who dost in ev'ry Country change thy shape!
Here black, there brown, here tawny, and there white;
Thou *Flatt'rer* which compli'st with every sight!
    Thou *Babel* which confound'st the Ey
    With unintelligible *variety!*
    Who hast no certain *What,* nor *Where,*
    But vary'st still, and dost thy self declare
    Inconstant, as thy *she-Professors* are.

Beauty, Loves Scene and *Maskerade,*
So gay by *well-plac'd Lights,* and *Distance* made;
False *Coyn,* with which th' *Impostor* cheats us still;
The *Stamp* and *Colour* good, but *Metal* ill!
    Which *Light,* or *Base* we find, when we
    Weigh by *Enjoyment,* and examine Thee!
    For though thy *Being* be but *show,*
    'Tis chiefly *Night* which men to Thee allow:
    And chuse *t'enjoy* Thee, when *Thou least art Thou.*

Beauty, Thou *active, passive* Ill!
Which *dy'st* thy self as fast as thou dost *kill!*
Thou *Tulip,* who thy stock in paint dost waste,
Neither for *Physick* good, nor *Smell,* nor *Tast.*
    Beauty, whose *Flames* but *Meteors* are,
Short-liv'd and low, though thou wouldst seem a *Star,*

Who dar'st not thine own *Home* descry,
Pretending to dwell richly in the *Eye,*
When thou, alas, dost in the *Fancy* lye.

   Beauty, whose *Conquests* still are made
O're Hearts by *Cowards* kept, or else *betray'd!*
Weak Victor! who thy self destroy'd must be
When *sickness storms,* or *Time besieges* Thee!
   Thou'unwholesome Thaw to *frozen Age!*
Thou strong *wine,* which youths *Feaver* dost enrage,
   Thou *Tyrant* which leav'st no man free!
Thou subtle *thief,* from whom nought safe can be!
Thou *Murth'rer* which hast *kill'd,* and *Devil* which
      wouldst *Damn me.*

Ode upon Doctor Harvey

   Coy Nature, (which remain'd, thô aged grown,
A beauteous Virgin still, injoy'd by none,
   Nor seen unveil'd by any one,)
When *Harvey's* violent passion she did see,
Began to tremble and to flee,
Took Sanctuary, like *Daphne,* in a Tree:
There *Daphne's* Lover stopt, and thought it much
   The very Leaves of her to touch:
But *Harvey,* our *Apollo,* stopt not so,
Into the Bark and Root he after her did go:
   No smallest Fibres of a Plant,
For which the Eye-beams point doth sharpness want,
   His passage after her withstood;
What should she do? through all the moving Wood
Of Lives endow'd with sense she took her flight,
Harvey persues, and keeps her still in sight.

But as the Deer, long hunted, takes a Flood,
She leap'd at last into the Winding-streams of Blood;
Of Mans *Meander* all the Purple reaches made,
   Till at the Heart she stay'd,
   Where turning Head, and at a Bay,
Thus by well-purged Ears she was o're-heard to say.

Here sure shall I be safe (said she,)
None will be able sure to see
   This my Retreat, but only He
   Who made both it and me.
The heart of Man, what Art can e're reveal?
   A Wall impervious between
   Divides the very Parts within,
And doth the very Heart of Man ev'n from itself conceal.
   She spoke, but e're she was aware,
   Harvey was with her there,
And held this slippery *Proteus* in a chain,
Till all her mighty Mysteries she descry'd,
Which from his Wit th' attempt before to hide
Was the first Thing that Nature did in vain.

   He the young Practice of New Life did see,
   Whil'st, to conceal it's toilsome poverty,
It for a Living wrought, both hard, and privately.
   Before the Liver understood
   The noble Scarlet Dye of Blood,
   Before one drop was by it made,
Or brought into it to set up the Trade;
Before the untaught Heart began to beat
The tuneful March to vital heat,
From all the Souls that living Buildings rear,
Whether imploy'd for Earth, or Sea, or Air,
Whether it in the Womb or Egg be wrought,
A strict account to him is hourly brought,

How the great Fabrick does proceed,
What Time, and what Materials it does need.
He so exactly does the Work survey,
As if he hir'd the Workers by the day.

Thus *Harvey* sought for Truth in Truth's own Book,
  The Creatures, which by God himself was writ;
    And wisely thought 'twas fit,
Not to read Comments only upon it,
But on th' Original itself to look.
Methinks in Arts great Circle others stand
  Lock'd up together hand in hand,
    Every one leads as he is led,
    The same bare Path they tread.
A Dance like Fairies, a Fantastick round,
But neither change their Motion, nor their Ground.
Had *Harvey* to this Road confin'd his Wit,
His noble Circle of the Blood had been untroden yet:
Great Doctor, th' art of Curing's cur'd by thee,
  We now thy Patient Physick see
From all inveterate Diseases free,
  Purg'd of old Errors by thy Care,
New Dieted, put forth to clearer Air,
    It now will strong and healthful prove,
Itself before Lethargick lay, and could not move.

These useful Secrets to his Pen we owe,
And thousands more 'twas ready to bestow;
Of which a barbarous War's unlearned Rage
    Has robb'd the ruin'd age;
Oh cruel loss! as if the Golden Fleece,
    With so much cost and labour wrought,
And from afar by a great Heroe brought,
    Had sunk even in the Ports of *Greece*.
Oh cursed War! who can forgive thee this?
    Houses and Towns may rise again,

And ten times easier 'tis
To rebuild *Pauls,* than any work of his.
The mighty Task none but himself can do,
   Nay, scarce himself too now,
For tho' his Wit the force of Age withstand,
His body Alas! and Time it must command.
And Nature now, so long by him surpast,
Will sure have her revenge on him at last.

Andrew Marvell

(1621–1678)

The Nymph Complaining
for the Death of Her Faun

The wanton Troopers riding by
Have shot my Faun and it will dye.
Ungentle men! They cannot thrive
To kill thee. Thou neer didst alive
Them any harm: alas nor cou'd
Thy death yet do them any good.
I'me sure I never wisht them ill;
Nor do I for all this; nor will:
But, if my simple Pray'rs may yet
Prevail with Heaven to forget
Thy murder, I will Joyn my Tears
Rather then fail. But, O my fears!
It cannot dye so. Heavens King
Keeps register of every thing:
And nothing may we use in vain.
Ev'n Beasts must be with justice slain;
Else Men are made their *Deodands*.
Though they should wash their guilty hands
In this warm life-blood, which doth part
From thine, and wound me to the Heart,
Yet could they not be clean: their Stain
Is dy'd in such a Purple Grain.
There is not such another in
The World, to offer for their Sin.

Unconstant *Sylvio*, when yet
I had not found him counterfeit,
One morning (I remember well)
Ty'd in this silver Chain and Bell,
Gave it to me: nay and I know
What he said then; I'me sure I do.
Said He, look how your Huntsman here
Hath taught a Faun to hunt his *Dear*.
But *Sylvio* soon had me beguil'd.
This waxed tame, while he grew wild,
And quite regardless of my Smart,
Left me his Faun, but took his Heart.

Thenceforth I set my self to play
My solitary time away,
With this: and very well content,
Could so mine idle Life have spent.
For it was full of sport; and light
Of foot, and heart; and did invite,
Me to its game: it seem'd to bless
Its self in me. How could I less
Than love it? O I cannot be
Unkind, t' a Beast that loveth me.

Had it liv'd long, I do not know
Whether it too might have done so
As *Sylvio* did: his Gifts might be
Perhaps as false or more than he.
But I am sure, for ought that I
Could in so short a time espie,
Thy Love was far more better then
The love of false and cruel men.

With sweetest milk, and sugar, first
I it at mine own fingers nurst.
And as it grew, so every day
It wax'd more white and sweet than they.
It had so sweet a Breath! And oft

I blusht to see its foot more soft,
And white, (shall I say then my hand?)
NAY any Ladies of the Land.

It is a wond'rous thing, how fleet
'Twas on those little silver feet.
With what a pretty skipping grace,
It oft would challenge me the Race:
And when't had left me far away,
'Twould stay, and run again, and stay.
For it was nimbler much than Hindes;
And trod, as on the four Winds.

I have a Garden of my own,
But so with Roses over grown,
And Lillies, that you would it guess
To be a little Wilderness.
And all the Spring time of the year
It onely loved to be there.
Among the beds of Lillyes, I
Have sought it oft, where it should lye;
Yet could not, till it self would rise,
Find it, although before mine Eyes.
For, in flaxen Lillies shade,
It like a bank of Lillies laid.
Upon the Roses it would feed,
Until its Lips ev'n seem'd to bleed;
And then to me 'twould boldly trip,
And print those Roses on my Lip.
But all its chief delight was still
On Roses thus its self to fill:
And its pure virgin Limbs to fold
In whitest sheets of Lillies cold.
Had it liv'd long it would have been
Lillies without, Roses within.

O help! O help! I see it faint:
And dye as calmely as a Saint.

See how it weeps. The Tears do come
Sad, slowly dropping like a Gumme.
So weeps the wounded Balsome: so
The holy Frankincense doth flow.
The brotherless *Heliades*
Melt in such Amber Tears as these.

   I in a golden Vial will
Keep these two crystal Tears; and fill
It till it do o'reflow with mine;
Then place it in *Diana's* Shrine.

   Now my Sweet Faun is vanish'd to
Whether the Swans and Turtles go:
In fair Elizium to endure,
With milk-white Lambs, and Ermins pure.
O do not run too fast: for I
Will but bespeak thy Grave, and dye.

   First my unhappy Statue shall
Be cut in Marble; and withal,
Let it be weeping too: but there
Th' Engraver sure his Art may spare;
For I so truly thee bemoane,
That I shall weep though I be Stone:
Until my Tears, still drooping, wear
My breast, themselves engraving there.
There at my feet shalt thou be laid,
Of purest Alabaster made:
For I would have thine Image be
White as I can, though not as Thee.

A *Dialogue Between the Soul and Body*

SOUL

O who shall, from this Dungeon, raise
A Soul inslav'd so many wayes?
With bolts of Bones, that fetter'd stands
In Feet; and manacled in Hands.
Here blinded with an Eye; and there
Deaf with the drumming of an Ear.
A Soul hung up, as 'twere, in Chains
Of Nerves, and Arteries, and Veins.
Tortur'd, besides each other part,
In a vain Head, and double Heart.

BODY

O who shall me deliver whole,
From bonds of this Tyrannic Soul?
Which, stretcht upright, impales me so,
That mine own Precipice I go;
And warms and moves this needless Frame:
(A Fever could but do the same.)
And, wanting where its spight to try,
Has made me live to let me dye.
A Body that could never rest,
Since this ill Spirit it possest.

SOUL

What Magick could me thus confine
Within anothers Grief to pine?
Where whatsoever it complain,
I feel, that cannot feel, the pain.
And all my Care its self employes,

That to preserve, which me destroys:
Constrain'd not only to indure
Diseases, but, whats worse, the Cure:
And ready oft the Port to gain,
Am Shipwrackt into Health again.

BODY

But Physick yet could never reach
The Maladies Thou me dost teach;
Whom first the Cramp of Hope does Tear:
And then the Palsie Shakes of Fear.
The Pestilence of Love does heat:
Or Hatred's hidden Ulcer eat.
Joy's chearful Madness does perplex:
Or Sorrow's other Madness vex.
Which Knowledge forces me to know;
And Memory will not foregoe.
What but a Soul could have the wit
To build me up for Sin so fit?
So Architects do square and hew,
Green Trees that in the Forest grew.

To His Coy Mistress

Had we but World enough, and Time,
This coyness Lady were no crime.
We would sit down, and think which way
To walk, and pass our long Loves Day.
Thou by the *Indian Ganges* side
Should'st Rubies find: I by the Tide
Of *Humber* would complain. I would
Love you ten years before the Flood:
And you should if you please refuse

Till the Conversion of the Jews.
My vegetable Love should grow
Vaster then Empires, and more slow.
An hundred years should go to praise
Thine Eyes, and on thy Forehead Gaze.
Two hundred to adore each Breast:
But thirty thousand to the rest.
An Age at least to every part,
And the last Age should show your Heart.
For Lady you deserve this State;
Nor would I love at lower rate.

But at my back I alwaies hear
Times winged Charriot hurrying near:
And yonder all before us lye
Deserts of vast Eternity.
Thy Beauty shall no more be found;
Nor, in thy marble Vault, shall sound
My ecchoing Song: then Worms shall try
That long preserv'd Virginity:
And your quaint Honour turn to dust;
And into ashes all my Lust.
The Grave's a fine and private place,
But none I think do there embrace.

Now therefore, while the youthful hew
Sits on thy skin like morning dew,
And while thy willing Soul transpires
At every pore with instant Fires,
Now let us sport us while we may;
And now, like am'rous birds of prey,
Rather at once our Time devour,
Than languish in his slow-chapt pow'r.
Let us roll all our Strength, and all
Our sweetness, up into one Ball:
And tear our Pleasures with rough strife,
Thorough the Iron gates of Life.

Thus, though we cannot make our Sun
Stand still, yet we will make him run.

The Fair Singer

To make a final conquest of all me,
Love did compose so sweet an Enemy,
In whom both Beauties to my death agree,
Joyning themselves in fatal Harmony;
That while she with her Eyes my Heart does bind,
She with her Voice might captivate my Mind.

I could have fled from One but singly fair:
My dis-intangled Soul it self might save,
Breaking the curled trammels of her hair.
But how should I avoid to be her Slave,
Whose subtile Art invisibly can wreath
My Fetters of the very Air I breath?

It had been easie fighting in some plain,
Where Victory might hang in equal choice,
But all resistance against her is vain,
Who has th' advantage both of Eyes and Voice,
And all my Forces needs must be undone,
She having gained both the Wind and Sun.

The Definition of Love

My Love is of a birth as rare
As 'tis for object strange and high:
It was begotten by despair
Upon Impossibility.

Magnanimous Despair alone
Could show me so divine a thing,
Where feeble Hope could ne'r have flown
But vainly flapt its Tinsel Wing.

And yet I quickly might arrive
Where my extended Soul is fixt,
But Fate does Iron wedges drive,
And alwaies crouds it self betwixt.

For Fate with jealous Eye does see
Two perfect Loves; nor lets them close:
Their union would her ruine be,
And her Tyrannick pow'r depose.

And therefore her Decrees of Steel
Us as the distant Poles have plac'd,
(Though Loves whole World on us doth wheel)
Not by themselves to be embrac'd.

Unless the giddy Heaven fall,
And Earth some new Convulsion tear;
And, us to joyn, the World should all
Be cramp'd into a *Planisphere*.

As Lines so Loves *oblique* may well
Themselves in every Angle greet:
But ours so truly *Paralel*,
Though infinite can never meet.

Therefore the Love which us doth bind,
But Fate so enviously debarrs,
Is the Conjunction of the Mind,
And Opposition of the Stars.

The Mower Against Gardens

Luxurious Man, to bring his Vice in use,
   Did after him the World seduce:
And from the fields the Flow'rs and Plants allure,
   Where Nature was most plain and pure.
He first enclos'd within the Gardens square
   A dead and standing pool of Air:
And a more luscious Earth for them did knead,
   Which stupifi'd them while it fed.
The Pink grew then as double as his Mind;
   The nutriment did change the kind.
With strange perfumes he did the Roses taint.
   And Flow'rs themselves were taught to paint.
The Tulip, white, did for complexion seek;
   And learn'd to interline its cheek:
Its Onion root they then so high did hold,
   That one was for a Meadow sold.
Another World was search'd, through Oceans new,
   To find the *Marvel of Peru*.
And yet these Rarities might be allow'd,
   To Man, that sov'raign thing and proud;
Had he not dealt between the Bark and Tree,
   Forbidden mixtures there to see.
No Plant now knew the Stock from which it came;
   He grafts upon the Wild the Tame:
That the uncertain and adult'rate fruit
   Might put the Palate in dispute.
His green *Seraglio* has its Eunuchs too;
   Lest any Tyrant him out-doe.
And in the Cherry he does Nature vex,
   To procreate without a Sex.

'Tis all enforc'd; the Fountain and the Grot;
  While the sweet Fields do lye forgot:
Where willing Nature does to all dispence
  A wild and fragrant Innocence:
And *Fauns* and *Faryes* do the Meadows till,
  More by their presence then their skill.
Their Statues polish'd by some ancient hand,
  May to adorn the Gardens stand:
But howso'ere the Figures do excel,
  The *Gods* themselves with us do dwell.

The Mower to the Glo-Worms

Ye living Lamps, by whos dear light
The Nightingale does sit so late,
And studying all the Summer-night,
Her matchless Songs does meditate;

Ye Country Comets, that portend
No War, nor Princes funeral,
Shining unto no higher end
Then to presage the Grasses fall;

Ye Glo-Worms, whose officious Flame
To wandring Mowers shows the way,
That in the Night have lost their aim,
And after foolish Fires do stray;

Your courteous Lights in vain you wast,
Since *Juliana* here is come,
For She my Mind hath so displac'd
That I shall never find my home.

The Mower's Song

My Mind was once the true survey
Of all these Medows fresh and gay;
And in the greeness of the Grass
Did see its Hopes as in a Glass;
When *Juliana* came, and She
What I do to the Grass, does to my Thoughts and Me.

But these, while I with Sorrow pine,
Grew more luxuriant still and fine;
That not one Blade of Grass you spy'd,
But had a Flower on either side;
When *Juliana* came, and She
What I do to the Grass, does to my Thoughts and Me.

Unthankful Medows, could you so
A fellowship so true forego,
And in your gawdy May-games meet,
While I lay trodden under feet?
When *Juliana* came, and She
What I do to the Grass, does to my Thoughts and Me.

But what you in Compassion ought,
Shall now by my Revenge be wrought:
And Flow'rs, and Grass, and I and all,
Will in one common Ruine fall.
For *Juliana* comes, and She
What I do to the Grass, does to my Thoughts and Me.

And thus, ye Meadows, which have been
Companions of my thoughts more green,
Shall now the Heraldry become

With which I shall adorn my Tomb;
  For *Juliana* comes, and She
What I do to the Grass, does to my Thoughts and Me.

The Garden

How vainly men themselves amaze
To win the Palm, the Oke, or Bayes;
And their uncessant Labours see
Crown'd from some single Herb or Tree.
Whose short and narrow verged Shade
Does prudently their Toyles upbraid;
While all Flow'rs and all Trees do close
To weave the Garlands of repose.

Fair quiet, have I found thee here,
And Innocence thy Sister dear!
Mistaken long, I sought you then
In busie Companies of Men.
Your sacred Plants, if here below,
Only among the Plants will grow.
Society is all but rude,
To this delicious Solitude.

No white nor red was ever seen
So am'rous as this lovely green.
Fond Lovers, cruel as their Flame,
Cut in these Trees their Mistress name.
Little, Alas, they know, or heed,
How far these Beauties Hers exceed!
Fair Trees! where s'eer your barkes I wound,
No Name shall but your own be found.

When we have run our Passions heat,
Love hither makes his best retreat.

The *Gods,* that mortal Beauty chase,
Still in a Tree did end their race.
Apollo hunted *Daphne* so,
Only that She might Laurel grow.
And *Pan* did after *Syrinx* speed,
Not as a Nymph, but for a Reed.

What wond'rous Life is this I lead!
Ripe Apples drop about my head;
The Luscious Clusters of the Vine
Upon my Mouth do crush their Wine;
The Nectaren, and curious Peach,
Into my hands themselves do reach;
Stumbling on Melons, as I pass,
Insnar'd with Flow'rs, I fall on Grass.

Mean while the Mind, from pleasures less,
Withdraws into it happiness:
The Mind, that Ocean where each kind
Does streight its own resemblance find;
Yet it creates, transcending these,
Far other Worlds, and other Seas;
Annihilating all that's made
To a green Thought in a green Shade.

Here at the Fountains sliding foot,
Or at some Fruit-trees mossy root,
Casting the Bodies Vest aside,
My Soul into the boughs does glide:
There like a Bird it sits, and sings,
Then whets, and combs its silver Wings;
And, till prepar'd for longer flight,
Waves in its Plumes the various Light.

Such was that happy Garden-state,
While Man there walk'd without a Mate:
After a Place so pure, and sweet,

What other Help could yet be meet!
But 'twas beyond a Mortal's share
To wander solitary there:
Two Paradises 'twere in one
To live in Paradise alone.

How well the skilful Gardner drew
Of flow'rs and herbes this Dial new;
Where from above the milder Sun
Does through a fragrant Zodiack run;
And, as it works, th' industrious Bee
Computes its time as well as we.
How could such sweet and wholsome Hours
Be reckon'd but with herbs and flow'rs!

An Horatian Ode
upon Cromwel's Return from Ireland

The forward Youth that would appear
Must now forsake his *Muses* dear,
   Nor in the Shadows sing
   His Numbers languishing.
'Tis time to leave the Books in dust,
And oyl th' unused Armours rust:
   Removing from the Wall
   The Corslet of the Hall.
So restless *Cromwel* could not cease
In the inglorious Arts of Peace,
   But through adventrous War
   Urged his active Star.
And, like the three-fork'd Lightning, first
Breaking the Clouds where it was nurst,
   Did thorough his own Side

His fiery way divide.
For 'tis all one to Courage high
The Emulous or Enemy;
    And with such to inclose
    Is more then to oppose.
Then burning through the Air he went,
And Pallaces and Temples rent:
    And *Cæsars* head at last
    Did through his Laurels blast.
'Tis Madness to resist or blame
The force of angry Heavens flame:
    And, if we would speak true,
    Much to the Man is due.
Who, from his private Gardens, where
He liv'd reserved and austere,
    As if his highest plot
    To plant the Bergamot,
Could by industrious Valour climbe
To ruine the great Work of Time,
    And cast the Kingdome old
    Into another Mold.
Though Justice against Fate complain,
And plead the antient Rights in vain:
    But those do hold or break
    As Men are strong or weak.
Nature that hateth emptiness,
Allows of penetration less:
    And therefore must make room
    Where greater Spirits come.
What Field of all the Civil Wars,
Where his were not the deepest Scars?
    And *Hampton* shows what part
    He had of wiser Art.
Where, twining subtile fears with hope,
He wove a Net of such a scope,

That *Charles* himself might chase
To *Caresbrooks* narrow case.
That thence the *Royal Actor* born
The *Tragick Scaffold* might adorn:
  While round the armed Bands
  Did clap their bloody hands.
He nothing common did or mean
Upon that memorable Scene:
  But with his keener Eye
  The Axes edge did try:
Nor call'd the *Gods* with vulgar spight
To vindicate his helpless Right,
  But bow'd his comely Head,
  Down as upon a Bed.
This was that memorable Hour
Which first assur'd the forced Pow'r.
  So when they did design
  The *Capitols* first Line,
A bleeding Head where they begun,
Did fright the Architects to run;
  And yet in that the *State*
  Foresaw it's happy Fate.
And now the *Irish* are asham'd
To see themselves in one Year tam'd:
  So much one Man can do,
  That does both act and know.
They can affirm his Praises best,
And have, though overcome, confest
  How good he is, how just,
  And fit for highest Trust:
Nor yet grown stiffer with Command,
But still in the *Republick's* hand:
  How fit he is to sway
  That can so well obey.
He to the *Commons Feet* presents

A *Kingdome,* for his first years rents:
   And, what he may, forbears
   His Fame to make it theirs:
And has his Sword and Spoyls ungirt,
To lay them at the *Publick's* skirt.
   So when the Falcon high
   Falls heavy from the Sky,
She, having kill'd, no more does search,
But on the next green Bow to pearch;
   Where, when he first does lure,
   The Falckner has her sure.
What may not then our *Isle* presume
While Victory his Crest does plume!
   What may not others fear
   If thus he crown each Year!
A *Cæsar* he ere long to *Gaul,*
To *Italy* an *Hannibal,*
   And to all States not free
   Shall *Clymacterick* be.
The *Pict* no shelter now shall find
Within his party-colour'd Mind;
   But from this Valour sad
   Shrink underneath the Plad:
Happy if in the tufted brake
The *English Hunter* him mistake;
   Nor lay his Hounds in near
   The *Caledonian* Deer.
But thou the Wars and Fortunes Son
March indefatigably on;
   And for the last effect
   Still keep thy Sword erect:
Besides the force it has to fright
The Spirits of the shady Night,
   The same *Arts* that did *gain*
   A *Pow'r* must it *maintain.*

Index of Titles and First Lines

14-400